MW01128857

The Kennedy Assassination

The Kennedy Assassination

A Historical Novel by

J. Arthur Jensen

-JENS

To order additional copies of this book, contact:
Xlibris Corporation
1-888-7-XLIBRIS
www.Xlibris.com
Orders@Xlibris.com

The Kennedy Assassination is fiction.
Actual quotes are distinguished in italics.
All have one or more references.

*To the full release of all government files on
Marilyn Monroe and to a reappraisal of her role
in history, this book is earnestly dedicated.*

In 1961, President John F. Kennedy approved a plan to deal with the Communist government in Cuba: assassinate Fidel Castro. A private citizen learned of the operation and tried to stop it: her name was Marilyn Monroe. Could the film star have seen the moral conflict which might have cost John Kennedy his life? Based closely on the historical record, *The Kennedy Assassination* presents one of the most controversial historical hypotheses of our time.

J. Arthur Jensen graduated from Harvard College and Yale Medical School. Following training in surgery at Stanford University, he specialized in plastic surgery at U.C.L.A. where he currently serves as an assistant clinical professor. This is his first novel.

Chapter 1

"Let's be firm on Monroe Doctrine: Who will be the next ambassador to Monroe? This is one of the many problems which President-elect Kennedy will have to work on in January. Obviously you can't leave Monroe adrift. There are too many greedy people eyeing her, and now that Ambassador Miller has left she could flounder around without any direction."

Art Buchwald
Los Angeles Times
November 9, 1960

Marilyn Monroe looked in the mirror at one of the most beautiful, seductive, and recognized faces in the world. It did not please her. She stared at the dark circles beneath her eyes, and then studied the small lines radiating away from her mouth. She was 34 years old and her youth was starting to fade.

On this morning, she did not have time to worry. Almost two months earlier, John Kennedy had been elected President of the United States, and Marilyn wanted to know if she should make plans to go to Washington for the Inauguration. She had been unable to make contact with Jack, and had some difficulty getting in touch with Peter Lawford. When she had finally been able to get through to Peter, he had proposed a walk on the beach for that morning in January 1961. She was already late.

The coastal mist was still hanging over Santa Monica even though it was late morning. It was not a good day for the sun worshippers, but a beautiful day for Marilyn Monroe. She liked the mist because she felt that the sun would make her skin age too quickly. And a girl had to think about her skin, particularly a girl who had made a career out of looking beautiful and seductive.

Driving down San Vicente, a boulevard divided with grass and Coral Trees growing between the lanes, was usually pleasant, but Marilyn felt discouraged. It hadn't been a very good year. While they were filming a movie in Nevada, her husband, Arthur Miller, had started a relationship with a photographer on the set. Then, an old boyfriend was elected President of the United States. It was not bad that her marriage with Arthur Miller was ending, nor was it bad that John Kennedy had been elected President; it was just that sometimes she got the feeling that she had gone to the wrong party, that she had missed some big opportunities.

How could she feel unlucky? No one thought she would make it in Hollywood when she arrived. The entire town seemed like it was full of critics. Many people told her that she should go to acting school. Others told her that there were too many blondes. But things worked out. She worked the angles, the same way anyone has to work the angles, and she had won. She had started the fifties with nothing, but by 1960, hers was one of the most famous acts of all time.

Joe DiMaggio helped. He was one of the most prominent athletes of his generation—the best man on the best team ever assembled. And even though the relationship hadn't lasted, it had still been worth it. The publicity alone was beyond anyone's wildest dream. It was a match made in heaven: the biggest star with the biggest star. But he didn't understand that she wasn't a traditional Italian mother, and when he tried to put her into the mold, she didn't fit. Then he tried to make her fit. She tried to keep that part quiet.

Arthur Miller was another great move. People should have seen the symmetry there—but they chose to ignore it. They should have understood that the world's best writer could not be in love with a woman just because she was beautiful. There had to be more. She must be more complicated, more delicate and beautiful than anyone thought. And thoughtful. Arthur Miller was a sensitive writer—she must be a sensitive actress. But they didn't understand it—it was still Marilyn Monroe the seductive, full figured blonde bombshell. She was a famous actress, but not an artist. She wanted people to know that she was thoughtful and sensitive to the world's problems—Marilyn wanted to be taken seriously.

The sun broke out from behind its misty shroud briefly as she turned off San Vicente and on to 7th, a road that curved down Santa Monica Canyon to the beach. She slowed down as she passed a gas station and then an elementary school mid way down the canyon. Children were running around on the playground. On any other day, she might have stopped and watched them play, but Peter would probably be drinking, and she wanted to get to him while he was still coherent. She passed a bar and a restaurant, then turned left on the Pacific Coast Highway and drove past the few beach clubs and private residences that lined the ocean front. She parked her car and went inside.

Marilyn always got a thrill when she entered the Lawfords' beach house. The house had originally been built for a film executive and it had all the trappings of wealth. Dark wood with elegant carvings lined the halls. The light fixtures had been imported from France. Downstairs the house had a screening room, large living and dining rooms, a kitchen, pantry, and a swimming pool off the patio. Peter would never have been able to afford a place like this had he not married into a very rich family.

Marilyn Monroe knew Peter Lawford before either one of them had become famous. He came out to California from Florida, where his parents settled after leaving England. His father was a decorated military man from the first World War—a general who had actually been knighted in the field for his courage. That meant that Peter's father had some measure of social rank, but that didn't translate into money or opportunity for Peter.

When they first met, Peter was a golden boy—an actor of modest prominence who spent his days surfing and playing volleyball at State Beach. Friendly and very attractive, he spoke with just a trace of a British accent, which made Marilyn think he must be very intelligent. They went out for a time, but they were both young dreamers—long on ambition and potential, short on cash. Marilyn needed a bigger star to bring attention to herself, and Peter needed someone with the social rank and the money he longed for as a child.

That time seemed a long way off because so much had changed. Peter met Patricia Kennedy at the National Convention in 1952 and realized she would be a good match. They married and Patricia's brother, Senator John Kennedy, was an usher at the wedding ceremony.

Marilyn knew John Kennedy in the early 50's, but at that time he could barely get out of bed. He was an attractive young politician with a big smile and a lot of promise. But Joe DiMaggio was a far bigger name in the early 50's than John Kennedy. Marilyn pursued the sure thing, but when John Kennedy came out to California, he always wanted to see Marilyn. And she had seen him. The question was whether she would be able to backtrack in her life, and find a way to have the world's most powerful man. With DiMaggio and Miller, she married two of the most prominent men of her generation. Could she have the President? Marilyn was only sure of one thing: if she didn't try, she'd never know.

Peter Lawford poured the Dom Perignon into a champagne glass. Marilyn always wanted champagne and she always wanted Dom Perignon. So he made sure he always had it around. It was just easier that way. Marilyn was a woman who always seemed to get her way. For himself, he dropped a couple of ice cubes in a glass and measured out some Scotch. He wasn't sure why he bothered to measure it. He was going to have as much as he wanted anyway. And then some.

He handed Marilyn her glass and they went out on the patio

where they could see the waves. As she walked in front of him, he couldn't help looking down at her bottom, maybe the most famous bottom in the world. Of course, he'd had Marilyn. He'd had Marilyn any way he'd wanted to before he'd ever facilitated things with Jack. Now, she wouldn't even consider his approaches. That's gratitude for you. Introduce her to the political world, and she starts to think of you as the hired help.

"When are you going back?" Marilyn asked.

"Next week," he replied. "There are so many parties. So many people to meet."

"Aren't you excited?"

Peter swirled the Scotch and the rocks and looked out over the ocean. He didn't want to look too excited. Sure, it was great to have your brother in law elected President of the United States, but it could also be a pain in the ass. There was a time when Jack bragged about knowing Peter Lawford. Now, it was Peter who felt like the unknown. But Jack was a great guy. A funny guy. A guy's guy. A guy who liked girls. And Peter knew the girls. They were going to have some very good times in the next few years. Peter was going to enjoy all the free publicity of being the first brother in law. And when it was over, he would be one of the biggest names in show business. But in the meantime, he had to be a good guy for Jack. He had to be content to be in Jack's shadow. But with all the parties, and all the girls, it wouldn't be such tough duty. He smiled to himself.

"Oh, I suppose I'll get through it," he replied. "I've seen these big celebrations before."

"Do you think Jack will want a little company?" Marilyn asked with a coy smile. "Or will the First Lady take care of him?"

"What did you have in mind?" Peter asked bluntly. "I don't think Jackie is going to miss the festivities. This will be her time to shine."

"So you don't think he wants anyone else around?"

Peter looked at her innocent face. He hated to break bad news.

"You know Angie is going to the Inaugural Ball?"

"Angie!"

"I thought you knew."

Marilyn's skin burned with embarrassment. She took a deep breath and tried to hide her disappointment. Of course, Jack had many girlfriends and she knew she was only one of them. Still, she was hurt that she hadn't been asked. She took a deep breath and looked down.

Peter could see that Marilyn was disappointed and tried to rationalize why she had not been asked to come to Washington. "You are a married woman. Jack is going to have to be particularly careful to avoid anything that might bring in an angry husband—you know that."

"Married woman? What are you talking about?"

"Aren't you still married?"

"Technically, I guess."

"That's what I'm talking about. You are a married woman."

"It didn't make any difference during the campaign."

"This isn't the campaign."

"Why didn't you tell me before?"

Peter studied her face. She was actually worked up. Why was she taking this so seriously? She knew Jack had other girlfriends. The last thing he needed right now was Arthur Miller writing something about presidential philandering. Better to play it safe, for now.

"Marilyn, you know the score. The President is married. Anything he does on the side has to be kept strictly confidential."

She looked stunned for moment and then gazed out over the ocean. She hadn't quite accepted the fact that life had moved on for Jack Kennedy as well. He was married and had children. Marilyn was trying to work through her dream.

"Do you think he's happy in his marriage?"

"What does that have to do with anything?" Peter asked.

"What if he wants someone else?"

"Look, Marilyn, Jack is now the President of the United States. He can't get divorced. Furthermore, his wife is one of the most gracious women in the world. She is well educated, refined, artistic, and beautiful. She's the perfect woman to have in the White House. She's perfect for state functions—entertainment—"

"—I've entertained."

Peter leaned back and laughed. Marilyn had entertained troops in Korea with her raunchy song and dance act. She couldn't be serious.

"That's not exactly the kind of entertainment expected of the First Lady!" He laughed and then drank the rest of the scotch.

Marilyn felt her face begin to burn. She had scratched her way to the top of the movie business, but felt confined. With limited education and no acceptable social background, Marilyn felt she was from the wrong side of the tracks—just a lucky girl who had become famous. She stood up suddenly and walked off the patio, toward the beach as tears welled up in her eyes.

Peter felt the first blush of his drink as he watched Marilyn stand up and walk away. Where was she going? It was just a joke. Actually, it wasn't even a joke. It was true. He watched her walk. What an act! He wondered for a moment whether the drink had made him say something he shouldn't have said. Pat was always nagging him not to drink so much, particularly around the old man. But what the hell? This was Marilyn, and he had only been saying the obvious. He put the glass down, stood up, stumbled a half step, and followed her out to the beach.

The sky was gray right on the beach, keeping the temperature down. A strong surf was pounding up on the sand. Marilyn began walking West, into a slight head wind, toward the beaches collectively known as Malibu. Through the low hanging clouds, she could barely make out the little jut of land called Point Dume. That's where I'm going, she thought, toward doom.

A couple of young men had dared the strong surf, but looked as if they had had enough. They were paddling their boards back to shore.

Marilyn walked along the curving wet line of the beach, where the water occasionally rushed over her feet. She wiped her eyes and pulled her long, light skirt up so that it would not get wet. Peter, who had been in pursuit, was finally catching up.

"You don't have to become offended so quickly, you know."

Marilyn wouldn't look at him. "You don't have to be such a jerk."

"Look, I was just making a joke. Maybe it wasn't a good one, but you can't run away every time I make a bad joke."

"In this country, it isn't just how well you are born that counts."

"I know. It's not that way in England—not completely that way."

"I think the world should allow people from poor backgrounds to rise to the top—to whatever level their personalities and skills allow."

"That is a noble wish."

"Just because someone has had to put up with the indignities of working their way up, doesn't mean they can't entertain or interact with all sorts of people."

"I'm sure you'd do just fine."

Marilyn wiped her eyes again and looked out at the ocean. Waves slowly rose up from the dark blue green water and then crashed in front of her. The water rushed up the beach and covered her feet.

"Maybe Jack Kennedy isn't the right thing for me now. Maybe I need someone who can give me more time and a family of my own. Just because he's President doesn't mean that I want to spend my life with him."

"Of course not."

Marilyn looked down the beach a few hundred feet where a dolphin had beached itself and was struggling at the water's edge. She began to walk quickly toward it. "Look, Peter! The fish is trapped on the sand."

"Beached dolphin," he said without much concern. He felt his empty pocket for a package of cigarettes.

"Come on! We have to save it," Marilyn yelled as she ran toward the dolphin. She waved for him to follow.

Peter could tell Marilyn was about to spin off on another hysterical mission of mercy. Marilyn had a way of trying to save every little thing from its natural end. He had been with her when she had tried to save sick birds. Once she insisted on pulling a dog that had been hit by a car back to her apartment in an effort to save it. The dog's blood had ended up all over Marilyn's carpet.

"Marilyn, it's just a fish."

"Just a fish!?" she asked incredulously. Pushing against the massive fish, Marilyn could not make it move. She stood up and wiped her hands on her dress.

"Peter, get over here."

Peter shuffled across the sand without enthusiasm. He really didn't want to get his hands covered with fish slime.

"Marilyn, this kind of thing happens. They get sick and wash up on shore. Life has to end sometime."

"We have to help it!" she exclaimed as she turned around on the beach.

Several hundred feet back down the beach, the two young men were drying themselves from their attempts to surf the rough waters. Marilyn screamed for them, jumped up and down, and waved for them to come. Upon seeing her, the men looked at each other and ran toward her.

Within a few minutes, the men were pulling the dolphin with a towel back toward the ocean. Marilyn pushed as the young men pulled. The dolphin rolled. Much to Peter's surprise, when the fish reached the water, it seemed stunned for an instant, but then quickly darted away. Marilyn kissed each one of the young men and stared into Peter's face.

"See! You can't tell. Everything wants to live."

Peter saw anger in her eyes. "Marilyn, it was just a fish," he pleaded.

"How would you like to be a fish and have someone walk past you when you needed them?"

"A fish isn't exactly a human being."

"How do you know what a fish thinks? If someone isn't from just the right family, you would just let them drown."

"Really, Marilyn."

"Well, there are those of us who want to do what we can for anything we can—regardless of its place in your little view of the world."

Peter looked at her strut away. He could only shake his head. She could be so damned stubborn. And when she thought she was right, well, there was simply no reasoning with her. As he followed her over the sand, he worried that maybe she would really want John Kennedy. When she really wanted something, she always ended up getting it. It was what had made her a success. As Peter saw her go into his beach house, he was reminded of one of the terms of the classical Greek dramas—something about success and failure. He stopped and stared out at the gray clouds and the dark ocean. He looked up the beach as the cool wind blew into his face. There was a word that described Marilyn's desire to have John Kennedy. But he couldn't remember what it was.

Chapter 2

*"Let every nation know . . . we shall pay any price, bear
any burden, meet any hardship, support any friend,
oppose any foe to assure the survival and the success
of liberty."*

John Fitzgerald Kennedy
January 20, 1961

The snow fell onto the windshield making it difficult from
the back seat of the limousine for him to see the road ahead. John
Fitzgerald Kennedy was going to the White House as a Senator for
the last time. Tomorrow, he would take the oath of office as the
35th President of the United States. But tonight, he was going to
enjoy the greatest celebration any man can ever enjoy—his own
inaugural ball. First, he had to have his sign out meeting with Ike.

He deserved the celebration. Getting there hadn't been easy.
He remembered the lonely, gray, cold winter days of his youth—
the days when he had been sent to boarding school. There had
been whispers about him then. He had been the runt. He had
been the skinny, sickly Kennedy boy who was headed nowhere.
Joe was the real Kennedy. Joe had been given the perfect body—
the mass, the reflexes to play the competitive games and delight
his father with achievements on the athletic fields. The doctors
were worried about poor Jack. He kept getting sick.

So he'd had to make a decision early in life. He could give

up and stay in bed, feel sorry for himself, and have others wait on him. Or, he could take a little extra pain—actually take a lot of extra pain—and give it the good fight. And after trying it out both ways, again, and again, he decided to make a fight of it. He decided long ago that he would try to make the most of every minute of his life, realizing, and being so advised by his doctors, that he might not have many minutes left. He had to make the most of every day.

He reached into his pocket and pulled out the latest copy of his inaugural address. There were only a couple of spots he was uncomfortable with. Tomorrow he would be center stage, speaking not only to America but also to the world. The address called a nation to attention and the free world to action. As the great Churchill had rallied the English people during their hour of greatest need, and so established himself as a leader without peer, so John Kennedy would step into the void and speak for free men everywhere who opposed the tide of Soviet fascism. This speech would do it. It had the words and the rhythms. And he was going to give it. He just didn't want to bungle any of the lines.

The limousine stopped under an arch and the door was opened. The President-elect took off his reading glasses, folded the papers back up and slid them in his pocket. He stepped out of the limousine and glanced at the White House entrance where Marine guards stood at attention. He paused for a moment and then went in.

The meeting with Eisenhower had a formal air to it. The sitting secretaries of Defense, State, and the Treasury were seated next to Kennedy's men. Eisenhower conducted the meeting according to a distributed outline. As the discussion began, Kennedy realized that it had all started. Someone was taking notes. Ike and he were going on the record and history was being made. He clenched his teeth with this realization and watched Eisenhower direct the meeting.

It was the best and worst of Eisenhower, Kennedy thought. Eisenhower's ideas were well reasoned and well informed. But they were derived from a process that was as bureaucratic as the military. The White House was working like one giant military headquarters: staff people interpreting data, other staff people processing and arguing about it, and finally, a select few presenting options to the commander. The whole pyramid could be replaced with a single man, Kennedy thought, if he were the right man. He tapped on his teeth with his fingernail.

Ike tried to make a point about Laos. He looked up from his notes and paused, as if to give his words on this particular subject greater emphasis.

"This is the cork in the bottle of the Far East. If Laos is lost to the free world, in the long run we will lose all of Southeast Asia."

Kennedy didn't like the idea of actually fighting. The idea of sending men into combat—that lives could be lost carrying out his orders was a new one to him. He wasn't completely comfortable with its implications.

"You are going to have to put troops in Laos," Eisenhower went on. *"With other nations if possible—but alone if necessary."*

"If the situation was so critical," Kennedy interjected, *"why didn't you decide to do something?"*

Eisenhower stopped and looked at him as if the answer were perfectly obvious.

"I would have, but I did not feel I could commit troops with a new administration coming to power."

Logical enough, Kennedy thought as he sat back in his chair. Would have been easier for me if you did. But you didn't.

The discussion went on to China, to how long it would take to move troops around the world, to how many small wars could be fought at one time, and then to Berlin. The Communists had to do something to stop the flux of refugees leaving East Berlin and fleeing to the West.

So, the line had been drawn. The Communists were contained in Asia. They had been fought to a standstill in Korea. The line was holding in Southeast Asia. There was no mention of gaining ground in any of these areas—only of holding what was already pro-democracy.

"*Should we support guerrilla operations in Cuba,*" Kennedy asked?

Again, the venerable old President fixed the young President-elect in a stern gaze.

"*To the utmost,*" Eisenhower replied. He then mentioned the possibility of guerrilla infiltration and trying to topple Castro with his own countrymen. There were some proposals being made, but no final plans had been decided upon. Eisenhower concluded by saying that "*We cannot let the present government there go on.*"

Kennedy let Eisenhower tell him about the plans for Cuba as though he were learning about them for the first time. Actually, he learned about the plans during the campaign through channels of his own. He worried that the CIA would get rid of Castro in the weeks before the election and hand Nixon a certain victory. In the debates, Kennedy suggested that the United States support Cubans who wanted to overthrow Castro. It had been an easy way to flank Nixon on the right. But now John Kennedy was President of the United States. If he wanted to take Cuba, he was going to have to pay the price. He was going to have to bear the burden.

After more than an hour the meeting broke up and the President-elect shook hands with Eisenhower and his departing cabinet members. He was ushered back through the halls of the White House to his limousine. On the way back to the hotel, Kennedy noticed the snow had started to gather on the streets of Washington and his mind began to wander. Containing the Communists wouldn't be easy. There could be problems in Asia. He had fought there before. He didn't like the idea of sending men there. And if he moved on Cuba, what were the Soviets likely to do in Berlin? The snow continued to blow against the windshield. Perhaps there wouldn't be any inauguration after all. Perhaps the snow would keep everyone away, and Eisenhower would simply have to go on for another four years.

No. He was going to do it. He was going to stand up there and give his inaugural address, if he had to do it in the dining hall. And he was going to be the President of the United States. And why not? He had been bred for it, born to it, his father had wanted it, his brother had deserved it, and he had gotten it. Eisenhower was retiring to his farm in Pennsylvania and John Kennedy was going to be the leader of the free world.

"Do you think I look all right?" she asked. Jacqueline Kennedy was dressed in an elegant black dress—her hair up and diamonds dangling from her ears.

"No woman has ever looked better," he replied as he paced around her dressing room. He couldn't believe he was going to be late to his own inaugural ball. "Now, we have to go."

"Jack?" she said as she rose from her dressing table and looked at her tuxedo clad husband in the mirror. "There won't be any nonsense tonight, will there?"

"Jackie, we're ten minutes late right now. We have no fewer than five parties to attend in our honor. Do you really think this is the time to help me with all my shortcomings?" He walked toward the door, stopped, and waited.

She looked over at him and smiled. It was a beautiful smile, a smile that reflected perfect taste, perfect education, and just the right degree of displeasure.

"I just want to make one thing clear before we start: I can only do my part if I am afforded the dignity of my position. If you humiliate me in front of our friends, in front of our country, I will go home. Do we have an understanding?"

"And you've never strayed?"

"Do we have an understanding?"

"Jackie, this is your night. You're the First Lady. You are by far the most beautiful woman I have ever known."

"I'm waiting."

"Of course we have an understanding. But, I would expect you to consider your place as my wife, and as the First Lady of this country. There are things to consider beyond the obvious. And I would hope—"

"I will go home. Keep that in mind," she warned.

He watched her pass in front of him and thought she looked almost regal. She was perfect for the role of First Lady, he thought, if only she could be a little more tolerant of his needs.

Jacqueline Bouvier Kennedy's regal dress was a good match for the tone of the event. The Kennedy family was seated in a box above the rest of the guests. Like a royal family, the Kennedys looked down upon their guests, were cheered, and they waved back politely. Framing the family in the trappings of royalty had been Joe Kennedy's idea. If the Kennedys acted like royalty, Joe reasoned, maybe people would begin to consider them as such. It couldn't hurt.

Jack looked around the Presidential Box. The family seemed to be having a good time. Jackie was truly in her element. Smiling, waving, looking beautiful was really what she did best. He looked over at his father. If there was one guy who would be more bored with the whole scene than he was, it would be his father. And, true to form, the President-elect's father was in the process of excusing himself from the rest of the group. He nodded at Jack and left the box. Jack assumed, as did everyone else in the family, that the patriarch was off to transact some business. It was hard to keep him entertained for long unless there was some business on the line.

As it turned out, there was some business—important business. Within a few minutes an aide tapped Jack on the shoulder and told him that his father had asked that he come for a few minutes. Jack looked over at Jackie who glanced back at him suspiciously.

"Don't be long, Jack," she said.

"Really, Jackie," he said. "You could be just a bit more high minded."

"Maybe you could help me with that," she suggested with a smile.

Jack stood up to follow the aide, and as he did he felt a twinge of pain in his back. The pain, always with him, didn't stop him from following the man. He didn't grimace. He didn't limp. It wasn't that kind of pain. It was just enough to notice, enough to remind him that painful days had haunted his past, and painful days were ahead.

He followed the aide into an ornate room across from the Presidential Loge. As he entered the room, he saw a cloud of cigar smoke and through it, his father and two men rose. As they rose, his jaw fell. Only his father had the audacity to arrange such a meeting and not warn him well in advance. He felt his pulse quicken. He was about to sit down with two of the most powerful men in America—both enemies, both friends. His success had depended on these two men. And his future would also depend on them.

"What a great pleasure it is for me to introduce my son, the President-elect," his father said. "Jack, I think you know Director Hoover and the Mayor of Chicago, Mr. Daley."

Jack did know them. And he knew the gravity of the meeting that was about to take place. J. Edgar Hoover could destroy his political life with a single news leak. He had been able to do so before the election, and he would be able to do so at any point in the future. His father and Hoover had long been friends—in the way that men of great power and great ambition are friendly but it was a studied friendship, a strategic friendship. Hoover kept the secrets. He was a man with whom any President of the United States had to maintain only the best of relations.

Richard Daley was the ultimate big city boss—and he looked the part. He was brash and fat and certain in his knowledge that no one knew what was better for the people of Chicago than he did. He embodied the way politics had been done in his father's generation. And Joseph Kennedy's business dealings in the City of Chicago had been profitable for both Kennedy and the mayor.

Of course, Hoover had become famous while working for the F.B.I. in Chicago. He knew the way the city operated and how

Daley's machine worked. They all stood in a circle for a moment—eyeing one another.

"Yes, of course," Jack said as he shook their hands. "I'm honored you gentlemen have braved the elements this evening to pay me, to pay my family, this respect."

He looked at Hoover to see if he was in a conciliatory mood. But Hoover's face did not betray any of his emotions. He managed only a brief, strained half grin. The men sat down into the large red leather club chairs. Jack was offered a cigar and glass of brandy. He took them.

"I have long respected both of these great Americans, as I know you have, Jack," his father went on. "We've been associates for many years in politics and in business, and I'm very hopeful that our warm relationship will be carried on in the years to come."

"I'll drink to that," Jack said, raising his glass. He tasted the brandy, but not much of it. His fickle digestive system did not allow him to consume much alcohol.

"I'm sure this will come as something of a shock to you, Jack, but Mr. Hoover has uncovered some irregularities in the voting in Cook County," his father reported.

"No," the President-elect said, feigning disbelief. Reports of voter fraud had been the biggest crisis of the election. For weeks after his 'victory,' Kennedy wondered whether Nixon would contest the outcome.

"But Mayor Daley has assured the Director that while there may be some confusion about how the registration and voting systems work in Cook County, there was certainly no systematic bias with respect to the voting."

"Of course not," the Mayor grumbled.

"And Mr. Hoover believes the time has passed to have the House of Representatives become involved."

"Mr. Nixon did not wish to pursue any questions about the vote," J. Edgar Hoover said with a grim smile. He did not mention that he knew of several other districts where the vote had been tainted and he had strongly encouraged Nixon to make formal charges of voter fraud. "With the Communists challenging us in every corner of the world, Dick thought it would send the wrong message to developing nations to call into question the integrity of our tradition of free and open elections."

Jack glanced at each of the men. He didn't want to acknowledge that there had been irregularities. To do so would be an admission that his father, through his contacts in Chicago and elsewhere, had in fact stolen the election of 1960. Again, Joseph Kennedy broke the tense silence.

"That's a noble thought on Mr. Nixon's part," the old man said and then cleared his throat. "And I quite agree. This would not seem to be a time to undermine the authority of the United States or our system of government by pointing to some election procedures which might be getting a bit out of date."

They all knew the truth. Daley knew how to throw an election. Hoover knew. For Joseph Kennedy, influencing the outcome of an election was a normal business expense. And they all knew that Illinois could not elect a President. But then, that's why Lyndon Johnson was on the ticket. He knew how to get the vote counted in Texas.

"Mr. President," Mayor Daley interjected, "Cook County needs federal money to update and systematize our voting processes."

"Cook County's needs will certainly be considered by the administration," Jack replied, holding a straight face. "We will look forward to working with you on modernizing your electoral system."

"Under local guidance," Hoover suggested with a smile. He knew Daley had no intention of actually changing anything about his election apparatus.

"Under local guidance," Daley agreed.

So it was all right, Jack thought, as he gazed into the faces of the old power brokers. The old man had paid the price, some of Daley's friends had "gotten out" the vote, Nixon was taking the high road, and he was going to be the next President of the United States. Hoover was going to keep the peace, Daley was going to get some much needed federal money, and Joseph Kennedy was going to see his son realize the prize he had been denied. No, he hadn't won the Presidency outright. But he had won. And if his past had taught him anything, it had taught him not to question his good breaks. Just take them. Take them, and run. He stood up. All of the men stood up. Jack wanted to run.

"There is one other concern," Hoover grumbled as he realized that his opportunity to extract any kind of favor from the President elect was fast ending. "I'd like to clarify the attitude of the Attorney General on the subject of the Negro."

Jack marveled at Hoover's instincts. He had raised just the issue to bring Daley to his side.

"Yes," Daley said. "Some of my friends in Chicago have voiced some concerns about that little fella, Bobby."

The Ambassador let out with a good natured belly laugh. He slapped the Mayor on the back and puffed from his cigar.

"I don't think we have much to worry about with Bobby," he said. "I know his old man."

It was a good line, Jack thought. It was a line that carried the promise that the old man could keep Bobby in line. Bobby owed his job to his father's insistence that he be appointed Attorney General. Jack had not wanted to appoint him. Clark Clifford had argued Jack's case with the old man. But the old man had asked for only one thing and that thing was that Robert Francis Kennedy be appointed Attorney General of the United States. Nothing less would do. Jack didn't want to take the political heat for appointing his brother and campaign manager to the office of Attorney General. But on reflection, he had decided it was better to face down the press, and the public, and adverse world opinion if necessary, than to cross the old man.

"Is he the kind of man who knows his friends?" Daley pursued. No one from Daley's circle knew if Bobby was sincere in his efforts to shut down Jimmy Hoffa in the fifties or if he was just buying the family political credibility. Daley wanted assurances that Bobby could be controlled.

"You leave Bobby to me," Joseph Kennedy ans\
"Bobby's not going to be a problem in this administration
have my word on that."

"That's all I need," Daley said with a smile. Daley and Joe
Kennedy had always operated on the basis of personal trust.

Jack left them, still smoking their cigars and drinking their
brandies. He wondered as he walked away what Nixon's inaugural
party would have been like. Nixon didn't have a father who was on
a first name basis with the Mayor of Chicago or the Director of the
F.B.I.. He stopped for a moment as he was walking out. He looked
back at his father, and the two older men. He was struck with the
thought that Nixon must have had to do it on his own. He had no
deal maker. Imagine, a guy from Nixon's background actually coming
so close. He waved to his father. His father waved back.

Jack intended to go directly back to the Presidential Box. But
in the hallway, he saw a big contributor from New York and then
another friend from California appeared. And finally, the evening
turned into a continuous receiving line, punctuated only by occasional trips out to the limousines where the President elect and his
family would be moved on to a new party—with new faces and
new demands on his attention.

Amidst the faces, the handshakes, and the promises, Jack
saw his friend Paul "Red" Fay. Red had been with him in the
Pacific when the PT 109 had been hit by a Japanese torpedo. The
men had been presumed killed, but lived to tell their story. The
old man, grateful Jack had survived, arranged to have their story
published in the **Saturday Evening Post**. So they returned from
the war as national heroes. Red's mission that night did not involve putting himself in the line of fire. But it was, in its own way,
most perilous: he was assigned to escort a beautiful, young Hollywood actress to the evening's events.

Jack glanced around the room. His father stood in one cor-
ner, surrounded by career officers from the State Department.
His mother stood a few yards away, speaking with their wives.
Various political appointees, entertainers, and family members

were crowded into the room. Jackie was not among them. Jack nodded at Red, and looked over at a door. Taking the signal, Red led the actress through the door, and into the private room nearby.

Jack was listening to a Southern governor tell him why Eisenhower had made a mistake at Little Rock when he realized the time had come. He needed a break. Actually, he needed more than a break. He needed what almost all men need several times a week. His situation was slightly different—sometimes he needed it several times a day. Jackie's interests were more limited. She was only occasionally interested in him. Once or twice a week. Maybe.

"Governor, I couldn't agree with you more. We're not going to change a hundred years of history in one administration. Now, if you will excuse me for a moment."

After securing the door with a large secret service agent, Jack stood in front of one of the most beautiful women he had ever seen. She pushed a strand of hair behind her ear and looked up at him with calm, clear green eyes. This was going to be too easy, he thought. Just lower that dress half way down, maybe tip her over a bit. No problem.

But it was a problem. To his increasing amazement, the actress wanted to talk. After a couple of fairly promising kisses, and a little gratuitous groping, he realized that she didn't want to go forward. She asked him about mutual friends, and travel plans, and whether they might see each other in California. Didn't she understand why she was there? He made a couple of efforts to unzip her dress, but no use. She folded her arms across her chest and suggested they get together when things didn't seem so rushed. He left the suite thinking the whole episode had been an utter failure. He had spent much too much time getting nowhere.

He was so frustrated upon leaving the room that he didn't check his appearance very carefully. He thought of that when he opened the door back to the reception room, moved the massive secret service agent out of the way, and came face to face with Jackie.

"Been resting?" she asked with a raised brow. "Your hair looks like you've been taking a little nap."

"I've been looking for you," he said managing an innocent laugh. "I think we need to spend a few minutes together later in the evening."

"Were you looking for me in there?" she asked with a smile. "I suppose it's time I be getting home."

"Jackie, nothing happened. You said you'd stick around."

"I think we had an understanding. There's no point in discussing it here. We'll have plenty of time, later." She squinted at him, turned and walked away.

Peter Lawford watched Jackie walk through the crowd and he watched Jack look at her go. He walked over to the President elect, who was pushing his hair back into position.

"Jack, you must be having a hell of a good time, tonight," he said jovially.

"Actually, not as good a time as I'd planned."

"You'll never guess who is getting her divorce tomorrow," Lawford said.

Jack looked stunned. "Not Marilyn."

"Marilyn," Lawford said as he inhaled his cigarette. "She was a little disappointed she wasn't invited to join you this evening."

"She wants the headlines of her divorce to be in the same newspapers as my inaugural address. Do you think she's trying to send a message to me or to the world?"

"Both," Lawford said, blowing smoke out his nose.

"Actually," Jack said as he looked around the room for his next serious conversation, "things might have worked out better if she had been here, tonight." He flashed a smile at Lawford. "Couldn't have been any worse."

Chapter 3

"Don't think, honey, just throw. That's the story of your life. Don't think, do it."

John Huston to Marilyn Monroe
December 1960

Marilyn sat back in the chair, tipped her head back, and allowed the water to flow through her hair, gently rinsing the chemicals out.

"I don't know what we'll do. Maybe go over to a club. Maybe just dinner," she said to George, her hair dresser. "With all the considerations about security, I don't have much to say about it."

George nodded as he heard her reply. She needed her hair done on short notice because she was going to see the President of the United States. Likely story. But, she was Marilyn Monroe and he had heard rumors about the President. She was one of his few celebrity clients, and when she called, he needed to change his plans to accommodate her. What a job! But there was a certain element of artistry about it. As a hair dresser he could create something interesting, something new. And it paid well.

George took a step back. He was a well muscled, very attractive young man. He chose a comb and began to try to work it through her hair.

"It's been a while since you've washed your hair, hasn't it Marilyn?" he asked.

"Yes. It's been a few days."

A few days . . . right, he thought. More like a week. How could someone with the international reputation of Marilyn Monroe allow herself to completely neglect her appearance for so long? What if she were seen? What if she were photographed? Her hair was disgusting. The apartment was also a little on the disgusting side. He had always assumed his celebrity clients would live with elevated sensibilities. To see someone like Marilyn Monroe live in an apartment with stained carpets and shoddy furnishings, well, it didn't do much to support his fascination with movie stars.

"You really need to take better care of your hair, Marilyn," he said, trying not to be too condescending. "I'm going to have to get you on a regular program."

"Everyone wants me to get on a regular program," she said. "I'm not the regular program type."

She really wasn't the regular program type, George thought. She was a real mess. Her screen image was a far cry from her real life. There were other women like her, of course. Artists, mostly. And they tended to live down in the village. He could understand why women might choose to reject the life society expected of them—throw off expectations, avoid marriage, and write poetry in the coffee houses. He could understand all of that. He just couldn't understand why they lost any interest in their looks.

While her hair was drying, George began to rub makeup onto Marilyn's face. The irregularities, the slight blemishes seemed to completely disappear.

"He seems like such an attractive man," George remarked. "And vigorous. I've heard he exercises every day."

Marilyn sat up to apply her lipstick. She cast a glance at her hair dresser and lifted a brow.

"I just meant it must be exciting for you to be around him," he offered.

She looked at him for a long moment, then she looked back into the mirror as she smeared the red pigment over her lips.

"Yes," she said. "It is."

George looked in the mirror at her transformation. He was stunned. When he had started, his client had appeared positively vagrant, but with a bath, some shampoo, and a little makeup, she was the very image of Marilyn Monroe.

"George," Marilyn said, thinking of his perception that the President was vigorous, "remember that sometimes appearances are deceiving."

John Kennedy sat in a silk robe over his pajamas and turned the final pages of a paperback novel he had been reading that afternoon. He was comfortably ensconced in his favorite room in the Penthouse of the Carlyle Hotel, New York's finest, reading one of his favorite authors.

"Damn!" he exclaimed as he put the book down. "What a character!"

He was thinking about James Bond, master English spy. He loved the Bond books. Bond always won, and he always got the girls in the process. He was good looking, enterprising, daring, and virile—everything people wanted in a hero.

Kennedy pulled himself up and positioned his crutches beneath his arms. Using the crutches to keep his full weight off his back, he maneuvered past a commanding view of Manhattan and through an open door. When he came to a closed door, he used one of the crutches to knock against it. The door was opened for him.

"Are you fellows trying to keep me away from my command?" he asked with a good natured smile. He lifted himself along with the crutches into a room where a small group of men in white shirts and dark ties were reading, writing, and typing. All activities stopped, and one of the young men stood up as the Commander in Chief entered. He made it over to a rocking chair where he lowered himself.

"All right," he asked, "what are we going to do with the son of a bitch?"

A middle aged man with tortoiseshell glasses, short red hair, and freckles sat on the edge of a table.

"You were the one who said we couldn't tolerate a Soviet base on the island of Cuba. I realize that it was a debate and you wanted to embarrass Nixon, but you were the one who publicly proposed to send freedom fighters into Cuba."

"What was I going to say? Think about it, Mac. If Ike had toppled Castro, I wouldn't have to worry about being President."

"But that was in a debate. You're the President now. We have options."

"What options?"

"Just letting him stay there. What harm is he going to do?"

"Forget it. Castro has to go or during the next election we're going to have to explain why we talked tough and backed down."

One of the other senior advisors puffed at his pipe and cleared his throat. Kennedy looked over at him.

"The truth is, Jack, getting rid of Castro isn't going to be particularly easy. He has excellent security. The Russians are giving him security people as well as guns."

"—That's the whole point," Kennedy interrupted. "The people of this country will simply not tolerate Soviet expansion into this hemisphere. He's got to go."

"He happened on Eisenhower's watch. Ike didn't turn the Army loose on him."

"I wish he had," Kennedy replied as he rocked back in forth in his chair and looked out over the fading Manhattan skyline. "Have you guys seen those maps the right wing nuts like to show?"

The advisors looked at each other.

"They like to talk about the tide of history—the great red march. They show a large map of the world and then how the Soviets took over Russia. Communism sweeps Russia!! Then after the war, with a Democratic president at the helm, the Communists took over the countries of Eastern Europe. And the map is starting to look pretty red at this point. And then they show China going Communist. That's a big land mass. Then Korea. And as a viewer, you're starting to feel nervous. Then they focus on the Western Hemisphere and light up Cuba! The Communists are in Cuba."

"Latin America is certainly ripe . . ." one of the young men in the room began. He stopped talking when he saw the stern glares from the others.

"Exactly," Kennedy said. "What's your name?"

The young man told him.

"True, Castro came to power with Eisenhower at the helm. But if any more Latin American countries come under Communist influence, we're going to be seeing more of that growing red map in 1964 than we ever wanted to. Castro has to go. Eisenhower thought so. I ambushed Nixon with the idea. I don't think we can just forget about Cuba. What are our choices?"

The discussion was interrupted by a knock at the door. A secret service agent opened the door.

"There is a Miss Monroe here to see you, sir," he said soberly.

Kennedy glanced around the room as his aides tried to repress their smiles.

"Please show her into the reading room."

The secret service agent led Marilyn through the assembled staff meeting and toward the door Kennedy had used just a few minutes before. The men stared openly at Marilyn as she walked slowly through the meeting. She wore a black dress with a plunging neck line and a large fur to cover her partially covered breasts. As she passed him, Marilyn glanced over at the President, lifted a shoulder and waved. Then she turned and followed the agent into the reading room. After a few moments the conversation continued.

"Mr. President, perhaps we shouldn't be talking about CIA plans for Cuba under these circumstances," the senior aide said.

"Why not?"

"With all due respect, sir, I'm not sure Miss Monroe has security clearance."

"Security clearance?" the President asked rhetorically. "Does the **New York Times** have security clearance? You can read all you want about American plans to invade Cuba on the front page of the **New York Times**," he yelled. Kennedy was referring to an article published on January 10, 1961 under the headline: "*U.S. Helps Train an Anti-Castro Force at Secret Guatemalan Base.*"

Marilyn entered the room and was struck by the grandeur of the view. Manhattan was full of high rise buildings, but she had never had a more commanding view. The sun had set and the lights of the city were beginning to outshine the light of the sky. Then she turned and looked around the room. Tall, dark bookshelves lined the room and a thick dark red carpet covered the floor. On one table she saw a photograph of Winston Churchill which was inscribed "to the young Kennedy." Between the rows of books hung a painting of a young man in a three piece suit. It looked like one of Jack's brothers. A light was burning next to one of the reading chairs, and next to the light, on a small table, was a paperback book. She picked the book up and smiled.

What a choice, she thought. Surrounded by such classic works of literature, someone had been reading a James Bond novel. She stared at the handsome illustration of Bond on the cover. If Peter Lawford had not turned down the role of James Bond, he would still be working.

The voices from the other room spilled into the silence that surrounded her. She heard something about Castro and Cuba. Then she heard Jack yell something about the **New York Times**.

She wondered why tempers were flaring.

Within a few minutes the door to the meeting was opened completely and Jack pushed his way through, swinging his body on the crutches as he went. Then he turned and used one of the crutches to push the door securely shut.

"Like this place?" he asked.

"It's magnificent. Is that one of your brothers?" she asked pointing at the painting.

"Father," he replied. "As a young bank president."

"I thought your father was in the government or the stock exchange or . . . something."

"Actually, he was in the government. He was the Ambassador to the Court of St. James just as the war was starting. Before that, he served as Chairman of the Securities and Exchange Commission. And before that, he was in the stock market, in a way."

"He made a lot of money," Marilyn concluded.

"A lot of money," the President confirmed.

"Who is the man riding this horse?" She was pointing to a framed photograph.

Kennedy laughed again.

"Actually, that man is my wife. She's going over a jump on her horse."

Marilyn felt a little tightness as she realized that she was betraying her ignorance. But she wanted to keep moving. She didn't want him to think she was in over her head.

"Do you jump horses?" she asked.

Kennedy lifted the crutches he was standing on. "Not exactly," he confessed as he swung through the crutches. "These days I'm lucky to jump women." He smiled.

Marilyn laughed. It was an opportunity to leave the subject behind.

"It's a cold night," the President said. He made his way over to a table and picked up a small silver bell. Ringing the bell, he asked if she wanted a drink.

A tall man dressed in what Marilyn thought was an old tuxedo came in through a different door.

"Miss Monroe will have some Scotch," he said. "Could you bring it to the fireplace?"

The man left and Marilyn followed Jack through yet another door out of the library. He swung along on the crutches until they came to a large room.

"We can warm up in here," the President suggested.

Marilyn glanced around the room. A bed was covered with books and newspapers. A cup of tea sat on a silver platter on a small table next to the bed. Across the room, a fire burned in one of the largest fireplaces Marilyn had ever seen. Two chairs were on the periphery of a large, circular fur in front of the fireplace. Jack went over to one of the chairs and lowered himself. He grimaced as he did. Marilyn sat in the other chair as the steward arrived with her drink.

Kennedy talked for a time about the inauguration, about how much he had wanted her to be there, but been advised against it. As he spoke, Marilyn thought he looked tired and thin. All of the responsibilities of being president must be taking their toll on his health. But he seemed relaxed as he sat in the chair opposite her, the light of the fire reflecting off his face.

"Did you read that Arthur and I got a divorce?" she asked.

"I noticed that," he said. "Three days after my election, you announced your separation. The day of my inauguration, you got your divorce. Was there a message there?" He smiled at her.

"Maybe there was."

"You're not going to talk to the reporters about me, are you?" he asked.

"Of course not!" she said plainly.

"Do you have any idea how dangerous it is for me to see you? Honestly, I don't think this government could be brought down by a full Russian assault. But it could fall overnight if the press got word that the Commander in Chief was seeing Marilyn Monroe."

Hearing him say that made Marilyn feel suddenly more important. She was known, after all. She might be the best known actress in the world and she was glad he realized that. She was feeling the first effects of her drink.

"I don't need more publicity," she said demurely. She looked into the fire and finished the Scotch.

"Would you like some dinner? I can have something brought up," Jack offered.

She thought for a moment. Should she try? She wanted to go out and enjoy the excitement of going to a restaurant or club with the most powerful man in the world. But what if he said no? Marilyn liked to take risks.

"I was hoping we might go out," she said softly. She looked at him with her eyebrows slightly raised.

"I wish we could," he replied. "But I can't move around nearly as much as I once could. The Secret Service has to check out restaurants before I come in. The hallways have to be secured. Turns out, being president means I can't be as spontaneous as I like to be." He smiled his regret.

John Kennedy looked at Marilyn Monroe and squinted. True, his back hurt like hell, but he was the President of the United States, sitting atop one of the best properties in New York, staring at a woman who was not only beautiful, but sexual. Jackie was beautiful, but she wasn't much interested in being sexual. This woman knew how to be sexual, and there was something about her presence in a room which excited him.

The light flickered over Marilyn's crossed legs. His eyes followed her legs up to her abdomen. It was thin. Tight. Her breasts filled the top of her evening dress, but were partially covered by a fur hanging around her neck. He looked up into her face and saw that she was looking at him stare at her body. She smiled. She knew she had beautiful legs. She knew her entire body was beautiful and she liked the fact that men looked at her. Marilyn was a woman who enjoyed her sexual appeal.

It was perfect in a way. He had spent the day talking about foreign policy, about how he was going to save the developing economies around the world from the creeping threat of Communism. And at night? At night, he was in the company of the world's most seductive woman.

He found himself staring at her legs again. There was a slit in her dress that ran halfway up her thigh. It wasn't a dress Jackie would wear. Too risqué. But Marilyn would wear it. She liked being a bad girl. Marilyn lifted one of her legs slightly and was somehow able to drop a shoe from her foot. She pushed her unclad foot down to her other foot and wiggled that shoe off, as well. He looked up at her and took a deep breath. It didn't appear that she was wearing any stockings.

"The fire is so nice," she said as she removed the fur from around her neck. Her neck line showed the fullness of her breasts.

Her skin looked clean and soft. She leaned in toward the fire, rubbed her hands together, and held them out toward the fire as if to warm them. "Fires don't seem so nice in California."

She then uncrossed her legs and slid down onto the mink throw. She crawled over closer to the fire and knelt up to warm herself

The President tried to get out of his chair and slide down onto the mink covering. It had been on his bed earlier in the day. In anticipation of Marilyn, he had asked that it be put in front of the fireplace. As he bent forward, he felt a twinge of pain in his back. He grimaced. It wasn't going to be as easy as he thought. Getting down there was going to hurt. He sat back in the chair to brace himself for another attempt. Bond would be able to get down and roll around with the woman. But Bond never had a bad back.

"Did you have a busy day?" Marilyn asked as Jack sat back into the chair. She sensed that he was uncomfortable.

"Not bad. A meeting with the national security guys. Didn't get anywhere."

"You must go to a lot of meetings."

"Too many. I've got to do something about that. I get nothing done." He was distracted for a moment. He really didn't like all those damn meetings. "But we have problems to address, and we have to think them through completely."

"What's the problem?"

"Castro. Castro tried to get money out of the administration, but Ike wouldn't give him any. So he went to Moscow and talked to the Communists about spending some money on Cuban development. Naturally, they liked the idea of buying a base right next to the United States. The bastards! We're going to go down there and take it away from them."

"Why? So they have a base next to the United States? Who cares? We're not going to war with them."

Kennedy tapped on his teeth. He had been with some of the best minds in America all afternoon, discussing logical strategies for Cuba, and now he was going to get some advice from a movie star. He should just get down there and let Marilyn work her magic, but his back needed another few minutes of rest.

"Marilyn, you can't mention anything I say about Cuba, or anything else, to anyone. Do you understand?"

"Of course I understand. I told you I don't talk to reporters." She continued: "I can't believe you're thinking about taking over Cuba. Isn't there something else we could do?"

"Yes," the president said. He squinted and stared into the fire. "If we don't invade, the only other option I have would be to go down there and shoot him."

"Shoot him?!! How could you shoot him?" she asked in a high excited voice. Marilyn's heart skipped a beat and then began to race. She hated the thought of someone being killed.

"Marilyn, calm down. I wouldn't shoot him. The CIA would simply facilitate it. There is no shortage of Cubans who would love to shoot Castro. One of them would be facilitated. Facilitated. Castro took their lands. He took over their casinos and their businesses. One of them might get to him, anyway. I'm not going to shoot him." Jack didn't like the way the evening was progressing. He didn't want to spend the night explaining top secret foreign policy to someone of Marilyn's educational background.

"I was thinking that maybe you could send some students down to Cuba to help the people build bridges and roads. Why do you have to get rid of Castro?"

"That's actually a nice thought. We're going to set up a Peace Corps for other areas. But students aren't going to prevent the Soviets from putting a military base 90 miles off our shores. We have to get rid of the Soviets and of Castro. We can't get rid of them unless we get rid of him."

"That sounds so. . . . serious," Marilyn blurted out anxiously.

Kennedy laughed. It was serious. It was most serious. It could initiate a chain of events that might end life on the planet. He listened to Marilyn's thoughts. Maybe her thoughts represented how other Americans were thinking about Cuba. But then, maybe not. Most Americans were completely afraid of Communists.

Marilyn wanted to send in the Peace Corps. She was something else.

"You remember those men you saw today?" he asked her.

"Yes."

"They are some of the smartest people in the United States. One of them was a dean at Harvard. One of the others was a professor down at Yale. They have access to facts you don't have. They are working from an historical and policy framework you are not in a position to appreciate. I mean, I value your input, but these are serious matters, and they must be decided by the best and the most capable people available."

"I'm sure they are," Marilyn agreed.

She went from her kneeling position back onto all fours and stretched her back. Then she laid on the mink covering, facing him. He stared at her full figure, his eyes darting up and down her body.

"I think you need to hear more of my ideas," she said suggestively. Her smile had returned.

"Actually, I always want to hear everyone's point of view."

"I wonder if you need a little back rub."

He took another deep breath. Bond would be able to do it. It looked tough, but it was only getting down to the floor. He resolved to make his move. Pulling himself up, he moved through the pain, sliding off the chair and onto the floor. Then he stretched out, face down, and lifted his arms above his head. It was going to take a few minutes to judge the damage.

Marilyn massaged his back through the robe. His muscles were tight with spasm. But having her rub them made them relax and made his pain better. After a few minutes, he was able to roll on his side and face her. They lay in front of the fire, he in his pajamas and robe, she in her evening dress.

"You should have kept your shoes on," he said. "And taken off the dress."

She laughed. "I'm not sure there's any point in that. You don't look like you're in very good shape. I'm worried that physical activity might not be good for you—not good for the country," she teased.

The President smiled, but was not amused. He had worried

most of his life that he would lose public support because he was weak, underweight, and bordered on being an invalid. As his back had become worse over the years, he had taken steps to hide his disability from the public. But he was worried that word was leaking out, and that, at long last, the truth would be known.

During the next few minutes, clothes were shed, bodies were turned, and the President's virility was once again confirmed.

"My goodness," she said when it was over, and she stared into his face, "I think I made your back feel better."

"You did," he gasped. "Yes, I think you did."

After she left, Kennedy was back on his crutches and pleased with himself. Better to have the rumors be that he was getting too much than nothing at all. And if his back did not start to improve soon, he wasn't going to be able to walk. The idea of a truly spineless president, being wheeled around in a chair, confronting the brutal forces of Communism bothered him. But he wasn't going to let that happen. He was going to get some back experts and they were going to help him. He was going to keep making policy and he was going to maintain himself on a steady diet of beautiful women. And if rumors reached the press that he was bordering on a sexual superman, well, that was just too bad. The voters would have a choice: a repressed conservative Republican, or a healthy, virile, attractive and debonair Democrat.

He passed a mirror as he was going back into the bedroom. He looked at himself and smiled one of his big teeth smiles. "Bond has nothing on you, my friend. Bond should do so well." He then lifted the crutches forward and swung himself down the darkened hallway.

Marilyn was led down a long tunnel away from the Carlyle. It was too risky to have her seen coming out of the building itself, so the Secret Service was taking her to an adjacent hotel where she would get into a private car and be taken home.

She wasn't completely happy with the way the evening had gone. She wanted to say something important—she wanted to leave him with her thought that getting rid of Castro was just plain wrong.

It was wrong not because she was a former Harvard dean or Yale professor. It was wrong because it was wrong. It had always been wrong to take a human life under any circumstances. And it ways would be wrong.

She had wanted to go out to dinner. She had wanted to be seen with him. But that night, it was not to be. Marilyn blushed a little as she thought that she still needed to get dinner. She had gone over to the Presidential Suite, had sex with the President, and now was being led secretly away. It wasn't exactly an interaction which would be accepted in polite society. But she had done such things before.

That's the way it had happened in Hollywood, she thought. Initially, she had gained attention with her body. Then, she had secured a couple of roles with sexual favors. But finally, when given the opportunity she would not have had without using her sexuality, she had succeeded. She had become Marilyn Monroe. She had risen to a level of fame enjoyed by few other human beings. Maybe it would be that way again. Maybe now she felt like she was being used just as a sexual outlet for the world's most powerful man. But in the future, who could know? Maybe she would earn a different place, a better place, a place which would recognize the power of her thoughts and the high principles in which she believed. She got into the limousine and began the trip back to her apartment.

John Kennedy sat in his chair next to the blazing fire and read a top secret report while Marilyn watched the street lights pass the window of her limousine. Neither one realized that both of their lives would turn on the bearded dictator of Cuba.

Chapter 4

"The best way for me to find myself as a person is to prove to myself I am an actress."

Marilyn Monroe
Los Angeles Times
November 30, 1960

From the middle drawer of her bureau Marilyn picked out a brown bottle with a rubber stopper held in place by an aluminum band. She shook the bottle to see if there was anything left inside. There was, but not much. Demerol made her feel better, physically relaxed and mentally hopeful. Sad that she had to turn to a drugs to feel hopeful, but on some days she needed them.

Would there be enough? She held the bottle up to the light of the window of her apartment and tipped it in different positions to get an idea just how much she had left.

Getting Demerol was an occasional challenge. The doctor who supplied her with her last few bottles told her that he could get his license revoked for giving it to her. But she always got her way: every doctor who gave her the drug wanted the notoriety of being Marilyn Monroe's doctor, so he wasn't going to refuse his little moment of celebrity. And the authorities weren't going to pick up on a few bottles being missing from any one doctor. So her trick was to simply change doctors. Get one to give her a few bottles, then when they ran out, go to a different doctor.

She picked up the glass syringe she had been using for the last few months—the syringes were harder to come by than the Demerol—and took a hypodermic needle out of a closed bottle filled with alcohol. Someone had told her that she had to boil the syringe after every use. But she didn't. And it didn't seem to make too much of a difference. Needles were different: if she didn't boil the needles or keep them in the jar of alcohol, she found that she got little infections wherever she found a vein. And she didn't like little marks. They were hard to cover over.

The light seemed too bright to her, even though the windows were mostly covered. She went over to a chair near one of the windows and sat on a towel. After her warm bath, the veins in her feet seemed easier to find. She tied a shoelace around her ankle firmly and waited for the veins to get large.

The night had been spoiled by the anticipation of the morning papers and then the news hadn't been good. The newspapers had turned against her. Early in her career she anxiously bought papers and brought them back to her apartment, excitedly turning to the reviews to see her name in print. It hadn't mattered whether the critics had liked her performances or not. Seeing her name in print was good enough. But seeing her name in print was not good enough anymore.

For years she had been confined to the sexy roles. They had come easily for her. She had gotten her start, after all, posing for calendars. It seemed embarrassing to her now, but at the time, she thought it was easy money and a chance at the big time. Then she got roles where she would be the girl who was asking for it—in a nice sort of way. But she knew there was more in her than just showing off her body. She felt that she could act and she wanted an opportunity to prove it.

Getting married to Arthur Miller had been partially motivated by her yearning to be taken seriously. He had recognized in her the talent to actually play a real dramatic role. And who better to judge such talent? He had been around the theater most of his life. He knew talent when he saw it.

It was Arthur Miller who was struck by Marilyn's habit of trying to save the seemingly less important creatures in the world. Although her friends thought she was crazy, Marilyn made a point of trying to look out for life, no matter how insignificant. Arthur hit upon an idea for a movie that would dramatize how much she cared for life that the rest of society considered worthless. By trying to protect the lives of wild horses, Marilyn would be portrayed as the woman she felt she truly was—a woman with important moral values. It had been his first screenplay: *The Misfits*.

He gave her the play as a Valentine's present—it was to be the vehicle by which her talent as a serious actress would be proven once and for all. The money men in Hollywood loved the idea. Marilyn Monroe staring in a screenplay written by her husband, the most talented playwright of his generation—it had to work. They were so impressed with the idea that the executives convinced the legendary John Huston to direct her. With so much enthusiasm developing over the script, other film heavyweights wanted to come aboard. Clark Gable was signed up to play opposite Marilyn. After *The Misfits*, nobody would ever consider Marilyn to be just a sex star again.

It was a great script: Marilyn was married to a cowboy—Clark Gable—who rounded up wild horses on the deserts of Nevada and sold them for slaughter. But Marilyn was to emerge as a woman of substance, someone with a deep inner conviction. She had to convince Gable that killing the horses was wrong. Even though the horses were a nuisance, taking the life of another living thing violated an important moral law. In the process of making this argument, Marilyn would demonstrate the power of her moral vision, and Gable would realize that he loved Marilyn for reasons which transcended her physical beauty. It would be the first movie to look seriously at animal rights.

The Misfits was her big chance. But the papers brought her the news that the critics didn't like it.

Marilyn had known rejection throughout her life—first as a child put up for adoption, then in the various foster homes, and throughout her career in Hollywood. But now, with so much on the line, having made such a big emotional investment in *The Misfits*, getting poor reviews hurt her deeply. The film was not going to be a success. She was not going to be recognized as a artistic actress.

She lightly touched the vein on the side of her foot. She pushed the hypodermic needle in and pulled back until she saw blood come into the syringe. Then she pushed what she was able to collect from the bottle of Demerol into her vein. She took off the shoelace, sat back in a chair, and waited for the calmness, the hope to outshine the gloom that had overtaken her.

It didn't work. There hadn't been enough Demerol. The chair felt cold against her back and she could feel herself relax, but she did not experience any euphoria. She needed something more. After a few minutes of looking through her curtains down at the busy New York street below, Marilyn decided she would have to get some more Demerol. To get the Demerol, she was going to have to convince a doctor that she needed it. She fumbled through her address book, looking at the names and numbers, trying to find someone who might be sympathetic.

After making a couple of calls, Marilyn tried the office of Dr. Marianne Kris. Dr. Kris had seen her before, and even though she wasn't as sympathetic as some of the others, she could be convinced to see Marilyn that day. Marilyn showered and dressed and took a cab over to Dr. Kris' office.

"You know what the problem is," Dr. Kris said. They sat in chairs next to Dr. Kris' desk. The analyst's couch was left unused for this discussion.

"The rejection?" Marilyn suggested.

"No. It's the drugs," Dr. Kris asserted. "Let me ask you: how can you possibly enter into a stable relationship with a man if he believes you are always on drugs? Do you think he will trust you?"

Marilyn knew Dr. Kris was right, but she began to feel defensive. "I haven't had problems entering into relationships with men," she retorted.

"Do you want to make progress, or do you just want to argue?" the psychiatrist asked. "We've been over this before. You don't have problems entering into relationships. We both know that. The Marilyn side of you can always get a man into bed. What you want is someone who will have a real relationship with you— someone who will love you, care about you, and not just want to use you for a sexual release. Am I getting through?"

Marilyn stared across the desk at Dr. Kris and then past her, through the window, into the empty trees in the park beyond. It was a cold day in early February of 1961. The bare trees of winter reminded Marilyn of her own barren life. Even though she was regarded as one of the world's most desirable women, no one actually desired her. She could lure a man to her with her sexuality, but she couldn't keep him interested. She couldn't have a stable, normal relationship.

"When you don't have anything else in your life," Marilyn began, starting to cry, "drugs can make you feel better."

Drugs were part of Marilyn's life and had been for years. The studios hired doctors to inject her with uppers in the mornings and downers at night. When she started acting, drug use seemed like an accepted part of the routine. But after months, then years of the injections, they began to lose their effect. Her sleep cycle was thrown off, and she was dependent on more drugs, and in greater doses.

"Marilyn, the point is that when you have drugs in your life, you can't have anything else. If you want to begin to have normal relationships, you have to get off the drugs. It is as simple as that."

"It wasn't my idea to start using them," Marilyn claimed. "Everyone was getting shots."

"I don't care how you started," the doctor pressed, "you have to stop. Do you want to stop, or not?"

Marilyn looked at the psychiatrist, not an unattractive woman, and realized that the doctor was a woman with a sense of values. She had confidence in what she had learned, and she had the security to recommend her opinions to her patients. Dr. Kris was a strong woman. Marilyn was starting to listen.

"I know I need to stop. I've tried before. But it is just so hard. They are everywhere I go."

"You have to make the decision. You can go on the way you have. Or you can try to make a clean break of it. I think you need to make the break. And I think you need to make it now. If I admit you to the Payne Whitney, you will have an opportunity to make a break with the past. I think you should do it."

Marilyn studied the lines of her doctor's face. Clearly, going into the hospital wasn't the reason she had sought out Dr. Kris. But if she went into the hospital, it might not be so bad. She had been in hospitals before. And if the treatment worked, Marilyn would be far better off. She would be able to think with a clear mind. Maybe it wasn't such a bad idea.

"I guess I should do it," Marilyn announced, suddenly feeling better.

"You can do it," Dr. Kris encouraged. "But only you can do it. I can give you the place, and make it safe. But I can't commit your mind. Only you can do that."

"I want to try."

Marilyn agreed to go directly to the hospital. If she went back to her apartment, she thought she would lose her nerve and skip the treatment. So, she had Dr. Kris' secretary call for a cab, and she went over to check in.

She had been hospitalized for her drug use before. In California, her doctors would occasionally admit her to the hospital for a "rest cure." She would be escorted to a private room and pampered for a week or two. And during the hospital course, they would try to give her fewer and fewer pills—try to wean her from the dependency she had developed. In the past, it had been a gentle process, with no one, not even the doctors, believing she would actually be able to put the pills behind her.

After the cab ride, Marilyn stood in the lobby of the Payne Whitney wearing her enormous fur and wondering if she were doing the right thing. She had just signed the papers to go upstairs. But she was starting to wonder if the place didn't look just a little too serious.

The lobby seemed so depressing. It was dark and cold. The furniture was outdated. The whole place seemed so old and dirty, not like the new hospitals out in California. The elevator door opened and a man was wheeled past her and toward the clinic exit. He looked completely expressionless. He didn't even recognize her. Was she going to end up looking like him? Would they turn her into some kind of expressionless zombie?

"Mrs. Miller," a nurse addressed her. She had registered as 'Faye Miller.' Why she had used the name 'Miller' was unclear even to her. She had divorced Arthur only a month earlier. "Please come this way."

Marilyn took a last look at the lobby. If she didn't like it, she would leave. She could always leave. She followed the nurse into the elevator, pulling the fur more closely around her neck.

Marilyn got out of the elevator and stared around the psychiatric unit. She had never seen anything quite like it. The patients all looked completely stoned—blank looks and flat faces. As the nurse led her past the rooms she noticed that some of the doors to patient rooms were closed.

"Why are the doors closed?" she asked a nurse.

"Many of our patients need rest," the nurse replied, unconvincingly.

Marilyn followed the nurse into a room that mirrored the rest of the hospital: a bed with a plain covering, a sink, a mirror, no television set, a small window to the world. A light blue hospital gown, neatly folded, was on the bed.

"There is no telephone in here," Marilyn noticed.

"No. If you need to make telephone calls, you can make them at the nurses' station. You are limited to three calls a day."

"Why?" Marilyn asked.

"Policy," the woman replied. "Your doctor is supervising your care. You wouldn't be here if Dr. Kris did not think you needed this level of care."

Marilyn took a deep breath. It wasn't going to be fun. It was serious. But she needed something serious. She needed to make a break with the past. She picked up the hospital gown.

"You want me to put this on?" she asked with a smile.

"Yes. I'll be back in just a moment for your clothes," the nurse said with no warmth.

"Well, all right. I don't really understand why I have to wear this little hospital gown. Someone should be over here soon with my pajamas and robe."

The nurse looked at Marilyn quizzically. "If you will get into the gown and let me take your clothes and jewelry, please."

The nurse left the room.

Marilyn looked out the window. The view was terrible and the window seemed dirty and small. A bad combination. She sat on her bed, thinking about whether she should change into the little gown. She had told Dr. Kris she would cooperate. She told her that she would make the effort to really change this time, so she removed her clothes and folded them. She put on the gown, which did not close in the back, and sat back on the bed. She smiled as she felt her bottom touch the cold bed. Jack would love this little gown. Using the gown, she could tease him without mercy!

She smiled with this thought. Even as she sat in the bleak room, with its small, thick, dirty window looking out on the cold February day, she was warmed by the thought of his touch. She thought about how he would corner her against a bookcase and feel her bare bottom and then raise an eyebrow and start to smile. She thought about the warmth of his embrace and felt better that there was someone in the world who wanted to hold her. There was someone who thought her interesting and exciting enough that he would risk his political career to be with her. There was something about her, about the way she moved, about the way she made him feel that made it worthwhile for him. She shifted her weight on the bed and thought about how much attention it would draw to have him visit her there, in the small room. The powerful leader of the free world coming to a small hospital room to see a very special woman, a woman—

The nurse pushed the door of her room open and ended her fantasy. Marilyn looked up at her. The nurse was still acting so cold—no smiles, no hugs. Just doing a job. Marilyn watched her come over to the bed and pick up her clothes and place her bracelet and a cheap wrist watch into a small brown envelope.

"These will be stored for you," the nurse said lifting the envelope and the clothes. "If you need anything, please signal me using the call light."

"Oh, I'll get along," Marilyn said cheerfully. The hospital was starting to remind her of an orphanage she had been in for a time in her youth. They always looked depressing when you first went in them. But, things got better after a while. She always met someone and made a friend. "I'll just come out and get you."

"No," the nurse said, turning and facing Marilyn. "Use the call light."

Marilyn was stunned. The nurse was acting like a robot. She still hadn't smiled.

The nurse closed the door. Marilyn looked out the small, dirty window. Then she heard a click.

It was not just any click. It was a click of a lock being turned on her door. Marilyn stood up immediately. She went over to the door and turned the knob. The knob turned, but the door would not open. It was locked from the outside.

Her eyes widened as she tried to comprehend that she was in a small, cold room in the middle of a psychiatric unit, surrounded by strange people, and the nurse had just locked her door. She couldn't open it. She turned the knob and tried to pull the door open again, not quite believing that she was really locked in the room.

"Open the door," she said at moderate volume. "I can't be

locked up. They know—my doctors know I can't be locked up!!"
She felt her hands become moist.

"Open the door, right now!!" she screamed. She looked through
the small window and into the hallway. There were nurses passing
by her room, but they were not stopping. She banged her hand
against the door. Then she kicked the door with considerable
force.

"They know I can't be locked up!! Now, get this door open."

She saw her nurse coming back down toward her door. Marilyn
beat her fist against the door. Her heart was racing. "Open this
door," she screamed.

The nurse stood next to Marilyn's door and spoke through
the small window, which was open at the bottom. A space at the
bottom of the window was large enough to pass pills under the
window.

"Mrs. Miller," the nurse began, "please sit down."

"Open this door," Marilyn said. "I'm not the kind of person
who can be locked up."

"Mrs. Miller, you need to sit down before I will talk to you."

"Are you out of your mind?" Marilyn asked. "Call Dr. Kris
right now. Tell her to get me out of here immediately."

"Mrs. Miller, please sit down."

Marilyn lifted her hand and smashed it against the small window, which did not break.

"Listen to me! I want you to unlock that door, and I want you
to do it right now. I'm warning you, I'm not the kind of person who
can be confined. It's a medical condition. Now, open this goddamn
door!"

The nurse smiled lightly.

"I think we're going to have a little problem until we learn
what the unit is like. If you will sit down, we can talk."

"A problem?" Marilyn repeated. "I'll show you a problem."
Marilyn turned from the door and looked desperately around the
room. She picked up a small chair, turned and hurled it against
the nurse peering through the window. The chair leg hit the small

window directly and shattered the glass. Pieces of glass blew out of the window and into the hallway, skidding across the waxed floor.

The nurse jumped away from the exploding glass window just in time to avoid being hit by the flying glass. She gasped her surprise, made a determined grunt, and then walked confidently back to the nurses' station.

Marilyn looked at the broken glass window. It had taken some loud language, but she had gotten her point across. She couldn't be confined in a locked room. The nurse now seemed to understand that. Soon, Dr. Kris would be there, and the whole, ugly episode would be over. She sat on her bed and waited for the nurse to return. She wondered how long it would take Dr. Kris to get over there. After a few minutes, she carefully stood up and walked over to the window looking out of the hospital. It wasn't a dirty window, as she had at first assumed. It was a thick window. It was made of unbreakable glass. She shuddered with the thought that she was truly captive. But, Dr. Kris would be there soon, and Marilyn would be on her way home.

After what seemed to be a very long time, she heard another click from her door. She turned to see not the nurse, not Dr. Kris, but a large man in a white uniform enter her room. He was followed by a smaller man, also in a white uniform. The second man was carrying a canvas garment covered by straps and buckles. The first man smiled at Marilyn.

Marilyn pressed against the wall behind her. There was no place to go.

"Now, Mrs. Miller," the first man said with his eyebrows arching upward, "we have to get you into this little vest. Can you help us?"

"What the hell are you thinking about?" Marilyn asked in a sober low voice. "Do you know who I am? I'm Marilyn Monroe!! Now, put that little vest down and get out of here!! Call a policeman. Call Dr. Kris. But, do not even think about laying your dirty hands on me!!"

The orderlies looked at each other.

"She actually does look a little like Marilyn Monroe," the

smaller one said with a sheepish smile. The men looked back at Marilyn, both of them glaring at the curves of her body.

Marilyn smiled as she saw they were staring at her. At last, she would be able to make some kind of human contact get these men on her side. They would get word to Joe. But they had to know it was really her.

She turned herself halfway around and pulled in her stomach and stuck out her bottom. The men looked at the protruding flesh from the back of her gown. Then they looked back up at her face. She struck a pouty Marilyn pose and pulled the gown forward just a bit more to tease them.

"It is Marilyn," the taller orderly said. They both broke into broad smiles. Their friends were never going to believe this one.

"One thing you need to appreciate about me," Marilyn suggested seductively, "is that I can't stand to be locked up. I'm a claustrophobic or something. It scares me."

Hearing her say these words prompted the men to look at each other again. The smaller man shrugged.

"Marilyn," the taller orderly said, " we need to get you to put on this vest. We work here. It's our job to get this vest on people who become violent."

"I wasn't becoming violent."

"You broke that window."

"That nurse wouldn't unlock the door." Marilyn felt her heart begin to race again as she anticipated the possibility that they would actually try to put the vest on her. "All I want is to have Dr. Kris come over here and straighten everyone out. I'm not a crazy woman. I'm an actress. I may be a depressed actress. I may have some problems with the pills. But I'm not crazy and I won't let anyone lock me up or tie me down."

The larger of the two men held his hand in front of his co-worker. "We better be sure of this," he said. The two men backed away from Marilyn. Their shoes crushed the glass as they approached the doorway. Marilyn looked at the crushed glass on the floor and then up at the tall man blocking her exit. Maybe if he came toward her, she could get out. If she could only get him to come about halfway across the room.

Staring into the taller man's eyes, Marilyn reached the tie on the back of her neck and pulled it. She let the gown fall off her shoulders and onto the floor. The orderly looked at her body with utter amazement. Marilyn Monroe was standing in front of him, completely naked.

The nurse and the smaller orderly approached the doorway. The nurse gasped as she saw Marilyn standing naked in front of the gawking man.

"Mrs. Miller," the nurse began, "I'm afraid I must ask you to put your gown back on. These men have to get you into the vest."

"You get out of here," Marilyn screamed at the nurse. "I'm not going to wear any vest and I'm not going to be locked in any room."

The nurse looked at Marilyn and then at the two orderlies. "Put the vest on her," she commanded.

"No!!" Marilyn screamed.

"Get it on her," the nurse went on. "I'll get some medication."

The men began to slowly approach her, expecting her to try to escape around them. Marilyn cowered back toward the window. The men, with careful, straight faces, inched forward.

She screamed her raw fear as they came forward. Then she lunged between the men, trying to get out the door. They grabbed her. One man held her arms down while the other tried to put the vest over her head. Marilyn pushed back against the tall orderly who had his arms wrapped around her chest and kicked the small orderly directly in the groin. He fell to his knees and gasped. Then she kicked him again. The man rolled on his side and moaned. Marilyn struggled with the larger man now pulling her to the bed. Together, they fell on the bed, Marilyn trying to roll into a position to administer a knee to the big man, he trying to keep her from rolling.

The nurse entered the room with a syringe filled with a clear liquid. Marilyn struggled and pushed, but was out muscled by the large orderly. The nurse wiped a moist cotton ball over Marilyn's struggling bare bottom. She plunged the needle through the skin and pushed the clear liquid into Marilyn.

Marilyn felt the stick on her bottom and knew what was going to happen next. She quit struggling and simply lay on top of the man who was trying to restrain her.

"Let me tell you one thing," she said as she felt herself becoming more lightheaded. "Nobody controls Marilyn Monroe."

She turned her head toward the light coming in from the window. The window seemed to get smaller and smaller, and then it disappeared.

Chapter 5

*"I was always afraid I was crazy like my mother, but when
I got in that psycho ward I realized they were really in-
sane—I just had a lot of problems."*

Marilyn Monroe to Susan Strasberg, 1961

Marilyn stared at a dark circle on a light blue surface.
The circle was slightly darker than the surrounding surface. And
as she stared at the contrast, it occurred to her that the circle had
a texture, it was not completely flat. It had little bumps and folds.
She felt a pain in the back of her neck, but as she tried to move
her neck the pain became worse. She decided not to move after
all. Just relax. Just let things flow. The inside of her mouth felt
thick and dry. She pulled her tongue back into her mouth and
closed her lips. The dark circle was coming into better view. It was
like a fabric. It was like a moist fabric. She blinked her eyes a
couple of times to get a better view.

Her vision sharpened with the blinking. The dark circle was
on her lap. She blinked some more. She moistened her lips with
her swollen tongue and looked at the circle.

The dark circle was wet. It was a wet circle on her blue hospital gown. She blinked again. She heard a moan from somewhere to
her right.

She heard the footsteps of someone passing directly in front of
her. She did not try to look up. Too much pain in her neck. Gradu-

ally, her eyes came into clear focus. And just as gradually, she became more aware of the sounds and odors around her. She was waking up.

Marilyn lifted her head slightly, feeling the pain in her neck, but lifted it anyway. Memories of coming into the hospital, registering to go upstairs, the expressionless nurse, the broken glass, and the two men came back to her. She turned her head to the right and saw a row of chairs. In each chair was a man or woman wearing a blue hospital gown and a canvas vest with straps and buckles. Some of the people were awake, staring into space. Others slept, their heads hanging forward.

My God, she thought. I'm one of them.

She pulled her head up to a normal position and looked the other way. Nurses were gathered at a station, some writing, others talking, others carrying pills out of a small room in little paper cups and walking to rooms down the hallway.

Marilyn looked back into her lap and saw the dark, moist circle on her hospital gown. Finally, the thought occurred to her that the circle was her own saliva. She had been drooling on herself. She swallowed a couple of times and tried to stand up but was restrained by a strap at her waist. She was belted to the chair.

Marilyn rolled her head around on her neck and the pain seemed to ease. She wondered how long she had been belted in the chair, drooling on herself.

One of the nurses brought a tray of food and put it down on a small stand in front of Marilyn. She looked at the food unenthusiastically.

"You look better today," the nurse said. Marilyn had never seen the nurse before.

"Where is Dr. Kris?" Marilyn asked, the words sticking on her swollen tongue.

"Dr. Kris has been here off and on," the nurse replied. "You are so much more alert."

Marilyn stared at the woman. She felt no anger toward her.

"Can I make a telephone call?" Marilyn asked.

"You can make three calls every day."

"Will you help me?"

The nurse wheeled her over to the telephone and helped her dial a number in Florida. To the woman's amazement, the number was for the Spring training camp of the New York Yankees.

By late afternoon, Marilyn felt completely alert. She still was wearing the strapped vest, but she was able to accept it if she didn't think about it too often. Joe was on his way and she would be out of the hospital soon.

Joe DiMaggio showed up after lunch on the following day. He was a tall, broad man with dark eyes and large, bushy eyebrows. On his way into the hospital, Joe had been stopped several times to give his autograph. When Joe DiMaggio moved through the streets of New York City, he was recognized. Just as Marilyn was recognized throughout the world, Joe was recognized, almost worshipped in New York.

He married Marilyn because he thought there was a side of her which was thoughtful and beautiful and which needed to be protected. Initially, they seemed like an ideal couple.

But he couldn't understand why she had to behave like a whore. He wanted her to keep her act in one place in her life, and live in another place. But Marilyn could not turn it off. Every time there was a camera, Marilyn the act emerged. She postured and strutted. She simply could not act like a respectable woman.

Their marriage lasted less than a year.

But whenever Marilyn needed someone she could rely on, whenever she was in real trouble and needed help, she called Joe. And Joe, having fallen in love with Marilyn, accepted their divorce, but was never able to get over her. When she called, it was like old times. She needed him. He knew it was right for him to take care of her—it was how he had been raised. So when he got her telephone call, even though he was at the Yankee training camp, he changed out of his uniform, and started toward New York.

The director of the Payne Whitney was surprised to see Joe DiMaggio in his office. The director was a doctor who retired from the active practice of medicine to focus on hospital administration. He was also a Yankee fan. Although he met many famous people in his capacity as the director of the clinic, it gave him a special thrill to see the great DiMaggio.

Joe was not in a mood to talk baseball.

"All I can tell you Mr. DiMaggio is that she signed her consent to be hospitalized and to undergo treatment. We are treating her." The director sat back in his chair and nervously pushed his gray hair back over his temples. His framed diplomas covered the wall behind his desk.

"She told me that two men physically attacked her, and that a nurse gave her an injection against her wishes," Joe said solemnly. He stared into the hospital director's eyes with grave seriousness.

The director grimaced as he heard this charge. He shifted his weight in his chair.

"I can assure you, sir, that only standard procedures were used in her case, as they are in treating every patient at this facility." He wished that they could just talk baseball.

"It is standard procedure to knock people out with drugs?"

"Dr. Kris is her doctor. We have done everything Dr. Kris has asked us to."

"She has fired her doctors. She didn't understand that she was giving permission to be restrained."

The hospital director did not like what he was hearing. The issue of what constituted informed consent in psychiatry was being discussed for the first time at the national medical meetings. But most of his job was trying to keep the families happy. Marilyn had no family. Joe DiMaggio was starting to sound like her lawyer.

"We are here to serve people, Mr. DiMaggio. If Marilyn Monroe wishes to go somewhere else, we will do whatever we can to accommodate her."

Joe lifted one side of his face up ever so slightly into a half smile. Getting Marilyn out of the hospital wasn't going to be a big fight. This director fellow was going to be a good guy.

"Mickey Mantle has been hitting the ball well this Spring," Joe confided to the older man. "I think he's the best center fielder the Yankees have ever had."

"No, he's not," the director answered. "You were."

Joe sat with Marilyn in her hospital room while the preparations were made to move her to a different facility. Getting another doctor to give her the "rest cure" she wanted had not been as easy as he had hoped. But the appeal of being "Marilyn's doctor" was too much for anyone to resist. So a different psychiatrist at a different hospital was taking on the new title. She was to go to the new hospital with Joe. He had given his personal word that she would be delivered. But they had to wait for a few hours until the light began to fade in New York. Marilyn didn't want those pesky photographers to catch her in the daylight.

"I don't understand why you had to shed the hospital gown," he said.

"You weren't listening."

"I was listening. You have two men who have come into your room to put you in a vest—or whatever it was—and you stand in front of them and throw off the only thing you are wearing."

"I thought that it would make them realize that I was really Marilyn Monroe and that they shouldn't try to put me in a restraint," she answered.

"That's a good way to keep men away from you. Throw off your clothes," he said sarcastically.

"We're not married anymore, all right?" Marilyn answered defensively.

DiMaggio stood up and walked across the room and looked out the small, thick window. He was wondering why he had dropped everything in Florida and raced up to New York to be with Marilyn. Even when she was wrong, she wouldn't admit it.

"Well, I guess nothing has changed," he said.

"What do you mean by that?" she asked.

"Just what I said. Nothing has changed. You're still taking off your clothes anytime there's a guy to gawk at you."

"Now you're going to say I wanted to have sex with the two orderlies? And the nurse? I wanted to have sex with her, too?"

DiMaggio turned away from the window and stared at Marilyn. He wanted to see how she was going to react to his next sentence.

"No, I didn't say you wanted to have sex with them," DiMaggio said. "Why would you want to have sex with them, if you can have it with the big boy?"

Marilyn was stunned. She didn't understand how Joe found out everything she did. She looked down at the bed sheets and tried to avoid his gaze.

"I don't know how you hear about all these crazy rumors," she said, continuing to avoid eye contact.

"Because with you, the crazier the rumor, the more likely it is to be true."

"Can't I have any privacy?" Marilyn asked.

"So, it's true," he said nodding his head. "You're in bed with our fearless leader."

Marilyn paused. She knew it bothered him. Even though they had been divorced for over five years, and she had remarried, and been divorced again, it still bothered him that she was interested in other men.

"Maybe," she said. "I guess I just don't see anything wrong with two people enjoying each others' company."

"You're headed for more trouble, Marilyn. Every woman in the United States is falling in love with that guy. They think he's the greatest thing since Roosevelt. But he's not. I can tell you that."

Marilyn looked up at him, now taking the offensive in the conversation.

"Oh, you can? You know a lot about politics?"

Joe paused and met her stare directly.

"Maybe I know more than you think," he said and then paused for effect. "I guess you know the election was stolen."

Marilyn laughed. Men would stop at nothing to gain the advantage on one another. She couldn't believe that Joe seemed to still be competing for her affections.

"Joe, really!"

"Daley swung the votes in Cook County. Illinois was thrown. And I heard that Texas was thrown, too, but by different people. Nice to know who runs the government."

"Don't be silly. All I know is that John Kennedy is President of the United States." She smiled at him. She was involved with the President. He was hanging around his old baseball training camp.

Joe took a deep breath. He realized that he had wandered off his subject. He was there to help Marilyn, not to try to change the way politics worked. He sat down in the chair next to Marilyn's bed and looked at her with another one of his deep stares.

"You're wasting your time with the pretty boy," DiMaggio said. "You're never going to get him."

"What makes you think I want him?" she asked.

"I know you. Being Mrs. Joe DiMaggio wasn't a big enough thrill for you. You wanted more fame. You wanted to climb a little further."

Marilyn grimaced. His words were hurtful. There was also a little bit of truth in them, but she didn't want to acknowledge that.

"I don't need to derive fame from the man I'm with," Marilyn finally said. "I'm not exactly an unknown actress."

"But that's not the point, Marilyn. The point is that you want him. You think you can put him under your spell and launch yourself into even more publicity. It's the way you are."

"No, I'm not."

"And it isn't going to work. He can't be with you. You have to get that through your head. He is the President of the United States. He's not going to get a divorce and ruin his career for Marilyn Monroe."

Marilyn smiled. She liked the thought: the President of the United States powerless without her. When she was a girl, the King of England had given up his throne to be with his mistress—

Edward VIII had abdicated for Wallis Simpson. She remembered that much history.

"Do you happen to remember the name 'Wallis Simpson'?" she asked with a teasing smile.

DiMaggio couldn't make a connection. He shrugged.

"King Edward VIII?"

"Marilyn!" DiMaggio exclaimed as he made the connection. "That's exactly what I'm talking about. Maybe I should just leave you in this place. You really are nuts. Listen to me: there is no way, no way, that the President is going to leave his wife and marry you. Do you understand that? You have to understand because if you don't, you're going to continue to fool yourself and hold onto a dream that has absolutely no chance of being filled. And when you're disappointed, and I can guarantee you will be, you're going to go back to the hooch, to the pills, and you're going to end up in a place like this. Or worse. You have to face facts, and the facts are that the great John Kennedy is using you like a call girl."

He stopped himself. He was on a roll. But he had to stop himself because he was going to hurt Marilyn's feelings, and that wasn't why he had come. He had come to help her. He had come to try to convince her that there was a better way to live than to constantly seek something she couldn't have.

"All I really wanted to say," he continued, "was that there is another way."

"You want me to marry you and stay at home and knit sweaters and be happy," Marilyn summarized. "I couldn't live like that before. I don't think I can live like that now."

"You're in a mental institution. You're going to spend a few weeks at another one. Don't you think it's time you tried to make some changes?"

Marilyn began to cry. She knew how desperate she had been when she read the reviews of *the Misfits*. Maybe if she had more stability, more people who cared about her, a child, something or someone who she could love, reviews wouldn't be so hard on her. The truth was that she lived for her fame and she didn't really want to. She wanted to live for other things. But she didn't have the other things. He was right—she should seek a simpler life. She should seek solid relationships. She needed to make a change.

"I'm sorry, baby," DiMaggio said as he watched her cry. "I came up here to help, not make things worse."

"I know you did, Joe."

"Sometimes you need a little bit of a shock to be convinced you need to change things. I just hope I haven't made things worse by bailing you out of this place. Maybe this Dr. Kris is right on the money. Maybe you need to stay in here until you're really committed to change."

"I'm not crazy Joe. These people are crazy."

"You can't try to have something or someone that is beyond you. You have to be realistic."

"You had dreams, Joe."

"That's the problem," he agreed. "You're Marilyn Monroe because you dared to go for the top. And now you're at the top, and you want to go further. I just don't want to be the one who has to pick up the pieces."

"You don't? You don't love me, Joe?"

"Let's just say this: I don't want to have to pick up the pieces knowing I didn't try to do something about it. That's all. I can see where this is going. And I don't like it. I wish you could just go home with me and be happy."

Another tear rolled off Marilyn's face.

"I wish I could, too," she said.

Chapter 6

"Tell them I don't have Addison's disease . . . I used to take cortisone, but I don't take it anymore."

John F. Kennedy to Pierre Salinger, 1960

"It doesn't take a Price Waterhouse (accountant) to figure out that fifteen hundred Cubans aren't as good as twenty five thousand."

Former Secretary of State Dean Acheson to
John F. Kennedy, March 29, 1961

As he lay in bed, he could see the crowds cheering. He could see the Cuban flag being waved and the smiles and the waves as he went by. Without Castro, his life was going to be so much easier. No Communist trouble makers sneaking into Latin America to topple another government. No surging red tide on the global map threatening the American borders. The Cuban commandos start the counter revolution and then the people attack the Presidential Palace—and Castro falls. They would invite him down to show support for the first country to throw off the chains of communism and there would be parades and speeches and the world would know that he had been behind the counter revolution from the beginning. But it had all been a secret. Behind the scenes, those tricky guys at the CIA had orchestrated the downfall of Castro, but no one had known. A trick here, an accident there, some counter revolutionaries come ashore, and Castro is gone. Bond would be proud.

He rolled over and looked at the ceiling. His legs didn't want to move. His back was stiff, but not too painful. He had slept all night, but he didn't have the energy to get up.

Slowly, he rolled to the side of the bed and reached for a chair nearby. He pulled it closer. He put one hand on the chair and pushed his way up. After a few halting steps, Kennedy sat in a chair next to a small bureau where he kept medications in his bathroom. He opened a drawer and fumbled some bottles, finally selecting one with a typed label. He held it up to the light to see if there was anything inside. He shook it. There was enough. He drew the contents of the vial up in a clean syringe with a sterilized needle. With his left hand he rubbed alcohol over his right thigh. The thigh was discolored and scarred from multiple previous injections and implantations. He stuck the needle into the large muscle of his thigh without flinching and pushed the contents of the vial into his leg. Another day, another dose: it was the only way he could live.

In public, Kennedy would never acknowledge that he had Addison's Disease—a deficiency of a hormone necessary for normal life. Fortunately for him, doctors at the Mayo Clinic had discovered how to make the hormone in a test tube in 1939. By taking shots and having pellets of the hormone implanted into his muscles, he was able to function on a relatively normal level. Everyone around him knew he required daily injections. But the public did not know. The public thought he was active—even vigorous.

After getting dressed and having breakfast, the President sat in his rocking chair and looked through the raw intelligence data. The CIA had men in Cuba who were positioned to get to Castro. But as he looked at the cables, he wondered if the mission they were proposing for Cuba might not be a little on the grandiose side.

Kennedy worried about being too confident. One of his doctors told him that side effects of the steroids he was given for the Addison's Disease might make him too confident and increase his sexual appetite. He didn't worry about the increase in libido—he enjoyed that—but he wanted to be careful with overconfidence.

Kennedy moved to the Cabinet Room and waited for his national security team to arrive. If the intelligence guys didn't look well organized, he was going to have to cancel the Cuban invasion. He didn't want to cancel, but cancellation was a better option that failure.

Richard Bissell was the first to arrive. It was Bissell who had secretly called Kennedy before the election to let him know that plans were underway to kill Castro. If Castro had been removed prior to the election, there would have been a great outpouring of sentiment for Nixon. Kennedy certainly didn't want Castro to be removed prior to the election and Bissell assured him that he would not be—thus winning Kennedy's loyalty. Bissell was an economics professor at Yale before starting to work for the CIA and looked more like an economics professor than a spy master. At the CIA, he directed the development of the U-2 spy plane, bringing the plane in earlier than expected and considerably under budget. For reasons of personal loyalty and professional accomplishment, Bissell had Kennedy's confidence.

"I hope you guys know what you're doing," Kennedy said as Bissell lifted a large map of Cuba into position for the meeting.

"We've got men in position to do the job," Bissell explained as he adjusted his glasses. "Everything has been carefully positioned—now it just has to work."

As they chatted, the room filled up with top administration officials. The Joint Chiefs of Staff, Bundy, Rusk, and McNamara and their assistants sat around the large table in the Cabinet Room. Allen Dulles, the director of the CIA, entered last. Because he ran intelligence networks against the Nazis, he was considered something of a spy's spy. His integrity and experience gave the younger men greater confidence.

"We come ashore here," Bissell motioned to the map. "First we hit them with the air strikes, then we land the men here on the south coast—near the city of Trinidad. We're planning to land 1500 men."

"*Too spectacular*," Kennedy said. "*It sounds like D-Day. You have to reduce the noise level of this thing.*"

"We've also got to get the job done," Bissell countered. "We can't expect the Cuban people to rise up unless they know that their personal risk will be worthwhile."

"Am I missing something?" Rusk asked. "You're going to land 1500 men on the Island of Cuba and you think you can take on Castro's army? You can't be serious. How many men will Castro be able to bring to the coast on the first day?"

"We believe he will bring 25,000 men to resist the landing," Bissell said.

The Joint Chiefs looked at each other. This wasn't a military operation. It was an 'intelligence' operation. No experienced military commander could think that an amphibious landing of an invasion force could be accomplished with 1500 men.

"How do you expect to mount a successful invasion with a force of that size?" Rusk persisted.

"Let me just reiterate the ground rules here, gentlemen," the President interjected. "Number one: there will be no, repeat no, intervention by U.S. forces. Two: I want to be able to deny any U.S. involvement—I need plausible deniability. Three: I want you to move the landing to a more remote location. Four: I want to be able to call off the whole thing up to 24 hours prior to the landing."

Bissell made notes regarding the President's objections, but Rusk could not believe what he had heard. "I don't want to seem slow, Mr. President," he began. "But I must be missing something. There is no way 1500 men can invade Cuba with any reasonable chance of success. I must not have the whole plan. Is there more to the plan?"

There were uncomfortable glances around the room. There

was more to the plan. But no one wanted to talk about it. Not there. Not at that time. Bissell looked over at Dulles. Dulles shook his head sideways. This wasn't the time for a full discussion. They were in the Cabinet Room.

Bissell continued to explain how the exiles would operate once inside Cuba. He took some questions about the plans for transporting the Cuban exiles to the island and how they would be protected with superior air cover.

"If things look bad, the exiles will retreat to the Escambray Mountains and wage a guerrilla war," Bissell explained.

"Are you guys crazy?" Rusk asked, looking around the room. "You're going to land roughly a thousand men—not even trained soldiers—on a foreign beach and expect to prevail against an occupying force of over 25,000 men? And if they don't just knock over Castro's trained soldiers, they will just go into hiding? If they encounter even 10,000 Cuban troops, there won't be any need to hide. Those men will be either captured or killed. It's that simple."

"One other thought, Mr. President," Dulles said, ignoring Rusk's outrage. "If you decide to cancel the invasion, there will be a problem with dispersing the Cuban exiles who have trained for this operation. They are going to go out and tell their story."

"That's a concern," Kennedy said. He was ignoring Rusk as well.

"Concern?" Rusk asked. "That's a concern? I read about this invasion plan in the **New York Times**. I've been told that it is common knowledge on the streets of Havana. This is the worst kept secret I've ever heard about. Why would canceling the invasion bring on more embarrassment than landing a thousand men against 25,000 and expecting them to prevail? That would be the public relations problem I'd be thinking about."

Kennedy stood up. "You gentlemen know the ground rules?" he asked Dulles and Bissell.

"Yes, sir," Dulles replied.

"I will brief Secretary Rusk," the President said.

The President stopped to talk to Dulles on his way out of the

Cabinet Room. Dulles reminded him that more than a hundred Cubans were in Czechoslovakia learning how to fly Russian MiGs. If they delayed with the invasion, those pilots would be back in Cuba, able to defend the island against a future attack and the Cuban exiles would lose their superiority in the air.

Rusk followed the President out of the room. They walked through a hallway and then through another door. Kennedy smiled at Rusk and shook his head. He led him into the Rose Garden of the White House.

"Mr. President, I apologize if I said anything wrong," Rusk began. "That plan made no sense."

Kennedy stopped and looked at him. He took a deep breath and let it out.

"Dean, I know you well enough to level with you. We're in this together. There are things we don't talk about in the Cabinet Room."

"What things?"

"Things that can't be made a part of the official record. You realize that everything we say in there gets transcribed? There is a record for the historians. In addition, while I know everyone in there, and I trust them, there are things I cannot acknowledge publicly under any circumstances."

"Yes, sir."

"Do you really think I would send a thousand men to invade Cuba? Stop and think about it for a minute. What can a thousand exiles do against 25,000 trained Cubans?"

"Nothing. It would be a disaster."

"Exactly. So you can't know the whole story, can you?"

"No, sir."

"What if there were a popular uprising?" Kennedy asked.

"There might be some chance of success, if Castro had to use his troops to quell the uprising."

"Yes. But what if Castro were to be killed during the uprising? What if Castro were to be killed and a thousand men were to storm ashore? What then?"

"That would be a different situation. If Castro were dead, there might be a substantial revolt. There might be anarchy."

"Exactly."

"So the invasion would be in conjunction with killing Castro."

"Might be," the President responded with a wink.

Rusk considered this new revelation. Clearly, there was more to the plan, but something which the President could not or would not acknowledge even to him.

"How do we know that Castro would die? If Castro doesn't die, fifteen hundred men are going to be surrounded by 25,000."

"It's part of the game, Dean. An element of risk is part of the game."

"Mr. President, I still feel like this thing is poorly thought out. I've read about this invasion in our newspapers. Castro must surely know what's going on. Do you really think he won't be protected against an overthrow.

"It's a risk."

"It's a big risk. He's going to have anyone remotely suspicious locked up immediately. If Castro lives, this operation is going to be a bust."

Kennedy pushed his hands into his coat pockets. He looked around the garden.

"It's a risk. But you understand why we can't talk about killing Castro in the Cabinet Room?"

"I understand. I don't like it. But, I understand. Who's idea was it to kill Castro?"

"The CIA has been working on it for the last year or so. I don't know whose idea it was. But I don't think Eisenhower and Nixon let these guys work without oversight. The assassination idea came up on their watch."

"But it will be carried out on your watch," Rusk countered. "If they kill Castro, you better have plenty of deniability. Plus, I just don't think we ought to do that."

"I understand. But that's what the CIA does. It worked in

Iran. It worked in Guatemala. The CIA got the job done for Ike. Why not for me?"

"I guess I'm much more comfortable with everything on the table. I don't like the idea of training someone to go in and kill Castro.

"Look, Dean, Castro has got to go. Ike was planning to get rid of him. I don't want to call it off. What if Castro sends men into other countries of Latin America? Where do you want to fight this guy?"

"You're the President. My job is to give you advice. I think assassination is a bad idea—on general principles."

"What's the difference between shooting a man in war and shooting him to prevent a war?" Kennedy countered. "If we have to invade Cuba, there will be a lot of dead soldiers on both sides. Not to mention Berlin. It makes sense. Someone kills Castro, exiled troops invade, there is general revolt, and we show up to declare the Cuban exiles to be heroes. We didn't kill Castro. We didn't invade Cuba. The Soviets can't march into Berlin. It's a good plan when you think about it." The President smiled confidently.

Chapter 7

*"The invasion is an open secret . . . Resistance will be for-
midable and the United States will probably have to use
its own armed forces to win."*

> J. William Fulbright in memo to
> JFK, April 2, 1961

*"When lies must be told, they should be told by subordi-
nate officials. At no point should the President be asked to
lend himself to the cover operation."*

> Arthur Schlesinger, Jr. in memo to JFK,
> "Protection of the President"
> April 10, 1961

"I just needed to put it all behind me," Marilyn explained
to Jeanne Carmen. They were sitting in the shade on a patio behind 882 North Doheny Drive in Beverly Hills. "After losing the
baby, and having the whole thing come apart with Arthur, and
then losing confidence in Dr. Kris, I figured it was time to make a
complete break. I wanted to get out of the cold of New York and
come home."

Jeanne poured some more coffee into her cup and motioned
to see if Marilyn wanted more. Marilyn shook her head and Jeanne
put the coffee pot back down on the table. A Sunday edition of the

efort="6"

Los Angeles Times was scattered over the table, an adjacent chair, and on the pavement to the side of the chair. Marilyn had been reading the entertainment reviews.

"Don't feel defeated, Marilyn," Jeanne advised. "You've had a phenomenal run of good luck. You certainly don't owe anyone an apology."

"I've done all right, I guess," Marilyn conceded. Both she and Jeanne started out as models and cover girls, but Marilyn had gone on to stardom, while Jeanne was still waiting for some good luck. She had gotten a role in a B movie the year before and was hoping that her close relationships with Frank Sinatra and some of his friends in the movie industry would yield more opportunities.

"You should be looking forward, Marilyn, not back. Who do you think you'll marry next?"

Marilyn laughed. It was a relief to be back in California and among the people with whom she felt comfortable. In New York, she was always feeling like people expected her to change herself, to strive to be someone she was not. In California, being a super-star was enough.

"Something's got to work out," Marilyn answered. "Getting married to Frank would be the best, because he's in show business—he understands what it's like. At least there's some chance Frank would be interested in getting married. I'm not sure the other thing has much of a chance."

Jeanne stared at Marilyn and tried to understand if Marilyn harbored any hope of a relationship with the President of the United States. '

"It's hard to think that the President would leave his wife," Jeanne said. She sipped the coffee and tried to gauge Marilyn's reaction.

Marilyn did not immediately respond. She looked back at Jeanne and tried to think about John Kennedy.

"I guess we'll find out," Marilyn suggested. "I never imagined that I would get married to Joe DiMaggio, or Arthur Miller, and I think there was a time I could have married John Kennedy. But I think that time has probably passed. Even if we don't get married, he's still fun to talk to."

"Just as well," Jeanne replied, lifting up the front page of the **Los Angeles Times**. "Being President isn't an easy job. I've got a feeling they are about to get in trouble again."

Marilyn raised her eyebrows, reached over and picked up the front section. She began to scan the articles. "What's going on?" she asked.

"They are trying to get rid of Castro," Jeanne replied nonchalantly.

"What?" Marilyn asked, her voice rising. She started to read the front page article describing the invasion by Cuban refugees trained by American "advisors." "I can't believe this! When are they going to invade?"

"It doesn't say—just says that the invasion could come at any time."

Marilyn stood up and walked around the table while she was reading the article. "This is absolutely outrageous. Castro is going to be bigger than ever. This is only going to make him some kind of hero."

"They're going to take Castro out," Jeanne reported. "It isn't in the paper, but Johnny Rosselli has been talking about working for the President. He and Sam are in charge of getting rid of Castro." Jeanne knew Johnny Rosselli, the organized crime boss of Los Angeles, and Sam Giancana, the Mafia boss of Chicago, through her association with Frank Sinatra. She had heard rumors that the Mafia was involved in an attempt to kill Castro.

Marilyn looked at Jeanne in total disbelief. "That's not true. Jack Kennedy isn't the kind of person who would try to kill someone like Castro. He's not like that. He probably doesn't even know."

"Right," Jeanne said cynically.

"Come with me," Marilyn ordered her friend. They left the newspaper and coffee on the patio table and went into the apartment building.

Marilyn's apartment was unfurnished and filled with her suitcases and unpacked boxes. She walked over to her unmade bed and lifted a telephone from the bedside table. "We'll see about this," Marilyn said as she dialed the telephone.

Arthur Schlesinger, Jr. stood in the Oval Office listening to John Kennedy curse. As the President's assistant and unofficial biographer, Schlesinger found himself on the front lines of the Cold War.

"*I can't believe what I'm reading. Castro doesn't need agents over here. All he has to do is read our papers. It's all laid out for him,*" the President ranted. "We've got to get this fellow Ted Szulc working for us. For God's sake, there's no way this is going to be a secret."

"With all due respect, Mr. President," Schlesinger suggested, "it is not a secret now. We got word from the State Department that **Radio Moscow** is reporting that an invasion is imminent."

"**Radio Moscow**?" Kennedy asked.

"**Radio Moscow**," Schlesinger confirmed. "It is hard to think that it's a secret in Havana."

"I thought the Cuban papers were reporting that Castro was sick?" Kennedy asked. "I heard that he hadn't been seen for a while."

"They have been," Schlesinger said. "But we don't know just how sick he is. I just have to wonder how effective the invasion will be if the Cubans know it is coming."

"You're not getting paid to wonder about how effective the invasion will be," the President admonished. "You're getting paid to help me out, and seeing this story on the front page of every newspaper in the country is not my idea of getting helped out."

Schlesinger looked out the window and grimaced. Trying to influence the press was not exactly his idea of being a special assistant to the President. But he realized that loyalty was the most important quality Kennedy sought in any of his advisors, and if calling an editor here and there was necessary to maintain Kennedy's confidence, he would make the calls.

"Given the situation at this time," Schlesinger persisted, "I just have to wonder if you want to cancel the whole operation. You have the option until the men start out in the boats."

"You have to focus on what I'm saying," Kennedy sternly told his advisor. "The invasion is on. And it's a secret."

The telephone on the President's desk rang. Kennedy looked at it with some surprise because he could not imagine the White House operators putting anyone through unless there was an emergency of some kind. He glanced at Schlesinger and picked up the telephone.

"Yes," he answered. A broad smile broke out on the President's face as he covered the receiver and whispered to Schlesinger: "it's Marilyn Monroe. The White House operators think that if they recognize a name, they should put the call through. Amazing." He paused as the connection was made.

"Marilyn," he greeted her. "What a surprise to hear from you." He smiled at Schlesinger again and then seemed preoccupied with the call. "No, that's not true. There is no invasion being planned by the United States Government." Another pause. "I am the Commander in Chief. I think I'd know." He turned to Schlesinger and rolled his eyes.

Marilyn felt gratified to have gotten through the White House switchboard. How many people could call the President and get through. Maybe Jeanne would not be so fast to discount her relationship with John Kennedy. She paced around her bed.

"I also heard that an attempt was being made on Castro's life," Marilyn stated. She listened. "Absolutely ridiculous," she repeated for Jeanne's benefit. "That's what I thought, but I wanted to hear it directly from you."

Marilyn smiled at Jeanne and then seemed to slip off into her own world with the President. "No, Frank hasn't been around—I think he's in Hawaii. But, I'll let him know."

Schlesinger walked back through the White House halls

leading to his office. Kennedy was a very smart man. Clearly, he knew something that Schlesinger did not know. But just as clearly, he could be desperately wrong. If the President was gambling on Castro being overthrown during the invasion, he could be mistaken. The whole operation could turn into a disaster.

Schlesinger sat down in front of his typewriter. He had been working on a memorandum arguing that the president should cancel the proposed invasion. He read the last paragraph of the memo, and then tore it out of his typewriter and threw it away. He leaned back in his chair and put his feet on his desk. Then he looked up at a photograph of his father hanging above his desk. Arthur Schlesinger, Senior had been a well known and well liked professor of history at Harvard for a generation. Now, his son was in the White House seeing history made. It wasn't as glamorous as his father had made it out to be.

Was it possible, he wondered, that John Fitzgerald Kennedy had temporarily lost his senses? Was it possible that one of his medications, or perhaps one of those other drugs, were adversely influencing an otherwise rational mind? Kennedy could speak. He moved normally. He did not seem irrational. And yet, given the reality as Schlesinger was able to see it, Kennedy was about to make a colossal mistake.

What should he do? He drummed his fingers on his desk. If Kennedy did make a mistake, and was left with a major public relations disaster in its wake, what could be done? A president shouldn't quit. He shouldn't resign in disgrace. If the CIA operation were to fail, not just fail in a small way—but in a very big way, what would Kennedy do? What options would he have?

He fed a new piece of paper into his typewriter. He began to type *"Protection of the President."*

"When lies must be told, they should be told by subordinate officials. At no point should the President be asked to lend himself to the cover operation. There seems to me merit in Secretary Rusk's suggestion that someone other than the President make the final

decision and do so in his absence—someone whose head can later be placed on the block if things go terribly wrong."

He thought of who might be logically blamed if the invasion turned out to be the disaster he suspected it would be. Dulles? The Chief of the CIA was certainly culpable. The public might very well see the logic of Dulles. A young president comes into office . . . the CIA has a plan . . . they don't tell him . . . something goes wrong . . . the young president gets blamed. Yes. The public might buy that. They might forgive the young president. And, of course, in time, the CIA director would be replaced. That might be enough.

One option then would be to characterize the CIA as *"errant idealists and soldiers of fortune working on their own."* Yes, he thought. The public would buy that. If things go terribly wrong, Jack won't have to quit—they will blame the whole mess on the CIA.

He smiled as he pounded the keys of the typewriter. He dated the memo *"April 10, 1961."*

It's brilliant, he thought, as he took the memo out of the typewriter carriage. Then he looked up at the photograph of his father. Maybe better than writing history after it happens is writing history as it happens—to actually be part of history. Even better, he thought with a smile, was to write history before it happens. He laughed, then turned out the lights and left the room.

Chapter 8

"I want to say that there will not be, under any conditions, an intervention in Cuba by the United States armed forces."

John F. Kennedy
April 12, 1961

He had done it.

He had thought everything through. He had listened to his advisors. He had gone over the contingency plans. It was Sunday, April 15, 1961. The President had just made the call to Secretary of State Rusk. The invasion was on.

John F. Kennedy stood on a small hill at Glen Ora, an estate Jackie had rented in Virginia and looked out over his neighbor's cornfield. He could not see anyone watching him. Moreover, as he looked around, he couldn't see how anyone could see him. After looking around one last time, he unzipped a hand bag and emptied 20 or 30 golf balls on the grassy area in front of him.

The small hill he was standing on wasn't exactly a groomed golf tee, but it would have to do. Holding a little wooden tee in his hand, he picked up a ball and drove the tee into the soil, leaving the ball balanced on the stem. He set up 10 balls in a row and then picked up his driver. He stared out onto the cornfield and tried to guess the distance of a shed out in the field.

There really wasn't much risk to the Cuba decision, he thought.

Not if it was pulled off correctly. The United States wasn't involved. Sure, the CIA had trained the Cuban exiles—but that was more like facilitating what they wanted to do anyway. It wasn't like the CIA had hired them to cause problems for Castro. This clearly was not going to be an operation of the armed forces of the United States. If it were, our best planes would be bombing Cuba, not the rag tag bunch of old bombers that were being used.

He swung the driver a couple of times to loosen up his shoulders and back. Better to loosen up now, than tighten up later. He cleared away a small plant with the small spikes on his golf shoes and edged his way up to the first ball.

Keep your shoulders straight. Knees slightly bent. Even back stroke—stop—take it again. That shed is not more than 140 yards away.

He could hit it with a good drive. He went into the backstroke again and then swung at the ball. The driver hit the top of the ball, raising some dirt as the ball dribbled into the corn directly in front of him.

"Shit," he thought. "I hope that isn't a sign of my luck for this day."

He edged up to the next ball.

Castro had it coming. He tried to blackmail the United States Government into funding economic development in Cuba. When Ike wouldn't play ball, Castro sold out his friends in Washington. The Russians were more than happy to trade for a missile base so close to American shores. But, that was simply not going to happen. It would upset the balance of power.

The balance of power—what a delicate balance it was. The world was just starting to comprehend the power of nuclear weapons. No generation had ever tried to grasp the end of the world. They hadn't needed to. There was no way a war would end human survival on the planet before the atomic bomb. But now the Russians had the bomb, too. And for the first time in human history, everyone could potentially get wiped out. The people who survived a nuclear war would have to live with the fallout. Scientists, experts from around the world, all agreed that survivors might not survive long.

Atomic weapons could not be based in Cuba. Simple concept. If the Russians put a missile base in Cuba, that would be it for 1964. The Democrats wouldn't elect another president in this century.

But Castro had made a deal. He had taken Russian money for Cuban development and, in return, he was going to let the Russians put missiles in Cuba. The only way to keep the missiles out of Cuba was to get rid of Castro. So, it was get rid of Castro, or go toe to toe with the Russians over the missile base.

The CIA could do it. They had removed foreign leaders before. They knew what they were doing. But, no one else could know what they were doing. That was the tricky part. If the world knew that Castro was about to be killed, there would be an international uproar. He didn't want to be in the position of having to defend a new policy of diplomacy by death. He didn't want to be remembered as the president who had planned assassinations.

That was the reason why keeping the United States out of it was so important. If the world community thought the United States had participated in the invasion, then they might also think that Castro's death had been planned by the United States. That was all true, of course, but no one would ever find out.

He swung the driver again, hitting the ball squarely toward the shed in the cornfield. It veered a little to the right. Missed. He rotated his shoulder and stretched. Then he lined up another ball.

Boom. Clean shot. Headed directly for the shed. Just over. Would have gone over the green and half way to the parking lot. Better to leave them slightly short.

There was no reason to think that the operation would not work. The CIA had lined up a Mafia hit—a Mafia hit. Those guys didn't miss. There were going to be multiple gunmen, and they were going to have machine guns. Castro's own security force had been infiltrated by the Mafia tough guys. He gets a call that his airfields are getting bombed, he comes out of his headquarters to go to the security bunker. Bang. His own guys shoot him. Not once. Not twice. They shoot him like Mafia guys shoot people who crowd in on their business. And Castro had crowded in on their business. The Mafia had done a $100 million business in Cuba before Castro. They had motive. They had plenty of motive.

How could anyone blame the President of the United States? He had been hitting golf balls into his neighbor's cornfield all afternoon. He certainly wasn't commanding a strike on Cuba.

Keep that shoulder down. Pull it every time if that shoulder comes up. He edged up to another ball.

Castro dead. The Cuban military in chaos. Exiles come ashore. The people rise up to take back their old businesses. Communism turned away. Russians have to keep their missiles out of the Western Hemisphere. It was going to work. He could feel it was going to work. What could go wrong? When you really thought about it hard, what could go wrong?

Swing. Hit. The ball is in the air. It is straight enough. It is far enough. Crack!! On the money. The shed has been hit. He smiled. Maybe it wasn't going to be such a bad day after all.

Jackie and Caroline were still out in the field when he went back to the house. What could interest them about horses, he failed to comprehend. First you had to catch them, then brush them, then feed them carrots, then braid their manes—it never stopped. And for what? Who wanted to ride them, anyway?

It was a beautiful day at Glen Ora. The fields were green. Another spring had arrived. He stared out at Jackie leading Caroline on the horse. He waved at them. They waved back. He turned and walked into the large colonial Virginia house.

"How is Adlai holding up?" the President asked his Secretary of State. He was sitting in a leather chair drinking a glass of iced tea. The telephone was on his lap. Rusk was in Washington at his desk in the Department of State.

"He is denying that he knows anything," Rusk answered.

Adlai Stevenson, the U.S. Ambassador to the United Nations, was in New York trying to explain to the world community that the United States had no knowledge of any attack on a Cuban airfield.

"Then he's telling the truth," Kennedy laughed. "I'm not sure he was really told what was going to happen."

"The Cubans are saying that Saturday's air strikes are a prelude to an invasion."

"Are they buying the story that the bombs were dropped by Castro's own air force?" Kennedy asked.

"Who knows? Stevenson is showing the photographs of the plane that landed in Florida. It should hold them for a while," Rusk answered.

"Any word from Havana?"

"Not yet. But today's the day. Once the invasion starts, it's hard to see how anyone is going to get to Castro."

Rusk did not know Castro's own guard had been infiltrated. The details of how Castro would be killed were kept secret from even Kennedy's closest advisors.

"The Brigade is on its way?" the President asked.

"They are now at sea," Rusk confirmed.

"Then there's no going back. Not now," the President said soberly. "Do we know how well yesterday's raid went?"

Kennedy was alluding to U-2 reconnaissance photographs of the damaged airfields.

"Poor," Rusk said.

"Poor?" the President asked with disbelief. "How could they have missed? The fields were unprotected."

"Five planes disabled," Rusk said. "There is another strike tomorrow morning—just before the Brigade hits the beaches. That will be the entire exile air force—sixteen B26's."

"But nothing to connect them to us," Kennedy said.

"Well, nothing but the obvious. Where else would those Cubans get planes?"

"So, you think there is some risk?"

"Of course, there's some risk. Castro's boys are going to have their cameras out next time," Rusk said. "They can't wait to show Stevenson some photographs of attacking B26's. It's going to make Adlai look pretty idiotic."

"Yes," the President responded, "it's going to be pretty obvious with all those B26's." Maybe he had put Stevenson in a position from which his credibility would never escape intact. Kennedy experienced a brief moment of guilt.

But it passed. Soon, he was back out looking at Jackie and Caroline feeding the horse. He leaned against the white fence. The sun was getting lower in the sky.

The President had a daiquiri before dinner that night. And because he did not want to have trouble sleeping, he took a light green pill for sleep with his meal. It was some kind of sleeping pill, a barbiturate if his memory was right. He always traveled with a small bottle of barbiturates, but rarely used them. They had been a gift from Marilyn Monroe. That was one area Kennedy felt Marilyn had great expertise: sleeping pills. She used them every night. They had to be safe.

After dinner, Jack sat in the leather chair and called Dean Rusk again.

"Is there any news from Havana?" he asked.

"Same news," Rusk said. "They are anticipating an invasion."

"Damn!" Kennedy mumbled. "If Castro doesn't go down soon, the people won't have any reason to rise up. The timing of this thing will be all wrong."

"There's going to be plenty of news tomorrow, Mr. President," Rusk predicted.

"One other thing," Kennedy said. "I want to cancel that bombing raid tomorrow morning."

"Excuse me, sir?" Rusk said.

"Call off the B26's," Kennedy said. "*We've got to keep the noise level down on this thing*."

"Mr. President, that would mean the exiles will hit the beaches without any air cover."

"I just don't want Adlai to have to explain a formation of B26's at the United Nations. This operation is not going to turn on air cover."

"Are you sure you want to cancel their air cover, sir?" Rusk asked.

"Yes," the President answered. "I'm sure."

The President said good night to his wife and went to bed. He had no trouble falling asleep.

Chapter 9

"Admiral, I don't want the United States involved in this."

John F. Kennedy to Admiral Arleigh Burke,
Tuesday, April 18, 1961

John Kennedy was riding the popularity wave of his lifetime. Never before had a president been so popular in his first months in office. The week before the Cuban invasion, NBC had broadcast a television special devoted to the graceful lifestyle of the Kennedys. Jackie spoke about the pleasures of raising young children. Jack described his personal, take charge management style. Americans had fallen in love with their young leader. He was handsome, funny, intelligent—a kind of super human who read faster than anyone else.

As he put on his formal white tie and tails for a White House reception on Tuesday night, Kennedy was frightened. For the last 36 hours he had been acting like he was not responsible for anything that was going on in Cuba. But now, things were starting to unravel.

"You look very fine this evening, sir," his personal valet told him as he helped the President on with his formal jacket. "I don't understand why you are feeling so glum."

The President felt the tension build up in his chest and took a deep breath. He had to keep playing the act. He had to go out there and show that he had nothing to hide. But word was starting to come in that the men who were fighting at the Bay of Pigs would not be able to hold on. He was waiting for news that Castro had been hit, but in the meantime, men on the beaches were under attack. He had to appear calm, even jovial. He wasn't feeling jovial.

The White House was the stage for a lavish reception for the members of Congress. The crushed velvet ropes which usually confined visitors to just a few rooms in the mansion had all been taken down. Guests were wandering through the great home to presidents, impressed by the graciousness of its current occupants. Champagne was served and the Marine band played in the East Room. It was a moment of high style and elegance.

At ten o'clock in the evening, the President and First Lady of the United States appeared at the top of the stairway in the formal entrance to the White House. As they descended, the Marine band played the show tune, "Mr. Wonderful."

The President moved through the crowd as only Mr. Wonderful knew how. He shook hands and made jokes and flashed his beautiful teeth in his confident smile.

Finally, he could stand it no more. He left the smiles and laughs and toasts to the New Frontier and walked back to the Cabinet Room. There, the mood was dark. Advisors read dispatches from the CIA and grimaced. Men sat in small groups. Some sat alone. Ties were loosened around shirt collars. Disaster was in the air.

Richard Bissell walked over to the President.

"It is not too late. You can still turn this thing around," he pleaded.

"What can I do?" the President asked.

"You can send Navy jets to control the air over the beachhead. You can bring a destroyer up to knock out Castro's tanks. You're the Commander in Chief. Only you can do it!"

Kennedy rubbed his face. It was easy for these guys to push him deeper into trouble. They weren't thinking about the whole picture. They were only thinking about their little operation. If he invaded Cuba, the Soviets were going to invade Berlin. It was as simple as that. He had told them that there were limits to what he was willing to do before the whole thing started. And he had meant it.

"*Right*," said Admiral Arleigh Burke, the Navy Chief of Staff. "*Let me take two jets and shoot down those enemy aircraft.*"

"*No,*" Kennedy said. "*I don't want the U.S. to get involved in this.*"

"*Hell, Mr. President, we are involved,*" Burke said.

"*Admiral, I don't want the United States involved in this.*"

The men exchanged glances. Was the President mad? He had approved the invasion, and then inexplicably canceled its air cover. The men storming the beaches had radioed that they were being attacked by Soviet MIG's flown by Czech pilots. Castro had surrounded them with tanks. They had no chance unless the President okayed an air attack.

Kennedy stared at Bissell. It had been Bissell who had sold him on the plan.

"What's the news from Havana?" he asked Bissell.

"You know the latest news," Bissell responded.

"It looks like the first part of this plan failed," Kennedy said.

"That's right. But it may be that the what we thought of as the first part, our friends in Havana thought of as the second part. They may be waiting for us to show our muscle before they show theirs."

"So, you think that they are looking at the invasion as the signal?" the President asked.

"Apparently. They were supposed to move with the air strikes. But the first one was pathetic, and the second one never came." Bissell was not backing down. He stared directly into the President's eyes.

"You think they don't want to pull the trigger unless they see we are coming ashore?" Kennedy asked.

"Mr. President, someone has to show some faith here. Our friends in Havana have the most to lose. If they act, and we don't come ashore, they all die. How can we expect them to make the first move if we are not willing to let the Navy shoot down some old T-33's?"

Kennedy rubbed his face. There were too many variables. These guys made it sound so easy. But, it wasn't. They just weren't thinking deeply enough.

"Dick," the President addressed Bissell, "we don't know that they haven't tried. Our friends in Havana might have tried and failed. We don't know!!"

"Communication has been dreadful," Bissell conceded.

"There were several parts of this plan that were dreadful," the President said.

"But the plan was designed for each arm to work independently," Bissell countered, still unwilling to accept defeat. "We haven't lost this thing yet, but time is running out."

"Mr. President," General Lyman Lemnitzer interrupted, "*it's time for this outfit to go guerrilla.*" That had been the back up plan. But Lemnitzer had missed the fact that Kennedy had moved the invasion site. The Escambry mountains were a backup for the Trinidad invasion site.

"*They're not prepared to go guerrilla,*" Bissell countered. He pointed to a map of the Bay of Pigs. The men were pinned down on the beach head. Between the beach and higher ground was an impassable swamp. And waiting on the other side of the swamp, between the exiles and the mountains were 25,000 Cuban troops.

Castro had read about the invasion. He didn't know exactly when, although the air raids had telegraphed the timing, and he didn't know exactly where, but the CIA had conveniently chosen geography he was intimately acquainted with—the Bay of Pigs had been his favorite fishing spot. Castro had the exiles trapped. There was no place for them to go. They could either surrender, or die.

"Mr. President," Rusk approached the map. "The Revolutionary Council is starting to raise a fuss." The Revolutionary Council was a group of Cuban politicians who were fronting for the CIA. They were being essentially held captive at an abandoned air force base in Florida. The CIA was issuing fictional battle dispatches in their name. But word had gotten to the Council that the invasion was mired down in the swamps. Failure was at hand. One man had threatened to kill himself. Others had volunteered to go to the beaches to fight.

The President dispatched Adolf Berle, the Assistant Secretary of State for Latin America to go down to the Florida base and to calm down the senior, exiled Cuban politicians.

"*I can think of happier missions*," Berle responded.

The President turned and saw Arthur Schlesinger.

"*You ought to go with Berle*," he told Schlesinger.

"What are we going to tell them?" the surprised Schlesinger asked the President.

"You'll think of something," Kennedy replied.

Kennedy turned away from them and looked around the room. His brother, Robert, was pacing back and forth. Mac Bundy was studying the map, as if a better comprehension of the geographical layout of the island might provide some clue as to an escape. Rusk and McNamara were studying the typed CIA dispatches as they were brought into the Cabinet Room. Voices were held low.

The President decided to step out into the Rose Garden. He had to think it through clearly in his mind. He had to go back to first principles and work through what to do now. As he walked toward the door, he was again approached by the Admiral.

"Mr. President, we can still take control of this thing," Admiral Burke said

The President ignored him.

The air was cool as he stepped out into the Rose Garden. He looked at the rose plants and picked a rose bud from one of them. Men, brave men, were on a beach in Cuba. They were there because he had approved a plan to send them there. He could not escape responsibility for that decision. At some point, the press was going to discover that the whole thing had been a CIA operation from the beginning, and that he had approved the operation. Then they were going to discover that he had canceled the air

cover. He was going to look very bad. He was going to be accused of backing out while his men went forward. He was going
to be accused of being a spineless coward.

Castro was supposed to be dead. The plan made no sense
unless Castro was dead. He had assumed that the Mafia hit men
would do their job. It was the one part of the plan he could not
publicly acknowledge or discuss, and so it was the one part he
had not fully evaluated for failure. What were the odds that Castro
could survive a machine gun attack from his own guards? Zero.
But he had. Or he hadn't been attacked. Castro was still alive.

What could a president do? He couldn't go before the American people and say that the CIA had promised that the Mafia was
going to kill Castro.

They weren't going to risk their lives unless the invasion was
going to be successful. Or maybe, they had. Maybe they had been
discovered. Maybe they had been killed.

But that was all irrelevant. The question was what to do now.

If he authorized Navy jets to shoot down Castro's planes—
whatever they were—he could not deny U.S. involvement. But
what if they did shoot down the planes, what if they controlled the
airspace over the beach? The men were still pinned down. They
couldn't go anywhere. Castro was waiting for them on the other
side of the swamps. What did he really get by controlling the air?

The President didn't like his options. Send in the Navy jets,
you lose plausible deniability, and you don't really gain anything.
Hold the Navy jets back, the truth of the invasion gets out, you
look like a bum.

Wait. There had to be a way. What if you send in the jets,
control the air space, then evacuate the men? What if the U.S.
goes to the defense of the exiles? That wouldn't be such a bad
idea. We didn't plan the invasion, but we wanted to evacuate our
friends from the beaches. But what about the artillery? Castro had
tanks that would resist the rescue force. American lives would be
lost. But what if he brought in the U.S.S. Essex? What if the Essex
took out the tanks? Then what? What would happen?

The Soviets might move on Berlin.

Damn. There must be some way out of this thing.

What if the U.S. defended Berlin and just took out the God damn Cubans? It could be war. It could be World War III. Did he want to risk World War III over the Island of Cuba? Was it really worth it? Maybe a 80 million dead on the first day—all for Cuba? No. Maybe it was better to take the publicity. Manage the publicity. Ride out the criticism.

He walked back into the White House.

When he entered the Cabinet Room the first two men to their feet were Burke and Bissell. They walked over to the President with deliberate strides. Kennedy held his hand out to keep them away. He didn't want to hear the same suggestions. He looked at Bobby pacing over next to the wall. Bobby had not been involved in the planning of the Bay of Pigs intervention and did not understand that Castro was to be eliminated. On one level, Bobby was not someone who could give him the best advice, because he did not know all the elements of the operation. On another level, he was the perfect person to give advice, because he had only Jack's interests at heart, and would be able to assess how a failure of the operation might impact the political world. The President walked over to his brother.

Robert Kennedy looked agitated. There was anger in his eyes.

"*We've got to do something*, Jack," he said. "We're in an international struggle with the Communists. We make big noises that we're going to hold Laos. We move in ships. You go on TV but we don't do anything. It's all a bluff. Then the CIA invades Cuba. We send a bunch of amateurs in some old boats, protected by some old, beat up planes, to take on Castro's army. Then we cancel the old, beat up planes. We decide putting the old planes up involves too much risk! We look like a couple of kids. I mean—Jesus Christ—we talk big and then we act like we can run and hide in our mother's apron."

"Bobby, I don't want to risk World War III on this thing."

"You think the Russians are going to go to war over Cuba?"

Robert asked incredulously. "You think they will take up a position 10,000 miles from their nearest supply line? Jesus Christ!"

"What if they move on Berlin?" the President asked.

"They're not going to move on Berlin," his brother countered. "We've got them surrounded by nuclear missiles. We've got them in England. We've got them on submarines. We've got them in Turkey! That means we've got nuclear missiles right on their front door. They're not going to push us in Berlin."

The President looked over at Burke and Bissell. If his own brother thought he had to move, he had to move.

"Admiral," he called. *"I want you to send six jets from the Essex and clear out some air space over the beach."*

The Admiral stood up.

"Yes, sir," he said.

"That's a deeper commitment, Mr. President," Secretary Rusk asserted. He reminded the President that he had promised no U.S. armed forces would be involved under any circumstances.

Kennedy turned to his Secretary of State.

"We're already in it up to here," he said, putting his hand under his nose.

Admiral Burke and Bissell rushed off to transmit the President's order to the U.S.S. Essex. The aircraft carrier was just out of sight of the Cuban beach head. They wanted to get the jets in the air before the President had a chance to change his mind.

His mind went back and forth. Even if he ordered the United States Marines to invade right then, they wouldn't be on the beach for more than a week. There was no way. And by that time, the Soviets would be talking about their right to occupy Berlin. The hours passed slowly as Kennedy waited for reports from the Essex.

It was 4 o'clock in the morning. President Kennedy stood in the Oval Office with Pierre Salinger, his press secretary, and his old friend, Kenneth O'Donnell.

"If Castro is dead," he said, "and the United States formally invades Cuba, it will be apparent that we somehow planned his death. How else would we know to invade?"

The two men looked at each other. Neither one smiled. They were at the center of power—not just for the United States. For the world. Kennedy had been talking off and on for the last hour, making points, then back tracking. He kept saying that he had been betrayed. He had approved the invasion contingent upon the CIA getting Castro out of the way. But with Castro alive, he had been left holding the bag.

"What am I going to do?" the President asked his silent advisors. "Go to the public and say I thought we were going to assassinate Castro?"

He stared at their confused faces.

"A president can not order that another human being be killed! The public would never tolerate that!"

Salinger shifted his weight and stood up.

"Mr. President," he said, "I think we better get you upstairs and in bed. I think you need to sleep on this."

O'Donnell got up as well.

"Jack, it's time to get some rest," he agreed.

"Time to get some rest? Jesus Christ!! There are men getting attacked on that beach!! I'm the guy who put them there. You want me to get some rest? Let me tell you something—," he began.

Salinger and O'Donnell looked at the President. His eyes were bloodshot. His hair was disheveled.

But he did not complete his sentence. He stopped himself and walked over to the doors to the Rose Garden. He opened the doors and went outside.

For an hour, Salinger and O'Donnell watched him walk alone on the grass. He was still dressed in his white tie and tails.

Chapter 10

*"In a parliamentary system I would resign. In our system,
the President can't and doesn't. So you and Allen (Dulles)
must go."*

John Kennedy to Richard Bissell
April 22, 1961

They were actually applauding him. He couldn't believe
it. Earlier that day, he had considered canceling his speech to the
American Society of Newspaper Editors. But Bobby felt that the
more he disrupted his schedule, the greater impact the invasion
was going to have on the public. They had been quite successful
in keeping most of the facts away from the press. So even though it
was only April 20, 1961—36 hours since he had realized that the
invasion was going to be a terrible failure, it was a good time to go
out and sound some familiar themes.

And there they were, hundreds of them, newspaper people,
standing on their feet and applauding him. They were going to
love his speech.

It was the old call to arms speech. Two economic systems were
competing for world control: the democracies and the Communists. We had to beat them.

"The hour is late," the President warned in Churchillian tones.
*"The message of Cuba, of Laos, of the rising din of Communist voices
in Asia and Latin America—these messages are all the same: The*

complacent, the self indulgent, the soft societies are about to be swept away with the debris of history. Only the strong, only the industrious, only the determined, only the courageous, only the visionary who determines the real nature of our struggle can possibly survive."

The newspaper men clapped some more. They were not asking the difficult questions. They just wanted to hear that the United States was going to fight the good fight.

The President wanted to reaffirm his commitment: *"I am determined upon our system's survival and success, regardless of the cost and regardless of the peril."*

They loved it. Regardless of the cost. Regardless of the peril. It sounded good. It sounded determined. He could still hear their applause as he climbed back into his limousine. He liked the role of the warrior. The only problem with the role of the warrior, he thought as he went back to the White House, was that occasionally they expected you to actually fight. It hadn't been a good week for American resolve.

"We've got to do something," Robert Kennedy kept saying. "The Russians are going to think that you're a paper tiger—all bluff and no action."

"Maybe that's what they should think," the depressed President replied.

The brothers were alone. The President lay on a sofa. The Attorney General paced around the Oval Office.

"You're sounding like you're a beaten man, again," Bobby said. "People don't like a loser. They don't like a president who has been whipped."

"Holding the bag," Jack said. "It was supposed to be so easy. There were going to be popular uprisings. Castro was going to be gone. But when it collapsed, I was the one who got caught holding the big bag."

"Jack, you can't make excuses. We've been through this before. You've got to pull yourself together. It doesn't do any good to sit around and wonder if you're up to this job. You have the job.

You are the President of the United States and it's about time you started to act like it."

The President looked out the window. It had been a tough few days. The Cuban invasion had been an utter failure—the exiles who had not been killed had been mercifully captured. Now, Castro had a thousand exiles in prison—they were like hostages. He was going to hold them there as a reminder of the invasion. Every time the American press mentioned the prisoners, people would remember the Bay of Pigs, and be forced to the conclusion that it had been Kennedy's failure.

"How are we going to get those guys out of Castro's jails?" the President asked.

"Castro has got us by the nuts—no doubt about that," Bobby conceded. "We're going to have to get the exiles out of there, or there will be hell to pay. Thank God they're not Americans. If they were Americans, we'd have to go in and get them."

"You think anyone is going to buy the idea that it was the CIA's fault?" Jack asked.

"First, you have to realize that most people aren't looking for someone to blame. They are looking for a leader. Most people understand we are at war. It isn't an open war—but it is a war, nonetheless. In a war, you don't blame your leadership, you get behind them. There are newspapers all over the country calling for an invasion of Cuba!"

"I think I'm going to simply have to accept the responsibility," the President concluded.

"No!" Bobby shouted. "Sure, you mention that you are ultimately responsible, but you don't accept anything more than that. The truth is that the military should have told you the thing was going to fail."

"They did."

"No, they didn't," Bobby countered. Then he looked at his brother and wondered when the fight would return. He had been knocked down. He had been hurt. But it was time to get up now. It was time to fight back. "Jack, this is politics. You don't take failure in politics. You blame somebody else. Maybe it was your fault. At some level, it had to be. But that's not the point. The point is that you're the President and these are very dangerous times and you can't quit. You're going to accept responsibility, but then we're going to blame this thing on the CIA. It was their operation. They are going to have to take the blame. We leak it out over the next few months. They had a plan. You were fresh in office. You didn't know what you were getting into."

"That much is true."

"But you can't blame yourself. You have to make the best of it. You have to fight back."

The President looked at his brother. He was part younger brother, and part older brother. Joe had been all older brother. He had dominated. And when Joe died, the mantle was passed to Jack. He could either try to make something of himself, make something of the Kennedy name, make something of his father's ambition, or he could hold back. He had bad health. He could just resign himself to a life of wheelchairs and narcotics. But he had chosen to make the effort. And Bobby, rather than thinking of his own name, and his own ambition, had worked for Jack. He had managed each of his campaigns. He had been the one to organize the appearances, line up the support, orchestrate the old man's dream that one of his sons would be president. Jack had been the one who had run for the offices. But Bobby had been the one who had pushed him to success.

The President twisted his body and pushed himself up to a sitting position on the sofa. Then he reached out to Bobby, who pulled him up. He walked over to the windows and looked out. He remembered walking out on the cold, wet grass the night the news came in from the Bay of Pigs. It had been a lonely walk. His advisors had been there to encourage him when the operation looked promising. And, of course, most of them couldn't be told that Castro was going to be killed at the beginning. When the plan fell apart, and Castro survived, he looked like an idiot.

"I wonder if things would have been different if you were at

the CIA," the President suggested to his brother. "I need someone over there to protect me and to get control of those guys. If
we are going to count on the CIA, it has to work. Who do I have
over there that I can really trust?"

Robert Kennedy looked at his brother. He didn't want to go to
the CIA. He wanted to stay in the Justice Department. But, Jack
needed help and he was going to have to help Jack.

"Look, I don't think I should go over there."

"Why not?"

"No, if I go over there, there will be no plausible deniability.
It's a good thing to have Dulles over there. If word gets out that the
CIA was suppose to knock off Castro, it gets blamed on Dulles.
Dulles is a Republican. We're buffered. If I'm over there, and
something goes wrong, not only do I get blamed, you can't
reasonably say you didn't know about it."

The President tapped on his teeth with his fingernail. Bobby
had a reasonable point. Covert actions had to have plausible
deniability. Either the CIA should be dismantled, or it should be
used. The Communists had their secret agencies. The Americans
needed theirs. But it had to be deniable. The President's brother
would not be deniable.

"Maybe so," Jack conceded. "But, I need you to keep an eye
on these CIA bastards. First, you need to conduct an investigation. Find out exactly what did happen. And then I want you to
circulate a report that quietly blames the thing on the CIA."

"That's the stuff!" Bobby exclaimed. "Now, you're thinking
like a president again. Sure, I'll start to help out with some of this
intelligence stuff. If it means that I have to run the cloak and
dagger operations, then I'll run them. I think we're a lot better off
if I'm not too closely connected to what the CIA is doing, but I'll
run things if you want me to. Let me ask you, do you know how
the CIA was going to kill Castro?"

The President stared at his brother.

"I had no idea they were planning to kill Castro," he said plainly.

Bobby laughed. "You should have been an actor! You've got

me believing you. But, let me tell you, Jack. I'm going to find out what was supposed to happen and I'm going to kick some ass. And let me tell you something else. We're going to get those prisoners out of there if it's the last thing I ever do."

Jack laughed. He was starting to feel better.

"So you'll do the investigation?"

"Of course, I'll do it. But blaming the invasion on the CIA doesn't get Castro out of office. We've got to work with those guys. We've got a problem with Cuba. And from what I understand, we've got a problem with Laos. You can't just talk big. At some point, you've got to draw the line and fight."

There it was, again. If it was obvious to Bobby that he was talking one posture and acting on another, it was going to be obvious to everyone. The President could only give so many speeches promising he would "pay any price, bear any burden," "regardless of cost, regardless of peril." He was going to have to show some resolve. He was going to have to raise the flag somewhere, and fight to defend it.

"I did that an hour ago," Jack said.

"Did what?" Bobby asked.

"Drew the line."

"Jack, it has only been two days since we took the most embarrassing defeat in American History. It may be a little early to make any firm decisions, yet. What did you do?"

"I put Roswell Gilpatric in charge of a secret Task Force," the President answered. "I was thinking on my way back from that speech to the newspaper men that I was going to have to draw the line somewhere. At some point, we're going to have to show the Soviets that we mean business. We're going to have to show them that we will fight."

"What Task Force?" Bobby asked.

"The Vietnam Task Force. I'm asking General Lansdale to run it. And I want you to oversee it. I can only get pushed so far before I really will look like a paper tiger."

"What's the Vietnam Task Force supposed to do?"

"Simple. I directed it to one simple aim: *To prevent Communist domination of Vietnam.*"

"I think we need to analyze where we should be strategically. We shouldn't do anything too quickly at this point," Bobby cautioned.

"This is a global conflict," the President continued, peering out at the Rose Garden. "The Soviets would like to consolidate their position in Cuba. And from there, they would like to move into Latin America. We have to stop them. They are behind the subversion which is going on in Laos. They want all of Southeast Asia. We're going to have to stop them there, too."

"Jack, my sense is that we don't want to commit the flag unless we can win. We need to think these things over carefully before we make a commitment," Bobby said.

The President was feeling better. He was starting to feel in control again.

"*If we have to fight in Southeast Asia, let's fight in Vietnam,*" the President said. "*Vietnam is the place.*"

Chapter 11

"If we do not, on a national scale, attack organized criminals with weapons and techniques as effective as their own, they will destroy us."

Robert F. Kennedy
The Enemy Within, 1959

Robert Kennedy stood up from his leather armchair and pounded his fist on his desk. Everyone in his wood lined office at the Department of Justice looked up at him.

"Indict them!" he shouted.

The Attorney General had interrupted Assistant Attorney General Nicholas Katzenbach. Katzenbach was one of his best assistants.

"We can't indict on the basis of an illegal wiretap," Katzenbach argued.

"Nick," the Attorney General replied, "my signature makes it a legal wiretap. You know that."

"But you can't retroactively authorize a wiretap that was placed illegally," Katzenbach returned.

The Attorney General sat back down in his chair and swung his feet on top of his desk. If he wanted to keep quality attorneys like Katzenbach around, he had to listen to them. Nick made the legal point. He should have authorized the wiretap before the evidence was collected.

"All right, then," he conceded. "Gather some more evidence.

Make sure we're covered. The Patriarca gang is going to jail. Let's not give their lawyers a way to get them out. So much for Rhode Island. What are we doing in New Jersey?"

The Justice Department was mounting the most aggressive prosecution of organized crime in history and it was Robert Kennedy's passion. When he had been appointed Attorney General he had received a memorandum from J. Edgar Hoover that the Communist Party in the United States constituted the greatest threat to the internal national security. But Kennedy knew better. He knew that the Communist party membership had dropped dramatically since the 30's. The real internal enemy was the Mob and he was going to prosecute them. He was going to prosecute them like they had never been prosecuted before—he was going to break the Mob.

His father had not liked the idea. Joseph Kennedy argued with his son when Robert had decided to investigate labor racketeering in 1956. It was a bitter argument. The old man heard that Bobby, who was the chief attorney for the Senate Subcommittee on Investigations, was traveling out to the West Coast and talking to newspapermen about a story they had been trying to expose for years.

Labor unions were being infiltrated by tough guys with tough friends. The idealistic origins of American labor had succeeded, and the labor unions were growing in power and in wealth. The health and welfare funds, controlled by the unions, were becoming vast sums of money—large enough to attract interest from organized crime. But what had started as a utopian vision to elevate the status of workers had become controlled by people who hardly qualified as idealists. A reporter who had started to write about organized crime and the unions had been blinded when an assailant had thrown acid in his eyes.

When Clark Mallenhoff, a newspaper man, tried to interest Robert Kennedy in using the Senate Subcommittee to investigate the unions, he had taunted him with the question of whether

Kennedy had the courage to take on the Mafia. Robert Kennedy didn't like questions about his courage.

In his family, Bobby had always been the small brother. His older brothers, Joe and Jack, had fought downstairs, while young Bobby stayed upstairs with the girls. His father taught aggressiveness in every aspect of life and Bobby heard his message. He was bred to fight and when he came of age, he wanted to go to show his toughness.

Following Senate hearings, Dave Beck, a union leader in Seattle, was convicted of larceny and tax fraud and went to jail. Bobby had taken on the biggest name in organized labor and put him behind bars. That Christmas, Clark Mollenhoff, the newspaper man who had initially questioned whether Robert Kennedy had the courage to take on the mob, wrote him a letter:

"You have carried a candle that has been a beacon to hundreds of reporters and editors, thousands of politicians and labor leaders, and literally millions of the rank and file labor union members and their families . . . You may go ahead to higher office than committee counsel, but it is doubtful if anything you do will have greater force for good government and clean labor than what you have done this year."

After Robert Kennedy had conducted the Senate hearings, he was surprised that the Justice Department did not act quickly and decisively to prosecute organized crime. In 1960, the New York office of the F.B.I. had 400 agents assigned to investigate the threat of communism in the City, and 4 assigned to look into organized crime. Upon taking office, Robert Kennedy moved to shift priorities. In his first year as Attorney General, more than 100 indictments were brought against organized crime. The number was to increase every year he was in office.

"Do you want to authorize wire taps in New Jersey?" Katzenbach asked.

"I want to authorize wire taps anywhere we have probable cause," Kennedy replied. He sat in the leather chair with his tie pulled loose around his neck. His shirt sleeves were rolled up and his hair seemed out of place.

A secretary walked into the room.

"Mr. Kennedy, the Director is here," the secretary reported.

The assembled staff members, including Nicholas Katzenbach, Burke Marshall, and Archibald Cox picked up their papers and coffee cups and began to file out of the room.

J. Edgar Hoover was escorted into the Attorney General's office. He had entered the office under many different Attorneys General. He had assumed control of the F.B.I. the year before Robert Kennedy was born. He had molded the Bureau, sold it to the Congress and the public, polished its reputation. He was the very essence of governmental integrity to many Americans. And he like to think that he looked the part.

Upon entering the office, Hoover looked around. Robert Kennedy stood up from his desk and walked over to him with an extended hand.

"Thank you for coming over on such short notice, Edgar. I'm sure the President will appreciate your cooperation."

Hoover shook the young man's hand, but he did not like what he saw. Kennedy was not wearing a jacket. His tie was loose. He had his shoes on, this time, but he was wearing white, wool athletic stockings—hardly appropriate for the Attorney General of the United States. If Kennedy was an agent of the F.B.I., he would be fired on the spot.

Hoover glanced around the vast, walnut paneled room. The vaulted ceiling and stately fireplace reminded him of the formality the office held before Bobby Kennedy arrived. The dark walls and red carpet had given the room a presence which Hoover felt was essential to the proper function of government.

"When did you shoot the cat?" Hoover asked the Attorney General upon seeing a stuffed tiger next to the fireplace.

"I didn't," Kennedy replied. "I wish people wouldn't kill them. But it was given to me. There's something about a tiger. Something inspirational."

"And what's that?" Hoover asked, unable to hide his astonishment. He was looking at a crayon drawing which Kennedy had tacked to the walnut panel behind his desk.

"A drawing. My kids love to draw. David did that one."

Hoover couldn't believe his eyes. Since first visiting the Attorney General's office in 1924, he had never seen a child's drawing tacked into the paneling. It was nothing short of desecration of public property. These Kennedy boys were going to take some time to get used to.

"The subject you asked me about involves foreign affairs," Hoover began. "The F.B.I. was restricted to domestic surveillance. The Department of Justice does not ordinarily concern itself with governmental operations outside of the United States."

"I know nobody likes it," Robert Kennedy began, "but Jack wants me to get involved in foreign policy."

"That's highly unusual," Hoover admonished.

"That's too bad," Bobby replied. "That's the way Jack wants it."

The two men stared at each other.

"I have my friends, and I have my enemies," Hoover said. "But no one has ever said that J. Edgar Hoover did not understand the line of command. I may not always be easy to work with, but I know my job. I work for the Attorney General of the United States. And he works for the President. I stand ready to execute your orders. Let me add that when I do not feel like I can execute my duties, I will no longer serve this government."

Hoover wanted to remind Bobby that while he worked for the Kennedy boys, they could only push him so far. If he resigned, they would have to endure the public anger his resignation would incite. It was a standoff that would endure throughout the administration.

"Yeah, well, I'm not sure I like it either," Bobby countered. "But I work for Jack, and Jack wants me to be his unofficial foreign policy advisor. After the Bay of Pigs disaster, I think he needs all the help he can get."

"I assume this material falls in the *'Do not file'* category."

Hoover referred to a designation beyond the usual security classification. The 'Do not file' material was considered too explosive to put down on paper. The Attorney General nodded.

"We have learned certain things," Hoover continued, "which border on the official jurisdiction of the Bureau."

"I don't give a shit about jurisdiction on this, Mr. Hoover. I want to know the facts. This isn't going anywhere."

"We have learned that *Colonel Edwards of the CIA made the arrangements to assassinate Fidel Castro*." (Memorandum from J. Edgar Hoover to Robert Kennedy, May 22, 1961)

"You mean the operation originated in the CIA? We weren't just helping Cubans who approached us with the plan?" Bobby was shocked.

"The plan originated with the CIA."

"Jesus Christ."

"Colonel Edwards was directed to contact Robert Maheu, a former F.B.I. special Agent, who I personally fired for drunkenness. Maheu was chosen as a cut out to arrange for the death of Fidel Castro."

"What do you mean cut out?"

"Someone who could not be plausibly linked with the CIA. They could disavow any knowledge of Maheu's activities."

"Does Jack know about this?" Bobby asked.

"I have to assume he does," Hoover answered. Then he continued. "Maheu contacted a known hoodlum in the Chicago area—Sam Giancana. Johnny Rosselli, a small time operator based in Los Angeles may have been an intermediary. Giancana is well acquainted with Santos Trafficante, an underworld figure formerly of Havana, now residing in Florida. The Agency thought that the underworld organizations had a motive to kill Castro because he had expropriated their clubs and operations after seizing control of Cuba. The operation has been funded through the CIA."

Robert Kennedy stood up from his chair. He could not believe what he had just been told. He felt the skin of his face begin to burn slightly.

"Let me get this straight. The CIA hired a one time F.B.I. agent to contact the mob. Sam Giancana is working for the United States Government."

"That is Colonel Edwards's statement to us."

"So you're saying that the CIA was using a Mafia contact to kill Castro. They planned an invasion of Cuba based upon the promised cooperation of organized crime."

"Yes, sir."

He slammed his hand against his desk.

"I'll be damned! Don't they know that I've been going after the mob for last five years? What are those guys thinking about?"

The Director blinked his eyes and raised his eyebrows. He yawned. "Some of the families did support your brother in the election," Hoover reminded him. "I believe your father has had some business dealings with at least some of these so called families."

Bobby Kennedy let Hoover's comments slide. Surely he knew that there had been some involvement of the Chicago mob in influencing the election. And he also knew that his father had certain dealings with the families. Robert Kennedy's prosecution of the mob was partially to distance his family from any future criticism that they were involved with underworld figures. But it was also work that he knew needed to be done. He still could not accept the idea that the entire Bay of Pigs operation had been dependent on organized crime. Jack must have thought that the mob would cooperate with him on removing Castro because it would be good for the mob as well as good for the country. Clearly, something had gone wrong.

"Thank you, Edgar," he said after a moment.

The Director stood up and re-buttoned his coat.

"The F.B.I. stands ready to serve you in any way we can, Mr. Kennedy."

Bobby flopped back down into his leather arm chair. He kicked off his shoes and put his woolen sock clad feet back onto the desk. He rubbed his hair and looked at the conservatively dressed Director of the F.B.I..

"Did Jack know that the whole operation depended on the cooperation of the mob?" he asked Hoover.

"I'm starting to think he is the only one who knows what's going on here," Hoover replied. He stared at Robert Kennedy for a moment and then opened the office door and walked out.

Chapter 12

*"In time of 'clear and present danger,' the courts have held
that even the privileged rights of the First Amendment
must yield to the public's need for national security . . . All
that I suggest is that you add the question: 'Is it in the
national interest?'"*

John F. Kennedy
April 27, 1961

The President was taking notes. After the Cuban debacle,
he met with Richard Nixon at the White House and Dwight
Eisenhower at Camp David. Then, he flew to New York where he
addressed the Newspaper publishers (and scolded them for revealing the details of the Cuban invasion while it was still being
planned) and met with former President Hoover. Now he was listening to General Douglas MacArthur analyze the national
security. He considered MacArthur's words so important, he wrote
them down.

*'He does not feel we should intervene at this time in Cuba be-
cause it does not represent a military danger to us although the
time may come when we may have to do so.'*

The President was making the rounds. The Bay of Pigs had
been a disaster and he knew it. But problems with Cuba were not
over. He had to understand what his options were in Cuba and
pursue a consistent policy. Nixon had encouraged him to invade.

Get it over with. Castro would eventually allow the Soviets to place missiles on the island. Better to eliminate that possibility before it becomes a reality. Eisenhower had treated him like a confused battle commander—during a walk at Camp David, Ike had verbally lashed him for committing troops to a plan he did not fully understand or approve, and then for canceling the air cover. Canceling the air cover—what possessed him to cancel the air cover? Kennedy winced. Being President was a tough way to learn the basics of commanding troops.

But MacArthur had been more merciful. MacArthur blamed Eisenhower for the Cuban disaster. *"The chickens are coming home to roost,"* MacArthur had told the young president, *"and you live in the chicken house."*

Naturally, MacArthur would take his side, Kennedy thought as he boarded Air Force One. MacArthur hated Eisenhower and for good reason: MacArthur had been fired after the war while Eisenhower had become President.

After making the rounds in New York, the President flew to Chicago where he arrived at the Conrad Hilton Hotel before 5 PM that evening. The press was told that the President would be resting until 7 PM. He was scheduled to deliver a speech to the Cook County Democratic Dinner. Members of the press checked into the Hotel and prepared themselves to cover the dinner.

The President stood in his room and looked out the window at the Chicago skyline—it seemed like Chicago just kept getting bigger. The Daley machine, with its Mafia contributors, ran the city, and it certainly looked like a picture of prosperity. Money being made, jobs being hatched, buildings going up. He knew there was a dirty side to the prosperity, a criminal violent side, but you wouldn't see it by looking at the city grow. A knock sounded at his door.

"Car is ready, sir," the Secret Service agent said.

Kennedy loved intrigue. Glancing down hallways and over his shoulder, he followed the agent down to service elevator. The reporters had been cleared from the hallway. Using a key from the maintenance department, the elevator was commandeered to the parking garage where a limousine was waiting with open door. The President slipped into the limousine and was off.

Without police coverage, the limousine took the President to another hotel—the Ambassador East. There, a Secret Service agent was holding another elevator. The President followed his security men.

Once upstairs they walked down another secured corridor. An agent opened a door and the President saw a beautiful woman with dark hair in her mid twenties. Judith Campbell had been introduced to John Kennedy in Las Vegas during the campaign by Frank Sinatra. Stunned by her beauty, Kennedy pursued a relationship with the woman and had been seeing her ever since. But there was more to their relationship than her physical attractiveness.

When she saw the door open, Judith Campbell saw the agent and the President. She turned away from the agent's stare.

"If you want to stay on schedule, sir, I think you can't be long here," the agent advised.

Kennedy looked at Miss Campbell silhouetted against the fading light of the Chicago afternoon.

"Oh, I don't think we're going to upset the schedule," he said with a smile.

The agent closed the door.

It wasn't easy being president, Kennedy thought as the young woman undressed him. The job had stresses and there were nights he didn't get enough sleep. Still, there were certain advantages.

He reached out and gently rubbed her breasts. They rolled on the bed in front of the undraped window.

She knew his limitations and the special considerations he had to be given—Kennedy's back restricted the kinds of activity he could enjoy. But she was sensitive to those restrictions and she moved around him with the skill of a professional. The President was grateful that Miss Campbell understood her purpose. She did not ask him to explain foreign policy during their time together.

"When are you going to see your other boyfriend?" the President asked her.

"Tomorrow and I wish you wouldn't call him my boyfriend."

"He's not nice?" Kennedy teased her.

"He's very nice. But I only see him for you."

She sat up in bed. He rolled on his side and stared at her. She had a near perfect body: large breasts, thin, well muscled legs, not an ounce of excess fat. The truth was that she had a better body than Marilyn Monroe, and that was saying something. If he couldn't have sex with his wife, why not women who were perfectly made for the job.

"He's mad at you," she told Kennedy as she rubbed his chest.

"So I've heard," the President replied.

"He helped you in the election," she said.

"I remember," the President replied.

"Does your brother remember?" she asked with a laugh.

"He never knew the full extent of Sam's help," the President admitted. "Maybe I need to let him in on some family secrets."

Judith Campbell helped the President get out of the bed and back into his clothes.

"Am I supposed to give him something?" she asked him.

"If you don't mind," the President said. He reached into his jacket and pulled out a sealed envelope. The return address was "The White House, Washington, DC" The envelope was not addressed to anyone. She took the envelope and put it in her purse.

"I've delivered every time so far," she said as she pulled on her robe. She had been delivering packages from Kennedy to Giancana for almost a year. Sometimes they carried intelligence information regarding Castro's positions and activities. But Judith Campbell didn't know what they carried. That wasn't her end of the business.

"Yes, you have," Kennedy agreed. "You're a woman who knows how to deliver."

She scowled at him and he laughed.

"I think I'm playing a little more important role than that," she protested.

"Oh, you are," Kennedy said. He was silent for a moment and then serious. "What you are doing is very important. You have to convince Sam Giancana that Bobby might be pestering him, but nothing is going to happen. If anything, all this stuff Bobby is doing covers the operation. Plausible deniability. But Sam has got to know how important it is that he deliver on his Castro promise. I can't tell you how important that is."

"Sam is getting nervous."

"Sam doesn't have to be nervous," Kennedy told her. "He just has to deliver on his end of this deal. I'll deliver on mine."

Chapter 13

"... members of the underworld element ... Joe Fischetti
(a Giancana Associate) and other unidentified hoodlums
are financially supporting and actively endeavoring to
secure the nomination for the presidency as Democratic
candidate, Senator John F. Kennedy ... to assist Senator
Kennedy's campaign whereby ... hoodlums will have an
entree to Senator Kennedy ..."

F.B.I. Report, March 1960

Sam Giancana didn't like F.B.I. agents. They were a
bunch of straight laced bastards from little towns in the Midwest.
He couldn't bribe them. He couldn't threaten them. They worked
in teams and they all carried guns. A city cop could be bought or
influenced under the right circumstances. Making deals with politicians didn't challenge him. But Hoover had made a name for
himself fighting organized crime, and built the F.B.I. as an organization which couldn't be corrupted by the mob. Giancana could
work with Hoover and he could work with Kennedy, so why did
he have to endure the harassment of the rank and file F.B.I. agents.

When Giancana walked into a waiting room at O'Hare Airport
the evening of July 12, 1961, the room seemed full of them. Phyllis
McGuire, the tallest and most beautiful member of the popular
music group, the McGuire Sisters, was traveling with Giancana.
She was always complaining that her reputation was going to be

ruined by her Association with Giancana. When she saw the F.B.I. agents in the waiting room, Phyllis looked at Sam and sighed. How could she continue to have a relationship with a man who was being literally shadowed by the Federal Bureau of Investigation.

"I thought you said this was going to stop," she said to Giancana.

"It is, baby." Giancana looked around him. His two body guards were staring eye ball to eye ball with the F.B.I. agents.

"Why don't you try telling that to one of these goons," she said. "My name is going to end up in the papers and the act is going to be blacklisted."

"No, it won't. Believe me. Your act is going to be fine. These guys shouldn't even be here. I was told they were going to give me some room."

Giancana looked at all the dark suits, white shirts and dark ties. One of them approached him.

"Sam Giancana?" the agent said, flashing a badge. "I'm Special agent Thompson, F.B.I.. Is this Phyllis McGuire?"

"Who do you think it is? Jimmy Hoffa?"

"I would like to ask Miss McGuire some questions."

"Shove it, pal. I was told you guys were suppose to leave me alone."

"Mr. Giancana, I would like to remind you that you are addressing an agent of the Federal Bureau of Investigation. If you fail to cooperate, or make remarks degrading to my position as a law enforcement officer—"

"Yeah, yeah. Give me a break, will you?"

"I would like to interview Miss McGuire," the agent persisted.

"Yeah, well, you can forget about that."

"Mr. Giancana," the agent began, taking an envelope out of his pocket. "This is a subpoena for Miss McGuire to appear before a Special committee of the United States Senate in order to—"

Giancana snatched the subpoena from the agent's hand. He looked it over.

"What a lousy bastard," he muttered as he glanced over the document.

"Did I understand you to make a remark insulting an agent of the Federal Bureau of Investigation, sir?" the agent sternly asked Giancana.

"No. I was talking about your leader. I didn't realize freedom of speech had been outlawed."

"I can talk to Miss McGuire here, or she can accept this subpoena."

Giancana looked at Phyllis. She was angry. She didn't want to be interviewed by the F.B.I., and she didn't want to accept a Federal subpoena—it might create headlines.

"What do you say, baby?" Giancana asked her.

"Maybe I should just answer their questions for a minute," she replied. "What harm can it do?"

Giancana looked back at the agent and nodded. Phyllis McGuire handed Giancana her purse for safe keeping. She was escorted away by the F.B.I. agents. As they left, more F.B.I. agents, in the same dark suits and white shirts stood around Giancana.

Momo Salvatore (Sam) Giancana was a strong man. He spent seven years in penitentiaries before working his way to the top job in the Chicago underworld. Under his leadership, the Brotherhood of Electrical Workers had taken over the juke box, coin machine and cigarette vending machine business in Chicago. Some blood had been spilled in the process.

When Robert Kennedy brought Giancana before the Senate Investigation Committee in 1958, Giancana took the Fifth Amendment 33 times. Kennedy described Giancana as the "chief gunman for the group that succeeded the Capone mob." Giancana did not dispute the description.

In the official transcript of the committee hearings, Robert Kennedy pressed Giancana:

Mr. Kennedy: Would you tell us if you have opposition from anybody that you dispose of them by having them stuffed in a trunk? Is that what you do, Mr. Giancana?

Mr. Giancana: I decline to answer because I honestly believe any answer might tend to incriminate me.

Giancana looked around the waiting room. He walked over and sat in a chair. His body guards, still trading glances with the multitude of F.B.I. agents, sat down on either side of him.

If he could get one of these guys, or even a couple, alone, he would beat them, he would torture them—there would be blood. He would make an example that other F.B.I. agents would notice. This bullshit had to stop.

Before the election, Giancana believed that the Kennedys were friends. Joe Kennedy had done business with some of the families during Prohibition. And when the Democrats were selecting a presidential nominee, Joe Kennedy bought some influence in West Virginia. The underworld families had been led to believe that Kennedy would be good for business. They helped out in the primaries. They counted votes in the election. Then the bullshit started.

Bobby Kennedy was supposed to be controlled. But they made him Attorney General. During the year before the Kennedys arrived in Washington, the Justice Department had prosecuted ten or twenty cases involving Mafia families. Now that the little bastard Bobby was Attorney General, almost one hundred cases had been filed. It was just flat out deception: the Mafia families had been lied to. Sam wondered if the Kennedys were prosecuting the families because they felt there were political rewards, or because they worried that the real story of the election would get out. If someone discovered the relationship between the Kennedys and the families, the Kennedys could point to the increased prosecution of organized crime as clear evidence that they had not been tainted. But tainted they were, and they still wanted Giancana's help with Castro.

But he should be safe. He was Sam Giancana. He worked for the government. Other Mafia families might be prosecuted, but he should be protected. He couldn't believe that having the F.B.I. stop and harass him was Jack Kennedy's idea of protection.

There was movement from the room. Phyllis came out of the room, followed by the F.B.I.. She walked toward him. Giancana stood up. He picked up Phyllis' purse and walked toward her. Upon seeing Sam Giancana carrying a woman's purse, a group of F.B.I. agents laughed.

"I wish I could get a purse like that," one of them heckled him.

"Is that where you carry your lipstick, Sam?" another chimed in.

Giancana felt his face flush and his blood boil. Approaching her, he handed Phyllis her purse. Then he turned on the F.B.I. agents.

"You can tell this to your boss, and your super boss and your super super boss. You know who I mean, I mean the Kennedys. I know all about the Kennedys, and Phyllis knows a lot more about the Kennedys, and one of these days we are going to tell all."

Phyllis McGuire pulled on his arm. They walked to their waiting plane.

Giancana's anger was not short lived. A few days later, in Las Vegas, Giancana joined Frank Sinatra at a casino table with Peter Lawford and Marilyn Monroe. He had a message for the President and he wanted to make sure it got through. Both Marilyn and Peter Lawford knew Giancana.

"Your man Kennedy don't know who his friends are," Giancana told Sinatra. "You write songs for him, you sing the songs, your friends get votes for him, and now he don't know who his friends are."

"Momo, you seem upset," Sinatra replied.

"I am upset. I helped this man. The families helped this man. Now he turns on us."

"What has he done?" Marilyn Monroe asked. Her voice was light and sweet.

"Marilyn, you've had too much to drink," Sinatra said. "Maybe you could let me talk to my friend from Chicago."

Marilyn stared over at Frank. She seemed hurt by his suggestion that she was drunk.

"Go screw yourself, Frank," she said in a lower voice. She glared at him. Sinatra shook his head and looked back at Giancana.

"This little bastard Bobby has me followed all the time. My house is staked out. I get stopped in airports. I can't play a round of golf without these F.B.I. thugs following me around."

"Momo, have you been arrested?" Sinatra asked.

"No."

"Has your family been injured?"

"No."

"Is your business suffering?"

"No."

"Then why are you mad at the President? He is a complicated man. He has many issues to understand, many personalities to work with. Sometimes he must appear to be doing one thing, when his intention is to do another. Maybe he likes you better than you think," Sinatra argued.

"I hope so," Giancana replied. "But I'm starting to wonder. Can he control the brother, or not?"

"He's the President," Sinatra said. "The Lieutenant must listen to the Don."

"I hope you're right," Peter Lawford chimed in. "I think Bobby has a mind of his own."

There was a long silence as Giancana stared at Lawford. Lawford nervously consumed the rest of his drink.

"See what I mean?" Giancana asked, turning to Sinatra.

Sinatra cast a harsh glance at Lawford, took a drag from his cigarette, and then looked back at Giancana.

"Jack's in a tough spot," Sinatra went on. "Take that Cuban invasion. It looked to me like he got left high and dry."

"Maybe there is a message there," Giancana suggested. "Maybe if he don't want to work with the families, maybe the families don't want to work with him."

"The President was deceived by the CIA," Marilyn interrupted. "Jack didn't know that they were going to ask for American help. He was honor bound not to use American troops."

The men looked over at Marilyn and then exchanged knowing glances.

"Marilyn, you need to go check your lipstick," Sinatra suggested.

"A woman can't know anything? Maybe I know a little more about the President than you think," Marilyn countered. "All Castro wants to do is spread the money around a little bit. Why should all the money be kept by the big corporations?"

Sinatra shrugged and leaned back in his chair. Marilyn was too independent for his taste. She was a star in her own right, and she wanted people to know it. She was talking with at least two men who hated women they couldn't control.

"You think Kennedy likes this man, Castro?" Giancana asked her.

"No. But the President would never order another man to be killed. He's a man of refined values."

Giancana snorted his disagreement.

"What about the families?" Giancana asked her. "Do you think he will be loyal to the families?"

"What families?"

"The Italian families. The people who supported him."

"A lot of people supported him. I'm sure he'll be fair with the Italian families, just like he will be fair to the Jews. And I think he's going to do a lot for the Negroes."

Sinatra shook his head. "Jesus, Marilyn," he said.

"There is no reason he should not be fair to the Negroes. They're Americans."

"He's not going to treat the Italians like Negroes," Sinatra said to Giancana.

"I think they will let the Negroes do whatever they have the legal right to do. And I think they will let the Italian families do whatever they have the legal right to do," Marilyn said.

"This is bullshit," Giancana said, shifting his gaze from Marilyn to Sinatra.

"If the Italian families are doing something illegal, then I think the Kennedys will stop them," Marilyn concluded.

"I've got news for you, Miss Know it All," Giancana said to Marilyn. "The Kennedys want Castro dead. They are paying to have him killed."

Marilyn looked stunned for a moment. Then she took another sip of her drink and stared for a long moment at Giancana.

"You're misinformed," she told the Mafia Don.

Giancana took a deep breath and shook his head. He knew he shouldn't say any more, but he couldn't help himself.

"The CIA is paying to have Castro killed," Giancana told her. "I know because I'm the guy making the arrangements."

Marilyn stared at Giancana in utter disbelief. John Kennedy had talked about whether he should have someone kill Castro, but she had argued that it was wrong. And he had listened to her. Perhaps there were forces in the government more powerful than the President. Maybe the CIA was working on its own.

Chapter 14

"Greenson had very considerable concerns that she was being used in these relationships. However, it seemed so gratifying to her to be associated with such power-ful and important men that he could not declare him-self to be against it."

Robert Litman, M.D.
Notes from interview with Dr. Greenson
1962

J. Edgar Hoover pulled the lower drawer of his desk open revealing his private files. He looked over the neatly typed labels at the top of each of the alphabetically organized folders. The la-bels were typed and spaced perfectly. There were no smudges. The folders were neatly hung, not crowded in the file drawer. The clipped nail of his index finger lightly tipped back the labels— Johnson, Lyndon Baines . . . Kennedy, John Fitzgerald . . . Kennedy, Joseph (Joe) . . . Kennedy, Robert Francis. He lifted his private file concerning the Attorney General of the United States out of the drawer and placed it on his desk. He slid the drawer closed.

Robert Kennedy was generally regarded as a family man. He did not have the interest in prostitutes his older brother did. In general, he stayed with his wife and raised his children. In general. But a report had just been filed from the Las Vegas office of the F.B.I.

documenting a threat against the Attorney General. Photographs had been taken with a telephoto lens showing the nation's top law enforcement officer on a blanket with two naked women. The threat had come from someone complaining about the Attorney General's interest in organized crime. Hoover looked over the report.

How convincing could such a photograph be? Pictures taken with telephoto lenses were usually fuzzy. Hoover wanted a copy of the photograph. It would be a nice addition to the file.

His intercom clicked on.

"Mr. Hoover, a meeting is beginning in the projection room," his secretary informed him.

Hoover reached over to the intercom box and pressed down the button.

"Meetings do not begin until I arrive," he replied.

He opened the file drawer once again, and went back to the K's. His file on his boss was returned to its proper place.

When the director walked into the projection room, he heard no noise. Five men, all quietly sitting in the last row of fold down chairs stood up as he entered. Hoover walked to one of two large, leather chairs at the center of the room and sat down. His right hand man, and lifelong companion, Clyde Tolson, sat in the other overstuffed leather chair.

The Director picked up a small knife from a table between the two club chairs. From his coat pocket, he pulled out a cigar. He cut the end off the cigar. Clyde held a match while the Director lit the cigar.

"Let's go," he muttered.

One of the men from the last row approached the front of the room and stood next to the screen. He was dressed in a navy blue blazer, a white shirt, gray slacks, and wore a thin, dark tie. His hair was cut closely, and he did not wear glasses. All special agents of the F.B.I. had good vision.

A photograph of a woman was projected.

"Paula Strasberg. Currently Miss Monroe's drama coach. Formerly a member of the American Communist Party."

The slide changed.

"Arthur Miller. Writer. Liberal. With the encouragement of Miss Monroe, Mr. Miller would not cooperate with Senator McCarthy's committee. Marriage to Miss Monroe dissolved on the day of the President's inauguration.

A photograph of Marilyn was projected.

"Marilyn Monroe. Well known actress with access to the highest levels of our government. Imagines herself as an activist for liberal causes. Lent her name to SANE—the Committee for a Sane Nuclear Policy—a committee advocating elimination of the atomic bomb. Is believed to actually support the efforts of Mr. Castro in Cuba. Her psychiatrist is Ralph Greenson."

The slide changed.

"Dr. Greenson has surrounded Miss Monroe with individuals who are loyal to him—many of whom are known to be members of the Communist Party. Dr. Greenson's mother, Katherine Greenschpoon, has a long term friendship with Frederick Vanderbilt Field. She served on the board of directors of Mr. Field's American Russian Institute. Frederick Vanderbilt Field—"

Again, a new face was projected on the screen.

". . . is the heir to the Vanderbilt fortune. Exposed by Louis Budenz—the Soviet defector—Mr. Field chose to leave the United States and live in Mexico rather than face investigation. He remains a member of the Communist Party.. Thought to be a well established source of information for the Russians. Our concern is obviously that information effecting the national security of the United States could be leaked from our Chief Executive to Marilyn Monroe, and then to Dr. Ralph Greenson and on to Frederick Field. The Communists have essentially an open line to our Commander in Chief."

Hoover puffed at his cigar and rubbed his forehead. Joseph Kennedy told him once that *he should have gelded Jack as a young boy.* Hoover was starting to understand why. Marilyn Monroe was clearly a security problem. She had Communist contacts in

Mexico and access to the highest levels of the U.S. Government. The slide show continued.

"The President meets Miss Monroe in the beach front home of this man—the first Brother in Law." A slide of Peter Lawford was projected. We have no way of knowing whether national security secrets are discussed with Miss Monroe, because the house is not under surveillance. Incidentally, the house is also frequented by Mr. Frank Sinatra and Sam Giancana."

"Amazing," Hoover muttered. "What a mess." He puffed on his cigar as the lights were turned on. He had the habit of talking into space and having his assistants strain to listen to his instructions. "You have to ask yourself if it makes any difference whether the Soviet Union knows what the secret plans of the United States Government are. We've always thought that secrecy was important, and given the recent embarrassment in Cuba, I've got to think it's terribly important now. I want that house on the beach installed with some microphones. I want it staked out. If Sam Giancana is visiting the President's brother in law, we have to know about it. If we happen to overhear Miss Monroe and the President, well, perhaps those transcripts should come to my desk, only. Is that understood?"

"Yes, sir."

"No copies made."

"None."

"And I'd like to know more about this fellow Ralph Greenson. I don't remember hearing much about him before. Find out how he fits into the picture."

Hoover continued to puff his cigar. He didn't like the idea of bugging the President of the United States. And so, he wouldn't. He would bug Peter Lawford. There were clear reasons why Lawford's house should be put under surveillance. There would be no wiretaps on the telephones. That would be illegal without the Attorney General's written authorization. But putting a few microphones in selected locations—not to collect evidence for a crime, merely to protect the national security—well, that could be justified.

After the meeting, Hoover and Clyde Tolson returned to the Director's Office. Tolson sat in a chair beneath a framed letter from Joseph Kennedy encouraging J. Edgar Hoover to run for President of the United States in 1956. J. Edgar Hoover stared out the window.

"We know that he is passing classified material to Sam Giancana through a young lady by the name of Judith Campbell. I have to assume that he is giving Giancana intelligence reports on the movements of Castro, because we know that Giancana is working with the CIA to kill Castro. But, Good Lord!"

"Not exactly according to the book," Tolson remarked.

"To have the President of the United States passing classified information to a Mafia Don? No, I'd say that isn't exactly according to the procedure manual. But these Kennedy boys have no respect for procedures. The Attorney General is now running the CIA operation on Cuba."

"No!"

"Yes. Robert Kennedy is no longer merely running the Department of Justice. He is now in charge of the Cuban operation."

"Ill advised," Clyde remarked dryly. "Ill advised."

"What is the President thinking about?" Hoover asked as he went over to his desk and sat down. "Why would any president take that kind of risk?"

The intercom broke the silence.

"Mr. Hoover, the White House on line 2."

Hoover cast a glance over at Clyde. He lifted up the telephone.

"This is Hoover," he said.

After a moment's pause, the President came on the line.

"Have you seen **Newsweek?**" the President asked.

"No."

"There is no security in this government!" Kennedy exclaimed.

"I have grown more concerned about security leaks, as well. What can I do , Mr. President?"

"I want you to find out how **Newsweek** learns about proposals from the Joint Chiefs of Staff regarding Berlin before I have seen them. Get some F.B.I. agents at the Pentagon and find out how this is happening." The President was livid.

"I will take it upon myself to look into security leaks in this government," Hoover promised. "We know the Cubans were able to get information from our own press, but my question is whether there is even more sensitive information being leaked. I believe it is a real national security concern."

"This shit has got to stop. We've got to stop this," Kennedy concluded. After the Bay of Pigs, he was particularly sensitive to the inability of the government to keep anything out of the news. He welcomed Hoover's promise to determine exactly how the information was getting out.

Hoover called to an assistant and explained the situation. He requested a copy of the most recent **Newsweek** and passed on the President's concerns. Hoover wanted a report before morning.

"Clyde, it's time," Hoover said to Tolson after he had ordered agents to investigate news leaks at the Pentagon. That was Hoover's signal that it was late enough in the afternoon to have a drink.

Tolson walked over to the door to Hoover's office and turned the bolt. Then, he went over to a row of books in one of the bookcases and undid a latch. An entire panel of books folded down, revealing a small bar. Clyde poured some whiskey into glasses. Into his glass, he added some water. To the Director's glass, he added some ice. He put a small peel of lemon into each glass.

"I don't know, Clyde," Hoover said after he had been served the drink. "John Kennedy is an attractive man—no question about that. He has seduced the public and press. But, I've got to say that I'm worried—I've never seen a president take such liberties with our system, and believe me, I've seen some liberties taken. But I just wonder if the President and his brother want our help."

Hoover emptied his glass and handed it to Tolson who poured some more whiskey and added some ice.

"Do you think we should leave Washington, Clyde?" Hoover asked as he began to nurse his refilled drink.

Tolson looked at him. Hoover was coming up to mandatory retirement age for all Federal employees. There was going to be pressure on him to step down.

"Don't talk that way, John," Clyde said softly. "The country needs you more now than it ever has. The President will extend your appointment. He clearly needs someone with some experience around here. I think there are some real concerns about what the Communists know and how they are getting their information. Frankly, I'm starting to wonder if John Kennedy knows what he is getting into."

"I should have closed out his political career a long time ago," Hoover lamented. "Have I ever played the Inga tapes for you?" He smiled.

"I always enjoy the Inga tapes," Clyde said.

Hoover got out of his chair and walked over to a cabinet. He took a key out his pocket and opened the cabinet door. The cabinet was full of carefully labeled audio tapes. Hoover began to load a tape into his tape player.

Inga Arvad was a 28 year old Danish journalist when she arrived in Washington in 1940. As a reporter for the **Washington Times Herald**, it was her professed ambition to learn the news. So rapid was her ascent through social circles in Washington that by late 1941, before America had entered the world war, Inga had been successful in her efforts to meet J. Edgar Hoover. His friend, Clyde Tolson, had introduced Inga to the Director at a party.

But by early 1942, suspicion had built that Inga was in Washington to spy for the Nazis. Photographs showed that Inga Arvad had been in the box of Adolf Hitler in the 1936 Olympic Games in Berlin. There was speculation that Inga may have been sexually involved with the German leader. The F.B.I. put her under surveillance.

Alarms began to sound in the intelligence community when Inga Arvada started to sleep with an officer at the Office of Naval

Intelligence. The officer was regarded as a potential target for a Nazi spy—his father was a known Nazi sympathizer, and had served as the Ambassador to England. The young officer was John F. Kennedy.

Kennedy was transferred out of Washington, but the affair continued. Agents of the F.B.I. listened to hidden microphones in Room 132 of the Fort Sumter Hotel in Charleston, South Carolina as the couple talked and made love. If Inga learned anything from young Kennedy which might have benefited the Nazis, the F.B.I. never learned about it. Hoover's agents never proved she was a spy.

"Listen to this, Clyde," Hoover said with a broad smile as he turned on the tape player.

"You've got to think we'll invade through France," the voice of the young Kennedy predicted. His voice and accent were immediately recognizable. "You can't get to Germany by going through Greece. We'll have to go through France."

Hoover shook his head. "That was 1942!" he exclaimed. "Wouldn't this make a great news story? 'Hitler's lover in bed with future president.' I love the sound of that." Hoover slowly unloaded the tape, put it carefully back into its case, and locked the cabinet.

"Clyde, what are the odds that a woman who is photographed with Adolf Hitler in 1936 is recorded in bed with a future president."

"I'd have to say that they were pretty thin," Clyde answered.

Hoover returned to his chair to finish his drink.

"I'd have to say they were very thin," Hoover concluded. "And if I'd leaked that tape, John Kennedy would be back in Boston counting his father's money."

"Why didn't you leak it, Edgar?"

"Oh, I don't know," the Director said wistfully. "I've been very careful with the information we've learned through the years. Our purpose is to protect the country, not embarrass it. And I guess I liked his old man."

The two men, both in their 60's sat in the light of the late Washington afternoon. Hoover glanced around his office at the photographs of himself with presidents and senators. He had been at the F.B.I. for 40 years. The F.B.I. had been his home. In a sense, it has been his life, his marriage. He had given it everything he had. But he was 65 years old, and the President of United States would have to exercise his power to extend the Director's term.

"I think he'll ask that you stay, John," Clyde Tolson said.

"What should someone in my position do when he learns that a young, attractive President is his own worst enemy?" Hoover asked. "John Kennedy was a security risk in 1942 because he was in bed with a woman who I still think was passing information to the enemy, and now, unless we are completely off the mark, he's in bed with a woman who is doing the same thing. It's amazing this country survives."

Chapter 15

"*Castro kept Santo Trafficante, Jr., in jail to make it appear that he had a personal dislike for Trafficante, when in fact, Trafficante is an agent of Castro. Trafficante is allegedly Castro's outlet for illegal contraband in this country.*"

Federal Narcotic Bureau document,
July 1961

Joseph Kennedy pulled his driver from his golf bag and took a couple of practice swings to loosen up his shoulders. It was a warm, fall afternoon in September 1961, and the president's father was enjoying the temperate climate of Palm Beach. A slight breeze was blowing in from the Southeast. The old man looked at the sky and then picked up some grass and let it fall, in order to better judge the wind.

"The wind shouldn't bother us today," he said to his guest.

Joseph Kennedy's guest that fall afternoon was a man with whom he had played golf on occasion for many years, John Rosselli. Rosselli was a short, well muscled man, ten years younger than the elder Kennedy. His dark skin contrasted with Kennedy's light Celtic coloring. Both men were impeccably dressed.

Rosselli's caddie was a stocky, young man who wore a jacket in the warm weather. Kennedy's caddie, a secret service agent, also wore a jacket. The two men eyed one another suspiciously.

They were the only two caddies on the country club course that afternoon who wore jackets. Kennedy and Rosselli were the only two golfers to go out on the course as a twosome. Everyone else played in groups of four.

The men teed off and then began to walk together down the fairway. The caddies walked separately, some distance behind. Joe Kennedy had transacted a considerable amount of business on golf courses. Today would be no exception.

"This whole disaster with the Russians is really your fault," the President's father told Rosselli. He was referring to the President's clash with Khrushchev in Vienna. So frightening and real was the prospect of nuclear war, that Americans were building bomb shelters in the basements. Both governments had recently resumed atmospheric nuclear testing.

Rosselli didn't flinch. He had come to play golf with Joseph Kennedy, and he knew that some understandings needed to be clarified.

"I can only do what I can do," Rosselli replied.

"You know as well as I do that there wouldn't be any of this saber rattling if there hadn't been that mess at the Bay of Pigs."

"That wasn't my fault."

"It was somebody's fault," Kennedy continued.

Joseph Kennedy had served on the President's Board of Consultants on Foreign Intelligence Activities during the Eisenhower Administration. The Board had the official responsibility to oversee the activities of the CIA. Kennedy realized that the CIA could not put all of its plans and schemes on paper, so it was difficult to establish exactly who was blame for a failed operation.

"The Agency provided me with some poison pills," Rosselli explained. "I passed them along to my contacts. Castro was supposed to have been poisoned before the invasion began."

"What happened?" Joseph Kennedy asked.

"The word that came back was that the pills were put in his drink, but that they didn't dissolve."

"Jesus," Kennedy muttered. "What an operation!"

"The Agency gave me the pills," Rosselli appealed. "I didn't test them. I had to assume that they had been tested."

The two golfers did not let their conversation change the rhythm of their game. They continued to play as if they were discussing politics or women.

"Let me ask you something," Kennedy said as they walked up to a green. "How was it that my son got the idea that Castro was going to be shot?"

"Shot?"

"Yes. Jack thought they were going to shoot him. He didn't see how they could fail."

"I don't know how he got that idea. The CIA gave me the pills. I gave them to my contact."

"You guys made Jack look pretty stupid," the Ambassador went on. "You tell him you're going to kill Castro and he sends a bunch of half assed exiles ashore expecting they will be received with open arms. Instead, they get met by Castro's army."

"We didn't make him look stupid. We were just trying to do our government a favor."

"Some favor," Kennedy retorted.

Rosselli missed a putt. The conversation, although conducted at a low volume, was making him angry. It seemed to him that the Kennedys were always asking for favors, but then didn't want to give the families any breaks.

"Your sons haven't been repaying any favors, you know," Rosselli said as Kennedy was trying to line up a putt.

"What's that suppose to mean?" Joe shot back.

"Sam Giancana is getting trailed around, you know," Rosselli continued. "We did our part in the election, and now our friends are getting arrested. Is that how you like to do business?"

"You know the way these CIA things work," Kennedy said. "You have to look like you're doing one thing, and really do another. That's the whole idea."

"Sam don't like F.B.I. agents around his house."

"Did you hear what I said? If somebody talks, Jack and Bobby need a way out. Who is really going to believe that a Mafia chief is going to be working with two guys who have his house staked out? Get it? It gives them plausible deniability." He paused. "You guys probably don't think too much about plausible deniability."

Rosselli looked up at him and snorted. "You think Sam don't know how to cover a hit?" he asked.

"He didn't deliver on the last one," Kennedy persisted. "Say nothing about covering it."

"Me and Sam weren't the only ones in on that," Rosselli reminded Kennedy. "We got the pills to Santos. Santos took it from there."

"Trafficante?"

"Yes. Santos is running things on the island."

"I didn't know Santos Trafficante was in on this," Joseph Kennedy said. "That puts a little different light on things."

"How so?"

"You know how so. Trafficante is Castro's man. Trafficante has a deal with Castro."

"Castro took over his casinos," Rosselli said. "He put Santos in jail. How good a friends do you think they are?"

"Yes, but Trafficante is out of jail now. He's running operations in Florida. And I'm going to guess that he made a pretty good deal with Castro. Something tells me that the drugs are still going through Havana and ending up in Florida. Santos Trafficante is out of jail, but he's still making money and Castro's getting his share of it."

"Might be," Rosselli said with a vague smile. "I wouldn't know. Bobby Kennedy is trying to make a name for himself at our expense. We put him in office, and now he tries to shut down our operations."

"Bobby's just doing what he has to do," Kennedy said to Rosselli.

"The hell he is."

"No, I'm serious. The public is demanding that the Justice

Department clean up some of these rackets. Bobby is just doing his job."

"Joe, don't bullshit me. Bobby is going after the families like we're a bunch of Communists or something. He's after Jimmy Hoffa and anyone else with an Italian last name. We deserve more."

"You got paid for your work," Kennedy shot back. "That was business. You got paid."

"Sure, we took some money for expenses. But we figure we deserve better than being followed night and day by the F.B.I.. Sam can't even play a round of golf."

Joseph Kennedy was silent for moment.

"You're telling me that the CIA left it to Santos Trafficante to pull the trigger on Castro."

"Right."

"They're idiots. There is no explanation for that."

"I can only tell you what I know."

"They are a bunch of goddamn idiots. The whole idea of the operation was that the Mafia had a motive to kill Castro because he took their casinos—he was bad for their business."

"I guess."

"But now, Castro is good for business. He's certainly good for Trafficante's business. And Bobby Kennedy is bad for business. Castro is letting you use his ports to ship the dope to the U.S., and Bobby Kennedy is trying to arrest you for doing it. I can see why Santos had a little problem keeping his end of the deal," Kennedy concluded.

"I don't want to say I agree with you," Rosselli said. "But if Santos has a motive to hit anybody, he's got a motive to hit Bobby Kennedy, not Castro."

Joseph Kennedy stopped walking. Then Rosselli stopped and looked at the Ambassador. His eyes were bulging.

"What are you suggesting?" he asked Rosselli.

"I'm not suggesting anything."

"Are you saying Trafficante is threatening Bobby Kennedy?"

"No. I didn't say that."

"Is anyone threatening any Kennedy?"

"Not that I know of."

"Let me tell you something. You guys aren't dealing with families anymore. We're not talking about who gets to run the numbers in Chicago. You guys are dealing with the United States Government. Bobby can have everyone of you guys taken out tomorrow morning and shot."

Joseph Kennedy and John Rosselli were standing in the middle of a fairway, staring eye to eye. The discussion was heated. Other golfers were now staring at the two men.

"And if anything should happen to Robert Kennedy, or any of his children, or the President, or any of his children, there's going to be a war for you guys like you've never had a war before. There's going to be an open season on every one of the families. Do you understand that?"

"Joe, I wasn't saying anybody's going to go after Bobby."

"You guys took the money to eliminate Castro. Now, you've got to deliver on your end of the deal."

Chapter 16

"What would you think if I ordered Castro to be assassinated?"

John F. Kennedy to
Tad Szulc, Reporter, **New York Times**
November 8, 1961

"It's not much of a body," the President said. "I've got all these scars on my thighs and a big hole in my back. The God damn steroids make my face puffy and make my arms and legs look like sticks. If I have to start using a wheelchair, that will be it. I'll never get re-elected with this body."

"I like it," Marilyn said. She and the President were naked.

"You do?" the President asked.

She rubbed her hand on his bare abdomen. They were lying on a bed in Peter Lawford's beach house. It was late afternoon on November 19, 1961. The surf could be heard rolling intermittently up on the beach.

"I do," she whispered. "There are parts of it that are really nice."

He laughed.

She leaned over him and began to kiss the skin of his lower chest. She continued to rub his lower abdomen, then his thighs. She kissed him on the flank.

He took a deep breath and let it out.

"Is this all right?" she asked innocently. "I don't want to hurt you."

"This is just fine," he answered.

In a small rented apartment, a mile or so away, agents of the Federal Bureau of Investigation adjusted their instruments and flipped their tape recorder on. They had been monitoring the Lawford house on the instructions of the Director of the F.B.I.. As the love making became intense, they looked at each other and smiled. Their report would go only to J. Edgar Hoover.

During a long period of silence, another agent came into the rented apartment with a pizza. He asked why the television had been turned off. He was hushed to silence, as the other agents followed the scene to its completion.

"What's going on?" he finally asked, hearing nothing from the monitors.

"They're doing it," one of the other agents said.

"Doing what?"

"That's what were trying to figure out."

The agents could not fully understand what had transpired at the beach when voices again returned to their monitors. They were there to find out what the President told Marilyn. But that wasn't what they most wanted to know.

Marilyn looked out over the beach. She and the President and one of the President's old friends were sitting on the patio of the beach house. Jack was talking with Senator George Smathers, but Marilyn found herself bored with their conversation. Smathers was in Los Angeles for a Democratic Party meeting and had been invited out to the Lawford beach house for a private meeting with Kennedy. They had been friends since their early years in Congress. George Smathers had been in John Kennedy's 1953 wedding.

Marilyn wondered what it must have been like to have gotten married to John Kennedy. She had seen the photographs of the wedding—Jackie had chosen a white dress which was elegant in its simplicity. The bride's maids were beautiful women, the groom's men were handsome, and the setting in Newport, Rhode Island, seemed idyllic. Why couldn't Marilyn have a wedding like that? She smiled.

The waves crashed on the beach, sending up a little mist right at the water's edge. The sun was blocked out by a bank of gray clouds. Marilyn pulled her sweater up around her neck. She was getting cold.

"What would you do?" the President asked his friend, George Smathers.

Marilyn liked George Smathers. He was an attractive man, about Jack's age, with none of the physical frailties. Marilyn had a feeling Smathers did all right with the women.

"I think you have to get rid of him," Smathers answered.

"I know that," Kennedy replied. "And I'm sure everyone in Florida would be happy if the Cuban exiles could just go home. But, that's not going to be possible as long as there is a Communist government in Cuba."

"I thought you told me that Castro was going to be killed before the Bay of Pigs," Smathers recalled.

"That thing made no sense if he didn't die," Kennedy said. "I can't believe the United States Government, the strongest power in the world, cannot get rid of one half assed dictator, but we can't. They keep telling me they're going to do it, and he keeps blowing cigar smoke in my face. What an operation!"

"Do what?" Marilyn asked.

Kennedy glanced over at Marilyn. He couldn't remember how much she knew.

"Oh, yes. I'd forgotten. Marilyn wants to send in the Peace Corps." Kennedy laughed. He picked up a cup of hot tea and sipped its contents.

Marilyn looked over at the President. She was no longer fantasizing about a Kennedy wedding.

"Did you say that we've been trying to kill Castro?" Marilyn asked him.

"No," Kennedy said, smiling back at Marilyn. "I want the son of a bitch to out live me. We're just trying to figure out a way to get him to retire before the congressional elections." He winked at Smathers.

"When you think about it, what he is doing in Cuba is good for the people," Marilyn remarked. "He reclaimed all the property that has been stolen from the Cubans over the years, and is trying to give it back to the people."

"Please, Marilyn," the President said. "This isn't your strongest subject."

"You agree that things were very bad before Castro took over?" Marilyn asked him. "You've told me that you hated the Batista government."

"It was horrible," Kennedy conceded.

"It was basically a police state to protect business interests," Marilyn persisted.

"It was not a good government," Kennedy agreed.

"In a way, Castro was good for Cuba," Marilyn concluded.

Kennedy again sipped from his tea and looked out over the ocean. Fighting Castro was the top secret priority of his government. No effort was being spared to rid the Cubans of Fidel Castro.

"Do you realize that your friend Mr. Castro had all of his political opposition taken out and shot?" the President asked Marilyn.

"He did?" Marilyn responded.

"He did," Kennedy confirmed. "Not only did he steal property, he used the experience of his Communist friends to deal with his political opposition. And he continues to lock up anyone who disagrees with him."

"But we're not going to know if his government can do a good job if we don't give it a chance," Marilyn persisted. "He overthrew Batista and now he wants a chance to prove that he can do a better job. It might take some time to make things better for the people."

Smathers now interrupted: "I can't understand why the Hollywood film community continues to think that Communism should be given a chance. You people have enjoyed such amazing capitalistic success and yet you swimming pool Communists continue to play like you are revolutionaries. Is it guilt?"

Marilyn couldn't believe she was under attack. "Are you serious? First, not everyone in Hollywood thinks the same way, thank you. Some of us have minds of our own. Second, what right does the United States have to decide who will govern the people of Cuba?"

Smathers laughed. He didn't know how seriously to take Marilyn Monroe—was she a sex goddess or a pain in the ass? He looked at Kennedy for an explanation.

"Look Marilyn," Kennedy said, "there are things you might overhear me say that are actually top secret."

"But you're not trying to kill Castro."

"I'm certainly not. I have a different job."

"But you're not arranging to have him killed, are you?" Marilyn wanted to know.

"I'm not. But there may be others in the government who want to see him gone. I can't speak for them."

"But you're the President. If someone in your government is planning to kill Castro, you're ultimately responsible."

"This isn't really a subject I can discuss with you, Marilyn. Suffice it to say that I am discharging my duties to the best of my abilities. I run a big government and I'm doing the best job I can."

"So you are going to have him killed," Marilyn deduced.

"Cuban policy is enormously important and enormously sensitive," Kennedy told her. "If you talk about it, a lot of people could get hurt. Do you understand that?

Marilyn stood up on the patio and looked at the President and Senator Smathers. "We should send in the Peace Corps," Marilyn said sternly. "If you're trying to kill Castro, you're not playing a fair game!" She turned and walked back into the beach house.

The men looked at each other and laughed.

Chapter 17

"My nightmare is the H-bomb. What's yours?"

Marilyn Monroe

Ralph Greenson looked out the window of his home on 902 Franklin Street in Santa Monica to see if Mrs. Murray had arrived. She had not. Greenson didn't worry much about whether Marilyn would come to her appointments with him. Ever since he had replaced Ralph Roberts, Marilyn's trusted masseur and driver with Mrs. Murray, he knew she would arrive. Roberts was not a dangerous person, Greenson thought, but he did have an independent mind, and therefore needed to be replaced. If Greenson was going to be able to continue to dominate Marilyn's life, he was going to need to control as much as possible. Marilyn had not wanted to give up Roberts, and had resisted Greenson's advice to do so, but in the end, she had relented. Marilyn believed Greenson could keep her from despair.

Initially, their relationship had not been so close. Marilyn had sought out Dr. Greenson because she was told that he was one of the foremost psychiatrists on the West Coast. Born and raised in Brooklyn, he had attended medical school in Europe, and ended up studying with some of Freud's own trainees in Vienna. Frank Sinatra's agent, Mickey Rudin, recommended Dr. Greenson to Frank and Frank had recommended him to Marilyn. Initially, neither one of them knew that Dr. Greenson was Mickey Rudin's brother in law. There was a lot they didn't know.

Greenson walked back into his study to fill his pipe. He struck a match and pulled the flame over the packed tobacco and walked back to the window to wait for Marilyn and Mrs. Murray to arrive.

It was an ideal set up. Marilyn Monroe was a major movie star, and he was a major psychiatrist, or wanted to be. She suffered from the loss of reality that all movie stars seemed to suffer from and needed a good social and personal support structure, and he invited her into his home to meet his wife and children. After her psychiatric sessions, Marilyn frequently joined the family for conversation and dinner. She was involved with the President of the United States, and he was very interested in what the President had to say. Ralph Greenson had always been interested in politics.

What Greenson couldn't tell Marilyn and she would never fully understand was that Greenson and his family, and many of their friends had direct connections to the Communist Party. Earlier in the decade, the Hollywood film community had been polarized over the question of loyalty. Marilyn's sympathies were firmly on the side of the so called Communists, many of whom were more interested in the philosophical roots of Marxism than they were in the nuts and bolts of revolution. The McCarthy hearings forced many in Hollywood to go underground with their political affiliations. Even though they did not consider themselves to be revolutionaries, they did consider themselves to be open to all points of view. Of course, there were also committed Communist idealists in Hollywood, with genuine connections to the Communist Party, and they would remain in Hollywood after Senator McCarthy fell into political exile.

Mrs. Murray's Dodge pulled up and stopped in front of Dr. Greenson's house. Greenson left the window and went back into his office and shut the door.

Marilyn stepped out of the car and walked into the Greenson

residence. It was a Spanish style white stucco house with a red tile roof. On the inside, the exposed hand hewn beams braced the high ceiling and gave an airy and almost foreign feeling to the house. An enormous fireplace was adorned with hand painted tiles. Mrs. Murray led her up the stairs and knocked on Dr. Greenson's door. After a moment's hesitation, the door was opened and Marilyn saw Dr. Greenson sitting behind his desk, smoking his pipe, and reading from a psychiatric journal.

"I've got something important to talk about today," Marilyn told the psychiatrist.

Greenson laughed. "It's all important to me, Marilyn. Come in and let's get started."

Mrs. Murray excused herself and closed the door to the study. Marilyn and Dr. Greenson sat in two large, comfortable chairs near a large window which had a view of the growing community of Santa Monica.

"I think the President has been lying to me," Marilyn reported after the usual pleasantries had been exchanged..

"Oh, I wouldn't be too hard on him," Greenson said, baiting her. He jotted down some notes in a spiral notebook. "What did he say?"

"Well, he tells me one thing, and then later he tells me something else. The two things are mutually exclusive. Now, either he doesn't want me to know, which I guess is his choice, or he doesn't think I'm smart enough to have an opinion on these matters."

"What matters?"

"Earlier this year, when I saw him in New York, he told me that he was considering an operation to invade Cuba and kill Fidel Castro. Or maybe it was that they were going to kill Castro and then have the exiles come ashore in Cuba. But I told him that I thought that was a very bad idea, because killing people is really not the right way to solve the world's problems."

"I think you are on firm ground there," Greenson said.

"He agreed with me, or at least I thought he did. I remember when I moved back out to Los Angeles, I was having coffee with Jeanne when she showed me a story about the invasion being planned. I called him. I called him right in front of Jeanne and asked him whether the story was true."

"What did he say?"

"He said it wasn't true. He said that the United States had no such plans and that the idea that we would be trying to kill Castro was ridiculous."

"Thank God. Our leaders have some sense."

"But, Jeanne said that Johnny Rosselli was looking into ways to kill Castro—you know Johnny. He's one of Frank's friends. I'm sure Mickey Rudin knows him. Anyway, I didn't believe that the President would actually do something like that. So that's the reason I asked about whether they were going to try to kill Castro. I should have put this together earlier."

"What together?" Greenson asked.

"I ran into Sam Giancana in Las Vegas. I was there with Frank and then Sam Giancana came by our table. And I think he told me that the President wanted Castro dead, and Sam was taking care of the arrangements. I should have remembered what Jeanne said about Johnny Rosselli. Of course. They are trying to kill Castro.'

Greenson pulled on his pipe and blew some smoke through his nose. He couldn't believe what he was hearing.

"Marilyn, are you sure that the President said he was thinking of having Castro killed? There's a big difference between wanting Castro to be gone, and hiring someone to kill him."

"That's just it. Last week, you know, I was with Jack and his friend George Smathers who is a senator, or something. We were at Peter's and Pat's house at the beach and Smathers and Jack were talking about Castro. I guess there are some political implications in Florida or something. But they were talking when I thought I heard Jack say something about Castro getting killed. And then I asked him—I asked him specifically if he was trying to get Castro killed, because, you know, it wouldn't be fair."

"No, it wouldn't—certainly not to Castro."

"And he danced around the issue a little bit, like he wasn't going to tell me. He said he wasn't going to kill Castro, because he had a different job, but that he couldn't speak for everyone in the administration."

"So he evaded your question?"

"Exactly. If he said 'no, we're not trying to kill Castro,' I would have believed him—I believed him last time. But now it is apparent that he lied to me. After the Bay of Pigs, I asked him why he told me that we weren't going to invade, and he said that we didn't invade. And, of course, I realized that we didn't. Those poor Cubans did and they're still in jail."

"Marilyn, I don't have to tell you that this is very sensitive material. You would do a disservice to the President if you mentioned this to anyone else."

"I'm not going to mention it to anyone else. I'm not going to hold a press conference and tell the world that the President of the United States plans to have the leader of Cuba killed. On the other hand, what do I do about it?"

Marilyn looked at Greenson and then out through the large windows of his study, across the buildings and houses of the community, and onto the Pacific Ocean in the distance. She pulled a strand of her white hair and twisted it around her finger. Greenson continued to smoke his pipe.

"There are different ways to think about this," Greenson pointed out. "On one level, we should think about what this says about your relationship with the President. On another level, what does it say about politics and the state of the world." He paused and drew on his pipe. "Do you really think that President Kennedy would arrange to have Fidel Castro killed? I find that hard to believe."

"I find it hard to believe. Maybe that's the reason it has taken me so long to realize this."

"But are you sure now?" Greenson asked. "How sure can you be of something that you do not have direct involvement with?"

"I wouldn't be, but as I think about things, it has to be true.

Jack told me more than he wanted to, and then tried to take it back. Then I heard it from Jeanne Carmen who knew that Johnny Rosselli was involved, then I heard it from Sam Giancana who claimed to be involved. And now the President himself won't deny that it is going on somewhere in the government. How many more hints do I need?"

Greenson remained pensive, trying to consider the importance of what Marilyn was telling him.

"Marilyn, I think both of us realize that your unusual relationship with the President puts you in a unique position. I will have to think about this for a day or two before I'm going to fully understand what it means. But I can tell you one thing right now. If what you have told me is true, it is one of the most important secrets of our government, and it has implications for the peace of the world. You should not tell anyone else about this. No one. If this rumor becomes public, not only will it ruin your relationship with the President, but it may put both of us at considerable personal risk, and it might put the world at some kind of risk of war."

Marilyn stared at Greenson as if she had not fully understood the implications of Kennedy's lie. She didn't respond to Greenson's advice.

"Just tell me right now that you won't tell anyone else about this," Greenson asked her. "Surely you don't want to spoil your friendship with the President."

"I want to keep seeing him."

"Exactly, he's important in your life."

"He means a lot to me and I think, or I thought, that I mean a lot to him. If he lies to me, how much could I really mean to him?"

"Perhaps he depends on your point of view to help him maintain a sense of proportion about things. Maybe he is surrounded by military people who want him to get rid of Castro and he depends on you to balance his own opinions."

"Maybe. especially after the Bay of Pigs. I told him that was a big mistake."

"You should gather more information as it comes to you—don't go looking for it—but we can discuss new things as they come up. And we can discuss what this means to you and to your obligations to the President and to others. I'm still not sure the President or anyone in his government would attempt to kill the leader of another country. But this is going to take some time to think about, and you need to be careful not to share it with anyone else."

Marilyn agreed.

Chapter 18

"... I had dinner last night with the Attorney General of the United States, Robert Kennedy, and I asked him what his department was going to do about Civil Rights and some other issues. He is very intelligent, and besides all that, he's got a terrific sense of humor . . . and he isn't a bad dancer, either . . ."

Marilyn Monroe in a letter to Robert Miller,
February 2, 1962

"I just want to see if you like it," Marilyn said to her press agent Pat Newcomb. Pat, an attractive young woman a few years younger than Marilyn, handled Marilyn press relations, drove Marilyn around, and served as a friend and confidante.

"Why don't you get a big house in Beverly Hills?" Pat asked. "That's where the stars live."

"I don't want a big house," Marilyn said. "In Beverly Hills, that's all anyone thinks about. I'm not looking for status in a house. I'm looking for some place to live. And something private."

Pat drove the car along San Vicente Boulevard until she reached Carmelina. She turned on Carmelina, stayed right at the Y and saw the Helenas—short little cul de sacs coming off Carmelina between San Vicente and Sunset Boulevard. "Nice neighborhood," Pat remarked. "I didn't know these little streets were over here."

"And you grew up here, didn't you Pat?" Marilyn asked.

"Sacred Heart High. But before that, we lived in Washington. My grandfather was a judge in Washington and father was a lobbyist. We came out here in 1946, just before I went to college. So I never really felt like I grew up here."

"I never knew your father was a lobbyist. You never talk about yourself."

"You're nice to ask, but it's not my job to tell people about myself and I've always been more of a private person."

Pat pulled the car into the cul de sac labeled 5th Helena and stopped. Marilyn got out of the passenger seat and called for Pat to follow her. Together, they walked along the high white wall which surrounded the house, through an ungated gap in the wall, and onto a brick driveway around which the white Spanish style hacienda which was built.

"It's small," Marilyn said as they glanced at the house, "but it is very private and I really want the privacy. There's a swimming pool in back."

"I like the trees," Pat said referring to a line of Eucalyptus trees which curved around the property. "It does seem very private, like you're not really in a big city. I like that."

"Tell me how you would furnish it," Marilyn suggested as they walked through the front door and into the living room. "Don't you like the open beamed ceiling? It gives it such an authentic Spanish air."

"Doesn't Dr. Greenson have a house a lot like this?" Pat asked.

Marilyn stopped in the middle of the living room and looked back at Pat. "He does have a Spanish house, and I love it. Actually, getting a house was his idea. Mrs. Murray helped me find it. Dr. Greenson only lives across the golf course. That's another plus."

"Sure seems like you're getting awfully close to him," Pat remarked. "Have you ever been so close to a psychiatrist? I thought they were supposed to keep some kind of professional distance."

"He's not just a psychiatrist, he's really become a close friend.

And I spend time with his children, too—they really treat me like family."

Pat walked through the dining room and into the adjoining kitchen. "It needs some work," Pat said looking at the old plumbing fixtures and worn counter tops. "But it has the potential. You can see the potential."

"I haven't signed anything yet, so I can still get out of it," Marilyn said looking at the old cabinets. "I'm going to have to put some money into it. We'll have to pick out some furniture when we go to Mexico."

Marilyn was referring to a trip to Mexico City which she was planning for later in the month.

"I don't see why we have to go there," Pat said. "I always get sick."

"I thought you wanted to go," Marilyn said.

"I do," Pat replied. "If you are going I want to go. But I just don't see why you want to go. You've got the movie coming up. We can buy all the Mexican furniture we want at a place about an hour from here."

Marilyn slid a glass door in the sun room open and walked out on a patio which surrounded the swimming pool in the back yard. She loved the California winters of sunshine and pleasant temperatures.

"I've always wanted a pool," she said. "It's going to be so nice to live here."

"So let's stay here and get nice tans," Pat suggested, trying to re-focus Marilyn on the trip to Mexico.

"You don't have to go," Marilyn said. "I'm serious, you don't have to. I wouldn't even want to, but Dr. Greenson thinks I should meet some people down there."

"Who are you meeting?"

"During the McCarthy hearings a group of Hollywood people were smeared as Communists. Dr. Greenson thinks that I've become something of a leader in the liberal community, the film community. So he thinks I should go down there to make some connections and talk about how much better things are now that McCarthy is gone and President Kennedy is running things."

"You're going to meet some Communists?"

"Not just meet Communists. They're not really Communists, anyway. They are just liberal thinkers who got run out of the country by the witch hunt. It's part of working toward one of my goals."

"What goal?"

"Just the goal to be taken seriously as something other than a sexy blonde actress. I'm going to be 36 years old this year and I can't play the dumb blonde roles forever. I think I have something more to contribute than just being cute on film. I think I could become someone who takes the voice of the poor people. I was poor once. Dr. Greenson sees this as a way to get back to my roots, to my people, while at the same time becoming something of a leader for tolerance and free speech."

Pat looked at Marilyn with her brows furrowed in a skeptical glare. "Wow . . . a leader of the Hollywood left . . . poor people. What does the President think about that?" she asked.

"I haven't exactly told him," Marilyn said. "Dr. Greenson thinks that the more seriously I take myself, the more serious the President will take me. He thinks that I balance out the President's advisors, who are probably a bunch of right wing military types. It's a different life for me. But when you think about it, I am part of the President's circle. Dr. Greenson thinks he has been interested in me because of my sexuality and my celebrity. But if I take positions he is interested in, then he will learn to respect me as a person, not just as an act. It's exciting."

Marilyn and Pat stepped back into the house and Marilyn slid the glass door shut. They walked back toward the entrance.

"And you're going to see Bobby tonight," Pat said. "We better get you back and ready to go to the dinner. "I wonder what the Attorney General will think of you talking to the Communists in Mexico."

"I hope it doesn't come up," Marilyn said with a wink.

Peter and Pat Lawford were hosting a dinner party in honor

of her brother the Attorney General. Robert Kennedy was beginning a trip which would take him to the Far East and Vietnam and the dinner was partially intended as a send off party. There were a few party leaders invited and some of the reigning Hollywood stars. Marilyn, reigning as one of Hollywood's biggest stars and as the President's favorite girlfriend, was a featured guest.

Upon arriving at the beach house, Marilyn smiled politely when she saw Ethel, the Attorney General's wife. Marilyn thought she looked like she had had about 6 children, which as point of fact, was true. She was pretty in a plain, modest way. But there was nothing glamorous about her. The curves were simply not there. Curiously, Ethel was seated at a different table from the Attorney General. In a different room. Bobby was seated next to Kim on one side, a young, pretty actress who was trying to compete with Marilyn for the sex symbol roles. Marilyn found her place opposite the Attorney General.

During dinner, Kim began to pepper the Attorney General about what he would do if there were more violence in the Civil Rights protests.

"Well, I think it's an embarrassment for the President," he said. "Here he is trying to convince the world that democracy is a better system, and then the newspapers show all these pictures of fights in our streets. I'm not sure that's good public relations."

"Can't you do something?" Kim wanted to know. "Isn't there a way of keeping them off the buses?" She was referring to the fact that black leaders were traveling around the South in buses to protest the lack of integration.

"We're certainly sensitive to those concerns," Robert Kennedy replied.

"What do you mean?" Marilyn asked.

"There are Negroes traveling around in buses throughout the South," Kim explained. "They are trying to cause trouble."

"The freedom riders?" Marilyn asked.

"You know about them," Kim remarked.

"Know about them?" Marilyn said, "after my next movie, I'm going to go down there and ride around with them."

Kim gasped. She looked over at the Attorney General who didn't say anything.

"That would be nice public relations for the President, don't you think, Mr. Kennedy?" Kim asked.

"The South is going to be tough in the next election. No question about that."

"So politics is more important than the rights of the American Negroes?" Marilyn asked. "Is that what I've heard you say?"

"No. We've stood by the Negroes."

"Of course, you have," Marilyn went on. "And you should. That's your constitutional duty. Do you think Mr. Hoover has a constitutional duty, as well?"

Robert Kennedy stared at Marilyn Monroe. He hadn't expected to be discussing Justice Department strategy with a table full of show business people.

"Mr. Hoover is from another generation," the Attorney General allowed.

"Well, I think you need to get rid of him," Marilyn offered. The other guests looked at each other and tried to hide their embarrassment. Kim stared at Marilyn in utter disbelief.

"I believe people should obey the law," Kim offered. "That's the first duty of citizenship."

"I believe the government should obey the law," Marilyn countered. "And J. Edgar Hoover is not obeying the law. He is working for the Klan. He should be working for the Constitution."

Robert Kennedy sat up stiffly in his chair. Marilyn was hitting all of his passions.

"We want to get rid of Hoover," the Attorney General said. "Mandatory retirement is coming up for him next year. I think the President is going to get a new director of the F.B.I.."

"Really?" one of the other guests said. "Who would replace him?"

"There are many good law enforcement people around,"

Kennedy said. "Chief William Parker right here in Los Angeles is one of them."

The guests looked at each other.

A few miles away, in a rented apartment, F.B.I. agents listened through their headsets and continued to tape the conversation. They smiled at each other.

"I can't see why the President is letting Castro stay in Cuba," Kim offered. She wanted to leave Civil Rights.

"You don't think the Cubans should have a say in who leads their country?" Marilyn asked Kim.

"He's a Communist!" Kim said.

"You really stay on top of the news," Marilyn remarked.

"Well, we can't let them keep missiles there," Kim continued. "If we let a Communist regime so close to our borders, who will be safe?"

"Who's safe now?" Marilyn asked.

"What I don't get," Kim persisted, "is why the President didn't just get rid of that man. Those exiles went ashore at the Bay of Pigs. It was a perfect opportunity. He should have just invaded Cuba and gotten the whole thing over with."

"There were people who wanted to invade," Robert Kennedy pointed out.

"I don't know about that," Marilyn said quietly. "If the President had invaded Cuba, I wonder what the Soviets would have done in Berlin? There might have been war. I think you have to give the President some credit for restraint."

Robert Kennedy looked around the table of astonished guests, and then directly at Marilyn.

"What did you say your name was?" he asked.

The guests laughed.

"My name is Marilyn Monroe."

"Well, Miss Monroe," the Attorney General said. "Would you like to dance?"

Chapter 19

"We are going to win in Vietnam. We will remain until we do."

Robert F. Kennedy on visiting Saigon
February 18, 1962

Marilyn Monroe looked out the window of the airplane as it taxied toward the terminal in Mexico City. She was terrified by what she saw. She turned in her seat in order to get a better look at a group of men who were standing in the receiving area of the gate. She reached up and touched her hair.

"Pat, look!" she said to Patricia Newcomb. "Those guys have cameras."

"That's impossible," Pat assured her.

"It's impossible, but that's what they have. I can't believe this. You said there was no publicity." Marilyn pulled a mirror out of her purse and examined her makeup.

"Marilyn, I swear to you. No one knows we're coming. There is no way they could know we are on this plane. The cameras must be for someone else."

"You are truly demonic!" Marilyn said to Pat. "You told me there wouldn't be any cameras. There are cameras!"

"Marilyn, calm down. The reservations were made in Eunice's name. There is no way that they could have figured it out." Pat jumped out of her seat to go to the opposite side of the plane to get a better look at the men at the gate. "I can't believe this, Marilyn!"

"Terry," Marilyn said to a man sitting behind her. "Get out the case. We're going to have to do what we can in the back of the plane."

The man stood up and lifted a makeup case from the overhead baggage compartment.

"Marilyn, we need towels and water," Terry objected.

"Get going. We're going to have to do the best we can," Marilyn ordered. "Pat, I want to know who tipped off the reporters. You better find out, and find out soon."

After the other passengers had exited, Marilyn and Terry went to the rear of the plane. Pat and Eunice Murray, were in charge of keeping the reporters at bay while Marilyn prepared herself for the camera.

The reporters were waiting for Marilyn when she finally got off the plane and tried to make her way through the airport. Her arrival had not been leaked by Pat, but rather by the F.B.I. who was carefully monitoring her visit to Mexico. One of the agents thought that having a media event would most easily hide their monitoring. No one believed that inviting a few reporters to the airport would lead to the near riot that ensued. But Marilyn was popular in Mexico and the local press was anxious to photograph her.

More than 5 hours elapsed before Marilyn could escape the attention and get to her hotel. The attention had been overwhelming, but on another level, it gave her some satisfaction to see the extent of her popularity.

After settling in at the hotel, Marilyn stood on the balcony outside her room and looked out on the courtyard below. Finally, a moment of peace. The airport had been an unanticipated frenzy and she still didn't understand how news of her visit had gotten out, but she was grateful to have made it to safety.

The air was pleasantly cool that evening, as Marilyn gazed over the cut stones which lined the courtyard. She looked up at the star filled sky and just the sliver of the moon when she heard a guitar play in the distance. Glancing down to the courtyard below, she saw a man walk toward her strumming a guitar. Another man followed him with another guitar. Marilyn turned and went back into her room.

"Pat," she called. "What's going on out there?"

Pat came out of the bathroom in a towel. She had been brushing her hair. She looked into the courtyard where a group of musicians had assembled beneath Marilyn's balcony. The musicians began to play a romantic tune.

"Is it some kind of joke?" Pat asked.

Marilyn turned out the lights of the room and went over and stood next to the exit to the balcony. More musicians were congregating. Pat got dressed and stood next to Marilyn.

"I don't know, Marilyn. Your life is just one long fairy tale. Who do you think sent those guys?"

"I'm starting to wonder if this whole trip has been planned for us. I seem to be the star, but I can't figure out whois producing this thing."

There was a knock at the door. Pat, who still had a towel wrapped around her head, answered it. A Mexican man in a hotel uniform brought a large silver plate of cut flowers into the room and put them on a table. He handed Marilyn an envelope.

Marilyn looked at the flowers, opened the envelope and read the card: 'True romance awaits you in the courtyard.' She put the card down and went over and stood by the window again.

"I can't believe this. Someone is putting me on," Marilyn complained.

The assembled musicians had divided themselves into two groups, one to each side of the balcony. As they continued to play, from the far reaches of the courtyard a Latin man walked toward Marilyn's balcony. He was young, attractive and better dressed and groomed than any of the others. He stood, surrounded by the musicians, and looked up at Marilyn.

It was the first time Marilyn had ever seen Jose Bolanos.

"He's handsome," Pat cooed to Marilyn. "Let's invite him up. How far wrong can we go?"

"Are you kidding?" Marilyn objected. "I get mobbed at the airport, then finally get to the room and some weirdo sends me a bunch of flowers and hires a couple of bands to make his entrance. Who's behind this?"

"Listen to that," Pat purred. "Those Latin guys are sure romantic.

Marilyn looked down at the attractive man below and listened to the soft music in the warm night. She began to soften. "This guy wants to meet me," Marilyn said. "I guess we should invite him up here. How far wrong can we go?"

After listening to the music, Marilyn beckoned the mysterious man to come up to her room. He was dark, lean, and very attractive. After some initial introductions, he told her that he was the heir to one of the great fortunes in Latin America but he had chosen to live with the writers and artists in Zona Rosa, the Hollywood community of exiles. Because he had worked in the film industry himself, and long admired her work, when he heard she was going to come to Mexico, he decided to try to meet her.

Beautiful women, Bolanos explained, were his passion. Truly beautiful women, he told her, were rarely satisfied by their men, because the kind of man a beautiful woman attracts is not always the kind of man who can satisfy her. He loved to be with truly beautiful women. And he loved to satisfy them. Marilyn glanced over at Pat who shrugged. At Marilyn's suggestion, Pat opened a bottle of champagne and poured for Marilyn and her new acquaintance.

After they finished the champagne, Jose offered to show Marilyn Mexico City and Marilyn, a romantic at heart, decided to take the tour. Like Marilyn, Jose was very sensitive to the plight of the poor and disaffected. He thought social justice would soon come to Mexico, and when it did, he would welcome it. Marilyn asked why he did not come to California to write. Wouldn't his work have a better chance of being produced there? Balanos explained that he did not want to get too far from his Latin roots, which he regarded as the source of his work. He might like to get to California more often, but he could not leave the art colony of Zona Rosa.

Later that night, Marilyn found herself in an unusual situation. Usually, she felt that it was her responsibility to satisfy the man she was with. On that night, she felt like the important celebrity that she was as her Latin lover endeavored to satisfy her.

Chapter 20

"Meet my brother in law, Churchill Murray," Eunice Murray said as Marilyn approached the car. Churchill Murray had pulled his car up to the hotel curb.

"Your brother in law?" Marilyn replied. "What a small world it is! So nice to meet you Churchill," Marilyn said smiling. "How long have you lived in Mexico City?"

"I've been down here for ten years or so," Churchill said. "Came down in the early 50's."

"Are you in business?"

"Actually, I run a radio station down here," Churchill said. "I used to be in the business of organizing labor, but things didn't really work out in California."

"Pat was a little upset that she wasn't invited to come," Marilyn reported to Eunice Murray. "But I told her that I didn't feel like I could invite her since you didn't think that Mr. Field was planning on her."

"Pat does your press relations," Mrs. Murray observed.

"You're not going to need press relations today. I think her presence might make Mr. Field a little uncomfortable."

"Do you think he would mind if I invited a new friend of mine along?" Marilyn asked. "He's a Latin screenwriter, maybe you've heard of him—Jose Bolanos."

Mrs. Murray looked over at the handsome Latin man standing near the hotel entrance. "Jose Bolanos?" she muttered to herself. Then she turned back to Marilyn.

"Marilyn, my sense is that you should spend some time with Mr. Field by yourself, rather than with Jose. I'm not sure Mr. Field has planned for so many people to come."

Marilyn turned back toward the hotel and waved good bye to Jose and then they all loaded into the car and were off. Churchill navigated around a traffic circle, through the interweaving traffic, and finally to a highway. Marilyn was amazed to see chickens and dogs right along the roadway, and boys herding small groups of cattle armed only with long sticks.

Frederick Vanderbilt Field lived with his wife Nieves in a large hacienda surrounded by a beautiful garden. Nieves was a former model and had been active in political circles. As Churchill's car pulled up in front of the hacienda, Field and his wife came out to greet their guests. Field escorted Marilyn and the Murrays around the property, showing them his gardens and animals. After the tour, they went into the house for lunch.

"We're so happy you have come to Mexico City, Marilyn," Field said at lunch. "We've heard so many good things about you."

"And I've heard good things about you," Marilyn replied. "You have a reputation as a man of conscience. Dr. Greenson told me you should be one of the members of this community I should try to meet—so I feel lucky that you extended an invitation for me to come."

Field and Eunice exchanged glances.

"Yes, of course." They sat around a table on a screened verandah with servants bringing the various courses of the lunch. Their conversation focused on the subject of politics—a subject about which both were passionate, and from which both were well removed.

"Do you think the President will allow the Civil Rights Movement to continue in the United States?" Field asked her.

"I think so," Marilyn said. "There are some problems, particularly with the F.B.I. But the Attorney General recently told me that the President was going to get rid of Hoover as soon as possible. They think he's a *psycho*."

"A psycho?" Nieves repeated. She had seen a recent movie by the same name. She had long thought of Hoover as some sort of closet maniac. To hear that the Attorney General had come to the same conclusion comforted her.

"And we've heard that he has been aggressive about keeping the big corporations from unreasonable profits," Field pursued.

"Yes, he had the fight with U.S. Steel. I think that defined the attitude with respect to big business."

Field sat back in his chair. "So he sounds like he is positive on the domestic front," Field concluded. "Why do you believe that the administration is not accepting the government of Cuba?"

"I don't know exactly what they are doing in Cuba," Marilyn confessed. "What I do know isn't good."

"We know what they're doing," Field said. "The secret police—the so called CIA—are doing everything they can to stir up anarchy: they set the sugar cane fields on fire at night, they blow up bridges, they sabotage the electrical utilities. My question is why?"

"The Bay of Pigs was a big embarrassment to the President," Marilyn explained. "The President doesn't want the government there to continue."

"We've heard that the CIA has plans to kill Fidel," Field stated.

"You have?" Marilyn asked. "What have you heard?"

"We've learned through some friends at the Cuban Embassy in Mexico City that the CIA has sent several individuals over to try to kill Castro. Up to now, they have been discovered and captured.

Two of them have confessed that they were trained by the CIA to kill Fidel."

"Is that right?" Marilyn said. The circle now closed for Marilyn. Clearly the President was trying to get rid of Castro by the most direct means—assassination. "It doesn't seem fair," Marilyn almost whispered."

"It isn't fair," Field stated plainly. "We heard that Che Guevara, acting as Castro's direct surrogate, approached the President's aide, Richard Goodwin, and suggested that the two leaders agree not to try to kill one another."

"Really?" Marilyn exclaimed. "Castro has captured trained assassins. That's amazing. Now he must know what's going on. And he's proposed a truce."

"That's what we understand," Field persisted. "Obviously, Kennedy cannot expect to send assassins into Cuba with the intent of killing Castro and not think that Castro will not find some way of trying to get back at Kennedy."

Marilyn was stunned as she considered this possibility. She sipped from her tea.

"Well, yes, I suppose that the President doesn't really imagine that the door could swing both ways. In the United States we just assume that because we are the most technologically advanced country in the world, that we can do whatever we want. I'm not sure the President really understands that his plan for Castro could backfire."

"You are technologically advanced," Field said, "but rifles work the same way whether they are being used to illegally gun down the leader of Cuba or the leader of the United States. And if the policy of the Kennedy government is to kill the leaders of foreign governments, those foreign leaders will devise their own plans to kill Kennedy."

"That makes sense," Marilyn sadly concluded. "If you threaten your neighbor with a gun, your neighbor is going to buy a gun to protect himself. If you take a shot at him, he's going to take a shot at you. Actually, if he thinks you are going to try to kill him, he's going to try to kill you first."

"It seems obvious, doesn't it?" Field asked.

"It does."

"Then tell me why Kennedy rejected Che's proposal that the two governments just call this whole cloak and dagger episode off and try to live as neighbors?"

"Did the President reject the idea to call it off?" Marilyn asked.

"He rejected it," Field confirmed. "Che wasn't asking for an endorsement, he was only asking that some way be worked out for both leaders to live in their separate worlds."

"Does Castro have the power to send people to the United States to try to kill Kennedy?" Marilyn asked.

"Of course he has the power. What power does that involve? He even has the assassins. At least two of the men who are in Cuban prison for bringing in weapons to try to kill Fidel are members of organized crime—Mafia hit men. They are now offering to go back to the United States and kill Kennedy."

"Really?" Marilyn asked.

"Consider their choice," Field went on. "The punishment for attempting to kill a president in Cuba is death. So if they can convince Castro that they would be willing to try to kill Kennedy, what harm does it do Castro to let them try? What harm would it do them to try? They could rot in jail or be executed themselves otherwise."

"Why wouldn't Castro simply send them?" Marilyn asked.

"You have to think that he wouldn't want to kill the president of another country, particularly not President Kennedy. If Castro sent men to kill Kennedy, and it were discovered, Cuba could be destroyed. It is in Castro's interest to make a deal and try to get along with Kennedy. But if he can't do that, what choice does he have? I think no man will willingly simply accept his own death."

"My God!" Marilyn exclaimed as she realized the harshness of Castro's position. "Someone has to convince the President that he has to accept Castro. That's the only way out of this."

"That's exactly right," Field agreed. "I've been thinking about this, as I know you have, and I've come to the conclusion that you are that person."

"Me?" Marilyn laughed defensively. "Why me?"

"You're the only one in a position to talk sense to the President. You are known to be willing to stand tall in the face of pressure, as you did when you supported Arthur Miller during the McCarthy hearings. No one else has the access to Kennedy. He is surrounded by people who agree with him, or want to invade Cuba. But believe me, invading Cuba is no longer an alternative. The President has to accept Castro and he must stop sending assassins over to try to take Castro's life."

Marilyn stared back at Field. She was stunned with the thought that she could do something so important for international peace. But as she considered it, she realized that he was right. She was the only one who had the access to the President and the knowledge that trying to kill Castro was a dangerous game for Kennedy to play. Playing a part in preserving the peace of the world struck Marilyn as a very serious role indeed.

After lunch, Mrs. Murray asked Frederick Field if he would like to meet Marilyn's new friend, Jose Bolanos.

"Jose Bolanos?" Field asked. "I think I've heard of him. How do you know Jose Bolanos?"

Marilyn was embarrassed that Eunice had brought up Bolanos at the end of her meeting with Field. She explained that Bolanos had welcomed her the previous evening with several Mararchi bands and taken her to some nice places in the city.

"Be careful of this man Bolanos," Fields advised her. "He is a man who is sympathetic to the Left, but drives expensive cars and wears expensive clothes."

"I wear expensive clothes," Marilyn confessed.

"But your heart is with the people," Fields observed. "You may be the most famous woman in the world, and yet your sympathies are with the powerless and the downtrodden."

"I was one of them," Marilyn said. "And I still am."

"I could sense that," Fields told her. "But your friend Bolanos is not from a rich Mexican family like he says. No one knows where he's from. And while he says he is sympathetic to change, he wishes to live like an aristocrat. He is known to the Left, but he is not trusted."

"Really?" Marilyn said.

"Be careful of this man," Fields told her.

Chapter 21

"Information has been developed that Judith E. Campbell, a free lance artist, has associated with prominent underworld figures Sam Giancana of Chicago and John Rosselli of Los Angeles. A review of telephone toll calls from Campbell's Los Angeles residence discloses that on November 7 and 15, 1961, calls were made to Evelyn Lincoln, the President's secretary at the White House."

Memo from J. Edgar Hoover to John F. Kennedy
March 22, 1962

The Director's limousine stopped beneath the archway and the door opened. J. Edgar Hoover got out of the limo and walked into the White House. He carried a small black, leather valise and glanced out at some tourists lined up behind a fence. They were waving to him. He waved back. A cold day in Washington on March 22, 1962, the sun shone brightly through the clear air. It was one o'clock in the afternoon.

Hoover walked down the hallway toward the Oval Office. He heard that the Kennedys had redecorated the White House— thrown out all the imitation furniture and brought in only authentic and expensive American pieces. Hoover glanced at the furniture. It looked the same to him.

J. Edgar Hoover had walked down this hallway toward the Oval Office since the 20's. He had seen presidents come and he had seen them go. He had liked some, disliked others, but always been reappointed. The young Kennedy boys were talking out of school. Hoover had learned that they were thinking of replacing him. He had asked for this meeting with John Kennedy to alert the President to a serious breach in the National Security and, also, to remind him of the value of old friends.

"Mr. Hoover, it is always a pleasure," Kennedy said as he shook Hoover's hand. "Please sit down."

Kennedy sat in his rocking chair. Hoover glanced around the Oval Office. He sat down in a chair opposite the President.

"I am disappointed that you saw fit to send me that memo last month discussing Sam Giancana and Johnny Rosselli."

"And Judith Campbell," Hoover added.

"Yes," the President said. "And Judith Campbell."

"How is your father, Mr. President?" Joseph Kennedy had suffered a stroke during the late fall.

"He seems to be getting better. His speech is garbled, but he can communicate. Not everyone thinks that's a positive thing."

The Director laughed.

"He was really something," Hoover said.

"He really was," Kennedy agreed.

"I was disappointed to receive that memo," Kennedy reiterated.

"I'm not sure this is the best place to talk about it, Mr. President."

Kennedy looked around the Oval Office. Light was streaming in through the window and falling onto his desk. All of the doors were closed.

"I believe you had a tape machine installed in this office," Hoover suggested to Kennedy.

"I believe I did. I think that's right."

"To help you with your memoirs, no doubt."

"That's right."

"I'm not sure what we have to discuss today should be included in your memoirs, sir," Hoover advised.

"That's a good point."

"In fact, one of these days a president is going to get caught taping what is discussed in this office. It will come back to haunt him. You don't want to be that president."

"I certainly do not."

"Perhaps we could talk somewhere more secure?" Hoover suggested.

Kennedy led the Director to the White House elevator. After a short ride, they walked to the Employees Dining Room.

"Much better," Hoover said as he again sat down with the President. They were sitting at a table routinely used by the White House staff.

"Memos have a way of resurfacing, Mr. President," Hoover said. "They don't have to, but sometimes they do." He opened his valise and took out several files. From one of the files, he pulled out a sheet of paper which had been stamped "Top Secret."

"I've learned recently that you and the Attorney General might like to see some new leadership at the F.B.I.," Hoover said.

Kennedy smiled. He had never seriously thought about getting rid of Hoover.

"I can't imagine trying to run the government without you," Kennedy said. He had wanted to get rid of Hoover, but realized that Hoover had far too much information on him. He thought he was much more dangerous out of government than inside.

"You're kind," Hoover said. "I think it has been very important to have a loyal friend in my position. In the future, I think it will be even more important."

"How so?" the President asked.

"On May 22, 1961, I sent the Attorney General a letter to inform him that I had discovered an association between the Central Intelligence Agency and organized crime figures—specifically, Sam Giancana and Johnny Rosselli. The purpose of the association was to recruit the criminals to assassinate Fidel Castro."

"I didn't know you sent that memo to Bobby."

"Perhaps he remembers," Hoover suggested. "On February

27th, last month, I sent you and the Attorney General a memorandum to bring you up to date on this subject. We now know that Sam Giancana and other members of the so called Mafia continue to work for the CIA in an effort to assassinate a foreign leader. We have learned that a woman by the name of Judith Campbell is a frequent companion of these men."

"Who is Judith Campbell?" Kennedy asked Hoover.

"I thought you might know," Hoover replied with a restrained smile. He then pulled the top secret memo out of his papers and handed it to the President. "Today, I wanted to hand deliver this memorandum to you."

Kennedy took the sheet of paper from Hoover and began to read it. The memo Hoover handed him documented that the President had called Judith Campbell more than 60 times from the Oval Office. Kennedy passed the memo back to the Director.

"What do you want?" he asked the Director.

"I only want to serve this government," Hoover replied. "I think you can see how important it is to have an old friend at my desk."

"Edgar, there is no chance I would ever want someone else at your desk. You were my first political appointment."

"And Allen Dulles was your second," Hoover reminded him. Kennedy had asked Dulles to resign after the Bay of Pigs, as a way of pinning the blame of the disaster on the CIA.

"You are a friend of the family," Kennedy argued. "You are the last person I would want to see retire at this point."

"Your brother Robert may have other ideas."

"Don't give that a second thought," the President said. "I can assure you that when I next see him I will tell him, as I have told you, that I have every intention of reappointing you. He has nothing but the highest respect for you."

Hoover looked at the President and nodded his understanding.

"I just don't see the point of writing a memorandum on a subject which is as sensitive and secret as Castro," Kennedy repeated. "As you said, memos have a way of resurfacing. As far as

I'm concerned, the less of a paper trail created on this subject, the better."

Hoover took a cigar out of his pocket. He then reached into his pants pocket and removed a small knife. He cut the ends off from the cigar, then he lit a match and started the cigar. Hoover stared around the room for a few moments and blew some smoke into the air.

"I'm your friend," he told the President. "I have a tape of you and Inga in a hotel room which I could have leaked anytime in the last five years and seen your political fortunes evaporate. I didn't. I have medical reports describing your Addison's disease—a disease you denied having in the campaign. I could have leaked them. I have evidence that Mayor Daley conspired to throw the election of 1960 by having dead voters miraculously turn up at the polls. I've never leaked s single story. Do you really think I'm such a bad man?"

"So why did you write this memo?" Kennedy asked him.

Hoover puffed some more on his cigar. "To try to bring you to your senses. You and your brother are getting into some real trouble."

"How so?"

"Just because some lunatics at the CIA planned an invasion of Cuba by a band of amateur soldiers didn't mean that you had to go along with it," Hoover said. "You could have simply canceled the operation."

"I could have," Kennedy conceded.

"But you didn't," Hoover argued. "You didn't carefully think about it. You allowed yourself to be taken in by those drunks over at the CIA. Now, they've got you involved with something else—something worse than the Bay of Pigs."

"Killing Castro?"

"Killing Castro," Hoover repeated. "Giancana was hired before you took office. You didn't have to go along with this plan. You could have simply canceled the operation. Instead, you have passed classified material to Giancana through this woman Judith Campbell. That was a serious mistake."

"Castro isn't dead."

"That's exactly right. And you should be grateful he isn't. This country should not have a foreign policy of political assassination . . . but I'm not making foreign policy. My job is internal security and unfortunately, sometimes the two become mixed. I have another uncomfortable topic to discuss with you."

The President stood up and walked around the cafeteria table, then stopped and stretched his back.

"I can't wait," he told Hoover with a smile.

"As you know, your friend Marilyn Monroe sees a psychiatrist in Santa Monica, California."

"I guess so," Kennedy replied.

"As you know, Miss Monroe recently traveled to Mexico to visit Frederick Vanderbilt Field, the founder of several Communist front organizations and an individual well known to pass information to the Soviet Union. We have reason to believe that Miss Monroe may have passed security information to Mr. Field."

The President sat back down at the table and looked over at Hoover. "What have you learned?" Kennedy asked.

"I'm sure the CIA also monitored Miss Monroe's activities in Mexico, and I suspect your information on this subject is better than my own," Hoover said. "This raises the question of whether there is any secret this government has which it does not want the Soviet or Cuban governments to have. Is nuclear testing a secret?"

"The Soviets know when we test," the President replied. "And we know when they test."

"Is the operation to assassinate Mr. Castro a secret of this government?" Hoover asked.

The President squinted at Hoover and thought for a moment. "Yes, you'd have to say that those efforts should remain secret."

"There is no greater secret in this government—is there Mr. President?" Hoover persisted.

"No greater secret," Kennedy agreed. "And yet, I believe the Cubans know we are trying to topple the current government of Cuba."

"That's right," Hoover said. "But they don't know that you are dedicated to assassinating Castro. If they knew that for sure, you would be in significant danger."

"That's probably true."

"I would suggest to you, Mr. President, that there is a security leak in this government, and that it starts right at the top. I am not critical of your sexual relationship with Miss Campbell or Miss Monroe, but I am concerned about the risk of either of these individuals, or individuals in the Mafia, confirming for the Russians or the Cubans the precise nature of our top secret foreign policy operations."

"You have a point, but I think that Marilyn Monroe cannot give anyone certain information regarding secret CIA plans. Any government which acted on the basis of a rumor from Marilyn Monroe would be acting recklessly."

"That is a judgment that only you can make," Hoover asserted. "My job is to give you information as I learn it. I am very concerned about your plan to kill Castro. If Castro knows for sure that that is your intention, you will undoubtedly face significant risk to your own life. Your security and the security of this country are my greatest responsibilities."

"And I appreciate your efforts, Edgar," the President said.

The Director went back down the elevator and back to his limousine. The time had passed quickly. By the time he went outside, he noticed that the light was starting to fade. His private meeting with the President, a meeting from which there would never be any official notes, had taken four hours. The Director went back to his F.B.I. office that afternoon. Over a couple of drinks, he and Clyde replayed some of their favorite recordings.

Chapter 22

". . . possible visit of President Kennedy in Palm Springs during the weekend of 3/23/62 . . . Sinatra reportedly has this house adequately wired for teletype facilities, has five private telephone lines, and enough cable available to handle a switchboard."

". . . special agent at Palm Springs has been advised by the Palm Springs Police Department that they have been contacted by the Secret Service . . . that the President is going to stay at Bing Crosby's residence."

F.B.I. Reports

Pat Newcomb stood behind Marilyn's hairdresser as he combed out her hair. It was a warm Saturday morning in Santa Monica, California. Marilyn had been in her new house for almost a month. They heard footsteps from the hallway.

"Is anybody home?" Peter Lawford said as he entered the room. He was dressed in a well pressed sport shirt and slacks.

Lawford had been assigned by the President to escort Marilyn to Bing Crosby's desert home in Palm Springs. His large frame filled the doorway to the room.

"We didn't hear anyone knock," Marilyn said to Lawford, who had come in without knocking.

"I didn't know if this was the right house," Lawford explained.

"It's so small, I didn't know if it was a famous movie star's house or a place for her servants." He laughed.

"It's both," Marilyn replied. "It's small because I had to buy it with my own money."

"Ouch," Lawford said. He took out a cigarette and lit it. He thought that Marilyn had always been jealous that he had married a rich girl from the East. Then the rich girl turned out to have a brother who ran for President of the United States. Then Marilyn became very jealous. And very involved. It had always seemed to Peter that Marilyn couldn't understand why he could marry into the Kennedy family, but that she, a bigger star, could not. He took a drag on his cigarette and looked around the perimeter of the room.

"Have something against furniture?" he asked.

"I wanted to decorate the house in a Spanish theme," Marilyn said. "So I'm having some furniture made in Mexico. They are going to bring it up next month."

"I like this place, Marilyn," Lawford said, coming back into the room. "It's very private. Nice gardens. Maybe a little small."

"I don't have a family," Marilyn said. "Or, maybe you don't want to hear that this early in the day."

Lawford laughed. Marilyn had a habit of getting drunk and pouring out her heart to Peter. She had told him that she wanted more than anything to find the right man and get married. She wanted children. He couldn't understand why she was involved with his brother in law. He certainly wasn't going to marry her. But they had been over that idea before, as well.

"I just want to get on the road," Lawford said as he picked a tin Indian mask off a nail on Marilyn's wall. "What's this?"

"Don't you love it?" Marilyn asked him. "I got it in Mexico. Masks are so interesting. I wonder why there are masks in primitive cultures. What purposes do they serve?"

Marilyn was having her final makeup applied.

"They allow people to imagine themselves as something they are not," Peter said.

Peter Lawford and Marilyn looked out the windows of the black limousine as it sped along the desert highway. They saw the flowering cactus plants, standing like soldiers in formation, with their arms gesturing at the heavens. The air blowing through the windows was warm and dry.

"Frank will probably never speak to me again," Lawford said.

"It wasn't your fault," Marilyn replied.

"Yes, but he'll take it out on me. It was Bobby's fault. Bobby's the one who won't play ball."

Lawford lit a cigarette. He threw the match out the window.

"I can't believe that guy," Lawford muttered.

"He's the top cop in the country," Marilyn said. "I can understand why he doesn't want to look like he's friends with the Mafia. And he wrote that book about fighting the Mob. They are turning it into a movie at Fox."

"Believe me, I know," Lawford said. He rubbed his head and took another drag from the cigarette. "Frank has been a peacemaker. Frank has been our friend. I can't see doing this to Frank."

"Do you think anyone will really notice?"

"Frank will notice. His friend Giancana will notice. Everybody in the business knows that the President just stiffed Frank to stay with Bing Crosby. Great move. Screw Frank. Stay with Bing. Let Lawford take the heat."

He blew more cigarette smoke into the warm desert air.

"The old man was a friend of the families but now he's had a stroke. Jack has been friendly. Then Bobby comes along and starts to cause trouble. And Frank was defending him—Frank was trying to keep the peace. Now they throw out Frank. I don't like it."

"What can they do?" Marilyn asked. "They might be powerful families, but they are dealing with the government. I don't think they are in any position to ask for favors from the President."

"I'm not so sure about that," Lawford said.

Bing Crosby's desert estate was built in clusters. The main house was at the center. There, the President and his advisors held their meetings. Marilyn was taken to a small cottage, down a dirt trail from the main house. The complex was distinctly modern with a steel frame, high ceilings, and giant windows which looked out over the desert.

From her bedroom, Marilyn could see a wide and uncluttered expanse. The air smelled fresh and dry. Some white wisps of clouds caught the sunlight above the dark shapes of the distant mountains. The shadows were growing long on the desert floor as the sun dropped closer to the horizon. She heard voices and footsteps as she looked out over the desert landscape.

Finally, Marilyn felt his hands gently rub her back and shoulders. His touch was light, and very sensitive.

"It's going to be a nice sunset," the President said.

Marilyn loved his presence. The time always seemed to pass so quickly when they were together. She wanted to slow it down and bathe in the warmth of his attention.

She turned and looked at him. John Kennedy was 44 years old—young, but showing wear. His red-brown hair was coarse and stood on end. Small lines radiated from the corners of his eyes. He was still staring out at the desert. The light caught his eyes, making them seem almost brilliant. Then he smiled, and his perfectly formed teeth reflected the light from the window. He was dressed in a dark turtleneck shirt, khaki pants and loafers.

"Let's take a walk," he said.

"Don't you need to check that out with your people?" Marilyn asked, thinking of the Secret Service.

"To hell with them," Kennedy whispered. "Not everything in life can be planned."

He took her hand and they walked out the door next to the window, then down a couple of steps to the dirt trail. The sun began to set as they walked among the giant cacti, and then down a dry wash. He leaned against a large boulder which seemed out of place on the desert floor. Marilyn leaned against him and he held her, his arms draped over her frame. They looked at the changing colors of the sky.

"It's a beautiful thing to see, if you have the time," Marilyn said.

"You need to take the time," Kennedy said. "They won't give it to you. You have to take it."

She stayed in his grasp. She didn't want the sun to set. She wanted to stay there and feel his body surrounding hers. But, set it did, and soon, hand in hand, they were walking slowly back up the wash, along the dirt trail, toward the main house.

A group of people had gathered in the courtyard next to the main house. As they approached, Marilyn saw a bar had been set up and attractive, well dressed people were mingling. She recognized some as members of the film community and thought the ones she did not recognize were in politics.

A young man dressed in a striped tie and blue blazer approached the President and Marilyn. He was accompanied by an older man who was dressed more casually.

"Mr. President," the older man said, "this is Phil Watson. He's the one who is running for Assessor. He's been loyal to the party."

The President extended his hand and young Watson shook it.

"You know Marilyn Monroe, Phil?" the President asked.

"No, sir."

"Miss Monroe has a strong interest in politics," Kennedy said. "I've got a feeling she's going to have an ever more important voice in the process."

The two men looked at Marilyn—Kennedy smiling as if he was amusing himself, and Watson with the straight face of the young politician. Marilyn shrugged. She had never been introduced by the President before as someone who might have a place in politics.

Later that night, after the party was over, and Marilyn and the President had consummated their afternoon together, Marilyn lay awake. She knew that the next morning would come all too soon, and that Jack would be gone. Still, she didn't want it to be over.

She drew a fingernail lightly over the President's bare back.

"Do you really think I could ever have a place in politics?" she asked him.

"What do you think?" he replied.

"I think I could," she said.

"I think you have proven you can do almost anything you want to," Kennedy said. He opened his eyes and stared through the window at the desert sleeping in the moonlight.

"Could I have you?" she asked.

"You had me," he said smiling. "That's all there is."

"No, could I ever have you in your world?"

Kennedy turned to face her. He positioned a pillow under his head. He glanced over the curves of her body, now shrouded lightly under the sheet. Then he looked into her face. Marilyn Monroe was 35 years old. Her skin, now washed clean of makeup, was unblemished and almost white in the moonlight. Her white hair and dark eyes provided a stark contrast.

He tried to understand her question. They had been intimate for more than a year. They had met in apartments, hotels, his sister's beach house—everywhere short of the White House. He wondered if, for some reason relating to the physical presence of the White House itself, Marilyn wanted to meet there.

"Yes," he said. "We could work that out."

Marilyn took a deep breath and swallowed. John Kennedy was heaven. He was smart, funny, attractive, and the most powerful man on earth. And she was with him. She had been with him for more than a year. And now he had said that anything was possible. Maybe anything was possible. She had always aimed for the stars and eventually, she had arrived.

She reached out and lightly kissed his lips. Then she fell back onto the bed and closed her eyes. That was enough for one day. She wanted to sleep with her fantasy.

Chapter 23

*"In the event that Miss Monroe absents herself on the dates
of May 17 and 18, the same will constitute willful failure
to render services pursuant to her contractual agree-
ments . . . Such action will result in serious loss and material damage to Twentieth Century-Fox."*

Frank Ferguson (lawyer for Fox) to Marilyn Monroe
"Warning Letter," May 16, 1962

*"Happy birthday to you, happy birthday to you, happy
birthday Mr. President, happy birthday to you."*

"It's terrible," the President said.

"You don't like it?" Marilyn asked. She was talking to the
President over the telephone while her $12,000 Jean Louis dress
was being fitted on her.

"I don't like it," the President repeated. "It was great before. I
want you to sing it the way you did last time."

"They won't let me," Marilyn purred.

"Of course, they'll let you," he replied. "The way you just sang
it is the same way people sing it every day. But the other way, the
sexy way—that makes it unique."

"I hope you'll like the dress," she said, looking at herself in
the mirror.

"I have a feeling I'm going to love the dress," the President
said.

Jean Louis looked at Marilyn from a corner of the room. The dress was nothing short of magnificent. It would have its own place in the history of American fashion and might have its own place in American history. Marilyn had been vague in the beginning about why she wanted him to make the dress. She had only requested that he *"design a truly historical dress—a dazzling dress that's one of a kind."* When he had asked her where she planned to wear the dress, she told him that it was a *"state secret."*

At that time, the dress designer had no knowledge that Marilyn was going to wear his creation to the Presidential birthday party. He was completely unaware of her involvement with Kennedy. So he looked through photographs of Marilyn and tried to envision a dress which would reflect her temperament. Finally, it had come to him. A nude dress. A dress made of a light mesh—with sequins and beads. Because Marilyn did not wear underwear, a series of heavier panels were sewn into the dress so as to cover certain strategic areas. But the effect of the dress was to accentuate Marilyn's physical proportions.

Elizabeth Courtney, one of the most accomplished fitters in Beverly Hills, stood at Marilyn's side, trying to decide what areas of the dress needed modification. She pulled on the fabric on one side of the movie star's thigh, thinking that perhaps this area could be tightened.

"I guess the cat's out of the bag, now," Marilyn said to Elizabeth after she had hung up the telephone. "Everyone is going to know, anyway."

"I'll never tell," Elizabeth assured Marilyn. "I can't believe you are going to appear at a birthday party for the President. Do you think this dress is appropriate for the President's party, Jean?" she asked the designer.

"In France, it would create a utter scandal," he replied. "Here, I don't know. Are you sure you want this effect?" he asked Marilyn.

"I'm sure," Marilyn said. "Everything has been secret for so long. At last, Jack wants everyone to know."

"Know what?" Elizabeth Courtney asked.

"Know about us," Marilyn answered without emotion. "We've been together for more than a year. Now, I think he wants something more public."

Jean Louis shot a glance over at Elizabeth. He lifted his eyebrows.

"That was the President on the telephone," Jean Louis said. "I'm sure he knows what effect we are trying to achieve with this dress. I'm just wondering what kind of effect he's trying to achieve."

"It's the 60's," Marilyn said. "He wants to lead the nation into a new place in history."

"This is a wonderful start," Jean Louis said. "This is the most beautiful dress in the world, on the most beautiful woman in the world, to sing for the most powerful man in the world. I predict it will be a moment to be remembered."

Milton Gould sat at his desk atop the Fox headquarters in New York City. It was going to be a very ugly meeting. The prospect of facing more than 300 angry shareholders made him want to go home. And angry they were. He had been elected to the Board because of his ability to turn around troubled companies like Fox. They had trusted him. But the stock had continued to go down. Fox management was on the ropes.

The problem was clear: Fox was working with actresses. Actresses were driving the future of the company. Gould couldn't imagine a worse fate. His future, his company's future, his money's future was now in the hands of a couple of talented, but highly temperamental actresses.

Elizabeth Taylor and Richard Burton were making *Cleopatra* in Rome. It was over budget, out of control, and drawing criticism from the Pope. Usually, even negative publicity was still publicity. But when the adulterous affair between Taylor and Burton had become public, even the Pope could not hold his criticism. Even that Gould could stand. It was the daily losses. There was some question as to whether the company had enough money to continue operations.

And then Marilyn Monroe became sick. Fox had the world's leading actress still signed to do a final movie on her old contract. It should have been easy money for Fox—they were paying Marilyn only $100,000 to star in *Something's Got to Give*. They were paying Elizabeth Taylor $1,000,000 for her role in *Cleopatra*. *Something's Got to Give* should have been a sure winner. But Marilyn, who would only work when she looked her best, had been sick with something her doctors called "sinusitis."

Dr. Lee Siegel, the Fox doctor, examined Marilyn on multiple occasions and ordered her to remain in bed. She had been sick from April 23 to April 27. She was able to work for a few days, but then left again from May 5 to May 11. The word had passed from the fabled Fox lot to the New York headquarters that Marilyn was not really sick. But every time Gould had asked Dr. Siegel to go over to look at Marilyn, he had been told that she was sick, and that the movie could not be shot until she was better.

Gould looked out his window at the smaller buildings beneath him. Spyros Skouras, the President of Fox, was going to show some clips from the two movies he hoped would save the company—scenes from *Cleopatra* and a test reel from *Something's Got to Give*. If someone asked a question about how the filming was progressing on *Something's Got to Give*, Spyros would simply have to lie.

"Mr. Gould," the intercom interrupted his thoughts. "It's the Attorney General of the United States."

Gould turned and stared at the box on his desk. Then he walked quickly over to his door and opened it to see his secretary directly. She motioned for him to go back to his desk. He had to assume that it was the real thing. He shut the door and walked back to his desk and picked up the telephone.

"Milton Gould?" an operator asked.

"Yes."

"Stand by for the Attorney General," the operator requested.

"Milton?" Robert Kennedy said.

"Yes, Mr. Kennedy," Gould responded. They had met when

Bobby set up a film version for his book **The Enemy Within**. He chose Fox because the Chairman of the Board, Samuel Rosenman, was a loyal Democrat, and had been in government with Joseph Kennedy in the Roosevelt Administration. President Kennedy had appointed Rosenman to several labor relations panels. Indeed, Robert Kennedy's father in law's corporation had bought prime real estate from the Fox Corporation. Robert Kennedy knew the leadership of Fox on a first name basis and their loyalty was deeper than first met the eye.

"How is Judge Rosenman?" Kennedy asked Gould.

"Just fine, Mr. Kennedy," Gould reported. "He is grateful that you helped steer him into the steel strike negotiations."

"Give him our best."

"I certainly will."

"I have a favor to ask you, Milton," Kennedy said. "It is going to seem a little complex, but I'm sure you understand that we are trying to juggle many considerations here."

"I understand," Gould replied.

"I want you to warn Marilyn Monroe that she will be fired if she goes to the President's birthday party. Have one of the lawyers send her a formal letter."

"I thought you wanted her to go to the party," Gould remarked.

"I do, but I also want to get a little leverage on her. I can't explain it all now, but you may be asked to help us out a little bit with Marilyn."

"I think you have pretty strong relationships here," Gould said. "We'll do whatever we can to help."

"I know you will," Kennedy said. "Your loyalty is appreciated, but this borders on the top secret national security stuff and I'm going to have to ask you not to mention it to anyone. Please issue her a warning, but don't bring us in on it. We want her to come. You don't want her to come. That's the understanding."

"I get it," Gould replied. "We'll lay out our position for Miss Monroe."

"Thank you," the Attorney General said.

Gould hit the intercom and his secretary answered.

"Get Frank Ferguson in here," he barked. "Marilyn needs to know how important this is to the studio."

Marilyn Monroe sat in her dressing room on the Fox lot. She knew very well that *Something's Got to Give* was the only movie being made on the lot. Things had gotten so bad for the company, that Fox had been forced to sell off a big part of its real estate, complete with stages and fake western towns, to a another company. As she sat in the dressing room she knew that less than a mile away, bulldozers were literally pushing down the old movie sets to make room for a new office park—something the developers were referring to as 'Century City.'

George Cukor came into the dressing room and asked everyone else to leave. Cukor was the director of *Something's Got to Give*. He had directed Marilyn before in *Let's Make Love*. They had not always gotten along well, but they had been able to get the movies done. Cukor had gray hair which was combed directly back. He wore a plain white shirt, open at the neck.

As Marilyn's various assistants left the room, Cukor sat down in a chair behind Marilyn's dressing table. She turned and faced him.

"Apparently, there is some issue about your plans to go to New York," Cukor began.

"Not really," Marilyn responded.

"You're not going?" Cukor said.

"I am going," Marilyn said.

"That's not my understanding. I just spoke with Milton Gould in New York. The entire Fox Board discussed whether they could allow you to go. You know that *Cleopatra* is in trouble."

"I know."

"Well, the Board is worried that the trip might throw you into a relapse. You were only able to work one week in the last four and we are obviously well off schedule. My understanding is that the trip is off."

Marilyn looked at him. He seemed calm and reasonable.

"I want to go," Marilyn said.

Cukor wiped his forehead and pushed his hair back.

"It's not a question of what you want to do, Marilyn. It's a question of what is best for your career. If you leave the set without permission, you will be in breach of your contract. It's as simple as that. You could be fired."

"Fired?"

"Yes. You signed a contract with Fox. Fox has paid dearly to have all of these people here, all of the set managers, and hair and costume people, the other stars. If you leave, the studio is going to lose a bundle and you're going to lose your job. You know the truth, Marilyn?"

"What? Tell me the truth."

"The truth is that you were made by Fox. When you started at Fox, you didn't have the money to buy a newspaper. The company made you what you are today. Now, I know that this is your last picture under contract, and next year you will be making a lot more money, but you owe it to the company to live up to your end of the contract."

"Fox would fire me?" Marilyn asked.

"That's what I'm trying to get across," Cukor said.

"But this is something for the President of the United States," she muttered, as if Cukor failed to realize the importance of the appearance. "There's going to be unbelievable publicity around this event—it will be good for the movie."

"Marilyn, 30 years from now nobody is going to remember which actress sang for which president at which birthday party. Trust me. But people will always remember the performance of Marilyn Monroe in George Cukor's *Something's Got to Give*." Cukor beamed a confident smile.

Jacqueline Kennedy walked into the Oval Office. The First Lady rarely bothered herself with the workings of government, and almost never came to his office. She was dressed in a simple dark dress without sleeves. Her hair was meticulously styled in her trademark circular coif.

"To what do I owe this honor?" the President asked.

"Jack, I've heard some very unpleasant rumors," she began.

The President sat back in his chair. He sensed a fight in the air.

"You're worried about the Gala?" he suggested.

"Just tell me. Did you invite Marilyn Monroe to sing at the Gala?"

"Actually, I didn't invite her. The writer-producer, Dick Adler, invited her. He invited her a long time ago, before—"

"—Before you started carrying on with her."

The President tapped at his teeth with the finger nail of his index finger.

"Right. Before any of that."

"I've heard she is going to dress in something transparent. She's going to sing Happy Birthday to you in front of a public gathering in a very provocative dress."

"That's the word."

Jackie walked over to one of the paintings on the wall of the Oval Office and stared at it for a moment. The First Lady turned and looked at the President. A faint smile came to her lips.

The President waited for his wife to say something. She knew about his sexual indiscretions. She welcomed them. She didn't want to have sex with him—not the way he needed to have it. His physical frailties restricted what he could do, and certainly restricted what she could enjoy. If the President had to trade on his position to get what he wanted, that was all right with her. But, it was not all right to have his behavior publicly known. And it was not all right to humiliate her in a public forum. That had always been their understanding.

"I hope you know what you're doing," she said.

"I hope I do, too."

"You realize that she has started to say that you intend to get a divorce and marry her?"

"I don't think she's actually said that."

"She has."

"I don't think so."

"Jack, why do you think you want her to perform for you in front of 10,000 people at Madison Square Garden? Don't you see what message this sends?"

"It sends the message that I'm a healthy man. I'm doing what every man in America would like to do. That's what a president should do. It's a psychological message."

"You may think it sends that message. Maybe it does. Maybe people will think you really are a healthy man, who enjoys a normal sex life. You're worried that the word will get out how bad your health really is."

"That might be part of it."

"But I'm concerned about this poor girl who thinks you love her."

"She knows I don't love her."

"Really, Jack. You know she thinks you do. And you know how disappointed she will feel when she learns the truth."

The President turned his chair around and began to look out the windows behind his desk. It was just like Jackie to think about the feelings of the mistress. But maybe she had a point. Maybe Marilyn needed to understand the reality of the situation. He stared out the windows and wondered if Marilyn actually could think that he could marry her.

"I will not be going to your birthday celebration," Jackie announced to him. "I think we have a clear understanding about your public behavior. Caroline and I will go to Glen Ora on Saturday and ride the horses. Maybe I will have the Deputy Secretary of Defense come down for dinner."

She was flaunting the fact that she was having a relationship with Roswell Gilpatric, a friend of Jack's. If Roswell were transferred out of Washington, Jackie had told the President, she would go with him.

"It won't be a public dinner," she continued. "I'll save you that indignity, for now."

Chapter 24

"But we settled all that. I said 'No,' the studio said 'No.'
Period. She can't go."

George Cukor
May 17, 1962

Peter Lawford looked down on the parked cars and back-yard swimming pools of the west side of Los Angeles. The large circular blade of the helicopter pounded above his head. The rhythmic sound of the propeller reminded him of the sound of a steam engine pulling a train. He wondered how long it had been since he heard a steam engine. The memory took him back to England, to his school days, long before he had become the President's brother in law, long before he knew Marilyn Monroe.

Bobby called him with an assignment. When Bobby told him to do something, it had to get done. Life was just easier that way. But Peter thought it was a mistake. The studio didn't want Marilyn to go to the Birthday Party. Jack and Bobby did. Fox said 'No.'' They said 'Yes.' Now, Peter had been assigned to pick up Marilyn and bring her to New York.

Howard Hughes allowed Peter the use of the helicopter. The Kennedy brothers thought sending in a Marine helicopter might bring on renewed criticism about their aggressiveness. A private helicopter would do. Lawford would simply go to the studio and take Marilyn. If Fox had a problem with that, let them complain to their local police.

The enormous helicopter floated down from the sky toward the Fox lot—to the cement pad adjacent to soundstage 14. Lawford looked at people on the ground running to get out of the way.

"I've heard they're using these things in Vietnam, now," Lawford said to the pilot.

"That's right," the pilot said. "Can you imagine what it would be like to bring this thing down in a jungle?"

Marilyn Monroe sat in front of her dressing mirror. She was supposed to get dressed to begin filming, but, instead, she sat in her Jax slacks and high heels and watched the final touches being applied to her hair. Her Jean Louis beaded gown was in a sealed suit bag, hanging next to a suitcase.

"Marilyn, I have a bad feeling about this," Patricia Newcomb warned her.

"You don't like to fly?" Marilyn asked.

"I just think it's a mistake," Pat continued. "It is going to be too public. You can't do some kind of seduction number for the President of the United States in front of ten thousand people and think the affair is going to be a secret."

"Who said it was going to be a secret?" Marilyn responded.

"Do you think the country will put up with it?" Pat asked. "Do you really think the moms and pops across the country will approve of a sexy movie star offering her body to the Commander in Chief?"

Marilyn tilted her head to one side and shook her hair slightly. She motioned to a spot which needed further attention.

"It's a chance," Marilyn said.

"It's a big chance," Pat repeated. "And you are going to lose your job over this."

"Who told you that?" Marilyn asked.

"Everybody on the lot knows that," Pat said. "You've been warned. The lawyers sent you a letter."

Marilyn did not acknowledge that the letter worried her. She continued to inspect her hair and makeup.

"That's being worked out," Marilyn said without emotion. "Bobby said he would take care of that."

"You look like a movie star," Paula Strasberg, her drama coach, asserted. Paula and Pat had packed their things to accompany Marilyn on the trip.

The women were startled as Peter Lawford threw open the door and strode into the room.

"Jump!" he commanded. "Let's get out of here before Cukor tries to kill me."

Marilyn looked up at Peter.

"Peter, has the thing with Fox been worked out?" she asked.

"What thing?" Peter asked, playing dumb.

"They said it was all right to go?"

Peter picked up Marilyn's suitcase and draped the suit bag carrying the Jean Louis dress over his arm.

"Yes. Bobby's working that out with the people in New York. What are they going to say? He's the Attorney General. Let's go."

"It's not worked out!" Pat exclaimed.

"It's not worked out?" Marilyn asked again.

"I don't know," Peter said. "My job is to get you to New York. Let's get out of here."

Pat sensed a moment of equivocation. Marilyn looked confused.

"If you go to New York," Pat said, looking into Marilyn's face, "you will end your relationship with the President. And you will end your job at Fox. Stay here, and the President will be able to continue to see you, if he wants to, and you will finish your movie."

"Jesus, Marilyn!" Lawford shouted. "We don't have time for the school girl intrigue!"

Marilyn looked at Paula Strasberg. Paula shrugged. Then she looked into the mirror and checked her hair from different angles. After a few moments, a smile came to her face. She walked over to Peter and reached for his arm. They began to walk toward the door.

"Marilyn," Pat called. She wanted an explanation.

Marilyn stopped and faced her.

"Jack and I are in love," Marilyn said to Pat. "Jack is taking a big risk to have me come to New York. He's taking the risk for a reason. And I have to take the risk, too. That's the way love works: one person takes a risk, and the other person also takes a risk. Both people take risks and things are never the same, again."

Pat stared at Marilyn. There was a moment of understanding between them before Marilyn smiled confidently. Then she walked out the door on Peter's arm.

Strapped into her seat on the helicopter, Marilyn looked out the window at the circle of stage hands and secretaries who had surrounded them. Pat Newcomb climbed into the seat behind Marilyn. Paula Strasberg sat next to her. The doors were slammed shut and bolted. The propeller began to pound faster. The noise was deafening. The helicopter lifted off the ground. Marilyn was on her way to New York.

George Cukor saw the big, blue helicopter rise from the ground. He held one hand over his hair as he charged toward the circle of onlookers. Dirt and paper was scattered by the force of the spinning propeller.

"What's going on?" Cukor demanded of a camera man.

"It's Marilyn," the man said. "Lawford picked her up."

"Marilyn?" Cukor repeated. *But we settled all that. I said 'No,' the studio said 'No.' Period. She can't go.*"

The two men looked at the helicopter rise higher into the sky and then circle the lot. After a single circle maneuver, the craft darted off in the direction of Los Angeles International Airport.

George Cukor rubbed his forehead and bit down on his lip. The Kennedy brothers were aggressive men. The idea of Eisenhower using the powers of the State for his personal entertainment was inconceivable.

Cukor watched the helicopter disappear over the hills and into the mist of the Southern California morning. Marilyn Monroe thought she was going to New York, Cukor mused. But she really didn't know where she was going. And neither did he.

Richard Adler was a composer. He had written *You Gotta Have Heart*, and the music for *Damn Yankees*. He wasn't new to show business. But nothing he had ever done had prepared him for the cross fire he found himself in as director of the President's Birthday Gala.

He looked at the stage which had been erected in Madison Square Garden. The other stars who had been invited to participate in the event had all taken his direction. But Marilyn Monroe had not. He had told her how to sing 'Happy Birthday' to the President, he had even recorded himself singing the song and sent it to her. He wanted something clean. He didn't want to be remembered as the man who allowed Marilyn to tarnish the reputation of the highest office in the land, or its current occupant.

But Marilyn had crossed him. Initially, he thought she might change her delivery. Then, for reasons he didn't understand, she had gone back to a baby voiced breathlessness which had characterized some of her film work. He wondered if it was too late to fire her.

"Jack, you have a sense of these things," he said as he approached his old friend, Jack Benny.

Benny greeted his question with an amused curiosity.

"What things?" Benny asked.

"Marilyn's appearance is stirring up quite a reaction," Adler confided to Benny.

"How's that?"

"When news that she was appearing started to break last night, I got calls from all over the country. Democratic leaders are mad. Even friends of the Kennedy family are mad."

"Mad about what, Dick?" Benny asked.

"Mad about Marilyn's appearance," Adler explained. "She's going to sing 'Happy Birthday' to the President."

Benny looked quizzically at Adler. Men of Benny's generation could not conceive of any production which might cast doubts on the integrity of a national leader. During the hard days of World War II, there might have been very restrained debate about presidential policies. But no one would level a morals charge against the President—any President. The President wasn't just a man, he was an office. He was the integrity of a government.

"You asked Marilyn Monroe to sing to the President?" Benny asked.

"Well, yes. That's what I'm asking you about. There's been criticism of having her appear. And she won't take any direction. I told her how I wanted the song done. She won't listen. She's going to infuse it with sex."

Benny blinked his eyes a couple of times. He was having trouble understanding Adler.

"How is she going to sing it, Dick?" he asked. "There's only so much you can do with 'Happy Birthday.'"

Adler cleared his throat. Affecting a flat facial expression and pouting his lips, he began his imitation of Marilyn singing the song.

"Happy Birthday to you. Happy Birthday to you. Happy Birthday, Mr. President—"

"What the hell?" Benny interrupted him.

"That's what she's going to do," Adler said.

"*Get somebody else,*" Benny said angrily. "*What kind of schmuck are you, anyway, getting Marilyn Monroe to sing 'Happy Birthday' to the President of the United States?*"

Adler looked at Benny. Of course, Benny was right. Adler had known that Marilyn's rendition violated any standard of decent taste when he had first heard it. He was directing the show. He was going to fire her. He had to move. And move now.

He walked quickly away from the stage toward his office. He felt his hands break into a warm sweat. The show was going to be a disaster. And he was going to be responsible. He walked into the office and slammed the door.

Shirley MacLaine was in town. She knew the President. She had common sense. Maybe she would do it.

He called Shirley MacLaine.

"*Can you work up a rendition of 'Happy Birthday' this quickly?*" he asked her after making telephone contact.

"*It'll be okay, Dick. Marilyn is only one part of a long evening full of stars,*" Shirley responded.

"*But it's the finale. I want you to sing it.*"

Shirley MacLaine thought for a moment. She was close friends with Frank Sinatra. She knew that the President and Marilyn had been carrying on an intense relationship. She wondered what cancellation of Marilyn might mean to her, and to the President.

"Think of the repercussions—both public and private," she advised Adler.

Adler put down the telephone. He knew that having Marilyn coo to the President would be explosive. Jack Benny had expressed his revulsion to the very idea. The Democratic Party leadership had sent him telegrams. Opposition was intense. It was a difficult decision. It would either be a moment which would shine out in history, or it would be a moment that history wanted to forget. Finally, he decided. As important a choice as it was, only one man could make it. It was the President's call. He had to get to the President himself and let him make the decision.

Adler called his contact at the White House but the President was already in New York. He was given a number to call at the Carlyle Hotel. Adler anxiously dialed the number. After he had identified himself, and explained the urgency of his request, Adler spent the next ten minutes waiting for the President to pick up the call. Finally, he heard the famous Boston accent on the other end.

"Mr. President, she's going to sing 'Happy Birthday' in a slow, breathy tone, just like she did in Gentlemen Prefer Blondes," Adler explained in a sober—but nervous—voice.

"Believe me, Dick, it'll be all right," John Kennedy reassured him.

Richard Adler put down the telephone. John Kennedy was taking a big risk by having Marilyn Monroe perform her sexy serenade. But the decision was his. John Kennedy was the Commander in Chief. Adler only hoped the President was right.

It was May 19, 1962. Marilyn Monroe had less than 3 months to live.

Chapter 25

"I don't think I have seen anyone so beautiful; I was enchanted by her manner and her wit, at once so masked, so ingenuous and so penetrating. But one felt a terrible unreality about her—as if talking to someone under water. Bobby and I engaged in mock competition for her; she was most agreeable to him and pleasant to me-but then she receded into her own glittering mist."

Arthur Schlesinger, Jr.
Diary, May 19, 1962

"Tonight we have with us a representative of probably the most controversial organization connected with Cuba in this country. The organization is the Fair Play for Cuba Committee. The person, Lee Oswald, secretary of the New Orleans Chapter for the Fair Play for Cuba Committee. This organization has long been on the Justice Department's blacklist and is a group generally considered to be the leading pro-Castro body in the nation."

William Kirk Stuckey, host of the
"Latin Listening Post" Radio Program
WDSU (New Orleans)
August 17,1963

Richard Adler sat in the control booth. Black and white television screens showed different views of the stage in front of him. Between him and the stage sat the President and Attorney General. The television monitors showed a close up of the man Adler could see from his booth. Peter Lawford was teasing the crowd with allusions to Marilyn. But every time he had introduced her, the spot light had gone to a corner of the stage and no Marilyn had appeared.

Adler's misgivings about Marilyn's appearance crested immediately before the show. Mac Bundy, the President's closest advisor called him to request that some excuse be found to cancel Marilyn's participation in the Gala. Then he got a call from a member of the Joint Chiefs of Staff. Finally, a member of the President's own Cabinet called him to protest Marilyn's participation as bad for the country.

Adler wondered why they were calling him. He was only the Director. The President had insisted that Marilyn be allowed to sing. True, Adler had invited Marilyn before he had known of her involvement with Kennedy, but the President himself had given the go ahead. Adler sensed that the President might not be telling his advisors the details of his involvement with Marilyn's appearance. That way, if the star's appearance backfired, he could claim it was Adler's fault.

"Would John Kennedy set me up?" Adler wondered.

Marilyn couldn't walk up the steps to the stage. The Jean Louis gown was too tight. If she tried to lift her thigh to climb the steps, the dress was going to rip open and she wouldn't be able to perform.

"You have to get up there now, Miss Monroe," a man in a white shirt with a clip board said.

"Can't you see there's a problem?" Marilyn asked.

"What's the problem?"

"I can't climb the stairs. The dress is going to rip."

"Larry!" the stage manager called to an assistant. "We've got to get Marilyn up on stage."

"We can't lift her up there," his assistant objected. "We'd drop her."

Marilyn gave the man a stern glance.

"I don't think the President wants me dropped," she whispered.

She stood silently in her 'flesh and beads' gown, waiting for the men to figure it out. Finally, she was surrounded by a group of men, some looking like they were about to do something a little shameful. The men picked her up and passed her up the stairs. Like a piece of unyielding sculpture, she was passed from firm grip to firm grip until was delivered at the top of the stairs. There, at the edge of the stage, she was balanced in the upright position. With little, calculated steps, she shuffled into position. Just to her right, she saw an enormous five foot high birthday cake.

Marilyn looked into the darkness. Twenty thousand New Yorkers sat in their formal dress. She looked up at the highest reaches of the cavernous arena. Then she looked forward, into the light, where Peter Lawford was moving through his introduction.

The spot light began to move closer to her. She took a deep breath and let it out. It was a performance. It was just another performance. She just didn't want to move so much that she ripped the dress. It was a performance with only one take.

"Mr. President, because, never in the history of show business, perhaps there has been no one female who has meant so much, who has done more . . . Mr. President—the late Marilyn Monroe . . ."

Marilyn made her move. She sprang into the circles of the light and listened to gasps from the crowd. After the initial gasps, a roar enveloped her. They were excited. The crowd was excited to finally see her.

She gently danced onto the stage, holding an ermine wrap to cover her shoulders and chest. Every eye was on her. She looked out into the darkness again, where she could see people standing and pointing at her. She stopped.

Marilyn stood in the lights and waited for the roar of the crowd to quiet.

Then, like a butterfly stepping out of a cocoon, she let the fur slide off from her shoulders. She looked up into the lights and around the arena. The noise was palpable. 'They are loving it,' she thought. 'They can feel the magic.' Marilyn could feel it, too.

She stood in front of the microphone and waited for the crowd to quiet.

"*Happy birthday to you*," she sang in a slow sexy voice. "*Happy birthday to you*," Marilyn sang the song like it had never been done before—throwing in some gestures which only a bad girl would know. But they loved it. They loved her. Things were going to be all right, because the people loved her. The crowd whistled and screamed.

"It was like a wave of electricity passed through the crowd," Isadore Miller told Marilyn. "Everyone was full of energy. With all the screaming and yelling, it was like a moment of mass sexual panic." They were riding in a limousine to an exclusive party.

Marilyn didn't know exactly what to make of her former father in law's comment. She wasn't sure exactly what a moment of mass sexual panic was. All those men out there, screaming, whistling, howling their delight was a moment of some kind of mass sexual expression. Marilyn didn't think it was exactly a panic. But, maybe it was. She had invited Arthur Miller's father to escort her to a party after the event at Madison Square Garden. He was the closest thing to a father she had ever had.

"Did you like it?" she asked simply.

"Like it?" he answered. "I couldn't hear myself think. How would I know if I liked it?"

Isadore had always been very supportive of her. Even after her separation and divorce from Arthur, he had been willing to keep her as family. And, in return, no matter what she was doing, when a call came in from Isadore Miller, she interrupted her activities to take it.

They got out of the limousine and walked through the doors of Arthur Krim's exclusive Manhattan residence. Krim, a wealthy

Democrat, was hosting a reception for the President. They took a private elevator to the penthouse.

When Marilyn stepped out of the elevator, she noticed that something had changed. Before she sang for the President, she was an easily recognized celebrity. But now, a few hours after her performance, she was attracting an unusual amount of attention.

Dressed in her Jean Louis gown, she went from small group to small group—as a hostess might have done. She introduced herself and her former father in law. Every time she moved, she noticed that heads turned, comments were made, and more heads turned. Because the First Lady was not at the gathering, and because her affair with the President had been essentially publicly acknowledged at the Gala, Marilyn had the reserved confidence that her relationship with the President extended the prestige of the presidency to her.

"You were always one of my political heroes," Marilyn said to Adlai Stevenson.

"And mine, too," Isadore Miller chimed in.

"You are kind to say so," Stevenson replied.

"Marilyn," Robert Kennedy interrupted, "I think you've met my wife, Ethel."

"Yes. Nice to see you again, Mrs. Kennedy," Marilyn said to the conservatively dressed woman.

Ethel Kennedy glared at Marilyn. There was a word for women like Marilyn Monroe, women who used their bodies to lure men away from their wives. And the word was on Ethel's mind every time she saw Marilyn. She managed a faint smile.

"I've never met you, Miss Monroe," a professorial man said, holding out his hand. "I'm Arthur Schlesinger."

"Junior," Robert Kennedy added.

"Junior," Schlesinger agreed.

"His father was the famous Harvard historian," Bobby continued.

"Bobby, I'm going to step over here, with the ladies," Ethel said to her husband. She looked at Bobby, but he did not acknowledge her comment. She took a deep breath and left the circle. Whatever Marilyn Monroe was, Ethel thought, she wasn't a lady.

"I've long admired your work," Schlesinger said to Marilyn.

"And I've admired yours," Marilyn assured him.

"Really?" Schlesinger said, wondering what of his Marilyn had ever read.

"Marilyn, why don't we go out on the floor and dance?" Bobby asked her.

She lifted an eyebrow as if to consider his interest.

The Attorney General led Marilyn Monroe past the revelers and onto the dance floor.

Across the room, Ethel Kennedy stood in a circle with some of the socialites she had known growing up in New York. Some of the women she had known from debutante parties, some from private school, some from her involvement in the church. None of the women would ever wear a dress which immodestly revealed her body. None would ever think of infusing the 'Happy Birthday Song' with sexual overtones.

"I can't imagine what Jackie was thinking about," one of the ladies commented to Ethel. "If I were the First Lady of the United States I wouldn't let some near naked woman publicly serenade my husband."

"I'm not sure she had any choice," Ethel said, defending Jackie. "I think the President just let it happen."

"Things like that don't just happen," one of the others objected. "Jackie should have drawn the line a little more forcefully. It sends a message to people everywhere, a message to men, women, and children. Frankly, I don't like the message it sends."

"I don't know if it's possible to control the President," Ethel countered. "He has his own sense of what's right and wrong. Thank goodness Bobby has a little different set of standards." She smiled her relief that she had married a man who could resist the sexual opportunities of his position.

"Ethel," the first woman said, looking across the room. "I think your husband, the one with the different standards, is dancing with the near naked one."

The women all stared over at the dance floor where the Attorney General and Marilyn Monroe were receiving more than their fair share of attention. Ethel turned away, pained by the sight.

"He's just trying to keep her away from Jack," Ethel reasoned. "He's just playing the family policeman, again. He's trying to keep her from being seen with the President."

"It would be better if she weren't here, at all," one of the others offered. "I don't know where this country is going."

Marilyn followed Robert Kennedy's eyes. For the President's brother, he was certainly spending a lot of time staring at her dress. The music ended, but Bobby would not let her leave the dance floor. He insisted on one more dance. As they danced she become more aware of him. He was shorter than the President, and more delicate. He weighed much less. Still, there was an energy to him. He had a certain spark that she always found interesting in a man.

Finally, the music stopped and Bobby offered Marilyn his arm. They walked off the dance floor and bumped into Merriman Smith, a reporter Bobby knew from the White House. Bobby watched the reporter look soberly at Marilyn and then at him. Smith was usually the reporter who would signal the end of a press conference by standing up and thanking the President. No questions were asked after Smith indicated that the session was over. Seeing someone of Smith's stature at the private party frightened Bobby.

"Merriman, I'm surprised to see you here," the Attorney General said to the White House reporter.

"It's a pleasure to be here," Merriman Smith said dryly. "I've always wondered how you fellows spend your weekends."

Bobby looked at the reporter. He couldn't imagine whose idea it had been to invite a White House reporter to such a private party. There was no point in being inhospitable, though.

Smith was there. Bobby might as well be polite to him, introduce him to people, and show him there was nothing to hide.

"Merriman, meet Marilyn Monroe," Bobby said. "She's the President's favorite actress."

"So I've gathered," Smith said.

Bobby managed to lead Marilyn further along, past the reporter, and back into the circle of White House aides and political confidants where she would be less of an exposure threat. He wondered if the President was aware that there were members of the national press in the room.

"Arthur, I wanted you to have an opportunity to talk to Miss Monroe about your work," Bobby said to the President's in house historian. "Merriman Smith is over there. Do you know who invited him?"

"No idea."

"I want you to keep Miss Monroe entertained with stories about the rich history of Harvard."

"The history of what?" Marilyn asked. She had only heard the last part of Bobby's comments with Arthur.

"You're going to need a drink, Miss Monroe," Schlesinger said to Marilyn as he lifted a glass of champagne off from the tray of a passing waiter. He handed her the glass. "Do you know much about the Puritans?"

Marilyn looked at Bobby weave his way away from her. She knew as much about the Puritans as she wanted to, but she listened politely.

Bobby left the circle of presidential loyalists and walked toward his brother. The President was enjoying himself. The crowd had loved Marilyn's performance and his cute line about being now able to retire from politics. He loved to get off a good line. The glamour associated with the film business gave a new radiance to the old formal workings of political fund-raisers.

After he pulled the President off to the side, Bobby voiced a concern.

"Jack, this may have been more publicity than we wanted."

"They loved it," the President said, smiling.

"They told me that the White House switchboard is swamped. The reaction has been one of outrage."

"Straight laced conservative types. Being a Republican can't be much fun," the President said.

"You've got to tell Marilyn she's got to go home before she comes over to the Carlyle."

The President leaned forward to look over the crowd. He squinted to make out a face at some distance.

"Is that Marilyn over there with that old man?"

Bobby couldn't see over the crowd. He took a couple of steps to see if he could see around a group of people to see who Marilyn was talking to. He couldn't.

"She's with Arthur Miller's father tonight," Bobby said.

"That's good," the President said. "I could have sworn she was talking to Merriman Smith."

A few minutes later, the President and Attorney General had successfully separated her from the White House reporter and spoke with her privately next to a bookcase. Bobby told two Secret Service agents to keep people away and to be sure no one took any photographs.

"He wanted to know how long I'd known you," Marilyn reported. "I told him that we've been friends since the 50's."

"Jesus," Bobby muttered. "All we need is a story like that right now."

"He's a very nice man," Marilyn went on. "He wanted to know about my movie at Fox. He told me that he had heard that Fox was in trouble financially, and he wanted to know how I had been able to leave the set in the middle of a movie."

The President and Attorney General exchanged glances. Then from the corner of his eye, the President saw someone to his left lift a camera. He turned his face down and away, but he was silhouetted by the flash. Bobby turned toward the man with the camera, but the man walked quickly away.

"I said no pictures," he said to a Secret Service agent. "Go get that guy."

"I can't leave the President, sir," the agent replied. He tried to see who it was that had taken the photograph.

"Look, Marilyn," Bobby continued, "we can't have you talking to reporters right now."

"I talk with reporters all the time, Mr. Kennedy," Marilyn replied curtly.

"I mean, we don't want you to talk with reporters about the President," Bobby explained. "I tried to get Fox to give you an official excuse for the Gala. They couldn't give an official excuse, but the fellow I spoke with—"

"—What do you mean? I thought it was all right to come."

"It was all right. It was fantastic. But we just need to be sure that you get back on the set on Monday. Believe me, Fox isn't going to fire you."

"Fire me?" Marilyn couldn't believe she had heard the words. She had never seriously thought that her future job at Fox or anywhere else might be seriously in question.

"They won't do it."

"How could they fire me? You said that things were going to be worked out."

"You're not going to get fired," the President assured her. "All you have to do is play by the rules, and everything is going to be fine."

"What rules?" Marilyn asked.

Marilyn left the party with her father in law. She went home, and then was picked up by two agents from the Secret Service and taken to the Carlyle Hotel. There, after hosting a small party of his own, the President entertained Marilyn with gossip, a discussion of nuclear testing and a brief physical encounter. At the end of their evening together, Marilyn and the President lay on his bed in the darkness.

"Do you ever worry that your plans for Castro will backfire," Marilyn asked John Kennedy.

"What do you mean," the President replied.

"What if Castro decides to play by the same rules as you do? What if he decides to send someone to the United States to try to kill you?"

The President was shocked.

"First of all, how do you know what we're doing with Castro?" Kennedy asked her.

"Everyone seems to know," Marilyn responded. "When I was in Mexico I spoke with that Communist guy—Frederick Field—and he seemed to know all about it."

"Surely, you did not tell him that we were trying to kill Castro?"

"No. I didn't have to. He told me that Castro knows that someone in the government is trying to kill him—he's captured some of the assassins. They've confessed. Castro assumes that you know what's going on."

"I don't know that we're trying to kill Castro," the President argued.

"Then why did Richard Goodwin reject the offer from Che?" Marilyn asked.

"Offer for what?" Kennedy asked.

"I was told that Che asked that you and Castro agree not to try to kill one another."

"Jesus Christ, Marilyn! What are you talking to some Communist spy about what we're doing?"

"He was telling me," Marilyn argued. "I didn't even know about Che."

"But you've told me that you think we're not playing fair with Castro. That has come up."

"That's right, but I didn't tell Field anything. He already knew. Field was very concerned that Castro would send someone into this country to try to kill you."

"You can't tell someone like Field that we're trying to kill Castro," the President stated flatly. "That man is an informant—and that would make you a spy."

Marilyn laughed. "Really, Jack! Marilyn Monroe is a foreign

agent. Where's my microfilm?" She picked up the pillow and looked beneath it.

"Well, you shouldn't be talking to someone like Field. You shouldn't talk to him at all but you certainly shouldn't tell him that we're trying to kill Castro," the President pressed.

"Let me say it one more time," Marilyn said, "Field knows. He told me all about it."

At 2:30 A.M., the journalist, Merriman Smith, was awakened by loud knocking on the door of his apartment. Agents of the Secret Service spoke to him about his appearance at Arthur Krim's party for the President. They wanted to know who had invited him. He told them he had been invited by Richard Adler, the show's producer. Later, he told Adler about the late night grilling he experienced at the hands of the President's private security detail.

"*They wanted to make sure I didn't write about Marilyn and Bobby. I wasn't going to write about them anyway. I'm not a gossip columnist,*" Smith told Adler.

Chapter 26

"We are contacting all groups (DOS) to organize one united front with a coordinator. You name him or we elect him. Tell us. Will try kill Fidel today. Andres OK but still hiding. His men gone to hill. Want to know what can be used."

Luis Jorge
May 3, 1961
Declassified CIA cable

J. Edgar Hoover got out of the limousine under the arch of the White House and again carried his black valise through the halls to the Oval Office. The weather had turned warm in Washington on May 24, 1962, and so had the news. Hoover had asked to see the President and Attorney General in a private meeting and his wish was immediately granted. John and Robert Kennedy were waiting for the Director of the F.B.I. when Hoover arrived.

"The more I look, the more I find," Hoover said as he sat in a chair in front of the President's desk. Robert Kennedy did not sit, but rather paced around the President's desk while Hoover spoke.

"And what plot have you uncovered today," the President asked Hoover with a twinkle in his eye.

"We'll, I think there is a plot, Mr. President, and I'll be frank with you, I don't like the direction this thing is going."

"What do you have, Edgar?" the Attorney General asked.

"This government pays for information, does it not?" Hoover continued. "For good intelligence, we are willing to give defectors and others money if their information is good."

"That's right," Robert Kennedy said. He was in charge of the darkest secrets in the administration.

"And we have to assume the other side is willing to pay out some money for good information?" Hoover said.

"Of course. Now get to the point," Robert Kennedy said. He wanted the information without the buildup.

"I keep hearing that I'm meddling in the private life of the President I serve," Hoover protested, "but I assure you that my motives have only been the welfare of my country. What you fellows do on your own time is fine with me, as long as it doesn't involve the security of our country."

John and Robert Kennedy exchanged glances and remained quiet.

"And I would like to apologize to you that this information does involve your private life," Hoover continued. "But I think you will soon understand that there has been a real and important reason for my concern about some of the President's friends. When I spoke to you in March, Mr. President, I was suspicious that Miss Monroe had passed national security secrets to Frederick Vanderbilt Field in Mexico City. You assured me that Miss Monroe did not have any significant national security secrets to pass because she did not know for certain that our government had plans to assassinate Fidel Castro."

"That's right," the President conceded.

"Is there any other secret Miss Monroe might have?" Hoover asked. "Is there anything else in this government as sensitive and dangerous as the plot to kill Castro?"

"No," Robert Kennedy answered. The Attorney General was the definitive source on secret national security operations.

"Let me ask, and I know it seems like a ridiculous question, but is this government trying to assassinate any other foreign leaders?" Hoover asked.

"No," the President affirmed.

"We are not trying to assassinate Mr. Khrushchev?" Hoover asked.

"Absolutely not," the President said. He turned to his brother.

"No," Robert Kennedy said.

"Marilyn Monroe sees a psychiatrist in Santa Monica, California by the name of Ralph Greenson," Hoover said. "Dr. Greenson—born Romeo Greenschpoon in Brooklyn, has been involved in Communist activities since his days in New York."

John Kennedy laughed. "Edgar, I can't believe you think this psychiatrist is a threat to our national security."

Hoover continued. "Ralph Greenson went to Switzerland for Medical School, where he met Hildegard Troesch. Her family ran the rooming house where Dr. Greenson lived. Her brother is currently the leader of the Communist Party in Switzerland. That means that Greenson has an open line to the Russians. But there's more. Dr. Greenson did his medical training at Cedars of Lebanon Hospital in Hollywood where he met Dr. Hyman Engelberg. Dr. Engelberg remains active in Communist Party activities in the Los Angeles area. He and Dr. Greenson have remained close personal friends. During the second world war, Dr. Greenson met John Murray, the founder of a Communist front organization. His wife, Eunice Murray, is currently Marilyn Monroe's housekeeper. It is not clear that Marilyn Monroe knows about Mrs. Murray's background or relationship to Dr. Greenson. John Murray's brother, Churchill Murray, runs a radio station in Mexico City which features pro-Communist propaganda. Churchill Murray met Marilyn Monroe during her recent visit to Mexico City and drove her to see Frederick Field. We believe that Miss Monroe's visit to see Mr. Field was orchestrated by Dr. Greenson."

Hoover paused and took a handkerchief out of his pocket and wiped his mouth.

"We appreciate your efforts, Edgar," Robert Kennedy said

and then smiled at his brother. "But we have also been keeping an eye on Miss Monroe. CIA agents followed her in Mexico City and we are generally well informed as to her activities there. We do not believe that she gave Mr. Field any national security secrets. It is not clear to me what she could give them."

"You would agree that if she told Mr. Field that our government was planning the death of Mr. Castro that our national security, indeed your personal security, would be violated?" Hoover asked.

"Of course. We understand that. But the Soviets aren't going to take Marilyn Monroe's word for that," Robert Kennedy said.

"I understand," Hoover said. "But if Marilyn Monroe's word were backed up in some meaningful way, then that would constitute very important information."

"It would," the President agreed. "It certainly would."

Hoover again wiped the corners of his mouth with the handkerchief.

"Three weeks ago, two weeks before the birthday party, Dr. Greenson left the United States and went to Switzerland," Hoover said. "We were surprised that he decided to make the trip at this time because he has an obligation, of which I am sure you are aware, to keep Marilyn Monroe working at her movie. She depends on him to keep her spirits up and when he is not around, she frequently can not work."

The President looked at the Attorney General. "I wasn't aware that her doctor was going anywhere," the President said to his brother.

"I didn't know," Robert Kennedy said.

"We have reason to believe that Dr. Greenson tapes his discussions with Miss Monroe, discussions which are obviously of a highly personal nature. We have reason to believe that Dr. Greenson may have taken some of these tapes on his recent trip to Switzerland."

"Why did he say he was going to Switzerland?" Bobby asked.

"He told the studio that his wife needed medical treatments at a special hospital there," Hoover answered. "We have determined that his wife is not ill. She has not been treated in any hospital in Switzerland."

"You think Dr. Greenson is making a little money in Switzerland?" the President asked.

"Dr. Greenson did not stay in Switzerland," Hoover went on. "He has now gone on to Germany. Our agents have lost contact with him there but we believe he may be in East Germany right now. We don't know what he's giving them."

"She's a spy," the President said blankly. "She's an unwitting spy."

"This guy Greenson sounds like he needs a little kick in the ass," Robert Kennedy said. "We ought to put him in a cell for few months and talk to him."

"Not so fast," the President said to his brother. "Maybe we need him on our side."

"We have to assume that Miss Monroe has told Dr. Greenson—perhaps on multiple occasions—what she knows about various secret operations," Hoover reasoned. "She has also told him about her relationship with the President. She has probably told him things that she thinks about, but would not talk openly about. Psychiatric interviews are not rehearsed, and I'm sure she doesn't even know what she's told him and that would make the tapes even more believable. Whatever the contents of the tapes, this fellow Greenson clearly has high level connections to the Communist Party and it appears to me that he might be using those connections to sell the Russians some material that they think is valuable."

"It's over," Robert Kennedy surmised. "Even if Marilyn is on our side, her friends are not. We have to cut off connections to Marilyn, and we have to get her to realize that she can't talk about national security secrets. This is potentially explosive. She could leak this whole operation to the press. This could cost us Cuba."

"Mr. President," Hoover began, "it is dangerous for you to continue to see Marilyn Monroe in any context. If she sees you, or speaks to you on the telephone, her words will be taken much more seriously by the Russians. I think you will need to cut her off completely."

"Consider that done," Robert Kennedy asserted. "I'll see to that. Her connections to the President will be terminated immediately!"

"We're going to need some real help here, Bobby," the President said. "We're going to have to figure out a way to damage her reputation, maybe circulate the rumor that she is a crazy drug addict, or something like that."

"That's right. We have to plant a seed of doubt in the minds of the Soviet leadership that Marilyn can't be taken seriously," the Attorney General agreed.

"If we can suggest that she is mentally ill or unstable, they will not be willing to take whatever they have heard from Greenson as hard evidence of our intentions."

"Yes," Bobby agreed. "And that's the nicest thing we can do for her. The alternatives are not as nice."

Chapter 27

"She was deliriously happy. What made that day different from any other day? I don't know. Maybe she was relieved because the scene contained only a few lines of dialogue. As I watched her, I thought to myself, 'Maybe we'll get this project finished after all.'"

Henry Weinstein
Producer, *Something's Got to Give*

Seeing the clippings from the newspapers brought it all back to her. It had been such a splendid moment. And they couldn't take it away from her. The photographs showed her standing in front of the President, her hand cupped around the lower part of her breast, seducing him with the *Happy Birthday Song*. At long last, she was escaping the world of make believe. Marilyn was not just an act of fiction anymore. She had crossed the line. She was involved with the President of the United States.

"Another glass of Dom," Marilyn said. She held up her empty glass and the Dom Perignon was poured. Marilyn was sitting in her bungalow on the Fox Lot, celebrating the end of a very successful week of filming *Something's Got to Give*.

"Careful, Marilyn," Pat Newcomb warned her. "You are still meeting Larry up at Schwab's. You're going to need your best judgment when you look at those pictures."

Pat was referring to Lawrence Schiller. He was a young photographer who worked for *Paris Match*.

On the Wednesday following the Gala, Marilyn did something she had not done for 15 years, and something a major movie star had never done: she had filmed a scene completely in the nude. Schiller recorded the scene with still photographs.

It had been Cukor's idea. There was a point in the script where Marilyn was trying to lure Dean Martin away from Cyd Charisse with a midnight swim. The scene was meant to give an impression that Marilyn was swimming naked. But she was to be actually covered by a Jean Louis designed silk bikini. The fabric used was from the same cloth as had been used to fashion her now famous dress for the Gala. But Cukor hadn't liked the illusion of nudity. The idea of a near nude scene wouldn't sell his film. So Cukor approached Marilyn with the idea that she spontaneously decide to do the scene completely nude.

Marilyn agreed instantly.

"This needs to be a spur of the moment thing," Marilyn said. She knew intuitively that her sexual appeal was more powerful when it was thought to be completely spontaneous.

Pat Newcomb called in Lawrence Schiller to shoot the stills. *"And bring plenty of film. Marilyn has that swimming scene tomorrow, and, knowing Marilyn, she might slip out of her suit."*

Marilyn knew that her nemesis, Elizabeth Taylor, had filmed a near nude scene in *Cleopatra*. For Marilyn to do a nude scene would force the press to carefully check who had the best body to flaunt. It was a comparison Marilyn was anxious to see addressed. Taylor was a little chunky. Marilyn was in perfect shape.

That Wednesday morning, Marilyn had been covered with a gooey body makeup to preserve her body temperature during the anticipated hours in the pool. Her hair was also specially treated to prevent damage from the chlorinated water. When she walked out in the blue robe, Schiller went into action. His motor driven Nikon camera caught Marilyn as she allowed the robe to gently slip from her shoulders. Then she got in the pool, where the water had been heated to 94 degrees. In all, she was in the water for more than four hours.

As Marilyn shrugged and posed and winked at the cameras inside the swimming pool stage, pandemonium broke out across the Fox Lot. Word that Marilyn was doing a nude scene quickly swept from office to office. It was necessary to post five extra guards at each entrance to the soundstage as the excitement grew. *Something's Got to Give* was going to have a tremendous publicity boost with the sensational footage being recorded.

The commotion exhilarated Marilyn. Seeing the security men hold back the crowd of Fox employees confirmed for her the power she had over the instinctual drives of men. She always knew she had it but it was nice to see her appeal had lost none of its power.

As she went to meet Schiller that Friday afternoon, she felt the best she had felt in years. She was one of the biggest stars in Hollywood, one of the most famous women in the world. Her performance at the Gala had given her a week of intense publicity. She was linked with the most powerful man in the world. And the nude swimming scene was going to be in every major magazine the world over. She needed to make sure that none of the photographs Schiller had taken showed too much of her. Marilyn knew there was a thin line between what was sexually interesting and what was grossly indecent. She had made a career out of walking that line.

When she saw the negatives of the photographs, she was sitting in Schiller's Thunderbird outside Schwab's Drugstore. Marilyn was holding the negatives up to the light and checking her positions. Any shot which was questionable, Marilyn cut in half with a large pair of scissors.

"You know what kind of response pictures like this will have in France?" Schiller asked her.

"They will be damned in France," Marilyn responded. "And every magazine showing them will be sold out."

Schiller laughed.

"I can't believe you were able to get through the shoot. I've heard that you've been sick."

"I've never felt better," Marilyn effused. "Things seem to finally be coming together for me now."

She cut another couple of negatives in half. Schiller was gathering the pieces of the negatives and shredding them further. Having the confidence of Marilyn Monroe could mean a lot to his career.

When she got back to her house on 5th Helena late that afternoon, Marilyn wanted to get some rest. Performing at the Gala had been a stress on her system but it had been important to Jack, and she had wanted to do it. Because she realized that her performance at the Gala had not gone over well at Fox, she wanted to be sure she put in a full week of work for Cukor when she got back. So the last week had been full of concentrated effort. The nude swimming scene was going to turn out to be one of her all time best. So all the effort was going to be worthwhile.

Next week was going to be hard, too. Cukor was going to work the cast as hard as possible. He wanted to get the movie in the can before somebody else got sick. So Marilyn needed to bank some rest over the weekend.

"Frank has been calling," Pat Newcomb said when Marilyn walked into the kitchen at 5th Helena.

"Frank Sinatra?"

"Yes. He's been calling from Australia. I have talked to him several times since I got back from work."

"What do you mean you've talked to him? What did he say?"

"Marilyn, why don't you call him back? I don't want to you to get all upset with me?"

"What did he say?"

"Call him. I don't know what he's going to say."

"You know. Why would he call me from Australia? Is somebody hurt?"

"Marilyn! Just call him. I'm out of this."

Marilyn went over to the telephone and asked an operator to connect her at a number Frank left with Pat. They were in Marilyn's kitchen and dining room area and Marilyn watched Pat boil some vegetables while she waited for the connection.

She kicked off her shoes and walked around the room with the telephone which was tethered by a long cord. Finally, Frank's voice came on the other end of the line. He was friendly and supportive as he asked her about the Presidential Gala. They talked about the nude swimming scene. But Marilyn sensed that he had some news. Frank must be calling for some reason other than to congratulate her on some publicity photographs.

"I think you need to brace yourself with Kennedy," Sinatra finally told her.

"Brace myself?"

"You know. Make sure you don't get too involved."

"Frank, I am involved. I've been involved for more than a year. I just put my entire career at risk to appear at his birthday party."

"I know," Frank said. "But, I just think you need to understand that this is an election year. The President isn't going to be able to take any negative publicity. He might not be able to spend much time with you."

Marilyn lay down on her couch and threw her legs over the back. She didn't like what she was hearing from Frank.

"It's not that kind of relationship. He wants to see me."

"I know he has," Frank said. "You just need to understand that he can take only so much heat before he has to pull the plug."

"What do you mean 'heat?'"

"Marilyn, it's obvious. He's the President. You're a sexy movie star. He can't be seen to be too close to you at this time—or any other, for that matter."

"It depends."

"No, it doesn't depend."

"It depends on what he has in mind."

"Marilyn, it doesn't have anything to do with what the President wants. He's the President. He can't be seen to be involved with an actress—no matter how big she is."

Marilyn was silent for a long moment. Pat was putting the dishes on the table for dinner.

"Frank, did Jack call you?"

"No," he said after a pause. "He didn't call me. I've just seen all the publicity out here. I know you're headed for a fall on this one."

"But he didn't tell you it was over or anything."

"No."

"Doesn't he like me?"

"Marilyn, will you stop it? Of course, he likes you. But it's obvious to me—it's an election year—he can't have pictures of you squeezing your tits in his face all over the newspapers and then visit you in your swell new house. It would be political suicide."

There was a pause as Marilyn tried to understand why Frank had called her.

"Marilyn, you need to think about what I've said. He's the President and he can't be involved with a movie star. There can't even be a hint that's he involved with you. Can't you see that?"

"We have a relationship!"

"You have to remember that I sang for Jack in the campaign. I sang for him and I organized for him. We were buddies."

"I know you were."

"But, we aren't any more. Jack wouldn't even stay at my house."

"I don't think you were involved with him in the same way as I am."

Sinatra let that one pass over his head.

"The point is Jack is a politician. That's all he is. He's not a movie star. If he gets bad publicity, he fails as a politician. So, if I happen to be friends with Sam Giancana and Johnny Rosselli, Jack can't be friends with me. It's that simple."

"And that's all right with you?"

"It has nothing to do with what's all right with me. It has to do with the fact that he can't be seen to be friends with a guy who is friends with certain Mafia types. Frankly, *I think the Kennedys just use you, and then they throw you out.* There were days I felt like Jack had thrown me out like so much garbage."

"You did?"

"Sure."

"And you think that's all right?"

"Marilyn, it's the whole political way. They use you for what you're worth, then they get rid of you."

Marilyn was quiet for most of dinner. She had never felt better than she had that afternoon. She was euphoric. Then she had come home and talked to Frank. Suddenly, she didn't feel very good. All she wanted was to be close to Jack. And she was. As she looked through the sliding glass door which led out to her pool, Marilyn sensed that her final conversation with the President might have gone too far, maybe she had been too strong in her argument that he call a truce with Castro."

"I'm going to call him," Marilyn announced.

"I wouldn't do that," Pat advised.

"Why not?"

"Let him call you. Don't start to chase him."

"I'm not chasing him. I just need to know where he stands."

Pat stood up and came over next to Marilyn and gave her a sisterly hug.

"I want it to work out. But if it doesn't, I still work for you. I want you to be happy, and I want you to be successful. Just because I warned you this might happen, doesn't mean you should take it out on me."

"What might happen? Nothing's happened. Frank called me. That's all that's happened."

Pat stood up and walked toward her bedroom.

"I hope it all works out, Marilyn," Pat said as she entered her room. "I hope it works out. And I hope we'll be friends forever." She shut her bedroom door.

Marilyn continued to stare out into space. Why would Frank call her? He might really want to brace her for some bumps in

230 J. Arthur Jensen

the road. Or, he might have known something. Jack might have called him. She looked over at the telephone.

There was nothing worse than chasing a man. Men don't like to be chased. They don't like to feel trapped. But there was no possible way Jack was going to stop seeing her. He liked the excitement she brought to his life. It was after 11 o'clock in Washington, but she was going to have to call him. She had to know if something was going on.

She dialed the President's personal number. She had dialed the number many times before. She didn't want Jackie to answer, but Marilyn had to know.

"White House," the operator answered.

"What do you mean 'White House?'"

"You've reached the White House. May I help you, Miss?" the operator said.

"This was the President's number. His private number."

"The President's private number has been changed."

"What's the new number?"

"I'm sorry, Miss. I can't give you the President's private number."

Marilyn's heart began to pound. She knew what was happening, but she didn't want to accept it.

She put down her telephone. Jack was cutting her off—there was no other explanation. After all the publicity of the gala, the President felt that he needed to not see her for a while. But why didn't he call himself? She had known John Kennedy since the early 50's. Why wouldn't he simply call her and explain the situation. She could accept that.

Marilyn went to her bathroom and took her bottle of Nembutal from one of the shelves. She took two pills. She washed them down with a glass of water. Then, she opened the bottle again, and took a few more. Because she took Nembutal almost every night, her body had grown quite tolerant of the medication. On a good night, she needed more than a couple just to fall to sleep. This wasn't going to be a good night. She felt alone, frightened, used, and she wanted to sleep.

"White House," the operator kept saying as Marilyn tried to fall to sleep. "White House." But the pills calmed her, and eventually, she felt less anxious, then less pained. Finally, she fell into a sound sleep.

Chapter 28

"The only way to get rid of Castro is to kill him . . . and I really mean it."

Robert McNamara as quoted by Richard Goodwin
May 1961

AM/GOOSE was not his real name. It was a name used only by the CIA. He was a well built Latin man with flashing dark eyes and a beautiful olive skin. Women were frequently attracted to him but they were not his passion. His passion was to reclaim what had been taken from him. He had been born into a prominent family—a family with significant holdings in Havana—and lived a life of elite schools and social clubs. But that had all changed when Castro took control of Cuba. His family's business had been "nationalized" and he had been left without money and without a future.

Like many displaced Cubans, AM/GOOSE wanted nothing more than he wanted to see Castro gone. With Castro out of the way, it was possible that he would get his land and lifestyle back. AM/GOOSE was recruited by the CIA, agreed to dedicate his life to the removal of Castro, and to never admit that he had been involved in a plot to remove the Cuban revolutionary. After months of waiting for his chance, AM/GOOSE was contacted by the CIA and told to go to a training facility where he would be taught the fine art of political assassination.

After he had established contact with the CIA agents in the old town of Antigua, AM/GOOSE was taken to a ranch outside the former capital city. The agents drove him to a building away from the main residence. Although the building was nicely furnished and had several typewriters set up on tables, a large pig ran loose in the courtyard. AM/GOOSE was impressed that a large pig would be kept in the courtyard of such a nice building.

AM/GOOSE stared at the two agents. Neither introduced himself. One was tall, had light brown hair, closely cut, and blue eyes. The other was shorter, heavier, with dark hair and dark eyes. The tall one was dressed in a gray business suit. The shorter man wore an open shirt and khaki pants.

"We keep giving you guys the tools, but you can't seem to get the job done," the tall man said.

"I don't know anything about what has been tried before," AM/GOOSE said.

"We'll it has been pretty pathetic," the tall man continued. "We give you guns, we give you poisons, we give you cigars which would kill him with a single puff. Nothing. Castro continues to enjoy excellent health."

"These things are not my fault," AM/GOOSE asserted.

"That's the other thing," the dark headed man said. "We never work with the same men. Every time we do this, we start fresh with a new recruit."

"Perhaps to keep Castro from suspecting something,"

The tall man sat down in a wooden chair. A framed black and white photograph of two boys walking on a sand dune hung from the white, plastered wall.

"The basic idea of this modality is to poison the target with something he routinely uses. Obviously, you will have to get close enough to him to be able to deliver the poison."

"If he takes something regularly, why would it poison him?" AM/GOOSE asked.

The two men looked at each other and exchanged smiles.

"Exactly," the tall man continued. "The public never thinks

that something you take regularly would ever kill you. But that is exactly the reason this modality is so effective. Every drug—from alcohol to dope—has a range of safety. If a man drinks too much, he can die. The dose becomes too great. Castro is reputed to use cocaine. We understand that he uses it as a stimulant. In small doses, particularly if it is chewed, cocaine is rather safe. But when it is snorted, or smoked, the amount delivered can be much greater—even toxic."

AM/GOOSE looked skeptically at his two CIA teachers.

"But you cannot simply urge him to smoke cocaine."

"We have some experience in these matters," the dark headed man said. "If you attempt to take someone's life, make sure you succeed. If you merely wound him, he will come back stronger than before and you can't predict what he might do. You must be certain that you deliver the entire dose to him. Never kill a man half way."

"How do I kill him?" AM/GOOSE asked.

The man with the light eyes stood up and walked over to a small, black suitcase on a nearby table. He popped up the clasps and lifted the top—exposing a set of medical syringes and small brown bottles of liquid covered with rubber stoppers. Aluminum bands held the stoppers in place. Large bore needles for medical injection were next to the small brown bottles.

"Cocaine is quite soluble in alcohol. If Castro were to drink this mixture, he would not be effected. The cocaine would be cleared by the liver. But if the solution of alcohol and cocaine is injected into Castro, he will die. It is that simple."

"Why don't you just let me shoot him?" AM/GOOSE asked.

The agents looked at him quizzically.

"We've been trying to get you guys to shoot him for a year and a half. We gave the people in the Dominican Republic guns and Trujillo was dead within the week. We give you guys guns and then we get a request for poison—then a request for a Botulinum laced cigar. The surest way to do the job is with a gun," the tall man concluded.

"But also the most obvious," his shorter companion added. "Perhaps they want it to look like a drug overdose so as to confuse the issue."

AM/GOOSE stood up and walked over to the table where the small carrying case displayed the syringes, needles, and bottles of cocaine and alcohol. He tried to pick one of the bottles out of the case. It wouldn't come.

"Yank it out of there," the tall man said. "You have to play with these things so you know how to use them. Now, take out one of the syringes."

AM/GOOSE pulled one of the syringes out of the case. He tried to slide the plunger back, but it seemed stuck.

"They sterilize these things and they get a little stuck," the tall man explained. "You have to get a bit of liquid in the syringe before you start. When you're ready to use it, you need it immediately. There is no time to get the thing ready. Attach one of the needles."

AM/GOOSE twisted the plunger against the cylinder of the syringe. It broke free. The plunger went up and down in the cylinder, but it was catching against the walls. He lifted up one of the needles and attached it to the syringe. He looked up at his tutors. They nodded their approval. With some force, he then pulled one of the brown bottles out of the case. He plunged the needle on the syringe through the rubber stopper on the brown bottle. He tried to pull back. Only a small amount of fluid returned.

"You have to push some air into the bottle," the tall man said. "There will be an air lock if you don't. Take the syringe out. Now, pull in some air. All right, now put the needle back in the bottle and push in the air."

AM/GOOSE followed instructions. A clear fluid returned into the syringe. He pushed in some more air. More fluid returned into the syringe. He filled the syringe and held it up.

"How do you propose that I get this villain to sit still for the shot?"

"There are two possibilities. You can recruit a doctor into

your plan and have him deliver the shot. Or, you can have another man or two hold him down. It's one shot. Once it is in, he will have an immediate change in his heart rhythm. His heart will fibrillate and he will die."

"Just like that?"

"Just like that. There are many drugs which will do the same thing. But this is something he is thought to use anyway. If the needle mark does not show, there is no way of knowing how the cocaine got into his system. If you put some cocaine in his nose, an obvious assumption will be made.

AM/GOOSE pushed a little bit of the liquid out the needle, spraying the clear liquid into the air.

"Do you feel like you can do it?" the shorter and thicker agent asked.

"If I can hold him down. Or, if we can devise a way to immobilize him, I should be able to do it. I would hate to have him pull free and escape."

"Have you ever caught a pig, my friend?" the shorter man asked.

"Not often, " AM/GOOSE admitted.

"You might gain a bit of experience here today. The drug you have in that syringe works equally well with pigs as with men."

The agents led him over to a door which opened out to the courtyard. There, the pig walked around on a paved surface. It seemed startled by the motion of the door.

For the next few minutes, AM/GOOSE chased the pig around the courtyard with the syringe in hand. The agents looked on. Finally, he put down the syringe and caught the pig by looping his belt around the pig's head. Then he dragged the pig over to the syringe. Holding the syringe with one hand, he forced the pig against a wall and plunged the needle into the rump of the animal. Despite the pig's attempts to escape, the syringe was emptied. Within a few moments, the pig quit moving. AM/GOOSE looked up at his CIA tutors. They nodded.

"There is only one other detail that needs reinforcement," the tall man said when the lesson was over and AM/GOOSE was ready to be taken back to town. "This is a national security operation. We have our rules. There is a penalty for talking about this operation and the penalty is death."

AM/GOOSE stared into the tall man's blue eyes. There was no hint of equivocation.

"Do you understand?" the agent asked AM/GOOSE.

"I understand," AM/GOOSE answered.

"The lives of a hundred million Americans might be endangered if this operation were to come to light," the tall man continued. "A war could start. We're not going to let that happen."

Chapter 29

"What happened," George Smathers told me, "was that she, like naturally all women, would like to be close to the president. And then after he had been associated with her some, she began to ask for an opportunity to come to Washington and come to the White House and that sort of thing. That's when Jack asked me to see what I would do to help him in that respect by talking to her." Monroe, Smathers said without amplification, had "made some demands." Smathers said he arranged for a mutual friend to "go talk to Marilyn Monroe about putting a bridle on herself and on her mouth and not talking too much, because it was getting to be a story around the country."

Seymour Hersh
The Dark Side of Camelot

Peter Lawford drove up the curved road from the Pacific Coast Highway and turned left on San Vicente Boulevard. It was almost 10 o'clock at night and there were few other cars going toward Brentwood. Marilyn was not going to like what he had to tell her, but tell her he must. Lawford lit a cigarette at a red light and then proceeded to Carmelina and the Helenas.

He pulled into Marilyn's driveway and stopped the car. Lights were on in Marilyn's house and Lawford walked up to the front door and rang the bell.

Mrs. Murray answered the door. Lawford went in and waited in the living room for Marilyn.

"Peter," Marilyn exclaimed as she came out of her bedroom in a bathrobe. Her hair was pulled back into a pony tail. She embraced him. "Eunice, bring Peter some Scotch."

Mrs. Murray went into the kitchen.

"I'm afraid I don't have anything good to say," Peter told her. He had already had something to drink.

"No, I didn't think you were here to give me good news," Marilyn replied soberly.

Lawford lit another cigarette and threw the match into the empty fireplace next to his chair. Marilyn handed him an ash tray and then she sat down on the couch opposite Peter. Mrs. Murray brought in a glass of Scotch and handed it to him.

"I can't believe you just call the White House and ask to speak to Jack," he started. "You always were willing to use a code name and keep the publicity to a minimum."

"Something's up," Marilyn retorted. "Jack won't talk to me."

"That's the reason I'm here," Peter said. He inhaled the cigarette smoke and blew it into the air above his head. "There are some problems."

"Just tell me," Marilyn said. "He's still mad that I saw Field in Mexico."

"That's part of it," Lawford agreed. "But I think it's more than that. The publicity is getting to be too much for him."

Marilyn leaned back onto the couch and crossed her legs.

"We've managed the publicity up to now," Marilyn asserted. "He's just acting like a big baby. He's wrong about Cuba and he hates to hear that he is wrong about anything."

"He thinks that you are a security risk."

"That's ridiculous and you know it."

"That's what Bobby told me. Look Marilyn, you can't call Jack anymore. Bobby told me that you are not to call either one of them, and you are not to write any letters—nothing. You stay in your world and they stay in their world."

Marilyn stood up and walked over to the sliding glass doors which separated the living room from the patio and swimming pool. "I can't believe it," she muttered. "They are really trying to cut me off."

Peter ground the tip of his cigarette into the glass ash tray, stood up and followed Marilyn. He continued to drink the Scotch.

"I don't know what you said to that guy in Mexico," Peter said. "It sounds like they think that you are trying to make foreign policy or something. They don't think that just because you've had a special relationship with the President that you have a right to press your views."

"I've overstepped my place," Marilyn suggested.

"Exactly," Lawford confirmed.

"Let me tell you something. I haven't overstepped my place. Anyone who knows what I know would try to help out. I know the President and I know some people in Mexico who think that the President is getting himself in trouble. I'm just trying to help prevent something bad from happening, that's all."

"It's over," Lawford repeated. "My job is to tell you that your relationship with the President is over. Bobby doesn't want any contact. Period. None. He was pretty emphatic about that."

"I can't believe this."

"Well, you've got to believe it. I don't think you know anything more about Cuba than I do. I don't understand why you think that your views are more important than the views of any other private citizen. If you're talking to some guy from Mexico or anybody else, then you're not playing by the rules. What choice do you give them?"

"I have a right to dissent," Marilyn said. "Any American has a right to dissent."

"We'll see about that," Peter replied. "We'll see."

Chapter 30

"Miss Monroe is not just being temperamental, she's mentally ill, perhaps seriously."

Peter Levathes
President, 20th Century Fox
June 8, 1962

John Kennedy looked across the Cabinet table at his Secretary of Defense, Robert McNamara. Next to McNamara sat Dean Rusk, Kennedy's Secretary of State. Other cabinet members circled the table. His brother, the Attorney General, was reporting on the latest negotiations with Castro.

"They don't want farm equipment," Robert Kennedy stated. "They want cash."

"If we give them cash for the prisoners, it is going to look like we caved into a ransom demand," Rusk said in a quiet voice. "We've already said that we're not going to pay ransom for the exiles."

They were discussing the fate of the Cuban exiles who had been taken prisoner at the Bay of Pigs. Castro had the exiles safely locked up and was arguing that the American government should pay reparations for all the damage the failed Bay of Pigs invasion had cost his government. When the Americans would pay up, he would release the prisoners.

"It's blackmail," the President said as he leaned back into his chair. "That guy has us right where he wants us."

"We could call it aid," McNamara suggested. "We could give him money as a humanitarian gesture—maybe soften the ransom idea."

"We need to get those exiles out of there as soon as we can," the President acknowledged. "If they start to die in Castro's prisons, there will be more calls to invade."

After the meeting, the Kennedy brothers waited for the others to leave. Then they stepped outside the White House and stood among the columns which ran along the courtyard.

"I can't believe we have to actually leave the White House to have a discussion," the President said.

"We do for this kind of discussion," his brother said. "I need to give you an update on the Cuba project. Out here, there is no chance that we'll be overheard."

"What's the report?" the President asked.

"We may have our first real break," Bobby reported. "The CIA has established contact with one of Castro's best friends—a man named Cubela. Cubela thinks that he can do the job."

John Kennedy squinted into the sunshine of the June day. He rubbed his chin. "We keep training them and nothing ever happens," he complained.

"I get the feeling that this is going to be different," Bobby said. "His name *is AM/LASH—Rolando Cubela Secades,* and our guys think that he's the real thing. I mean, we've been training some of the Cuban exiles, some of the malcontents, but they can't get close enough to Castro. Cubela is an insider."

"How so?"

"He was one of Castro's trusted lieutenants in the Revolution. The word on Cubela is that he was the one who killed Batista's Chief of Intelligence."

The President nodded and squinted into his brothers eyes. "What makes you think that he's not working for Castro?"

"That's the danger," the Attorney General agreed. "If he's still working for Castro, then hiring him to kill his boss is going to tell Castro what our intentions really are in completely indisputable terms. I'm worried about that. But the CIA thinks that he has become disaffected with Castro. Cubela—I guess we should call him AM/LASH—thinks that the Revolution has backfired, and he wants to work for us."

"I don't know," the President worried. "This would pose a new risk. How is this going to be different than using our own guys, other than increasing the risk?"

"We don't have anyone who can get anywhere close to Castro," Bobby admitted. "We send them in and nothing happens. We've tried to shoot him, poison him—no one has really come close. Cubela can do it, it is only a question of whether he's a dangle. If he's really working for Castro, then we're screwed."

The President walked down the colonnade and looked back through a window into the White House where a secretary was working on a typewriter.

"What does he want?" John Kennedy asked.

"That's where things get interesting," Bobby said. "He wants a *high powered rifle with a scope*, some *money*, and the *personal approval of Robert Kennedy*. He's making a big deal about whether I would personally approve the hit."

"He's trying to find out how high up in the administration the plots to kill Castro go," the President deduced. "They know men have been sent into Cuba to kill Castro, but they don't know for sure whether we're behind those men, of if they are working for themselves. The *personal approval of Robert Kennedy* leaves nothing to the imagination. If we tell this man that he has the *personal approval of Robert Kennedy*, then Castro knows I'm involved."

"*A high powered rifle with a scope?*" the Attorney General repeated. "Sounds like this fellow can get close enough to get off a pretty good shot but still wants the opportunity to make a run for it."

"I agree," the President said. "The question is whether he would actually take the shot, or would he find a bunch of reasons why it can't be done, in which case all we have accomplished is to blow our cover."

"From what Marilyn told you, Castro already thinks you're behind the attempts."

"Yes," the President acknowledged. "And if her psychiatrist is talking to the Russians, then they would know for sure. Do we have her under control yet?"

"She's about to be fired from the studio. Her doctor came back from Switzerland in time to argue his case, but she's going to get fired tomorrow. The studio is going to say she's nuts and that she's incapable of working. They're going to sue her."

"Jesus," the President said. "Don't you think that's a little extreme?"

"This situation is extreme," Bobby continued. "If she tells the newspapers that we're going to invade Cuba or try to kill Castro, we've got to have some way of defending ourselves."

"She wouldn't do that."

"We don't know what she will do. One thing we do know is that we need to get some leverage on her. We're going to start doing that tomorrow."

Chapter 31

ATTY GENERAL AND MRS. ROBERT F. KENNEDY
1962 JUN 13 PM
HICKORY HILL MCLEANVIR DEAR ATTORNEY
GENERAL AND MRS. ROBERT KENNEDY:
I WOULD HAVE BEEN DELIGHTED TO HAVE AC-
CEPTED YOUR INVITATION HONORING PAT AND
PETER LAWFORD. UNFORTUNATELY I AM IN-
VOLVED IN A FREEDOM RIDE PROTESTING THE
LOSS OF THE MINORITY RIGHTS BELONGING TO
THE FEW REMAINING EARTHBOUND STARS. AF-
TER ALL, ALL WE DEMANDED WAS OUR RIGHT TO
TWINKLE.

MARILYN MONROE

Ralph Greenson looked at Marilyn with all the
compassion he could muster. "I have failed, Marilyn,"
Greenson reported. "Fox has just announced that you have been
fired."

Marilyn rocked back in the chair next to her swimming pool
and closed her eyes. She would not remember June 8, 1962 fondly.
She had never been fired from a movie before.

"It is quite natural for someone to be upset at time like this,"
Greenson suggested. He had just driven over to Marilyn's house so
as to personally tell her the bad news. "I told them that you would

be able to finish the project—I gave them my personal assur-
ance that you would show up and work every single day. But
they weren't listening. They didn't really care what I said. They
have wanted to fire you since Monday and there was nothing
Mickey or I could have said to get them to change their minds.
The radio report said that Fox has filed a $1 million law suit
against you for breach of contract."

"You're joking," Marilyn asserted.

"I wish I were," Greenson replied. "They are claiming that
you are incapable of performing your duties on the set. They are
saying some very mean things."

"Like what?"

"They are saying that you are mentally ill. There have been
suggestions that you are using drugs and are incapable of
finishing your film."

Marilyn stood up and walked through the sliding glass doors
leading into her house. Greenson followed. She picked up the
telephone and placed a call to the White House. "This is Marilyn
Monroe," she told the White House operator. "I want to speak to
the President right now." She was put on hold.

"This wasn't Jack's idea," Marilyn stated to Greenson with the
telephone at her ear. "It had to be Bobby. Jack would never do
something like this, but that Bobby is mean."

"What makes you think that the Attorney General has anything
to do with this?" Greenson asked.

"Can't you see what they are doing?" Marilyn asked him.
"They are trying to destroy me. If I say that I've been the
President's girlfriend, they want to be able to say 'she's a drug
dependent nut case.' That's not going to work."

"Why would the people at Fox listen to what the government
says about an actress?" Greenson asked.

"I know how it works," Marilyn claimed. "That's what they
forget. I know how they got me fired."

"How?"

Marilyn paced around with the telephone in her hand and
waited impatiently.

"Fox is being run by some Wall Street types who are connected to the Kennedys. This Judge Rosenman is a Kennedy man—he was the one they got to settle the steel fight. Remember that? I'm going to guess that was a pretty good commission. And Ethel Kennedy's father is buying up the land that the Fox Studio is selling, or rather his company is buying up the land. Fox wouldn't do something like this to me. I'm their star. They have always made big money on me, and they are set to do it again. Why would a studio intentionally try to wreck their own movie? This hasn't come from the film side of Fox, this has Bobby Kennedy written all over it."

"Marilyn, you should try to calm down," Greenson suggested. "You're making some big assumptions there."

"No, I do not wish to have someone return my call. I want to speak to the President and I want to speak to him now!" she shouted into the telephone.

"Marilyn, I wouldn't . . ."

Marilyn slammed the receiver down and threw her telephone across the room where it banged into the wall and fell to the floor in a twisted mass of cords.

"Those dirty bastards," she screamed. She put her hands over her face and began to cry.

Greenson walked over and put his arms around her, but she pulled back from his embrace.

"First they tell you what they are doing, and then they don't want you to know about it," she said through her light sobs. "They think that they can intimidate me by getting me fired from the movie. Well, I have a few friends at Fox , too."

For the next few days, Marilyn made telephone calls to her friends at Fox. She was able to reach Spyros Skouras the day after she was fired. Skouras, her old friend and protector, was recovering from an operation in New York. Although he was the President of Fox, he had no real power. The day to day management was in the hands of the Wall Street lawyers headed by Samuel

Rosenman. Skouras denied that he had been involved in her dismissal.

Marilyn was also able to make contact with Darryl Zanuck a few days later. Zanuck, once the business genius behind the rise of the Fox Studios, was producing a movie in Europe. When he learned that Rosenman and the other lawyers were selling off the assets of the company, Zanuck was outraged. He was further outraged to learn that they had fired Marilyn Monroe. Although he did not think highly of Marilyn's work, he did have great respect for her box office value to the company. After a lengthy telephone conversation, Marilyn was able to enlist Zanuck's help to reinstate her to finish the movie.

After making contact with Skouras and Zanuck, Marilyn realized that there was a way she could finish her movie and not cave in to any pressure from the Attorney General. Skouras and Zanuck owned enough of Fox to upset the current management in a proxy fight. With Marilyn's encouragement, that's exactly what they planned to do. Judge Rosenman and his friends would be thrown out of the company, Zanuck and Skouras would reassume control, and Marilyn would finish *Something's Got to Give* without making any deals with Bobby Kennedy.

"I've got to write something," Marilyn said to her friend Pat Newcomb as they sat in the small kitchen of Marilyn's house on 5th Helena. "Is it June 13th?"

"Yes, it's the 13th, but I wouldn't write anything to Bobby," Pat Newcomb advised. "Didn't Peter Lawford say you weren't supposed to make contact with the Kennedys again?"

"That's what he said," Marilyn confirmed.

"Then I'd say just let it go. I wouldn't want to see Bobby Kennedy get irritated."

Marilyn was trying to write a telegram to the Attorney General and she wanted Pat to give her some advice on what to say.

"Bobby thinks that he can just deny me the right to voice a dissenting opinion," Marilyn asserted. "The Attorney General of the United States is trying to tell me that I don't have the right to have a minority opinion."

"What minority opinion?" Pat asked.

"Just what they're doing in Cuba. They think they have the right to get rid of Castro, I think they should stay out of what goes on in Cuba—leave that to the Cubans."

"And the Russians?" Pat asked.

"The Cubans have a right to pick their own allies," Marilyn retorted. "Look, I'm not saying that I like Communism or anything like that. I just think that I have a right to my opinion. And I think Castro has a right to his life."

"Let it go," Pat urged her. "Put the whole thing behind you and move on. You don't even know for sure that they got you fired."

"That's right," Marilyn agreed. "I'm not sure they got me fired, but I think they did. I think they got me fired because they wanted to discredit me and ruin my reputation. They think they can stamp out my dissent by trying to smear me with a bunch of lies, but it isn't going to work."

"Why won't it work?" Pat asked.

"It won't work because I'm going to fight back," Marilyn explained. "I'm going to do interviews with every major magazine in the world. You are going to make the appointments and the reporters and their photographers can come here and see for themselves. Let them ask their questions and take their pictures. Then let's see who believes that I'm some kind of crazy actress."

"But that won't get your job back, Marilyn."

"We'll see about that," Marilyn said as she penned the telegram. "Peter Lawford told me Bobby didn't want me to make any contact with him or the President. Let's see how he likes this telegram."

Chapter 32

"If my nose is broken, how quickly can we fix it?"

Marilyn Monroe to Dr. Michael Gurdin
June 14, 1962

Marilyn sat in the doctor's examination chair with a scarf over her head and her eyes covered with large, round sunglasses. Dr. Greenson paced around the room.

"Let me do the talking, all right?" Greenson asked his famous patient.

Marilyn felt a drop of fluid fall from her nose and she lifted up her finger to catch it. Touching her nose made Marilyn wince with pain. "Am I bleeding?" she asked her psychiatrist.

"No, it's just serum," Greenson assured her. "What is taking this doctor?"

They waited in the examination room for Dr. Michael Gurdin, a plastic surgeon in Beverly Hills.

"You didn't know who it was?" Greenson asked her.

"No," Marilyn whispered through her swollen nose. "Norman thought it was Joe DiMaggio. I've got news for him. That wasn't Joe DiMaggio."

Norman Jeffries, a handyman, was remodeling Marilyn's kitchen.

"I guess he could have been a thief, or maybe some kind of weird fan, or something like that," Dr. Greenson suggested.

"Right," Marilyn agreed. "Or he could have been trying to give me a message that I'm sticking my nose into other people's business."

"Oh, I don't know about that," Greenson said.

"He didn't stick around to say who sent him," Marilyn said, "assuming someone did."

Dr. Gurdin opened the door to the exam room and stepped inside. He wore a long white coat over a white button down shirt and tie.

"Marilyn!" he exclaimed with just the trace of a Southern accent. "I haven't seen you for years."

Marilyn shook his outstretched hand.

"I think it was when you worked on my nose the first time," she said. "I think you did a very nice job."

"Thank you," the doctor said, beaming his pride. "You've gotten very famous since then. But what have we here?" He looked at the swelling around Marilyn's sunglasses.

Marilyn slowly removed the sunglasses, revealing a black eye and a swollen nose.

"My goodness," Dr. Gurdin muttered as he looked at his patient. "When did this happen?"

"Last night—"

"—This morning," Dr. Greenson and Marilyn said in unison. They looked at each other without smiling.

"It happened late last night or early this morning," Dr. Greenson told the plastic surgeon. "Marilyn was trying to take a shower, and she slipped on the wet surface and hit her face on the way down."

"Unusual injury for a fall in the shower," Gurdin told Greenson, staring deeply into his eyes. "This is the kind of injury I see from bar fights."

"It doesn't make much difference how it happened," Greenson asserted. "She fell down in the shower, and got an unusual injury. That's all. The point is that she has it—the injury—and now we have to get it fixed."

Gurdin picked up a stainless steel nasal speculum, walked

over to where Marilyn was seated, and slid the speculum into each side of Marilyn's nose. He adjusted his light so as to get a good look at the internal anatomy.

"We should get some x-rays," Gurdin proposed. "I'm concerned that your cheekbone is broken."

"My cheekbone?" Marilyn asked anxiously.

"The zygoma," Gurdin answered. "This looks like it could be a standard zygomatic fracture. You might have broken one of your nasal bones or the zygoma or you could just have some bruising. I need an x-ray to tell."

Marilyn and Dr. Greenson were led by the doctor back into a part of his office reserved for taking x-rays. After changing position multiple times for multiple different x-rays, Dr. Gurdin escorted them back into the examining room.

"I don't see any displaced fractures on these films," he reported to her holding the films up to the light. "Of course, the cartilage of the nose can be torn and that doesn't show up on an x-ray."

"If my nose is broken, how quickly can we fix it," Marilyn asked.

"It might be broken and not displaced," Gurdin told her. "As long as it is straight, I wouldn't suggest you do anything. Just wait for the swelling to go down. If it is deviated at that point, then we need to push it back into place."

"That sounds pleasant," Marilyn said with a smile.

"I'd put in some local anesthesia," the doctor promised. "But I'm not sure you'll need anything done at this point. The most important thing I can tell you is to make sure something like this doesn't happen again. Take care of that shower, or whatever it was, and make sure you don't put yourself in a position where you might get hurt again." He looked at her as if he were concerned about the truthfulness of Greenson's story. "For some of my patients, that means they have to get to a place where they can avoid certain people or problems."

"We'll get someone to look at her shower," Greenson told

Gurdin sternly. "Maybe she needs something less slippery to stand on."

"Maybe so," Gurdin agreed. "My experience in this business has taught me that when something violent happens, it's a good idea to make some changes."

Chapter 33

*"I'm a lawyer and a politician and I live in my work.
You're an actress, and you live in your work, as well.
Besides, your work is important to the whole world. Stick
with it."*

> Robert F. Kennedy to Marilyn Monroe
> June 1962
> Quoted by Eunice Murray

*"I greeted Mr. Kennedy and showed him into the living
room that June afternoon."*

> Eunice Murray to Sylvia Chase (ABC News)

Robert Kennedy held his hand up and caught the keys.

"Thanks, Buddy," the Attorney General said. Robert Kennedy liked to get away from the government limousines when he was in Los Angeles. One of the members of his security team allowed Kennedy to borrow his car.

"Don't scratch it up," the officer said with a smile.

Kennedy drove the blue convertible down San Vicente Boulevard through Brentwood toward Carmelina and its multiply appendaged Helenas. He was officially in town to work on the preproduction of his movie *The Enemy Within*, but his real reason for coming to Los Angeles the third weekend in June, 1962 was to try to make peace with Marilyn Monroe.

After they learned that Marilyn's psychiatrist was meeting with the East Germans, the Kennedys decided that she was the security leak that Hoover had long maintained that she was. That meant that the President had to cut off any public contact with her. In addition, they needed to have a fall back position if she decided to speak out in public. Their friends at Fox had been willing to be good Americans and go along with the plan to put her mental status into serious question. But she was not showing any signs that she would relent. Quite the contrary, Marilyn was acting like she thought she could change American policy. In addition, she was making calls to the President's various residences and not using her code name—merely identifying herself as Marilyn Monroe and demanding to speak to Jack. That wasn't going to do. Marilyn was going to have to learn to be a good girl and know when to quit.

He drove into the cul de sac, pulled through the entry in the adobe wall in front of Marilyn's house, and parked the car. The Eucalyptus trees shaded the driveway and swayed gently in the breeze.

"I think anyone would feel hurt," Marilyn told Bobby. They were sitting on folding chairs at a table next to Marilyn's pool. Mrs. Murray brought out sandwiches and poured iced tea for Marilyn and her guest. "I've known your brother for almost ten years, and we've been very close. Just changing the telephone number and refusing to take my calls was not the way I thought the relationship would end."

"Jack became worried about security. There have been some significant security issues raised recently and we had to take some action. You weren't the only person who was affected by tightening the President's security. He felt very bad about what had to happen, but his advisors felt that he couldn't talk to you on insecure telephone lines."

"Frank called me but he really didn't tell me why," Marilyn

complained. Peter told me that you didn't want me to contact either you or the President.

"Security concerns," Bobby pointed out. "I'm sorry the time came when the President could no longer see you, but you have to understand that we are public officials and we have important work to carry out for the country."

"But why did you have to cut me out of your lives?"

"Because you are not just another acquaintance. You are famous in your own right, and if you say that we said something or other, then that takes on much greater importance than if someone less famous said the same thing."

"Why do you think the people at Fox fired me?" she asked.

"I called them about that," Bobby assured her. "That fellow Gould told me that they were using the President's birthday celebration as a legal excuse. Their real concern was that you simply didn't want to finish the movie because you don't think that you're getting paid enough to do it."

"They know that's ridiculous. Their own doctor told me to stay home. I had a fever."

"Well, they fired you," Bobby said. "That's the bad news. The good news is that now they have to hire you back."

"What makes you think that they want to hire me back?"

"I don't think they do," Kennedy said. "But you have some important people on your side. We can help you."

"Why do you think they tried to brand me as mentally ill?" Marilyn asked.

"I just think that they were angry that you didn't want to work for them. The Fox studio made you a star, or at least they think they did, and now they think that you don't want to finish your obligation to the studio. You owe them one more film, right?"

"Right."

"That's it. They felt like you had double crossed them and they wanted to take a little luster off your stardom as you left the studio."

Marilyn looked at the Attorney General. His explanations seemed possible.

"But you think you could get me hired back?" Marilyn asked.

"I think we could," Kennedy replied. "But I need to ask you to do a favor for us." He stopped and let her think it over. He sipped his glass of iced tea.

"What kind of favor?"

"You know some things now that properly come under the heading of national security. Whether you like it or not, the Cuban operation effects not only the people in Cuba, but a whole bunch of people who are working to free Cuba, and other people who had their land and businesses stolen by Castro. If you tell anyone about the American operation, even if they are your friends, or doctors, or anyone, you will be leaking very important national security secrets. You wouldn't know the secret if you had not been involved with the President. And out of respect for him, you shouldn't tell anyone about it."

Marilyn shook her head.

"I should have known this was what it was all about," she said. "I told Jack, and now I'm going to tell you that I didn't leak anything about Cuba or anything else. I talked with Fred Field in Mexico City and he told me that Fidel Castro's life has been threatened by gangsters who have been caught and forced to tell their stories. Castro knows that you guys are out to kill him because the gangsters told him. My side of this is simple: I don't want you to get hurt."

Kennedy laughed.

"We're not going to get hurt."

"How do you know?"

"Because we are running the most powerful country on earth, that's how I know. Castro illegally took property and businesses in Cuba and now he has to give them back. And he can't play like his right to govern is the same as our right to govern, or that his military is as powerful as our military. Castro is going to leave Cuba. That's it. He's got to go and now he's trying to play like he's got as much right to be there as we have to be here. That's nonsense."

Marilyn looked at Kennedy for some time after he had completed his argument. "Why do you think you can get my job back?"

"The Kennedy family has some friends at Fox."

"At the executive level?" She didn't want to reveal everything she knew.

"Let's just say that I can deliver on my end. Now are you willing to leave Cuba alone and go back to being an actress?"

"You think you can just pull a string and get me back at Fox?"

Kennedy paused and considered her question. He didn't want to make it look too easy. "I don't know exactly what it will take, but I do know it can be done. If we can bring the steel industry to its knees, I think we can get you back on the set."

Marilyn stood up and walked to the edge of the pool, then turned and looked back at Robert Kennedy. He looked up at her and saw that she had started to cry.

"What's wrong?"

"I don't know," Marilyn sobbed. "I just think you guys are too mean."

"Mean? We're going to get your job back."

"But with a big condition."

"But we are helping you."

"I just have to wonder," Marilyn said as she wiped away her tears.

"About what?"

"Why did you let them fire me to begin with. If you know people at the executive level, why did you say it would be all right to fire me?"

"We had nothing to say about that. They certainly didn't ask us."

There was a long pause in the California sunshine as Marilyn walked around the perimeter of the swimming pool, occasionally looking over at the gully where her gardens sprawled down the hillside. Robert Kennedy followed her to the other side of the pool and stood next to her. She wiped away her tears.

"Like the way my nose looks?" Marilyn asked the Attorney General.

"I guess I heard that you had a burglar or something. I didn't know you got hurt."

"You didn't send someone to teach me a lesson?"

Kennedy snorted. "Of course not! We don't operate like that. But, I'm sure you know that some of the operations that are on the periphery of our government are conducted by hoodlums. I can't control them."

"You think that somebody from the Mafia is trying to tell me to keep my nose out of their business?"

"Marilyn, I have no idea about those things. Both the President and I care for you a great deal. But we have to care for the country even more."

"You didn't get me fired from Fox?" she asked.

"We didn't get you fired," he assured her.

Marilyn looked back over the flowers blooming on the hillside beneath her and then back into Bobby Kennedy's eyes.

"I only told Jack about Field to try to warn him. I mean . . . I don't agree with trying to kill Castro, and Jack knows that, but if Castro is going to send someone up here to shoot first, I thought Jack should know that."

"We're not trying to kill Castro. If we were, he'd already be dead."

"I hope not," Marilyn said, "because if you are, you could end up getting your brother killed. I couldn't bear the thought— I don't want to stand by and see that happen."

"Don't worry," Robert Kennedy assured her. "You won't."

Chapter 34

"As far as I'm concerned, the happiest time is now. There's a future, and I can't wait to get to it!"

Marilyn Monroe
Cosmopolitan, July, 1962

"Sidney," Marilyn said to her hairdresser, "it looks too mean."

Sidney Guilaroff and Whitney Snyder were creating a new look for Marilyn for her meeting with Peter Levathes.

"That was the whole idea, Marilyn," Sidney argued. "You want to look formal and serious. Now let's try these." He put some horn rim glasses on Marilyn.

She laughed. "I could get a job as a businesswoman—something like that. Maybe I should ask him if I can produce the movie!"

Peter Levathes, the President of Fox production, was coming to 5th Helena for a meeting with Marilyn. It was Thursday, June 28, 1962, only 4 days since Robert Kennedy came to her house to ask her to do the Kennedy brothers a favor. On Monday, an executive in New York called Levathes and told him to sign Marilyn to complete the film. Levathes had advised New York that it was going to cost them some big money to sign her, but he was told that money would not be an object. Indeed, he was surprised to have the terms of her new contract outlined by the New York office . . .

When Levathes arrived at Marilyn's house, he was offered

some chilled caviar and a cocktail which he accepted. He looked around the modest house.

"Nice Aztec calendar," he commented to Pat Newcomb who had offered him the caviar.

"I got it in Mexico," Marilyn said as she came into the living room. She offered her hand and Levathes shook it.

He looked at her beige dress and no nonsense appearance.

"My goodness," Levathes said. "I guess we don't have to wait for your lawyer."

Marilyn cracked a smile. "Please sit down," she said gesturing at one of her new Mexican chairs.

Levathes outlined the studio's proposal to Marilyn.

"Of course we regret that we fired you, Marilyn," he explained, "but there was a big question in our minds about whether you were willing to go forward with the film. You were making $100,000 for Something's Got to Give. We know that you deserve much more, but this is the final film you have to do on your Fox contract. Nonetheless, if you would be willing to finish the film, you will make $500,000, and a bonus if the film comes in on time."

Marilyn lifted the horn rim glasses off from her face and looked at them. She put them back on.

"And we know that you have had certain problems with the script. We would be willing to go back to the Nunnally Johnson script if you do not like the rewrites that Walter Bernstein has submitted."

"George Cukor won't go along with that," Marilyn stated firmly.

"He won't have to," Levathes told her. "If Cukor doesn't like the script, we'll replace him with a director of your own choosing."

It had only been 16 days since 20th Century Fox had fired her. Now, they wanted her back on terms which she couldn't have even imagined two weeks earlier.

"Why are you guys doing this?" Marilyn asked Levathes.

"We want Marilyn Monroe back with Fox," Levathes told her. "You have always been one of our biggest stars, and if you want to stay with us, we want to pay you what we think you deserve. And we want to work with you in the future, when you are no longer bound to us by your previous contract. We will give you another half a million if you will star in a new musical called *What a Way to Go.*"

Marilyn made notes on a small pad she was holding. She was trying to hide her complete amazement.

"Let me see it in writing," Marilyn told Levathes as she stood up. "I'm glad Fox is changing its position. I think you did something very mean, and almost inexcusable when you fired me. But let me see this proposal in writing, and let me think about it."

"We'd like to get this project back on track as soon as possible," Levathes told her. "We'd like to start the filming again in July."

"Let me just think things over," Marilyn told him. "Send the contract to Rudin, and I'll talk to him about it."

Levathes felt very good on his drive back into Beverly Hills that afternoon. Although he had just given Marilyn the best terms she had ever been offered on a movie, he knew that the studio would make the money back. *Something's Got to Give* was going to be a big hit.

Marilyn took off the ridiculous horn rim glasses and had a drink with Whitney Snyder and Sydney Guilaroff to toast the Fox offer. Pat Newcomb gave her a big hug in what was shaping up as a celebration of Marilyn's victory over the forces that had tried to topple her. While the others were finishing the caviar and canapés which were brought in for Levathes, Marilyn changed out of the beige dress and into her slacks and a silk shirt.

"Aren't you happy, Marilyn?" Pat asked her boss.

"Very happy," Marilyn said soberly. "It is nice to have friends in high places." She put down her glass and walked toward the front door.

While the others laughed and drank, Marilyn walked down her driveway to check the mailbox. She stopped at the white adobe wall and tried to imagine what kind of gates she should have hung. Then she proceeded out to the street and opened the mailbox. There were a couple of bills, a letter from the actor's guild, and an envelope with Mexican stamps and no return address. Marilyn did not recognize the handwriting.

"Dear M." the letter began. "I am sorry not to have gotten in touch with you earlier, but I have worried whether your telephone line is truly private. The newspapers in Mexico reported that the studio fired you from *Something's Got to Give* and that the studio chief referred to you as mentally ill. Clearly they are trying to ruin your credibility and I suspect that you made some kind of attempt to tell your friend to call off his gangsters. I am sorry that my advice has led to this. The K. brothers will do what they can to silence you, and I sincerely hope that they will stop at merely trying to ruin your public image. However, I am deeply concerned that your life is in danger. If they went so far as to have you fired and have the studio chief say that you're mentally incompetent, they will go to other lengths which are even more aggressive. Of course, you could co-operate with them and agree not to be vocal on this subject. I suspect they will provide some nice incentives to do so. But I think you realize, as I do, that there is only one way to save everyone's life here, and that is for them to start playing by the rules of generally accepted conduct. Your decision as to what path to take will determine much more than is presently obvious. Because I feel some responsibility for having given you the advice that I did, I am making plans to come to the United States. If you feel threatened, simply get on an airplane and fly to New York City. I have a way to try to protect you there. Sincerely, FF."

Marilyn read the letter again to make sure she didn't miss anything. Clearly, Field felt that the Kennedys were involved in her job problems and that she might be in some kind of physical danger. She was going to have to go to a telephone where there were no taps and call Field. If he really felt that she needed a safe harbor, maybe she should listen. Marilyn tore up the letter from Field and the mailing from the Actor's Guild as she walked back to her garbage cans. She threw the little pieces of paper into the garbage.

"Get some bad mail, Marilyn?" Pat Newcomb startled Marilyn.

"Oh, Pat," she said. "You scared me."

"I was just wondering where you were," Pat explained. "I thought you were going out to get the mail, but I looked and didn't see you."

"Nothing important," Marilyn said. "Just some bills and something from the Actors' Guild. Sometimes, I don't even like to clutter up the house with this junk."

"I was just going to leave, and wondered if you wanted me to do anything with the proposal," Pat said. "Do you think we should plan a press release about the offer from Fox?"

"No, I don't think we should. Not yet. Let's let Mickey Rudin look at the deal first." Marilyn started to walk back toward the front of the house.

"You've got to love those terms," Pat said following her.

"Absolutely," Marilyn agreed. "Rudin himself couldn't have written a more generous offer."

"The money sure sounded good, and the offer for another film? Wow! Somebody must really love you."

"I think somebody does love me," Marilyn agreed as she walked back toward the house. "I'm just not sure who."

Chapter 35

"Dear Marilyn—
Mother asked me to write and thank you for your sweet
note to Daddy—He really enjoyed it and you were very
cute to send it—
Understand that you and Bobby are the new item! We all
think you should come with him when he comes back East!
Again, thanks for the note—
Love,
Jean Smith"

Letter from Jean Kennedy Smith to
Marilyn Monroe, undated

The football spiraled through the air and Peter reached out and pulled it in.

"Nicely thrown Bobby!" Peter Lawford shouted to his brother in law. They were playing football on the beach on July 4, 1962.

"Why can't you do that at Hyannis Port?" Pat Kennedy Lawford chided her brother. "Maybe after you practice on me and Marilyn, you will be able to score one on Teddy and Steve." She was referring to the family football game in Massachusetts where the defense would be a little more of a challenge.

"Nobody could have defended against that one," Bobby claimed as Peter Lawford spiked the ball into the sand.

Marilyn Monroe walked back to the pool side deck behind

Pat and Peter Lawford's beach house. It had been the girls against the boys and the girls hadn't done well. Upon stepping up on the deck, Marilyn noticed that a new face had arrived at the party. A tall, attractive man wearing a blue blazer and gray slacks sipped a vodka tonic.

"Do you know Jim Hamilton?" Bobby Kennedy asked Marilyn as he wiped his face with a white towel. "Jim is with the L.A.P.D. We worked together on the organized crime unit."

"Hi Jim," Marilyn said pleasantly. "I met you when you did Jack's security during the Democratic convention."

"I remember," Hamilton said. "I was trying to keep Jack from getting caught with his pants . . . well, I guess I was trying to keep him away from the press, or rather trying to keep the press away from him." James Hamilton ran John Kennedy's security detail during the convention in 1960, but his relationship with the Kennedys dated back to his work with Robert Kennedy in 1956. Hamilton was Chief William Parker's close associate and departmental ally. It had been Chief Parker's idea to have an "Intelligence Division" within the L.A.P.D. and to put Hamilton in charge.

"If Mr. Hoover steps down as director of the F.B.I., the President thinks that William Parker would be the best man for the job," Bobby explained to Marilyn. "And Jim Hamilton goes where Parker goes."

"You've always got to plan for the future," Hamilton remarked dryly.

"Has anyone worked up an appetite?" Peter Lawford asked his guests. "Nothing like a 4th of July barbecue to make you forget your diet!" Lawford laughed as he opened a bottle of beer, partially spraying Hamilton's shoes with its contents. In his embarrassment, he laughed again.

Hamilton smiled narrowly, stepped away from the small puddle of spilled beer, and turned back to talk to Marilyn. "I understand that you are working on a movie, Miss Monroe," Hamilton remarked.

"We're trying to get it back on track," Marilyn answered. "There have been some legal problems."

"You've got some powerful help with the law, I imagine," Hamilton said with a smile.

"It's nice when the Attorney General is in your corner," Marilyn agreed.

Marilyn sat down on a reclining beach chair and watched the others line up for a 4th of July lunch of hot dogs, hamburgers, chips, and beer. She made a point of trying to stay away from greasy foods, being secretly concerned that when the film was ready to resume, she wouldn't be ready for the camera. It was hard for her to keep from feeling discouraged with the way she had been treated by Fox. On another level, she was concerned that the Kennedys, despite their protests to the contrary, had really been behind her firing from the film in the first place. She had been around the film community for years and seen stars fight with directors and film companies all the time, but never seen a major studio try to ruin one of their major stars.

"Not having a good time, Marilyn?" Bobby asked. He put his plate down on the table and wiped his mouth with a starched cloth napkin.

"I've had better summers," Marilyn said flatly. "Not every day that a studio tries to ruin a film in production, not to mention one of their biggest names."

"But, they want you back under much better terms," Bobby protested. "You've been given five times the salary, a new director if you want one, and final say on the script. I think you've done pretty well there, with a little help from some friends."

Marilyn pushed her hair back and rubbed her eyes, her face still not showing much joy.

"Get up," Bobby urged her. "Let's take a walk on the sand."

Marilyn knew that he didn't want to talk in front of the others. Bobby didn't want anyone else at the party to hear her suspicions about why she really lost her job, or why she was really going to get it back. Slowly, and without enthusiasm, she stood up and began to walk off from the deck. Bobby followed.

"It is so nice to see you two together again," Pat Kennedy Lawford said looking at Marilyn and Bobby walking toward the beach. "I just hate it when people aren't getting along. Father always said that you were a Kennedy at heart, Marilyn," Pat continued.

"Really?" Marilyn replied. "He thought I'd be good in politics?"

"No," Pat confessed. "He thought you were stubborn like my brothers." Silence followed Pat's comment and so she felt that she had to add something to explain it. "You didn't have to grow up around them like I did. If you grew up around them, you learned how to get along." She laughed a lonely laugh.

Marilyn smiled. Funny that Joseph Kennedy would think that she was stubborn. Marilyn tried to remember what interaction they had shared in the past which would lead him to that conclusion.

Bobby and Marilyn walked out over the hundred yards or more that separated the beach house from the water. An occasional person would stop and look at them, but for the most part they walked without great attention.

"Fox wants to start filming in two weeks," Bobby told her. "I hope you're not going to play hard to get."

"Micky Rudin is looking at the contract," Marilyn said. "He has some legal questions that I don't understand." She had learned something about misdirection from her interactions with the Administration.

"Tell him that if he has any questions to call me directly," Bobby said. "I think anything can be quickly negotiated at this point, if it is done at the right level."

They walked over the sand to the water's edge. Marilyn stood at the curving wet line where the water raced up the sand and rushed over Marilyn's bare feet.

"I've had some nice times with Jack here," Marilyn said looking out at the calm surf.

"On the beach?" Bobby asked.

"No. In the house," she clarified. "You can't have any privacy with all these secret service guys in the shadows."

"I wonder how carefully they observe you in the house," Bobby said with a smile. "Could be pretty entertaining."

Marilyn managed a restrained smile. She felt a great distance between where she had been with the President a year before and where she was with him then. Jack had a joyful side. He liked to laugh and tease her and pull at her clothes. And when they got away from the others in the bedroom upstairs, he had rubbed her back, and then her bottom, and then they rolled on the bed with the ocean crashing in the distance. But that was all behind her. Jack didn't want to see her anymore because he couldn't accept the fact that she had opinions of her own, and that she had friends of her own. He thought that she would love him so much that she wouldn't care what happened to anyone else. When she told him that he couldn't go on with his plans, a major wall had sprung up in their relationship.

"I only told Jack about Mexico City because I felt he needed to know," Marilyn said to Bobby. "I never agreed with what you guys were trying to do, but that wasn't the point. The point was that Jack could be in some danger if everyone knows what you two think is a secret."

Bobby walked forward so that he would also feel the cold water rush over his feet.

"Jack always thought that you were on our side," Bobby said.

"I always have been."

"You're not on our side if you're down in Mexico City talking to a known Communist informant about the most secret plans of our government."

"I'm thinking of my country," Marilyn objected. "I just think that a government of some of the smartest people in the world should not be trying to dispose of their political problems by resorting to assassination. If those opinions are a crime, then I'm guilty."

"There is no crime in voicing your opinion, Marilyn," the Attorney General advised her. "But it is illegal to tell national secrets to our enemies. You will put innocent lives at risk."

"There are going to be lives at risk no matter what you do. I think you should simply have a press conference and announce that you will not invade Cuba and you will live with Castro. If you do that, then no one's life will be at risk. Even you and Jack will be safe."

"Marilyn, you have been in our camp—you've had a close relationship with the President. No one has seriously considered the idea that you could be working for the enemy."

Marilyn laughed.

"Working for enemy," she repeated. "This is the same problem we were having during the McCarthy hearings: anyone with a different point of view is considered a security risk. Let me tell you something. I wouldn't let Arthur buckle under the great purge of McCarthyism, and I'm not going to be intimidated into watching you guys kill Castro or waiting for him to kill one of you. If I have to take some bad press, so be it. I'm going to stop this fight while there is still time."

Robert Kennedy stopped and looked intensely into Marilyn's eyes. "Are you suggesting that you would attack us publicly?" he asked.

"I don't think I'll have to," she replied. "When you and the President really think this through, you'll see I'm right. It's time to call a truce."

"But that's what I'm talking about," Robert Kennedy said. "You shouldn't even know about that and neither should anyone else. It is a national security operation—it is top secret."

"But they do know about it," Marilyn argued. "They know about it in Mexico City, and Moscow, and even Havana. And the American people should know if their government is trying to kill a foreign leader. This isn't a police state."

Bobby Kennedy could not believe what he was hearing from Marilyn. There was no question in his mind that Marilyn had shifted her position—now she was making a threat to go public. "You're trying to blackmail us into leaving Castro alone."

"I'm not trying to blackmail anyone," she argued. "I'm telling you that I can't sit by and watch you kill Fidel Castro. I don't want to make it my cause—but I will if I have to. You and Jack should just think about it. How important is it that you do something which is this short sighted?"

"You're going to use your connection with us to try to save Castro's skin," the Attorney General concluded.

"I'm going to use my name to try to stop the killing before it starts. You guys announce that you will respect Cuban sovereignty, and I don't have to say a thing."

"And if we don't agree with you?" Bobby asked her.

"Then I will do as anyone else with a disagreement would do: bring attention to it, criticize your position, voice dissent. Don't think that I'm trying to save Castro, Bobby," Marilyn said, "think that I'm trying to save John Kennedy."

"We need to get you back on the set," Bobby told her. "If you have nothing else to think about, you decide to change foreign policy." He laughed. "I think you could help us change our minds about this thing—about a lot of things. We want your help. Our only concern is that you don't confirm our most secret plans to our enemies. That's not too much to ask, is it?"

Bobby Kennedy reached down and picked up Marilyn's hand. He lifted it up slightly and faced her.

"You have to tell me that you won't make this your cause," Bobby pleaded.

"I don't want to make it my cause."

"Then why can't you just promise me that you won't."

"You know I'm not going to do anything to embarrass you. I just want you and Jack to call a truce with Castro. Take Che's offer. Just tell them that the not so secret gun battle is over."

Bobby continued to hold her hand. They began to walk up the beach.

"I can't believe this," he said. "You know the President has a special feeling for you."

Marilyn remained silent and stared out at the ocean. Robert Kennedy thought that he could buy her silence with a movie contract. She could have any movie contract she wanted, anytime she wanted it. Sure, there would be ups and downs in her career. There had been in the past, there would be in the future. Bobby couldn't see the terrible real world conflict that she could see. The Kennedys thought that all they had to do was get her a better movie deal and she would forget the fact that they were trying to gun down a young, idealistic political leader. If she took the contract, they would think they had bought her silence, that she would not press them to give up their ill conceived plan. Maybe they didn't know her well enough. Maybe if they knew her a little better, they would understand that she wasn't just another flaky actress, but someone deserving of their respect. If they could only see the error of their ways, they would thank her for being courageous when all of the others were quiet.

"Jack wants you to finish your movie," Bobby asserted. "He thinks it will turn out to be one of your best."

Marilyn bumped up against Bobby's body as she turned back toward the Lawfords' beach house. They continued to walk hand in hand as they approached the other guests.

Chapter 36

*"Under the personal leadership of Robert Kennedy, at least
eight efforts were made to eliminate Castro himself."*

General Alexander Haig, 1997

Frederick Vanderbilt Field pulled his car into a service
station, edged up to a gasoline pump, and stopped. He opened the
door and stepped out into the heat of the late afternoon sun. A
young service station attendant, dressed in a dirty worn uniform
approached the car.

"Fill it?" the attendant asked.

"Please," Field replied. "How much further to St. Louis?"

"St. Louis is more than 100 miles from here, mister," the young
man replied. "You've got another few hours, at least. Can I check
your oil and water?"

Field looked at a dark car stop in front of the gasoline station.
Two men looked out at him as they sat in their car. "Sure," Field
replied to the attendant. He walked into the station where he used
the bathroom and drank some water from a fountain. When he
came out, the men in the dark car were gone. After paying the
attendant, Field walked over to a pay phone. He looked around to
see if anyone was watching him and then dialed Marilyn Monroe's
telephone number in Los Angeles. No one answered, so he got
back in the car and started for St. Louis.

Field had been on the road for almost a week. The trip had

been a slow one as the roads did not permit speeds much higher than 40 or 50 miles an hour. In Mexico, he was worried about hitting people or animals walking alongside the road. Traveling through Texas, he was able to make good time.

Traveling in the United States again made him nervous. Even though he was still an American citizen, he wondered how he would be treated if he were arrested. Going to New York involved a significant level of personal risk for Field and he would not have even thought of doing it were it not for his concern about the safety of Marilyn Monroe.

Field was worried that he had unwittingly gotten Marilyn into deep trouble. When she came to visit him in February, he knew that she was a friend of President Kennedy's but he didn't think she had anything serious to tell him. During their conversations, Field had discovered in Marilyn a kindred spirit of sorts, a person with considerable worldly wealth who believed in the cause of the poor. Initially, he suspected that she was merely repeating the political bias of some of her acting coaches, or her former husband, Arthur Miller, but then he became convinced that Marilyn was genuinely concerned with liberal causes. Because Marilyn had been poor, she felt a special kinship with the poor and disadvantaged, and that sympathy extended to poor and struggling countries.

Field looked in the rear view mirror and spotted the dark car following him on the highway. Since entering the United States, he had noticed different cars following him along his journey. If they had wanted to arrest him, they would have done so back in Texas. He was sure they were F.B.I. or other government agents but he could not understand why anyone would think that he would do anything of interest on his way to New York. Having two or more men follow him seemed like an enormous waste of resources.

Marilyn Monroe was worth protecting and Field was convinced that she would need protection. The Kennedys were on a collision course with Russians over Cuba, and Marilyn could see the danger. But rather than listen to what she had to say, the Kennedys accused her of siding with the enemy, or perhaps confirming the enemy's worst fears. Unfortunately for her, Marilyn seemed to enjoy this new level of importance. With every effort to shut her up, Marilyn had become more insistent that her views be heard. It was this characteristic stubbornness that worried Field. If she would only back down, and let the Kennedys and the Russians negotiate their differences, she would be safe. But if she continued to press her points with the Kennedys, she might be perceived as an enemy of her own government. That's where Field felt that he had some chance to help.

When Field read that Fox had fired Marilyn Monroe from the set of her movie, he realized that an effort would be made to destroy her and he suspected he knew the reason why. He had made contact with Marilyn and suggested that she might be in some danger. The question was how to best protect her. If Field went to Los Angeles, he had nothing to offer her. But if he went to New York, he could use his connections at the Soviet Embassy to the United Nations to shelter her. If it appeared that the Kennedys intended to silence her, perhaps he could convince Marilyn to return to New York and be hidden in the Russian Embassy. There she could tell her story to the press, and perhaps, if given the opportunity, make an appearance at the United Nations itself. By revealing what the Kennedys were up to, Marilyn Monroe could stop the secret American aggression against Castro and preserve the peace. Marilyn thought the idea was silly because she couldn't believe that she was in any personal danger, but she agreed to stay in close communication with Field. Because he was making the long trip on her behalf, and because she felt a political kinship with Field, Marilyn asked him to stay in her apartment in New York. This Field agreed to do.

Frederick Field, American aristocrat, Communist Party organizer living in exile in Mexico, wiped his brow and again looked at the government car following him. He wondered how much different the political system was in the Soviet Union. The American government prided itself on tolerating differences of opinion and protecting a citizen's right to voice a different opinion. But when the opinion bordered on an operation to murder the leader of a small island, it became part of the "national security." Marilyn Monroe had voiced her dissent about Cuba. The government had quickly acted to discredit her. What would they do if they thought she was actually going to make her criticism public? Field pressed harder on the accelerator and sped along the road to St. Louis.

Patricia Newcomb pulled her car into 5th Helena and then through the gates into Marilyn's driveway. She and Marilyn had been shopping that morning and Pat was driving Marilyn home. There was a dark blue Porsche parked in front of the house.

"Who's this?" Pat asked as she stopped and parked behind the Porsche.

"I don't know," Marilyn replied. "Nice car."

They carried their packages through the front door and into the living room. Marilyn glanced around the hallway to her bedroom, wondered if the telephone might have been moved, and then walked into the dining room and kitchen area. From the dining room, she could see someone sitting on a lawn chair next to her swimming pool. She opened the sliding door and stepped out onto the patio.

"Jose," Marilyn said as the Latin man stood to greet her. They embraced and lightly kissed each other. "When did you get back in town?"

"I came up last night," Jose Bolanos told her, as he walked over toward the swimming pool. "I hope you don't mind that I found my way to your pool."

"Not at all," Marilyn said. "Did Mrs. Murray give you something to drink?"

"Actually, when I realized you were not home, I just decided to wait here," Bolanos explained. "Mrs. Murray may not know I'm even here."

"I'm glad you did," Marilyn said, wondering how Jose had gotten back to her patio without going through the house.

A breeze blew across the hillside where Marilyn had planted her garden and stirred the tall eucalyptus trees which surrounded her property. A wind chime, hanging from a beam on the house, tingled in the warm gusting air.

"What a beautiful chime," Jose remarked to Marilyn. "I've been listening to it as I have waited for you."

"It is beautiful," Marilyn agreed. "It reminds me to look for the little things in life that are beautiful, not to always focus on the big, complex things that I can't change."

Pat Newcomb walked through the sliding glass door onto the patio where Marilyn and Jose were talking.

"Jose!" Pat greeted him. They also embraced and lightly kissed each other. "I haven't seen you since the Golden Globes." Pat was referring to the awards in March when Jose had accompanied Marilyn to the glitzy ceremony. "You were particularly handsome that night," Pat gushed.

"Such a sweet girl," Jose replied.

"What brings you to Los Angeles," Marilyn asked. "Are you trying to sell a script?"

"That is exactly it," he said. "I have been working on something about a Latin American worker who is frustrated with the landowners and attempts to organize a union."

"That's intriguing," Marilyn said. "Any takers?"

"My agent is looking at it. When I told him that I was going to try to have lunch with Marilyn Monroe, he suggested I take his car." Bolanos laughed.

The telephone rang inside and Mrs. Murray answered it.

"Marilyn," she called. "It's from the people at Fox—in New York!"

Marilyn rushed in to take the call and emerged from her living room a few minutes later.

"Unbelievable news!" Marilyn announced upon her return. "Darryl and Spyros did it! They threw the Kennedy people out of Fox."

"What?" Pat asked. "How is that possible?"

"Judge Rosenman and Milton Gould were Kennedy people," Marilyn explained. "You know that. Rosenman was friends with Joe Kennedy and he's very close with the President and Attorney General. Anyway, after they fired me, I got in touch with Darryl Zanuck and Spyros Skouras—I mean, I have some friends at Fox, too. They were outraged at what the studio had done. So they called a board meeting and voted the shares. Rosenman, Gould, and Loeb are out. Zanuck and Skouras are in, and I'm ready to sign a contract to finish *Something's Got to Give*."

In her surprise, Pat jumped up from her chair. "Marilyn, that's such . . . good news."

"It is!" Marilyn agreed, more enthusiastically. "It's great news."

"But you already had a contract to finish the film," Pat argued.

"I did but I didn't sign it," Marilyn retorted. "I'll never know for sure, but I think Bobby thought he could pull this little stunt to show me who's boss. Well, he gave it his best shot. I think he arranged to have me fired, arranged to label me as a drug addict, and arranged to have me return."

"Why would he do such things," Jose asked. "I don't see the point."

"The point is that if he controls my career, he thinks he can control me," Marilyn explained. "But he doesn't control my career and he doesn't control me."

"But why would he want to?" Pat asked.

"Let's just say that I've been around them long enough to know things that maybe are best left unsaid," Marilyn answered. "And I don't want to talk about them—I really don't. The Kennedys were always rich kids, they always got their way because their father had the most money. If they had ever been poor, they would understand that you don't start fights with people. If you do something violent, somebody else does something violent in return. First thing you know, there is a circle of violence. I just want them to treat everyone with respect. The world will be a better place."

"If you say so," Pat said laughing. "I've got to get back to work. Should we issue a press release about you going back to Fox?"

"Not yet," Marilyn said. "We need to take things slowly. Let's let the news of the change in Fox management sink in. I don't want people to think that I had anything to do with that. There will be plenty of time for them to put it together."

Pat said goodbye to Jose and Marilyn, leaving them to finish lunch on the patio. She hurried back to her office to make an important call.

Chapter 37

"In compliance with the desires and guidance expressed in the 10 August policy meeting on Operation Mongoose . . . We will hold an Operational Representatives work session in my office, at 1400 hours, Tuesday, 14 August. Papers required from each of you for the Tuesday meeting:
Mr. Harvey: Intelligence, political (splitting the regime), including liquidation of leaders . . ."

General Edward Landsdale's Memorandum to the
Special Group (Augmented), August 13, 1962

"Upon receipt of the attached memorandum, I called Landsdale's office and . . . pointed out the inadmissibility and stupidity of putting this type of comment in writing in such a document. I advised . . . that, as far as CIA was concerned, we would write no document pertaining to this and would participate in no open meeting discussing it."

William Harvey, CIA officer in charge of ZR/RIFLE
August 13, 1962

"Reference is made to our conversation on 13 August 1962, concerning the memorandum of that date from General

Lansdale. Attached is a copy of this memorandum . . . The question of assassination, particularly of Fidel Castro, was brought up by Secretary of McNamara at the meeting of the special Group (Augmented) in Secretary Rusk's office on 10 August. It was the obvious consensus at that meeting, in answer to a comment by Mr. Ed Murrow, that this is not a subject which has been made a matter of official record."

William Harvey's Memorandum to Richard Helms
August 14, 1962

"The subject you just brought up (the assassination of Fidel Castro)*: I think it is highly improper. I do not think it should be discussed. It is not an action that should ever be condoned. It is not proper for us to discuss and I intend to have it expunged from the record."*

CIA Director John McCone to Secretary of
Defense, Robert McNamara, August 10, 1962

John McCone didn't like what he was reading. McCone, a Republican who had been asked by President Kennedy to replace CIA Director Allen Dulles after the Bay of Pigs disaster, had experience with reading Top Secret reports. Most of them were worthless. But, the letters and documents he was reading that morning in late July, 1962 were particularly worrisome to him.

One letter was dated July 26, 1962. It was written by a Cuban and addressed to his family in Florida. The CIA routinely opened and read such mail.

"I was an eyewitness" the letter reported. *"Yesterday July 26 the Russian ship Maria Ulanova entered the port. It was painted white. It disembarked about 500 men, in my opinion they were military technicians."*

McCone knew that only one Soviet passenger ship docked

in Cuba during the first six weeks of 1962. In the month of June, more than 20 Soviet cargo ships unloaded military vehicles and sealed crates. More ships brought in troops. In the month of July, 30 more Soviet cargo ships had arrived and unloaded their contents.

One refugee interviewed in Miami by CIA agents reported *"driving by a long truck convoy. After about every third truck there was a long flatbed pulled by a tractor like vehicle. On each vehicle there was a round object as tall as a palm tree and covered by a tarpaulin."*

McCone, 60 years old, took off his wire rimmed spectacles and placed them on his desk. He rubbed his eyes. It was his job to tell the President some very uncomfortable news. He put his spectacles back on and looked back down at the reports. He re-read the reports of the tall, round palm tree like objects on the flatbed trucks. What could they be, if not missiles?

If the Soviets were placing missiles in Cuba, what kind of missiles were they placing? From the descriptions he read, McCone felt reasonably sure that SA-2's were being installed. But why would they place SA-2's? Was it possible that the Soviets were placing surface to air missiles so as to protect an even larger offensive weapon?

McCone felt himself break into a cold sweat as he realized that the Soviets might be planning to introduce offensive missiles in Cuba. That would mean that for the first time in American history, cities on the Eastern seaboard would be vulnerable to complete and near immediate destruction. There were good reasons why Khrushchev might try such a bold move. But, the United States would never allow him to get away with it.

Still, he could not get the thought out of his mind. If the Soviets put ballistic missiles in Cuba, it would mean a nuclear showdown. A nuclear showdown could mean the end of civilization.

"Mr. Director," his intercom interrupted. "The courier has just arrived from the F.B.I.. Can I show him in?"

McCone picked the reports up from the top of his desk and placed them in a folder. J. Edgar Hoover hated the CIA. Whenever Hoover wanted to share some information with the Agency, he sent it over in a sealed pouch. That way, there could never be any ducking responsibility for a security leak.

"Yes, I suppose so," McCone answered. He wondered what could be so important to Hoover that he would send it over in a sealed container.

The F.B.I. agent came into McCone's office and unsealed a leather briefcase in front of McCone. McCone lifted a black pouch out of the briefcase and smiled at the F.B.I. agent.

"Mr. Hoover should have been in charge of the CIA," McCone joked.

The agent managed a faint smile. He did not want to tell the Director of the CIA that Hoover shared that sentiment. After McCone signed for the delivery, the agent left the office.

John McCone opened the pouch and pulled out a standard F.B.I. report. He sat back in his chair and began to read the document. He scanned the report up to the transcript of the dialogue. Once he read the names of the individuals being bugged, he understood why Hoover liked to take such extreme security precautions. His eyes darted back and forth along the document. The electronic devices had picked up a conversation between Marilyn Monroe and Frederick Field.

After reading the transcript, McCone put the full transcript of Marilyn's conversation with Field down on his desk and again took off his wire framed spectacles and began to rub his eyes. Operation Mongoose was the biggest secret of the United States Government. High government officials did not even know of its existence. But a movie star, an actress who McCone had reason to believe was unreliable, knew about the operation and she was talking to a known Communist informant. The security of the United States was threatened by Soviet activity in Cuba. The CIA was taking steps to eliminate that threat, but the entire operation was compromised by a security leak at the highest levels.

Something was going to have to give.

Chapter 38

"Robert Kennedy personally managed the operation on the assassination of Castro."

CIA Director Richard Helms, 1975

"They are doing something," John McCone told the President and the Attorney General. A large photographic blow up of what appeared to be a construction site stood on an easel in the Oval Office. "We have intercepted letters from Cubans to their relatives in Miami which describe the transport of missiles from Soviet cargo ships to unknown locations in the country. There have been more Soviet cargo ships unload their contents in Havana this month than during the entire previous year. What else could they be up to?"

The President rocked back in forth in his rocking chair. There were few subjects he liked less than Cuba. From his earliest days in office, he had been attacked for not doing something more decisive about Castro. Now, his worst dreams were being realized. The Soviets were going to build a missile base. If he let Khrushchev get away with it, American cities would be vulnerable.

"I thought Khrushchev wasn't going to embarrass us before the mid-term elections," the President said to his brother.

"That's exactly right. That's what he said," Robert Kennedy confirmed.

"But, that's not the way it looks," the President said bitterly. "It looks like I've been screwed again."

"It looks like they are putting in some surface to air missiles—that doesn't mean they are putting in ballistic missiles," McCone argued. "But they may be putting in ballistic missiles."

The men stared at the photograph and traded glances at each other. The windows of the Oval Office were open on that warm summer afternoon.

"Why would they put in surface to air missiles?" the Attorney General asked McCone.

"Maybe they are worried about invasion," McCone replied. "What if they know about Mongoose?" McCone continued. "You told your friend Georgi Bolshakov that we would not invade Cuba. You told him that we would tolerate Castro's regime. He told you that they will not place missiles in Cuba. It looks like both governments are lying."

Both governments lying? The thought intrigued the President. He looked over at his brother.

"Georgi has always been completely reliable," Robert Kennedy said. "If the Soviets are putting missiles in Cuba, it may be that Khrushchev is lying to Georgi."

The President continued to rock in his chair and stare at the photograph of Cuba on display. McCone had also brought over an audio tape which had been loaded into a tape player on the President's desk.

"The other piece of bad news I have to share involves this audio tape," McCone said. "It would be worthwhile to listen to the entire tape," McCone continued. "There are some very disturbing things toward the end of the tape."

"Play the damn thing," the President said. John Kennedy didn't like listening to recordings.

McCone turned on the tape machine. He then sat back down in a chair and re-started his pipe. "It's a tape of Marilyn Monroe," he said. "The man she is talking with is Frederick Vanderbilt Field."

The President sat back in his chair as he listened to a conversation between Marilyn and Field. They talked about whether the United States would do atmospheric tests of nuclear weapons and then Field raised the question of Cuba.

"Are they still sending assassins in to try to kill Castro?"

"I don't know," Marilyn said. "The President doesn't want me to even talk about it. When I told him that you knew that attempts were being made to kill Castro, he all but accused me of telling you."

Field laughed. "If John Kennedy thinks he's fooling anyone about his Cuban policy, he's more confused than he was before the Bay of Pigs. He's out to get Castro and everyone knows it."

"That's the reason this has to stop right now," Marilyn told Field. "I've told them to just have a press conference and announce that no attempts will again be made on the life of the Cuban leader. I've even threatened to become vocal about it."

"That was very courageous of you, Marilyn," Field said. "But, I suspect that the Kennedys won't want you go say anything in public. They don't seem like they will tolerate public criticism. I hate to say this, but your own security might be at stake."

Robert Kennedy paced around the room while he listened. After the tape was over, he insisted that it be replayed in its entirety. He concentrated on the last part of the telephone record. "I have friends with the Soviet delegation at the United Nations" Frederick Field said on the tape, "and if you ever think your life is in danger, you could be sheltered in New York until the publicity insures your safety."

"What does that mean?" the Attorney General asked McCone and the President. "Is Field suggesting the Soviets could give Marilyn some kind of diplomatic shelter?"

"That would be a nice headline for the KGB," the President pointed out. "Marilyn Monroe defects to Soviet Union—claims Kennedy is out to kill Castro."

"I can't believe she's talking to a Soviet agent," Robert Kennedy said. "How could she do this to us?"

"She doesn't know he's passing information to the Russians," the President retorted. "Marilyn gossips all the time. She just doesn't understand how serious this is."

The brothers looked at each other and then over at McCone.

"I have taken the liberty of asking certain agents of Operation Mongoose to prepare contingency plans regarding Miss Monroe," McCone said. "If we think we can get rid of the leader of Cuba, we ought to be able to keep the lid on a movie star."

"You mean you're making plans to silence Marilyn?" the President asked.

"Yes, sir," McCone replied. "A top secret operation is in danger of being leaked to the press. As uncomfortable as this development is, contingencies must be made. The CIA stands ready to serve the national security in any way you deem appropriate."

The President looked out the windows of the Oval Office and grimaced. Clearly Khrushchev was lying to him about putting missiles in Cuba. And why not? He was lying to Khrushchev about tolerating Castro. Khrushchev had learned that the CIA was still conducting a secret war of sabotage against Cuba, so he was going to protect the island and counter the United States' bases in Turkey at the same time. Marilyn Monroe knew too much about Mongoose, but she didn't know that her involvement with Field endangered world peace.

"Do we have Marilyn under control, Bobby?" the President asked his brother.

"Hardly!" Robert Kennedy replied. "We've tried to get some influence over her, but I'm afraid that she just doesn't want to go along. We thought we could get her attention through Fox, but she succeeded in getting Rosenman and Gould thrown out and the Hollywood people back at the controls. What she is saying to us is that she can play hardball, too. We're trying to get some leverage on her and she is telling us that she won't be silenced. It seems crazy, but Marilyn wants to make policy."

"I wonder if she's right," the President said as he looked at his brother. "Field says that Castro knows we've been sending in killers. It's not a secret to Castro. Khrushchev probably has some pretty solid suspicions. That puts us at some risk."

"It certainly does," McCone agreed.

The President stood up, stretched his back, and walked around his desk. "Maybe we should listen to Marilyn. Maybe we ought to just stop our Cuban operations. What the hell? I'd rather send in the Peace Corps—I don't want those guys taking shots at me."

"Jack, we can't make friends with Castro," Bobby argued. "If the Soviets are putting missiles in Cuba, the Republicans are going to find out and we're going to look like we've been sleeping on the job."

"I can tell you one thing that won't work," the President said to McCone and the Attorney General. "We can't have Marilyn Monroe issuing press releases about Cuba. She might have a point about Castro, and that's a risk we need to talk more about, but we can't be trying to muscle the Russians around and then have her blind side us with a headline confirming the Russian position. If Marilyn has turned into a double agent, we're going to have to treat her like one."

Chapter 39

"A solution to the Cuban problem carries top priority in the U.S. Government. No time, money, effort, or manpower is to be spared."

Robert F. Kennedy
January 19, 1962

"Arriving home about twilight, they found Lee on the porch perched on one knee, pointing his rifle toward the street. It was the first time she had seen him with the rifle in months—and she was horrified.
"What are you doing?" she asked.
"Get the heck out of here," he said. "Don't talk to me . . ."
A few evenings later, she again found him on the porch with his rifle.
"Playing with your gun again, are you," she said sarcastically.
"Fidel Castro needs defenders," Lee said. "I'm going to join his army of volunteers . . ."

Marina Oswald as quoted by
Priscilla Johnson McMillan
Marina and Lee, (p 451-452)

Marilyn looked at the towering pines which surrounded the Cal-Neva Lodge and then down at the beautiful deep blue lake. She wanted to iron out some things with Bobby Kennedy but Bobby claimed that the risk of being seen with her in Los Angeles was simply too great. Marilyn was surprised and relieved when Frank Sinatra proposed that everyone come up to Lake Tahoe for the weekend and make peace. Frank's thought was that if everyone could just get together and enjoy one another, they would be reminded of why they had been friends in the first place and find a logical way to go forward. Marilyn flew up to the lake in Frank's private plane.

Almost as soon as her bags were put in one of Frank's private set of bungalows, Marilyn began to feel intimidated by the number of people who were arriving. Not only was Peter Lawford there, as she suspected he might be, but Pat Kennedy Lawford had flown out from Massachusetts specifically to see Marilyn. Peter and Pat were having problems in their marriage so Pat was essentially living with her mother in Hyannis Port. To have Pat come out meant that Bobby and Jack were serious.

"It's suicide," Peter Lawford told Marilyn Monroe as he and his wife sat with her on a deck overlooking the lake. They were all dressed warmly in the cool mountain air.

"It's not suicide," Marilyn argued. "It's dissent. The question is not whether I favor the Americans or the Russians, it is whether I think that trying to kill Castro is a good idea. You have to understand, it is not a secret in Havana."

"The point is that this subject is part of a national security operation, Marilyn," Pat Kennedy Lawford said. "National security operations are top secret."

"I understand that," Marilyn said. "But everyone seems to be missing here is that the operation is not a secret to Castro. Castro's the one you need to worry about. Who cares if Marilyn Monroe knows? If Castro knows, Jack's in danger and Castro knows."

"So what do you think Jack should do?" Pat asked.

"I think he should call the operation off just like I told him to do with the Bay of Pigs. That was another good example of a top secret operation."

"If he calls it off, how will that change things?" Pat asked.

"Castro will learn that he has called it off, and Castro will not send someone to the United States to kill the President."

Pat and Peter looked at each other. They had assured Bobby that they would be able to convince Marilyn to keep quiet about Cuba.

"Marilyn, this is not a choice," Pat emphasized. "There is a time to debate choices, and there is a time to be loyal to your country. The time to debate choices has passed, and now the country is going into battle. It is time to be loyal."

"Look, Pat," Marilyn began, "there is no question about my love for you or for your brother. Bobby, I could do without at times, but Jack likes to consider all his choices. I know that if he has time to consider this idea, he will see that he is in great danger. He's not going to accomplish anything trying to overthrow Cuba. The Soviets are going to build a base in Cuba if we keep threatening it."

"How do you know so much about what the Soviets are going to do?" Peter asked her.

"It's obvious. What else could they do? What did we do in Berlin when the Soviets started to make noises?" Marilyn asked.

"I think Jack should talk to her," Pat said to Peter. "Frankly, I think she's making some pretty good points."

"God damn it, Pat," Peter said impatiently. "This isn't the time to screw around. Marilyn has one choice and she has to accept it: she has to keep her mouth shut about national security stuff. She has to agree to just stay out of this—all of it—now and forever."

"I have a right to an opinion," Marilyn asserted.

"You had a right to an opinion," Peter said. "You gave up that right when you learned a bunch of things that no one else knows. Look, just promise me that you will go back to being an actress. That's not such a bad life."

"Why should I?" Marilyn asked.

"Because its your only choice," Peter answered. "Anything else is suicide."

Frank Sinatra finished holding the last note and then basked in the warm applause. He walked around the tables with the spot light still on him and shook hands with some of people he recognized, then sat down next to Marilyn at the VIP table. After Peter told him that the President couldn't stay at his house in March, Sinatra never thought he would have dinner with Peter Lawford again. But when the President of the United States asks you for a favor, it's hard to say no. So Frank sat with his old friend Peter Lawford and Lawford's wife, Pat Kennedy, and the First Girlfriend, Marilyn Monroe.

After a few minutes, two other people joined the Sinatra party. Frank introduced Marilyn and the Lawfords to a solidly built man named Tony, and his girlfriend who looked to Marilyn like she could be a hooker. There were still two places left empty at the table.

"Is Bobby coming?" Marilyn asked Pat. Marilyn had come up for the weekend with the understanding that Bobby would be there.

"Maybe tomorrow," Pat replied. "He got hung up with something."

Marilyn was enjoying the dinner, laughing at some of Frank's lines, when she saw a man in a dark shirt, dark tie, and sunglasses being led through the other tables by another well muscled, well dressed young man. Suddenly, Marilyn realized that the weekend might not have been designed to simply rediscover the friendship that had brought them together.

"Momo," Frank greeted Sam Giancana. "I was hoping you'd be able to make it."

"Takes me longer to get around now," Giancana complained. "Have to slip all those F.B.I. bastards." Everyone laughed and Giancana smiled. "If they catch me here, you'll lose your gambling license."

Sam had dinner with his body guard nervously looking around

the room. The conversation seemed pleasant enough until some-one got Giancana on the subject of Omerta—the Sicilian Code of Silence.

"We had ways to teach some of the shop owners in Chicago to keep secrets," Giancana told the assembled diners. "Occa-sionally, they would get the idea that there was safety in numbers. So one of them would make a call and start to talk to somebody at the newspaper. I always tried to find out who that one person was, and then I would shoot him in the mouth."

"Excuse me?" Marilyn slurred and then caught herself. "Frank, you're not making much money on these drinks." She was feeling a bit dizzy.

"I would empty a gun into his face," Giancana told her, "usu-ally in front of anyone else who wanted to talk to the newspapers." A stunned silence greeted his story. "There is nothing like seeing somebody shot in the mouth and face to make people remember not to talk," Giancana concluded.

"What did they do?" Marilyn asked slowly.

"They talked," Giancana told her. "No business works very well if people talk all the time." He stared at Marilyn.

"Why couldn't you do . . . doo something else . . . to get your point across?" Marilyn struggled to articulate her question.

"We had other ways," Giancana said. "Just being here in Nevada reminds me of some of those times where we would get someone we wanted some influence with and get them in a compromised position."

"What kind . . . of . . . position?" Marilyn asked.

"Let's say we had someone who didn't want to be seen with a pretty girl like Candy here," Giancana said to Marilyn. "You might like to party with Candy, but you wouldn't want to see the pictures in the newspaper, would you?"

Drugs placed in Marilyn's drink were now making everything seem funny to her. She laughed at Giancana's suggestion that she might like to be intimate with Candy.

Pat Kennedy Lawford excused herself to her room, which

was separate from Peter's, but the others proceeded to Sinatra's bungalow for another round of drinks. Marilyn hung on to the arm of Tony—the man who had accompanied Candy to the dinner. One of the people with Giancana remembered to bring along a camera.

During the next few hours, an orgy of sorts occurred with Marilyn as the most featured participant. Initially, Marilyn was reluctant to remove her clothing, but as time passed and the effects of the drugs became more profound, Marilyn rolled around with some of the other dinner participants on a large bed in one of the VIP bungalows. A camera recorded their positions and interactions.

Later in the evening, Marilyn slipped into a coma and a doctor was summoned. A tube was inserted into her stomach and the stomach was drained. The powerful drugs were no longer in her stomach, having been absorbed into her blood stream several hours earlier. Fortunately, she was able to continue to breathe while her body digested the drugs which had been slipped into her dinner drink. Sinatra, disgusted by the course of the evening's activities, insisted that Marilyn be flown back to Los Angeles where she could receive more expert medical intervention.

Marilyn routinely took sleeping pills and so her body rapidly processed the dangerous drugs she had been given. Although there was some concern at the lake that she might not survive the evening, by the time she arrived in Los Angeles, Marilyn was strong enough to walk. Pat Newcomb was located at the late hour of their arrival and recruited to keep an eye on Marilyn while she recovered further. Had she only told Peter Lawford that she would agree not to discuss any of the secrets she knew, Marilyn might have been spared her first encounter with 'suicide.'

Chapter 40

"I now live in my work and in a few relationships with the few people I can really count on."

Marilyn Monroe to Richard Meryman,
Life Magazine, August 1962

"If someone talks, he shoots them in the mouth," Marilyn told Dr. Greenson. They walked along a park near Dr. Greenson's house. Dr. Greenson attempted to show no emotion as he listened to Marilyn recount her memory of the weekend at Lake Tahoe.

"Did you get the idea that he was sending you a message?" Greenson asked. He kept his hands buried in his pockets as they walked.

"Of course. Now that I think about it, I think the whole weekend was designed to intimidate me. I'll bet it was Giancana who sent that guy out to break my nose. There must be a line of communication between the Kennedys and Giancana."

"Are you sure they took pictures?"

"Pretty sure. We were sitting at dinner and I had this feeling that I was getting drunk. Frank was being his usual charming self, but then Giancana came in and joined us at dinner. I knew when I saw him that he had come for my benefit."

"Doesn't he own part of the hotel?"

"I don't know," Marilyn said. "I know that Frank owns part, Mickey Rudin owns part, and Giancana may have an interest—

but what do I know about those things? You might have a piece of it as far as I know."

Greenson chuckled. "I'm not in that business."

"Giancana began to make rather pointed comments to me about staying quiet. He even mentioned that he would get compromising photographs of people right there in Nevada. I got the idea that he used the photographs to blackmail people into keeping quiet about business deals."

"You remember taking off your clothes?" Greenson asked. They sat down on a bench in the park. Except for a boy and his dog, the park was empty.

"I was pretty groggy by that time," Marilyn said. "I can remember being on the bed and having this woman try to kiss me and a camera flash went off. She was trying to take my clothes off me. The next thing I remember was waking up in the airplane with a tube in my nose. Everyone looked worried, like they thought I was going to die."

"It was clearly a weekend of intimidation," Greenson concluded. "They must consider you a very real threat."

"The message was that killing Castro is Mafia business," Marilyn surmised. "They are telling me that if I talk about killing Castro, I could be punished by being shot in the mouth. God—" Marilyn covered her mouth and took a deep breath. "That's a very ugly threat."

"It is," Greenson agreed. "There is no doubt that they want you to simply forget about Castro. Where does that stand?"

"I told Bobby that if they would say they were going to leave Cuba alone, I would just stay out of it. But if they continue to try to kill Castro or invade the island, I would voice opposition to their plans. Ever since I told Bobby that, they have completely ignored me. It's like now they want me to go away and forget about Cuba and just leave them alone. But, I can't do that."

"Why not?"

"Because I think I have a responsibility to try to stop them from trying to kill Castro. If I do that, Castro won't try to kill Jack, and there won't be a war over Cuba. Everyone will be better off."

Greenson put his fingertips together. He lightly bounced his thumbs and fingertips off each other as he thought about what Marilyn needed to do next.

"How real is the threat that Giancana would actually try to do you harm?" Greenson asked. "Killing Marilyn Monroe with bullets to the face would not be good for his business. I doubt he would want to do something which would draw worldwide attention to a secret operation."

"That's exactly the reason why I have to do this," Marilyn continued. "Someone else could just be quietly dealt with, but they can't get away with shooting me."

"Why not just let this go?" Greenson reasoned. "The world is a big place. You're not responsible for what the Kennedys do in Cuba. Why not just finish your film and let these guys run the government?"

"That would be easy enough," Marilyn agreed. "But I feel that I am in a unique position to help the President avoid a disaster. The hard part is that he doesn't see the tremendous risk that he is taking."

Greenson stood up from the park bench and paced around it.

"That's a good thought," Greenson said. "But the Kennedys don't seem to want your help. These are not idle threats made by idle men. They are real threats made by people who have the ability to carry them out. I fear for you, Marilyn. I'm starting to worry about your safety."

Marilyn looked at Greenson. "What should I do?" she asked.

"You're going to have to call the Attorney General and get this straightened out," Greenson advised. "Maybe you tell him that you want to put it all behind you and finish your movie. You don't want to play this game anymore."

"Then I watch them kill Castro."

"That's right."

"I can do better than that. I know these Kennedy brothers

and I think that they are just bluffing—mostly bluffing. They are not going to kill me over Fidel Castro. If they did, it would mean international headlines because it is known that I'm connected with the President. I don't see him taking that kind of risk, and I just don't think he would want to kill me. I mean, we've been . . . intimate."

"I think you are at risk," Greenson said. "You told the President that you heard that Castro knew about the secret plan to have him killed and the President quit taking your calls. Then they told you through Lawford to never contact them again. They must have thought that continuing any contact with you posed some kind of risk to them. But, you continued to call and then you got fired from the movie. You sent the Attorney General a telegram, someone came out and beat you up. You told Robert Kennedy that you might criticize them publicly, and now someone sent Sam Giancana out to tell you he will have your face shot off. They probably have photographs which would ruin your career. These men are not bluffing. It is time for you to call Robert Kennedy and tell him that you want to work with him. I wouldn't push these guys any further, Marilyn."

"You don't think they will listen to me."

"No, I don't. No one is more sympathetic to liberal causes than I am, but you can't put your own personal safety at stake for anything. You've never even met Castro. To hell with him. You've got to understand that these men mean business."

"Let me call Bobby," Marilyn said. "I'll see what kind of deal I can get."

Marilyn walked with Greenson out of the park and back to her car. She drove down the hill, around the golf course, and onto San Vicente. She always wore sunglasses and a scarf over her hair when she drove as a precaution against being recognized by other drivers. She drove down San Vicente to Carmelina, then up grade to the Helenas. It was such a nice day that she had trouble thinking that anyone would want to threaten her, least of all someone she had loved. It didn't make sense. People should look for ways to work things out, not ways to kill each other.

Marilyn reached her home on 5ᵗʰ Helena and took the telephone on its long cord out to her swimming pool. There she sat and looked at the water in the pool and the blue sky above her. Greenson thought it was time to make peace with Bobby and Marilyn was prepared to do that. She realized that each of Greenson's arguments as to why the Kennedys were serious was important, but on another level, she could not imagine that they would really do her harm. Still, there was the matter of Castro. Marilyn frowned when she thought that agents of her government were actually planning to kill him.

"This is Marilyn Monroe," she announced through the telephone to the secretary at the Justice Department. "I would like to speak to the Attorney General."

"What is this regarding, Miss Monroe?" Robert Kennedy's secretary asked her.

"Tell him I need to speak to him about his friend, Sam Giancana." Marilyn knew that the Attorney General would be shocked to hear Sam Giancana referred to as his 'friend.'

After a few minutes, Robert Kennedy answered the telephone: "I heard you had a tough weekend, Marilyn"

"Thanks to you," she replied. "I was expecting to see you and you sent your friend Giancana instead."

Kennedy grunted his disagreement. "I got caught up here in Washington. You know we have things to do."

"So you've told me," she said. "Don't you think having Sam Giancana tell me he would shoot me in the face if I broke the code of silence was a little too much?"

"I didn't even know Sam Giancana was going to be there," the Attorney General said.

"Yes, you did. Because if you were planning to be there, there is no way Sam Giancana would have been invited." She let the power of her logic sink in for Bobby. "So, you're calling out the Mafia to deal with me."

"If you know something that would make you a target for the Mafia, I hope you will let me in on it," Robert Kennedy said.

Marilyn got the idea that Bobby was choosing his words carefully and that the telephone line was probably tapped. She didn't care.

"I'm the one who is losing out here," Marilyn told him. "If I get you men to stop this nonsense with Castro, he benefits, you benefit, and I give up my relationship with the President. I save Jack Kennedy and he dumps me. That doesn't seem fair."

"It was your choice, Marilyn," Bobby reminded her. "You're the one who wanted to change things."

"Doesn't seem fair."

"You and the President are having a separation," he said. "You get to have the pleasure of changing our foreign policy, and we get all of our letters and things back."

"What do you mean?" Marilyn asked.

"You want us to say that we're not going after Castro, right?"

"Right."

"Then you have to give us your little book of secrets and all the correspondence that you've kept. I mean we can't say we're not doing something and then have you show information to the contrary. That's not fair. And you have to agree to remain silent about Cuba."

Marilyn thought about the tradeoff. She would give them back some letters, they would call off the Cuban operation. "That's fair," she concluded. "I can live with that."

"We don't like this," Bobby told her. "We want to get rid of Castro and you're basically telling us that we can't."

"I'm just trying to prevent Jack from getting shot," Marilyn said. "If it means that I have to give up my relationship with the President, I guess that's what it means. It hurts my feelings to think that he wouldn't ever want to see me again, but I'll have to accept that."

"Then we have an agreement," Bobby concluded. "I'll come down there this weekend and we'll get things worked out."

"I give you my records and you call off your thugs from Cuba," Marilyn summarized.

"That's the deal," Robert Kennedy confirmed.

Chapter 41

*"Marilyn Monroe is cooking in the sex appeal depart-
ment. She has appeared vastly alluring to a handsome
gentleman. A handsome gentleman with a bigger name
than Joe DiMaggio in his heyday—so don't write her
off."*

Dorothy Kilgallen
New York Journal-American
August 3, 1962

Robert Kennedy looked at the billowing clouds beneath
him. They were like floating cotton balls, he thought, pulled and
twisted by the high winds. As he sat in the airplane, he was trying to
read a typed speech he was scheduled to give to the Bar association
in San Francisco. But, his mind kept wandering away from the
speech. Marilyn Monroe was enjoying more publicity than she had
in years. On his way to the airport that morning, he had seen a large
poster of her mostly naked body. **Life** Magazine doing a feature on
her nude swimming scene. She was simply too large a presence to
ignore. Even though she was an actress, she commanded a certain
credibility in the press and it was that credibility in the press that
bothered him most that morning. Anyone else could just be dismissed
with a simple denial. Dealing with Marilyn was going to mean more risk.

"Mr. Kennedy," an officer called to him above the
background hum of the airplane.

Bobby looked up at the officer.

"It's the President," the man said. He handed Bobby the telephone.

Bobby glanced around the cabin. Ethel and four of his children were in the next cabin. Only his closest staff members were near him.

"Jack?" he said.

"Big trouble, Bobby," the President said. Through the mild static of the line, Bobby could hear a distinct tension in the President's voice. "It's Marilyn. It looks like we're about to lose our cover."

Bobby was struck with a terrible sinking feeling. For the last couple of weeks, he had sensed that Marilyn's involvement with the First Family was on the verge of making news.

"Has anything been printed?" he asked the President.

"I'm looking at a copy of the **New York Journal-American**," the President said. "It's a little too obvious."

"Are we mentioned?" the Attorney General asked.

"No. But, let me read it to you. '*Marilyn Monroe is cooking in the sex appeal department. She has appeared vastly alluring to a handsome gentleman. A handsome gentleman with a bigger name than Joe DiMaggio in his heyday—so don't write her off.*' Don't you love it?"

"Who wrote it?" Bobby asked.

"Dorothy Kilgallen."

"We're not mentioned," Bobby pointed out.

"It's hard to imagine anyone being bigger than Joe DiMaggio in his prime," the President said. "I think she's got the story. The only question is whether she'll go with it—whether her paper will go with it."

"Can't we get some leverage on the **Journal-American**?" Bobby asked.

"There's only so much we can do, unless we want another story about the Kennedys censoring the press. We've got to get some leverage on Marilyn. She's got to get back on our side."

"I'll try to make peace with her," Bobby said.

"If you can't make peace with her, I don't know what we'll do. I don't want to think about it."

"I don't want to think about it either, but McCone said they were making some contingencies. Marilyn's got to be controlled, one way or the other."

After the call, Bobby took his ball point pen out of his shirt pocket and began to make a drawing on the copy of the speech he had to deliver to the Bar association. Whenever he had to make a decision, he liked to draw little boxes. The boxes were possibilities. Lines came out of the boxes, showing the consequences of what might happen. Either Marilyn could come to her senses and play ball, or she could continue to be a pain in the ass. If she was a pain in the ass, she could be a pain in the ass on just a personal level, or she could choose to be a pain in the ass on a much bigger level. Bobby looked at the boxes and made a decision: she had to be controlled. That was only way it could work. Either she would agree to giving him the letters and book of secrets and tell him she would stay quiet, or she wouldn't. If she wouldn't play ball—he filled in one of the boxes with black ink.

When they arrived in San Francisco, Ethel and the children took a limousine to a ranch in Gilroy. The American Bar association provided him with a local sponsor, a loyal Democrat and Ethel and the children were going to spend the weekend at the Bates Ranch. After the speech, they were going to fly up to Washington State to meet the Supreme Court Justice William O. Douglas, an old Kennedy family friend. They were scheduled to enjoy two weeks of camping and recreation in wilderness areas. Bobby was looking forward to the vacation. But, first, he had to give a speech to the Bar association and he had to come to a firm understanding with Marilyn Monroe.

News reporters asked him questions as he arrived at the St. Francis Hotel in San Francisco. Bobby liked to spend time with reporters. Their friendship was important. But August 3, 1962 was not a day he wanted to spend with reporters.

A reporter for the **San Francisco Chronicle** wrote that "*Bobby was without his usual flashy smile and shook hands woodenly with those who welcomed him. Perhaps the cares of the administration are weighing heavily on him.*"

"Mr. Kennedy, there are rumors that the Russians are sending missiles to Cuba. Can you comment on that?" a young man asked.

"No. That's ridiculous," Bobby answered as he walked into an elevator.

"Is the Administration tough enough to keep the Russians away from Cuba?"

The elevator doors closed. The Cuban problem could explode in the press. Of all the issues he and Jack dealt with, they were most vulnerable on Cuba. Any headline would bring back the memory of the Bay of Pigs. After that crisis, the press had rallied to the support of the President. But if he and Jack let the Russians put offensive missiles in Cuba, the country was going to think they were not up to the job. The elevator doors opened. Bobby followed his security detail into a top floor suite which the Bar association had rented for his stay.

After the security men closed the doors, Ed Guthman, one of Bobby's closest aides, handed him a copy of the **Journal-American**.

"You're not going to believe this," Guthman told the Attorney General.

Bobby read over the piece. There it was in black and white. Marilyn was involved with a man bigger than Joe DiMaggio in his prime. He threw the newspaper across the room where it hit a window which rattled but did not break.

"Damn!" he said with his teeth clenched. "She's not giving us much choice."

"Dr. Greenson," the Attorney General said, after Guthman found Marilyn's psychiatrist on the telephone. "You need to help us out. Your patient has got to understand she can't use us for her own publicity. She needs to show some loyalty."

306 J. Arthur Jensen

"Mr. Kennedy," Ralph Greenson said, "Ethically, I can't discuss the care of Marilyn Monroe with you or anyone else."

Bobby did not immediately respond.

"Did I understand you to say that you had ethical problems with helping us out?" Bobby asked the psychiatrist.

"I know that seems like a technicality to you, but trust in a doctor is sometimes the most important—"

"—Trust in a doctor?" Bobby interrupted Greenson. "Let me tell you something about ethics, doctor. You acted as Marilyn's agent on this movie *Something's Got to Give.*"

"Actually, not as her agent. I was only—"

"Don't bullshit me. I know the facts. You selected the producer for the movie, didn't you?" the Attorney General was in no mood to have a civil conversation.

"Well, I suppose it—"

"You supposed right, Doctor. You guaranteed that you could get her to the sets on time. And you're in line to get a cut of the movie. Want to know how I found out about that?"

Greenson did not respond.

"Let's talk for a minute about ethics. Actually, let's talk for a minute about conflicts of interest. What do you think the medical board would do with a doctor who was taking a piece of a celebrity client's movie deal? I'm just wondering."

"Mr. Kennedy, my relationship with this patient is unusual because she is unusual. I have worked with her agents and the studio, but I have not violated my ethical responsibilities to her."

"Ethical responsibilities? I like that," the Attorney General mocked. "Do you think it was ethical for you to send your patient down to Mexico to meet with an old friend of yours who happens to be a Communist informant? Was it ethical for you to take recordings of your patient to Switzerland and East Germany? Was that ethical? We know that you talked with agents of the Soviet Union and you got paid for your trouble. That makes you a spy, Dr. Greenson."

The words stunned Ralph Greenson and he could not immediately respond.

"I have long admired the work you and your brother are doing," Greenson finally squeaked out. "No one has shown such courage on Civil Rights since Lincoln."

"You're kind to say so," Bobby said. He wiped his forehead.

"I know that sometimes there are conflicts, conflicts between doctors and patients, conflicts between politicians and their lovers. I am trying to help Marilyn Monroe. But, I want you to know that I understand the problems that she could cause for the Administration. Of course, I also realize that I have an obligation as a loyal citizen of this country."

"I'm glad you recognize the need to work with me on this," the Attorney General told Marilyn's psychiatrist. "If you were to be exposed as being an agent of a foreign government, that wouldn't really be good for any of us, would it?"

"No, I don't think so."

"No, it wouldn't. I don't want to indict you for being a spy. I don't even want to see your medical license pulled because I think we can work together, and we're going to need to work together if we are to help Marilyn Monroe realize that she only has one good choice."

"She has to stay quiet about Cuba," the psychiatrist summarized.

"That's right," the Attorney General agreed. "She has to stay quiet and you have to stay quiet. But I think if we work together, no one is going to get hurt."

Chapter 42

*"They argued back and forth for maybe ten minutes,
Marilyn becoming more and more hysterical. At the height
of her anger she allowed how first thing Monday morning
she was going to call a press conference and tell the world
about the treatment she had suffered at the hands of the
Kennedy brothers. Now, Bobby became livid. In no uncer-
tain terms he told her she was going to have to leave both
Jack and him alone—no more telephone calls, no letters,
nothing. They didn't want to hear from her any more.
Marilyn lost it at this point, screaming obscenities and
flailing wildly away with her fists. In her fury she picked
up a small kitchen knife and lunged at him. I was with
them at this point, so I tried to grab Marilyn's arm. We
finally knocked her down and managed to wrestle the
knife away. Bobby thought we ought to call Dr. Ralph
Greenson, her Beverly Hills psychiatrist, and tell him to
come over."*

Peter Lawford as quoted by C. David Heymann

Carrying a hand full of freshly cut wild flowers, Marilyn
climbed up the narrow dirt trail which coiled along the hillside
below her house. She loved the wild flowers, especially the bouga-
invillea which crawled up the whitewashed walls separating the
house at 5th Helena from the garden. Marilyn wiped her brow.

Even though it was still mid-morning, the low hanging cloud cover had already burned off and the temperatures were rising.

She had not slept well. Whenever she was dieting, she had problems falling asleep. Friday night, August 3, 1962, had been no exception. Marilyn had taken some Nembutal and still not been able to drop off. She was convinced that the diet pills themselves were keeping her awake.

Marilyn entered her house and walked to the kitchen. She took a vase from a cabinet and filled it with some water. Then, she moved the wildflowers around so as to discover the most pleasing arrangement. As she played with the flowers, Marilyn started to think about something Pat had said to her the night before. She had been at Pucini's with Peter Lawford and Pat Newcomb. The subject of Dorothy Kilgallen's column had come up and Pat told Marilyn that she should not have talked to Kilgallen. It was just like Pat to always take the Kennedys' side.

Another detail was lodged in Marilyn's mind. Bobby had made special reference to Marilyn's notebooks, her diary, and some letters that she had received from the Kennedys. He wanted to get all the material in exchange for calling the CIA dogs off from Castro. But how had he known about the notebooks and her diary? He might have guessed that she had some letters, but who would have mentioned her notebooks to Robert Kennedy?

Marilyn heard Pat Newcomb go into the bathroom. It was almost noon. Marilyn couldn't believe how long Pat could sleep.

Eunice Murray, Marilyn's housekeeper, walked into the kitchen.

"Up early this morning, Marilyn," Mrs. Murray commented.

"Are you going to report that to Dr. Greenson?" Marilyn retorted. Marilyn was becoming suspicious of everyone around her. She had a feeling that Eunice Murray was reporting Marilyn's conversations and visitors to her psychiatrist. Having Dr. Greenson know what went on at every hour of her day was becoming too invasive for Marilyn.

"Now, dear," Mrs. Murray responded with a gentle laugh.

"Dr. Greenson just wants the best for you. Would you like me to start on the laundry?"

"I'm expecting a very important visitor this afternoon," Marilyn told her housekeeper. "If you could set the table next to the pool, that would be nice."

"Shall I set it for two?"

"Yes," Marilyn answered. "You can set the table for two."

Mrs. Murray took down some crystal champagne glasses and began to rinse them in the sink.

"Nice rest, Pat?" Marilyn asked as Pat Newcomb came into the kitchen. She was wearing only a robe.

"Very nice," Pat said. She looked at Mrs. Murray drying the champagne glasses. "Bobby coming down today?

Marilyn put the flower arrangement down in the center of the table. She looked up at Pat with some confusion in her eyes because she had made a point of not telling Pat that Bobby was coming down that afternoon. She had wanted to say something the night before, but had been careful not to.

"Who told you that?" Marilyn asked her.

Pat wiped her eyes and used her hand to straighten her hair. She was not sure she was ready to start the day.

"I can't remember," she said, after a few moments thought. "I can't remember who told me."

Marilyn stared at her as she walked over to the refrigerator and poured herself a glass of orange juice. She wondered how Pat might have learned that Bobby was coming down to Los Angeles. Marilyn knew she had not told Pat.

"Did I tell you?" Marilyn asked.

"Yes, you did. That's how I learned. You told me."

Another few moments passed.

"When did I tell you that?"

"I don't know. Sometime during the week, I guess. What's with you today, Marilyn? Couldn't you sleep?" Pat sat down next to the table and began to look over the newspaper. She pushed Marilyn's notebook to the side.

"I never sleep that well when I'm taking the diet pills," Marilyn said. "They make me edgy. I just can't figure out how you learned that Bobby was going to come down here today.

"Is it a big deal?" Pat asked. "I didn't realize it was such a secret."

Marilyn smiled. Perhaps the diet pills were making her feel paranoid. She walked over to Pat and gave her a small hug as if to apologize.

"Well, he's coming here," Marilyn said. "We're going to have lunch and talk over some details."

Pat smiled warmly at Marilyn. "Must be nice to have the Attorney General coming to visit."

"It's not exactly a romantic occasion," Marilyn said.

Marilyn picked her notebook up off from the table. She wanted to go in her bedroom and finish her thoughts from earlier in the morning. In picking up the notebook, Marilyn made the connection.

"Have you ever mentioned my notebooks to Bobby?" she asked Pat.

"I might have, I don't remember," Pat replied. "Why would he know about your notebooks?"

"Exactly," Marilyn said. "I wondered how he might know about my diary or my notebooks. I certainly have never shared them with him."

"He probably just doesn't want you to show people like Dorothy Kilgallen the notebooks or diary," Pat proposed.

Marilyn considered this thought for a moment and then realized that the only way the Kennedys could know about her notebooks was through Pat. "You've known Bobby for many years," Marilyn suggested to Pat. "Has he ever asked someone for their diary?"

"Not that I can remember," Pat said absently.

"How many years have you known Bobby," Marilyn asked Pat.

"I don't know," Pat confessed. She realized that Marilyn was checking her answers for honesty. "My father worked for Ethel Kennedy's father. He was their lobbyist."

Marilyn absorbed this news without showing any emotion. Pat, someone she had trusted like a sister, was part of the Kennedy network. How could she have not known there was a connection between Pat and Bobby?

"So that's the reason that you think that I spoke with Dorothy Kilgallen. You work for me but you are really loyal to Bobby."

"Marilyn! You're making some big jumps there."

"But it's true. You must have known him before you knew me. It was Frank Sinatra who thought I should hire you. And you never told me that you knew the Kennedys from before."

Pat squirmed in her chair and pushed the newspaper away. She looked up at Marilyn and tried to remain calm. "I didn't know any of them very well. But, Pierre Salinger was my college professor and he wanted to work for Bobby Kennedy back in the days of the McClellan hearings. I called my father and he arranged to get Pierre an interview with Bobby."

"Pierre Salinger was your college professor?" Marilyn asked. She couldn't believe that the President's press secretary had a personal connection to Patricia Newcomb and she hadn't known about it.

"It all goes back to the Kennedys," Marilyn whispered to Pat. She buried her head in her hands and thought for a few moments, then looked back up at Pat. "Get out of here."

Pat was startled. Mrs. Murray turned away from the sink and stared at Marilyn.

"You've been reporting everything to Bobby," Marilyn asserted.

A light red tint came to Pat's face. She tried to answer Marilyn's charge, but couldn't find the words.

"I've never . . . why . . ." Pat stammered.

Marilyn picked up the notebook and took a swing at Pat. Pat jumped out of the kitchen chair and retreated away from the enraged Marilyn.

"You told him about the notebooks—you miserable little slut!

You've been spying!" In her rage, Marilyn threw the notebook at Pat.

Pat managed to dodge the flying notebook and then backed into the guest bedroom where she had slept and shut the door.

Marilyn sat down at the kitchen table and cried. She had always treated Pat like a sister, never suspecting that Pat might be disloyal. Now it was apparent to her that Pat had connections to the Kennedys that she'd never revealed. Pat knew about everything in her life and she had relied on Pat to be loyal to her, not loyal to the Kennedys.

Pat opened the door of the bedroom and walked down the hallway, away from the kitchen, and out the front door. She didn't say good-bye. Marilyn heard her start her car and drive away from the house.

Mrs. Murray continued to dry the plates she had just washed. She was ready to set the table for Marilyn's lunch.

"I wonder if you want to talk to Dr. Greenson before your guest arrives," she suggested to Marilyn.

Marilyn had stopped crying. She was angry, but she needed to focus on more important matters with Bobby than how he learned that she was keeping track of her thoughts in some old notebooks. This was a big day. She had to get prepared.

"I don't think I have time," Marilyn said. "I'm just going to have to do the best I can."

Marilyn went to her bedroom and changed her clothes. She began the ritualistic application of hair sprays and makeup.

Robert Kennedy wasn't in the mood to play nice. It was Saturday, August 4. He had traveled to Los Angeles aboard a military jet and then been taken to the Fox lot aboard a large blue helicopter, on loan from Howard Hughes, and reserved at the Los Angeles Airport for his use. Peter Lawford picked him up at the Fox lot. Bobby needed to collect the 'book of secrets,' any physical evidence of her association with the President or with him, and swear Marilyn to secrecy. This was a day of doing the family's business.

Peter tried to make conversation as he drove Bobby to 5th

Helena, but Bobby said nothing. After a few attempts, Peter realized Bobby wasn't going to talk and he quit trying.

"I need the letters and notebooks," the Attorney General told Marilyn Monroe when she greeted him at the front door. Bobby walked through the house and out onto the patio next to the swimming pool. Peter Lawford stopped in the kitchen where the lunch was being set out.

"My, my!" Lawford exclaimed playfully as he looked at the steaming meatballs.

Marilyn followed Bobby through the kitchen and out onto the patio.

"You're welcome to them," Marilyn told him. "You just need to announce that you will leave the Cubans alone.

Bobby laughed. "No," he said. "I need them today. Right now."

"That wasn't our deal," Marilyn reminded him. "You were supposed to announce that you will tolerate the government of Cuba. You quit harassing Castro, and I give you the notebooks or letters or whatever it is that you want and I don't talk about Cuba. That was our understanding."

Marilyn walked away from his uncompromising stare and looked down the hillside, at her wild garden. She sipped some champagne. Then, she looked across the pool and saw Peter Lawford picking at the lunch she had ordered in for herself and Bobby. It wasn't going to be a relaxed lunch given Bobby's mood, so just as well that Peter was enjoying it. She turned back toward Kennedy.

"I thought I was clear about the diary and papers," the Attorney General said.

"You were very clear," Marilyn agreed. "You were going to make a public statement announcing that the administration would tolerate Castro's presence in Cuba. I was going to give you whatever letters or notebooks you wanted."

"We can't play games, Marilyn," Bobby sneered.

"I'm not playing any games. That was our deal. Now, if you

want to behave in a civilized fashion, we can talk about the details over lunch."

Robert Kennedy turned away from Marilyn and walked into her house. She followed him.

"I didn't think you'd mind if I got a little jump on lunch," Peter Lawford said. He was finishing a plate of meatballs and washing them down with a glass of champagne as Bobby and Marilyn came in the house.

"I have to get those notebooks right now," Bobby told her. "We don't have time for this nonsense anymore."

"That wasn't our agreement."

"Where are they?" The Attorney General started to walk through the house looking for the notebooks. Marilyn followed him.

"You can't just start going through my house," Marilyn yelled. "You need a warrant."

The Attorney General entered Marilyn's bedroom and opened the closet. "Where are they?" he shouted. "I have to have them."

"Get out of my bedroom," she screamed at Bobby.

Robert Kennedy walked out of the bedroom, through the living room and dining room to Marilyn's kitchen. "Where are those goddamn notebooks?" he shouted.

"That wasn't our understanding," she responded. "You haven't done anything about Cuba."

They were standing face to face in Marilyn's kitchen. As they argued, they seemed to be drawn closer together.

"You're going to have to forget you ever heard about Cuba. You have to understand that. You have to forget about Cuba."

"Cuba, Cuba, Cuba," she mocked him. "I'll say it anytime I want to."

Robert Kennedy grimaced and pushed Marilyn away from him. She bumped back against the refrigerator and almost fell.

"You little bastard," she mumbled as she regained her posture. "You're big enough to push girls."

Something ignited in the Attorney General. Fire flashed in his eyes.

"Listen to me," he shouted. "You know things you shouldn't know. Now, you have to promise me that you won't talk about those things."

"I have to talk about them."

"No," he shouted. He reached out and took a firm grasp of Marilyn's shirt and pulled her toward him. "You have to be quiet. Either you shut up or we're going to have to shut you up."

He let her collar go. Marilyn blinked a few times as she tried to understand the implications of what Bobby was telling her. Their voices became low.

"Are you threatening me?" she whispered to the Attorney General.

"Marilyn, you have to stay quiet."

"Are you threatening me? Is that what you're doing?"

She stared into Robert Kennedy's eyes. He returned her stare.

"Yes," he said. "That's what I'm doing. I'm threatening you. You have to stay quiet. There's no other way."

Peter Lawford had been waiting out on the patio for the fight to end. After the shouting stopped, he saw no reason why he couldn't go in and get some more champagne. He walked into the kitchen, but stopped when he saw Marilyn and Bobby were within a foot of one another. Maybe this wasn't a good time to disturb them.

Marilyn, her eyes riveted to Bobby's, saw Peter approach from the side. She felt crowded as she realized that they had her surrounded. She was trapped by two men in her own kitchen.

In an instant, Marilyn pushed Bobby back and grabbed a small knife off the kitchen counter. She stood facing Bobby and Peter.

"Get away from me," she shrieked.

"Marilyn, for God's sake, put that knife down," Peter said. "Are you nuts?" He approached her with his hand out.

Seeing him approach, Marilyn realized that the two men had the power to overtake her. They were going to try to stop her—they were going to try to hold her down. She had no choice. She had to fight. Screaming, she rushed the two men.

Robert Kennedy reached up and caught Marilyn's arm, but

Marilyn was able to hit him across the face with her other hand. Peter Lawford, his hand reaching out for the knife, bumped into Marilyn and Bobby and the three of them fell to the floor. Marilyn landed on Peter and Bobby fell to Peter's side. Now, Peter had his hand firmly around Marilyn's wrist. He pried the knife out of her hand as the Attorney General of the United States held her on the floor. The more she screamed and the more she struggled, the tighter the men held her.

"What the hell are you doing?" Peter asked her. He was panting and sweating.

"Get off of me," she yelled.

With her head trapped against the floor, Marilyn saw another figure loom over her. She could not see a face, but recognized the shoes. Mrs. Murray was there! Mrs. Murray would help her.

"Call the police, Eunice!" Marilyn screamed.

There was a silence as Peter, Marilyn, and Bobby awaited Mrs. Murray's response.

"Should I call Dr. Greenson?" Mrs. Murray asked.

"Yes," Bobby Kennedy shouted. "Get Greenson over here. Marilyn's going to need an injection to calm her down. Get him over here."

Peter Lawford and Robert Kennedy restrained Marilyn until Dr. Greenson arrived.

Chapter 43

"Robert Kennedy was here, threatening me, yelling at me . . . You know, I know a lot of secrets about what has gone on in Washington . . . dangerous secrets."

Marilyn Monroe to Sydney Guilaroff (hairstylist)
August 4, 1962
Los Angeles Times, August 21, 1996

"The truth is, we knew Robert Kennedy was in town on August 4. We always knew when he was here.

Daryl Gates
Chief: My Life in the LAPD

Ralph Greenson sat next to Marilyn's bed and looked at his celebrated patient. Calmed by the injection he had given her, Marilyn spoke to him with her eyes closed. Occasionally, she slurred a word, but, for the most part, her speech made sense. It was the end of a warm summer afternoon on August 4, 1962.

"He said he would silence you?" Greenson asked.

"That's right. He said that I couldn't talk about Cuba or he would have to keep me quiet." Marilyn was quiet for a moment as she remembered the harshness of the exchange. "He was very clear. I've got to get to New York."

"New York?" Greenson repeated.

"I need a safe harbor," she said, her eyes darted around the room.

"Now Marilyn, calm down," Greenson told her. "Your thinking has become disordered. You need to slow down and think carefully."

Greenson shifted in his chair. He glanced over at Marilyn's bedside table. Several bottles of prescription pills littered the surface. A stack of scripts supported a single empty glass at the base of the table.

"I spoke with Robert Kennedy," Greenson told Marilyn. "There is no question in my mind that he feels responsible for the success of the Cuban program. If he said he would silence you, I think he means it."

"I'm sure he does," Marilyn agreed.

"I think you have to make peace with Robert Kennedy," Greenson advised. "I'd tell him anything he wants to hear at this point, but I'd be sure he understands that you've given up. You don't want to fight the entire United States government anymore."

Marilyn smiled. "I guess you're right. If it has come to this, maybe I've taken things too far."

"I think so," Greenson told her. "I respect what you've tried to do for Fidel Castro, but even Castro is thinking about his own skin. It is time that you started to think about yours."

Marilyn wiped her eyes.

"I think I've pressed them hard enough," Marilyn conceded. "Trying to get them to see the right thing to do is one thing, to lose your life doing it is another."

Greenson went on: "If they want some notebooks, give them the damn notebooks. He thinks you are trying to blackmail them with the notebooks. I told him that you are not, but he needs to hear it from you. You've done your duty to warn them."

A faint smile crossed Marilyn's face as she realized that she had taken things too far.

"No, I would never blackmail anyone," Marilyn said resolutely.

"I want you to tell him that, Marilyn," Dr. Greenson told her.

She laughed at the thought that the President and Attorney General of the United States were afraid of what she might do next. She opened eyes and squinted into the light coming through her window.

"All right," Marilyn agreed. "I guess I'll talk to him. This has gone on long enough."

Robert Kennedy was nervously pacing the living room when Dr. Greenson approached him. His shirt tails had been pulled out of his pants during his struggle with Marilyn. He had not yet tucked them back in. Peter Lawford was sitting on the couch smoking a cigarette. Mrs. Murray was in the kitchen cleaning up.

"Marilyn didn't intend to blackmail you, Mr. Kennedy. She can be a little stubborn. I think she was trying just a little too hard to get her way."

"Did you give her enough sedation, doctor," the Attorney General wanted to know.

"Yes. She's completely relaxed, but her thinking is disordered. She's talking about going to New York," Greenson reported.

"New York?" Kennedy asked.

"A safe harbor—something like that," Greenson said with a curious smile. "Barbiturates can sometimes mix up someone's thought processes. But let me assure you, Marilyn Monroe is no threat to you or your brother."

Robert Kennedy continued his nervous walk around the room and stopped to look out the sliding glass door at the swimming pool. "She won't be able to drive anywhere this evening, will she?"

"Oh, no. She should rest very comfortably this evening," Greenson predicted. Mrs. Murray will stay with her and will call me if Marilyn needs help."

"I would like you to stay here until I have a chance to leave," the Attorney General told Greenson. "Marilyn may need to talk to you again. You and I might need to discuss some contingencies."

Greenson stood in Marilyn's living room with Robert Kennedy. He stared at Kennedy until the Attorney General gave him his complete attention.

"I think you realize the depth of my loyalty to this country," Greenson asserted.

Kennedy stared back at Greenson. "I think we both know the depth of your loyalties," Kennedy told Greenson, "but let's hope it doesn't come to that."

Marilyn remained in her bed as Bobby entered her room. He sat in the chair vacated by Greenson and stared at Marilyn. She opened her eyes and returned his gaze. After a few minutes, Bobby stood up and pulled his chair closer to Marilyn's bed. He reached out and held her hand. She let him hold it. The time had come to make peace with the Kennedys.

"Things can get crazy," he said.

"They can," she agreed.

"I'm sorry things got so crazy this afternoon," he said.

"So am I."

Kennedy looked out the window in Marilyn's bedroom. Then, he looked back at her.

"I just spoke with the President."

"You did?"

"Yes. We talked about things."

"That's nice . . ." Marilyn said slowly.

"Marilyn, we want to ask something of you."

"What?"

The Attorney General squeezed her hand gently.

"We want you to forget about Castro and let us do our jobs."

"Forget about Castro," Marilyn repeated. "I wish I could forget this whole thing."

"You can," Bobby assured her. "Things have gotten very dangerous in the world and we have to know that you are with us. We have to know that you won't talk to the press about Castro and we have to know it right now."

Marilyn gazed into his eyes and he into hers.

"And if I don't agree to be quiet while you kill Castro?" she asked.

"You've got to be quiet about everything you know or think

you know about Castro, and you've got to give me those letters and notebooks. I wish I didn't have this job sometimes, but I do, and I have to guard the security of this operation."

"So, it isn't a deal anymore," Marilyn summarized. "I give you the notebooks, I agree to be quiet about Castro, and you go right on doing what you're doing."

"I'm afraid so," the Attorney General said. He squeezed her hand. "You're going to have to trust us to do what we think is best for the country—just like everyone else."

Marilyn thought about Bobby's demands for a few moments. The light caught the edge of his hair and gave his head an almost fuzzy look. She remembered the military haircut of her first husband and how the haircut translated into authority and the overwhelming priority of defense.

"I guess I have no choice," Marilyn said. "I guess I wrecked my relationship with the President and got nothing for Mr. Castro. I sure hope Jack will be all right."

"So you'll quit fighting us over Castro?" Bobby asked.

"I'll quit fighting you over Castro," Marilyn promised. "What you have planned for Castro is not fair—it wouldn't be fair for anyone. But I'll let you struggle with that one. I saw a threat to the President and like anyone who loves him . . ." her voice trailed off. She turned her head away from Bobby and swallowed hard as her eyes filled with tears. It all seemed so unfair to her that she should be thinking ultimately of the welfare of John Kennedy but like so much of the love she had shown him, her affections were not returned. She thought of him smiling and laughing at Peter's beach house. Then she thought of him criticizing her for having ever talked to Field, and then unfairly cutting her off. After a few moments, she was able to go on. "I tried to warn him. No one thinks I have anything important to say, but we'll see. I've done my duty."

"You have," Bobby confirmed. "You've warned us. But now you have to let us go it alone."

"All right," she agreed.

Robert Kennedy stood up from the chair.

"We'll be back in touch, Marilyn," Bobby assured her. "When things cool off, maybe something can be worked out. Where are the notebooks?"

"I have all the papers and things locked up," Marilyn told him. "I'll give them to Peter when I can get around a little easier."

"You can't get them now?" Kennedy asked her.

"Not after that injection," Marilyn said. "I'll feel better in a day or two."

The Attorney General was again stunned by her stubbornness: she wouldn't give up. As Robert Kennedy looked at Marilyn, a cold reality became lodged in his mind. Rather than agree with him on a very basic point, Marilyn wrestled him to the floor and needed an injection to sedate her. Now she was still unwilling to give him the papers he came to collect—and she was making references to trying to get to New York. The sad reality was that he could neither trust nor control Marilyn Monroe. The Attorney General nodded his understanding of the situation. He straightened his hair with his hand and rubbed his eyes.

"You're sure you can't give me those notebooks?" he asked finally.

"Not tonight," Marilyn told him. "I'll give them to Peter in a day or so."

Bobby lifted Marilyn's hand up and lightly kissed it.

"I think we'll see you soon, Marilyn."

Marilyn looked at him as he prepared to leave.

"I think you're right Bobby," Marilyn agreed cheerfully. "I have a feeling we're all going to be together again sooner than anyone thinks."

Robert Kennedy walked back out into the living area where Dr. Greenson stood up to receive him.

"I'll be in touch with you, doctor," he told Greenson.

Then, with Peter Lawford trailing behind him, the Attorney General walked out of Marilyn's house and got in Lawford's car. Together, they drove toward the beach.

Chapter 44

". . . Subject made reference to "bases" in Cuba and knew of the President's plan to kill Castro . . . Subject threatened to hold a press conference and would tell all . . . Subject made reference to her "diary of secrets" and what the newspapers would do with such disclosures . . ."

James Angleton
CIA Chief of Counterintelligence
August 3, 1962
Declassified "Top Secret" Report of Wiretap on
Marilyn Monroe's telephone

Although it was past 9 o'clock on a Saturday night, John McCone sat in his office in the large CIA Headquarters in Langley, Virginia and puffed on his pipe. He didn't have to be there. He could be at a country club with his rich friends enjoying the fruits of his successful career in business. But, such a life would not be of great service to anyone but himself, and that wasn't the kind of man he was. He wanted to serve his country. Duty to country was on the top of his list of efforts worthy of his time, so, even though he was a Republican, he had accepted the call to lead the CIA.

The Kennedy brothers needed his help. John McCone had known their father and liked him. But, the young Kennedys were a little bit reckless. McCone knew their kind. They were like the young men he had known in college who drove automobiles too fast, and when they got in accidents, got out and went on to the next party, letting someone else accept responsibility for their mess. It was behavior McCone associated with inherited money. If the fellows had any appreciation of how the money was made or who got hurt in their accidents, they would be a little more careful.

McCone put his pipe down and lifted his wire rimmed glasses off the desk. He polished the lenses using a special cloth he kept in the top drawer. When he was done, he neatly folded the cloth, placed it back into the drawer and put on his glasses.

He looked at the telephones sitting on his desk. One of the telephones was connected to his usual unpublished telephone number. The other telephone had no usual number. It was a telephone reserved for top secrets. It was constantly getting new numbers so that any calls made from the telephone could not be traced.

It was the evening of August 4, 1962. John McCone was waiting for a telephone call.

McCone met with Robert Kennedy's Special Group (Augmented) every day in early August. Intelligence reports indicated something serious was happening on the island of Cuba, something so serious, contingencies were being made to invade the island. Khrushchev had promised the President that he would not place offensive missiles in Cuba. In return, Kennedy promised Khrushchev that he would not attempt to remove the Communist government in Cuba.

But Kennedy was lying to Khrushchev and Khrushchev was lying to Kennedy.

The photographs taken by the U-2 planes were not lying. They showed missile silos being constructed on Cuba. Some of the photographs actually showed what appeared to be missiles on long flatbed trucks. The evidence was overwhelming.

What should McCone do? Should he allow his President—a man with such remarkable charm that he could lie successfully about his health and his women—to also lie about the national security? John McCone knew that the Soviets were building a missile base 90 miles from American shores. For the first time in history, cities on the East Coast from New York to Miami would be vulnerable to instantaneous foreign attack. Should he keep the secret? Was his first duty to his President or to the American people?

John McCone drew on the pipe and let the smoke blow out of his nostrils. He liked John Kennedy. But, he was not going to let those missiles go into Cuba without leaking the photographs to members of Congress. The public had a right to know.

McCone waited. The telephone did not ring. He continued to smoke the pipe. He leaned back in his chair and watched the smoke rise to form a cloud over his desk. The windows of his office were open, but it was hot and humid night in Virginia. No breeze would flush out the smoke.

Marilyn Monroe was not a foreign leader, so in a sense, her elimination was less of a moral dilemma. She was a private American citizen, though. The government was not in the business of eliminating private citizens.

It was a tricky business. McCone rationalized his agency's plans to kill Fidel Castro by weighing the cost of killing Castro against the cost of invading Cuba. There was really no comparison. It made sense to dispose of Castro and defuse what loomed as a showdown between the world's biggest superpowers. But, eliminating a movie star? He drew on the pipe.

By no fault of her own, Marilyn Monroe had learned about the CIA plans to remove Castro. She had no security clearance. She had never taken an oath to keep the government's secrets. But, now she knew one. She knew a very big one. And she was threatening to tell it.

The secret telephone rang.

McCone watched it ring. On the fifth ring, McCone picked it up. He said nothing. He glanced at his watch and looked at the second hand tick off the passing time.

He heard nothing from the receiver, except a muffled sigh from the caller.

Only one man had the number to the secret telephone that night. They had agreed that nothing would be said on either end for 20 seconds.

McCone watched the seconds pass.

Finally, he recognized the voice of the Attorney General.

"The game's up," Robert Kennedy said slowly. "The singer will not play." Kennedy paused, then repeated, "the singer will not play."

McCone did not respond. After another ten seconds of silence, he hung up the telephone.

There was no decision to make. He turned in his chair and smoked his pipe for another few moments. He had some calls to make, but facilitating the death of a young woman was not an action he relished.

AM/GOOSE looked at the waves rise on the Pacific Ocean and break along the beach. A light fog was rolling in off the water, but he could easily see the beach from the balcony of his motel room. The cool air felt refreshing against his moist skin. He was nervous. He had never killed a woman before.

The plan was simple enough. He had been given some bottles which contained the drugs. His job was to get the drugs into the woman. When he was done, he was to simply put the syringe and bottles back into the black carrying case and walk away. It was simple. He had been in the house before.

AM/GOOSE walked into the bathroom of the motel room and filled the sink with cold water. He threw some of the water up on his face and watched in the mirror as the water dripped away. He stared into his own brown eyes and studied what he had always considered to be the noble curves of his face. This was not work he had ever intended to do. He had grown up in privileged circumstances. When he had agreed to kill Castro, it was out of a sense of elevated purpose. Castro had taken his property and with it, the civility of his life. AM/GOOSE had no fight with Marilyn Monroe. She was one of the most beautiful women he had ever seen.

But if Marilyn Monroe was going to ruin the chances of a free Cuba, she would have to die.

He dried off his hands and walked over to the small desk on which he had placed the black carrying case. Flipping up the clasps, he lifted the top and exposed the syringes and dark brown bottles of liquid with the rubber stoppers. He lifted up one of the bottles and shook it in the light.

The telephone rang.

AM/GOOSE put the bottle back into the black case and walked over to the telephone. He lifted the receiver.

There was a long silence. He glanced at the second hand on his watch as he waited for his instructions.

After the empty pause, AM/GOOSE heard a voice from the receiver.

"Fifth Helena," the voice instructed him.

There was another long silence and then he heard a click as the connection was broken.

AM/GOOSE went back to the black carrying case and picked up the syringe from the case. He slid the plunger into the syringe and then fitted the needle. He pulled a little air into the syringe and then lifted one of the brown bottles up. Tipping the bottle upside down, he slid the needle into the rubber top of the bottle and pushed in the air. A clear green fluid ran back into the syringe. He pushed in some more air and more fluid came out. Then, he pushed the fluid back into the bottle and placed it back into the carrying case. He closed the top of the case and snapped the clasps back into place.

Marilyn Monroe sat in her living room and made telephone calls. Joe DiMaggio's son, Joe Jr., reported that he was breaking up with his girlfriend. It was just the kind of gossip she loved. She made a point of staying in touch with the friends she had made as she went through life, even if they were relatives of the men she had been involved with. Arthur Miller's father had called her earlier.

Marilyn called Sydney Guilaroff, her hairstylist. Sydney was always good for some entertainment.

"I want to get it done tomorrow," she told him, referring to her hair. "I've got some important meetings on Monday."

"With Fox?" Guilaroff asked.

"No," Marilyn answered. "I'm meeting with some Italian producers. They have promised me an $11 million dollar deal for four pictures. It's long range stuff, but if they're willing to pay $11 million, I'm willing to go to Italy."

"Can you imagine Rome on the day you arrived?" Sydney asked her. "Those Italian men would go completely nuts! You'd only be safe in the Vatican."

Marilyn smiled with the thought. Liz had conducted her affair with Richard Burton in Italy. It was time to show Liz who had the most star appeal.

"I've always liked Rome," Marilyn offered.

"But I thought you were still interested in that fellow from Washington," he said. "I think you're going to be busy enough here without going to Italy."

"*Robert Kennedy was here, threatening me, yelling at me . . . You know, I know a lot of secrets about what has gone on in Washington . . . dangerous secrets,*" Marilyn reported to Sydney.

"Marilyn," Guilaroff warned her, "If I knew some secrets about Washington, I think I'd try to forget them."

"You don't know the way these guys operate," Marilyn told him. "The more you scare them, the more attention they give you."

After she hung up the telephone with Sydney Guilaroff, Marilyn thought about who she could call next. The medication Dr. Greenson had given her by injection that afternoon was starting to wear off and she was feeling better with every call she made. Still, before he left, Dr. Greenson told her not to even think about going out that night. He was worried she would get into an accident if she drove. As she lounged on the couch in her living room, the telephone resting next to her, she looked at a script the Italian producers had given her.

Unable to concentrate on the script, Marilyn wanted to call Peter Lawford's house to try to speak to Bobby. The more she thought about it, the more ridiculous their fight earlier in the afternoon seemed to her. The Kennedys were playing her the same way they were playing Khrushchev—promise one deal, do something else. But there was a limit to how far she wanted to go to defend Fidel Castro and there was a limit to how far she would go to defend John Kennedy. Having a physical fight with the Attorney General was all the limit she needed. She had a movie to complete for an enormous new salary. And another one after that. And then her deal with Fox was over. The Italians were talking $11 million. The sky was the limit. Things wouldn't be so bad without the Kennedys.

She heard a noise outside her window. She got up to look outside.

Chapter 45

"Jose Bolanos, the lover who followed Marilyn from Mexico, says he telephoned Marilyn from the Ships Restaurant, not far from her home, between nine-thirty and ten o'clock. He will not reveal what they discussed. He does say Marilyn ended the conversation by simply laying down the phone . . . He thinks he was the last person to speak to Marilyn."

Anthony Summers
Goddess, 1986

". . . the day after Marilyn Monroe died, (Judith Campbell) Exner's own Los Angeles apartment was rifled. She later told the Times that her jewelry was untouched but her telephone records were stolen."

Los Angeles Times
September 26,1999

AM/GOOSE could see the lights burning in Marilyn's windows as he knelt behind a small shrub in her garden. There was just enough moonlight to allow him to see the outlines of the syringe and plunger and the dark bottles. He assembled the syringe and plunger, attached the needle, and drew the contents of two of the bottles into the syringe. Then, he stuck the needle into one of the bottles to prevent the liquid contents from leaking out. Standing up, he walked around the house. He placed the syringe and the bottle next to Marilyn's front door, then he continued his walk.

Through the windows of a back bedroom, AM/GOOSE saw an old woman reading a book. She rocked silently back and forth in her chair. AM/GOOSE continued to circle. When he saw Marilyn through the large windows of her living room, he wondered if he would be able to carry out his mission. He was moved by her beauty. She lay on her couch, reading a stack of white papers, printed on a single side, held together with two small clips. Her telephone rested on the floor beside her. She sipped something from a teacup. Seeing her in such a setting didn't convince him that she posed much of a risk to the national security.

AM/GOOSE stayed out of the perimeter of light coming from Marilyn's window. If he could get her to come out of her house, the job would be easy. From the side of the house, he picked up a small rock. He threw the rock at a piece of the pool furniture. It missed, landing quietly on some adjacent grass. He picked up a second rock. It hit.

Marilyn wondered what she had heard. She had lived in her house for almost six months and frequently read scripts late at night. She had never heard such a noise. It sounded like something had fallen off her table next to the pool. But why would it fall now?

She walked over to the sliding glass door which opened out to the pool patio. Nothing moved. Everything looked normal. She turned on an outdoor light and stared through the glass. What could it have been? Could it be a cat or a sick animal? Did something out there need her help?

Marilyn unlocked the sliding glass door and stepped out onto the patio beside her pool. There was nothing. She walked to the table next to the pool and looked around it. Nothing. She looked around her yard. Nothing moved. Still, she had heard something. Slowly, she walked back toward her house. A neighbor's dog had started to bark, but otherwise, the night was completely still.

Marilyn went back into her living room and slid the glass door closed. She latched it. Then, she went back to her couch and sat down. She decided to call her friend Jeanne Carmen. She had talked with Jeanne earlier in the day. Maybe, she could come over?

Lifting the telephone receiver, Marilyn dialed Jean's number. Then she held the telephone to her ear. She glanced around her house. Something was not right.

Marilyn heard a dial tone.

She tried to dial the number again, but the dial tone persisted.

Mrs. Murray must have been listening in on her last telephone calls, Marilyn thought. And then she hadn't had the sense to hang up the phone. The other extension must be off the hook. Marilyn slammed the telephone receiver back in its cradle and marched back to her bedroom. If Mrs. Murray was listening to her calls and reporting them to Dr. Greenson, she had to go. She should at least have the decency to not to listen from Marilyn's own bedroom.

Midway down the hall leading to her bedroom, Marilyn stopped. There were no lights in her room. She always made a point of leaving lights on in her house. Had Mrs. Murray turned the lights off? Or had someone else?

She peered into the darkness. Her skin became moist and she felt a slight chill.

Slowly, she crept down the hallway and looked into her bedroom. At the end of her bed, she saw her telephone. It was off the hook. Marilyn smiled. Maybe the diet pills were making her feel paranoid. She went into the room and picked up the telephone receiver. The door closed behind her.

John Kennedy couldn't sleep. Wearing his reading glasses, he sat in his bed. Copies of raw intelligence cables and aerial photographs of Cuba lay in front of him, but Kennedy was staring silently into the dark corners of the room.

The door to the President's bedroom squeaked open and the First Lady entered. She was dressed in a bathrobe and light slippers.

"Jack, I just wanted you to know that you were in my prayers," Jackie told him.

"I'll need some help with the Almighty, tonight," the President confessed.

"I read the most interesting article the other day," she went on. "A little boy was playing on some railroad tracks down in Georgia. A train was approaching and the engineer of the train saw the boy and immediately applied the breaks of the train. The wheels of the train locked, but trains have so much weight, it slid on the tracks."

The President lifted his glasses off from his face and placed them on a stack of papers. He rubbed his eyes.

"The boy was killed," the First Lady said. "The engineer did everything he could, but he could not stop the train quickly enough."

"The engineer was innocent," the President observed. "I'm not sure I'm so innocent."

"History is a train," Jackie said. "You might be the engineer, and you might want to stop the train, but you can't. There are going to be people killed by the terrible momentum of history. You couldn't have stopped the train if you were the engineer, and you couldn't have stopped it if you were the little boy on the tracks. History has a mass of its own."

"You are kind to be generous with me, tonight," the President observed. "Historians might not be so forgiving."

"You are doing the best you can do, Jack. These are very difficult circumstances. You can't derail the train for your friend, the actress. You are doing the best you can do."

After another few moments of silence, the First Lady turned and whisked out of the room. The President continued to stare into the darkness.

Two men in dark suits, white shirts, and narrow, dark ties got out of an unmarked sedan in front of a GTE office in Santa Monica, California. They glanced up and down the quiet street and walked into the telephone offices. The agents flashed their

F.B.I. badges to the security guard who summoned the night supervisor, a fat, bald man in middle age. The agents were brought back into the business offices where the supervisor scrutinized their papers.

"I've just never seen a Federal warrant before," the supervisor explained.

"This is a duly authorized national security action," the senior agent told the supervisor in a routine tone. "We need to gather the telephone records of one of your customers."

"But the bills haven't been processed yet," the supervisor objected. "The calls haven't been paid for."

"This action involves the national security," the agent continued. "Your supervisors will be given a procedure for payment of the bills."

"Which customer's bills do you need?"

"Marilyn Monroe, the actress."

The supervisor rubbed his neck and stared skeptically at the agents. Their identification certainly looked authentic. They were real F.B.I. agents.

"We keep the long distance records over here," the supervisor motioned. He led the agents to an area where a long row of open filing boxes was stored. "The calls are logged onto file cards, and then transferred to another facility for formal billing."

"We need all the telephone records for Miss Monroe," the agent continued.

"Could you accept copies of her records?" the supervisor asked. He was flipping through the MO's where he had located the cards for Marilyn Monroe.

"No, sir," the senior agent told him. "We need the actual records."

Marilyn had lifted up the telephone when she realized the door to her room was closing behind her. She spun around and found herself in the arms of a handsome Latin man with dark eyes. She gasped.

"Oh! You scared me," she said to the man.

"I'm sorry," he whispered.

"Things have been so strange around here, lately," she explained to him. "I've started to think everyone I know is out to get me."

"Yes," AM/GOOSE said.

"How did you get in here?" she asked him suddenly. "And why the telephone?"

A look of absolute panic came into Marilyn's eyes as she realized that the Latin man was there to kill her.

"I'm sorry," the man repeated.

"You work for them," Marilyn said softly. "You've always worked for them."

"It is so," he whispered.

Marilyn suddenly tried to break away from the man and get to her bedroom door. She knocked the man off balance, but his arms held onto her and they fell onto her bed. Grasping the telephone receiver, she swung wildly at the man, but missed. Then she squirmed and kicked and rolled as she tried to push him off from her. A needle went into her buttock and she felt the pain of an injection.

"You don't understand," Marilyn scolded the man. "I'm going to give them the stupid notebooks. I'm going back to make movies."

The man pulled the needle from her buttock, rolled the syringe away from the bed, and pinned Marilyn's wrist down to prevent her from taking any further swings at him with the telephone receiver.

"This is so great a tragedy," he whispered.

"But I don't want to protect John Kennedy anymore," Marilyn told him. "If you guys want to play games with Castro, you can take your own chances."

She felt the soothing wave of the drugs as they began to leech into her bloodstream. She yawned.

"I won't tell any secrets," Marilyn said, now slurring her speech.

The world was starting to spin around her. "I just want. . . . to be left . . . alone." She closed her eyes.

Marilyn felt the weight of the Latin man on her, but she did not want to struggle. At long last, she had the feeling that she was going to fall asleep. The spinning stopped and Marilyn could see a light in the distance. It was as though she were flying toward a light in a great sea of darkness. Then the light began to run out, and the darkness became larger and larger, and then she felt calm.

"Call it off! For the love of God, Bobby, call it off!" Peter Lawford pleaded as he followed Robert Kennedy out onto his patio on the Santa Monica beach.

Robert Kennedy wheeled around and slapped Lawford across the face.

"Shut up!" the Attorney General commanded his brother in law. "It's not the time for that. It's time for you to get in line."

They had just left a small group of friends with whom they had spent the evening. A Coast Guard helicopter was landing on the beach fifty yards away.

Lawford, who had been drinking all evening over Bobby's stern stares, collapsed into tears.

"Peter, you've got to be a big boy on this one. We're depending on you!"

"I shouldn't have ever arranged the meetings with Jack," Lawford whined.

"You've got to understand something," Bobby told him. "Everything depends on you doing your duty."

"I'll do my best," Lawford assured him.

"You know the rules," Bobby said. "There are no excuses. You've got to do your part and be a good soldier on this one."

"I just don't know . . ."

"What do you tell the press?" Bobby asked him.

Lawford wiped away his tears and took a deep breath.

"She was unhappy," Lawford said dryly. "She had attempted suicide before, this time she succeeded."

"That's the stuff," Robert Kennedy said.

"But if the cops come out for a statement, if I have to talk to the police—"

"We'll take care of the police," the Attorney General said. "You just have to do your part. But, remember, these are the rules. If you talk, no matter when, you will pay the price." He stared into the eyes of his brother in law.

"Jesus, Bobby," Lawford muttered. Bobby Kennedy's eyes scared him.

The Coast Guard helicopter was on the ground, its giant propeller popping overhead.

The Attorney General ran out into the darkness and climbed aboard the helicopter. The large rotating blade of the helicopter sent little bursts of sand up at the base of Peter's patio. The rhythmic pops of the blade pounded faster and the helicopter lifted off the beach and slipped out to sea.

Peter watched as the lights rose higher in the air and sound of the propeller became more muffled. Robert Kennedy had not been in Los Angeles at all. He had spent the entire weekend in Northern California.

Chapter 46

"I hope Mr. Hoover will continue to serve the country for many, many years to come."

Robert F. Kennedy
August 7, 1962

"I will tell you something that will rock you. Kennedy was trying to get Castro, but Castro got to him first . . . It will all come out one day."

Lyndon B. Johnson to
Howard K. Smith (ABC News) 1967
New York Times, June 25, 1976

Peter Lawford stood on the beach and looked back toward the city. A glow of pinks and reds stained the clouds over the Eastern horizon heralding the arrival of the sun. It had been a long night. Lawford had one more job to do before he tried to get some sleep—he had to call Jack.

He walked back down the beach toward his house and watched the surf pound up on the shore. Occasionally, water rushed up the sand far enough to rinse his bare feet. Despite the fact that he had been up for more than 30 hours, he didn't feel tired.

Most of the night, Lawford had walked through Marilyn's house trying to make sense of her death. He was shocked to see

340 J. Arthur Jensen

how Marilyn's body had taken on a blue hue—her fingernails looked dark. After the documents had been recovered and taken away, Dr. Greenson was called. When he arrived, Dr. Greenson was briefed and given instructions. At about 3 o'clock in the morning, Pat Newcomb returned to Fifth Helena. Upon seeing Marilyn's dead body, she began to hysterically scream. It had taken almost an hour to calm her.

The cleanup lasted almost four hours. Lawford returned to the beach before Dr. Engelberg called the police. When Marilyn's death was announced to the press, Lawford wanted to be out of sight.

Peter telephoned his other brother in law, the President of the United States, at almost 6 o'clock in the morning in Los Angeles on Sunday, August 5, 1962. The President took the call.

After he reported some of the details of the night to Jack, Peter found himself trying to apologize.

"I just wish I'd never facilitated this nonsense with Marilyn in the first place," Peter confessed.

"It's not your fault, Peter," the President assured him. "It's not anyone's fault. It was the force of history."

"I was part of it," Peter continued. "I helped kill her."

"You were an accessory," the President agreed. "We're all in this thing up to our eyelids."

"She had to be so damn stubborn," Lawford said. "It was her stubbornness that got her killed."

"Maybe," John Kennedy said. "But it was also her courage. It's hard to knock someone like Marilyn for being willing to stand up to the full authority of the Federal Government and tell us that we were wrong—but who knows how all this will end? She might turn out to be right. Then the President said, "I think I love her more now than . . ." His voice trailed off.

Peter continued to listen as he waited for his brother in law to compose himself. He was using a telephone on his outdoor patio.

"Marilyn will go on," the President said, his voice hoarse with emotion. "She was taken in her youth and in her beauty, so the world will never see her grow old. Her sacrifice will transform our memories of her—perhaps she will be molded . . . into myth."

"God, she loved the way you can speak, Jack," Peter sobbed. "I just have to wonder."

"Wonder about what?" the President asked.

"Do you think they'll ever find out? Do you think the public will ever understand what happened to Marilyn Monroe?"

The President did not respond to Peter's question—rather his question was left hanging as his connection to the President was terminated. In the silence which followed, it occurred to Peter that John Kennedy had not yet made his final peace with Marilyn Monroe.

Three days later, Joe DiMaggio organized a funeral for his former wife. Some of Marilyn's closest friends were in attendance. Patricia Kennedy Lawford, the President's sister, flew into Los Angeles from Hyannis Port to attend the funeral. But Joe DiMaggio would not allow Patricia Kennedy Lawford or her husband, Peter Lawford, to attend the funeral.. The former baseball star also turned away his long time friend Frank Sinatra from paying last respects to Marilyn Monroe.

An anonymous wreath was allowed at Marilyn's graveside. It bore the full text of an Elizabeth Browning's sonnet which concludes:

> *. . . I love thee with the breath.*
> *Smiles, tears, of all my life—and, if God choose,*
> *I shall but love thee better after death.*

Robert Kennedy spoke to the American Bar association meeting in San Francisco on August 6, 1962. He was scheduled to begin a family vacation during which time he would be in wilderness areas in the Pacific Northwest. The night before he flew to Seattle, the Attorney General had a long and private dinner with a single man—John McCone, the Director of the CIA.

Neither Sam Giancana nor John Rosselli was arrested or indicted during the remaining year of the Kennedy Administration. J. Edgar Hoover, the Director of the F.B.I., was appointed for another term.

Patricia Newcomb, Marilyn's press aide and occasional house mate, would never give sworn testimony on the subject of Marilyn's last days. On Wednesday, August 8, 1962, Pat flew to Hyannis Port where she stayed, away from the press, in the Kennedy family compound. One week after Marilyn's body was discovered, Peter and Pat Lawford, Patricia Newcomb, and the President's old friend Paul "Red" Fay went sailing with President Kennedy on the *Manitou* off the coast of Maine. Pat was photographed wearing the President's jacket.

Ten weeks after Marilyn's death, the United States and the Soviet Union began a showdown over missiles in Cuba which brought the world to the brink of nuclear war. During that tense confrontation, no one leaked information that the United States was secretly planning the invasion of Cuba or the assassination of Fidel Castro. The President was able to convince the world community that the missile placement was unprovoked by the Government of the United States.

The story of the CIA using the Mafia to plan the death of Castro was originally filed by the columnist Jack Anderson. In 1967, Anderson wrote that *"Bobby, eager to avenge the Bay of Pigs fiasco, played a key role in the planning."*

Operation Mongoose was investigated by a special committee of the United States Senate in 1975. As a result of that investigation, which was conducted by Senator Frank Church, the legal mandate of the CIA was changed. It no longer allows for the assassination of foreign leaders.

After the Church Committee scheduled meetings with Sam Giancana and Johnny Rosselli in 1975, both men met unfortunate ends. Sam Giancana was shot six times in the mouth and face while he cooked sausages in his Chicago kitchen. Johnny Rosselli's body was dismembered with a chain saw and placed in an oil drum which later washed ashore on a beach in Florida.

The Los Angeles Police investigation of Marilyn's death was handled by the 'Intelligence Division' under the direction of Jim Hamilton. Rather than eliciting sworn testimony from witnesses and gathering the evidence normally demanded by an unusual death, the investigation was shunted to something referred to as the 'Suicide Prevention Team,' the results of the investigation being a foregone conclusion. The members of the Suicide Prevention Team were all personal friends of Dr. Ralph Greenson. The Los Angeles Police did interview Peter Lawford about Marilyn's death—13 years later, in 1975.

Two months prior to President Kennedy's assassination, Lee Harvey Oswald was photographed at the Cuban Embassy in Mexico City. He also was photographed at the Russian Embassy where he met with KGB assassination expert Valery Kostikov. Kostikov is also known to have met with AM/LASH in Mexico City.

On November 22, 1963, the day President Kennedy was assassinated, AM/LASH secretly met with his CIA contact in Paris. AM/LASH, *Rolando Cubela Secades*, is now believed by some to have been a double agent. American involvement with AM/LASH was withheld from the Warren Commission which investigated the death of President Kennedy. When U. S. Ambassador Thomas Mann cabled the State Department that he feared that the Cubans were involved in the assassination of President Kennedy in November 1963, he was told to discontinue his investigation—at the request of President Johnson and Attorney General Robert Kennedy. The investigation was not pursued.

As he walked along the Santa Monica beach during the early morning hours of August 5, 1962, Peter Lawford thought about his days with Marilyn. She loved to walk along the water. He looked at the sea birds flying over the swells and he felt the cold ocean water rush over his bare feet. Then, just after the sun had risen, Peter came upon a starfish which had washed up on the beach. A starfish was quite a find, because they dried out so nicely. The children loved them. He lifted the starfish up and

-JENS

looked at it carefully. It had just washed up. Maybe there was a chance it was still alive. He looked at the fish carefully for a few moments and noticed its tentacles were still moving. Quietly, Peter walked out into the surf and put the fish back in the water. He continued his walk in the early morning light.

Peter kept remembering John Kennedy's words that Marilyn, because she died in her youth and beauty, would somehow be magnified in death to even greater glory than she had been in life. The thought captivated him as he watched wave after wave crash on the shore and rush up the sand. Maybe Jack was right. Maybe when young people die, they leave their hope and their promise and they become even bigger in death than they were in life. It was a thought he would have again and again in the years to come.

CPSIA information can be obtained
at www.ICGtesting.com
Printed in the USA
LVHW111403221022
731328LV00016B/608/J